Circle of Night

STEPHEN DE VILLIERS GRAAFF

Circle of Night by Stephen de Villiers Graaff

Published by S.J. de Villiers Graaff

3 Anura Road, Sitari Country Estate, Old Main Road
Somerset West, 7130, South Africa

www.devilliersgraaff.com

Copyright © 2022 Stephen de Villiers Graaff

Cover by S.J. de Villiers Graaff.

ISBN: 9798390334003 (print paperback)

1st Edition

Dedication

To my dad for reading to me when I
was too young to read myself.
Unbeknownst to us all, John Carter's
adventures on Barsoom sowed the
seeds of this project way back then.

*"With time and patience the
mulberry leaf becomes a silk gown."*
—Chinese Proverb

"In girum imus nocte, ecce et consumimur igni." (We circle in the night and are consumed by fire.)
—Heraclitus

*"The path into darkness is a gaping
maw, ravenous and alluring."*

—The First Book

Prologue

*"'All your promises are but errant songs.' Iudas wept.
'Each song a betrayal so sweet. Nothing but sultry
murmurs that wrap my soul in shackles.'*

*"And Eresophi, laughing at the ruin of Iudas, replied,
'Yours are naught but whispers and sighs: the empty
breathing of the damned.'"*

—The Fall of Iudas

The Kurgan Steppes
The Third Day of 368, Evening

Asakaran sat astride his horse and stared down from the hilltop to the massive army below. The ranks of the Guthur stretched the full breadth of the valley and reached back as far as the low hills to the north. Thousands upon thousands of banners, each depicting the totem of a Guthur clan, were tugged and snapped by the strengthening wind.

The captain of the horse rested a gloved hand on the pommel of his sword and tightened the grip on his shield as thin threads of lightning crackled across the sky. The deep, reverberating roll of thunder reached him a few seconds later, a sure sign of Guthur magic afoot. He spat with disgust.

A painfully bright flash of lightning forked down to the hills behind the army. The deafening crack that followed caused his horse to shy away nervously. He quickly retrieved the reins from the saddle horn and brought the animal under control. He leaned forward to soothe the frightened beast with a few gentle pats on its neck as the staccato patter of rain on leather and metal began.

"A pox on this weather," the man next to him growled. "What more do the gods want to throw against us?"

"Nothing to do with the gods Vayin," Asakaran said softly without looking at his lieutenant. "They could not care less who wins here today."

Vayin grunted sounding thoroughly unconvinced.

He's right though, the captain thought sourly. *The rain will make footing treacherous for the horses, and it's not as if we don't have enough against us already.*

There was another blinding flash, and in the brief dazzling light, he made out the massive misshapen creatures that stood between the Guthur soldiers. Some unfurled gigantic bat-like wings; some had flames curling over mottled, scaled skins, others were simply monstrous and defied description. It was impossible to see clearly at this distance, but he knew from the bitter experience of past battles that these creatures were deadly beyond compare. He remembered the eyes that blazed with hate and hunger, the jagged fangs and dagger-like claws perfect for rending flesh.

6

"Piss on the bastards. They have Nepyrim as well," Vayin growled, pointing to the enemy's left flank.

Asakaran squinted and caught glimpses of the towering, grey-skinned Nepyrim giants. The hulking warriors stood head and shoulders taller than the Guthur, dark and and terrible in their ebony armour. He nodded slowly. *This is not a battle that we can win.* A morbid thought he would never share with his men.

"Captain?" another voice called out behind him.

"What is it?" Asakaran asked, turning from the dreaded host in the valley below.

"The runner has returned with word from the khan."

Asakaran turned. A young boy stood shivering next to a burly warrior. The captain dismounted and handed the reins to Vayin.

"Thank you." He took the note from the boy, broke the seal, and read it quickly. The ink had run and smudged from the rain, but its message was unmistakable. He stuffed the note under his breastplate, placed a hand on the boy's shoulder, and lead him a few steps away. Asakaran then knelt down on one knee next to the boy, placed a hand on his cheek and looked into wide and terrified eyes.

"You have done well my son." he said softly with a warm smile. "I am proud of you."

"I'm afraid, Father," the boy replied, his voice trembling and tears filling his eyes. "I wanted to stay in the camp."

"But you did not. Despite your fear, you returned." Asakaran smiled. "That took great courage."

"But you are not afraid, Father." the boy said miserably.

The captain shook his head slowly. "Of course I am." He beckoned to another boy, who had run closer as his brother returned. The captain placed his hands on the shoulders of the brothers and looked deeply into their eyes.

"Of course I am afraid," he repeated. "All men are afraid of their end and what it might bring. But it is neither victory nor ruin that defines a man. It is how he meets that fate. Does he meet his end on his knees? Or does he breathe his last with sword in hand, a blazing light in the hour when it is darkest?"

Tears welled in the boys' eyes as the thinly veiled meaning of their father's words struck home.

"No." Asakaran shook his head and pulled the boys close to hold them tightly. "No. I would have it this way. I need to know you will be strong. You are my blood and my heirs and will need to take care of our house." He released the boys and squeezed their shoulders. Behind the tears, a new strength had begun to take hold.

"I am proud of you Karakuran and you, Perun." Asakaran smiled. "Now go."

They watched as their father strode away toward his horse. He swung into the saddle and bellowed to his men: "Mount up! We have more than two hundred thousand whoresons to kill. That's a thousand per man, so we had better make an early start of it!"

Laughter rippled through the ranks of horsemen as they mounted. Amid the creak of leather, the clank of armour and weapons, and the steady hiss of rain, all Karakuran could hear was his father's voice, steady, powerful, and sure as he issued orders and organised his men. He was the rock that the waves broke around. And no matter the how potent the storm, the rock would prevail.

The boys felt a heady surge of pride as their father's men fell into formation, their horses snorting and prancing in anticipation of the battle to come. Their father sat astride his horse, rain dripping from his face as he appraised his company. With a grim smile on his face, the captain drew his sword.

"I am proud to draw steel with you today." He traced the ranks of his men with the point of his sword. "In the valley, there are men bent on conquest. They have come here to take what is rightfully yours. They have come here with magic and monsters bent to their will. They come here to kill your families and burn your homes."

He looked up at the dark skies, and cold rain ran down the angular features of his face. "Even the gods have seen fit to piss on us this night." He looked back to his men, his eyes blazing. "There is an army numbering a quarter of a million waiting for us. But they are *men*. Not gods, not beasts. And they will bleed when steel meets their flesh."

His horse pranced with nervous energy, and thunder rolled and grumbled. "The khan marches. He will be here in less than two hours, and we are to keep the bastards occupied until he gets here. To victory!" Asakaran roared, stabbing his blade skyward. Lightning arced across the dark sky, and a deafening peal of thunder shook the ground.

"To victory!" roared the defiant voices of two hundred horsemen.

Amonaki dorj'Baatar wiped the rain from his face and tried, with little success, to hide his annoyance. Of the great many things that irritated him, being cold and wet was by far the worst. It was simply impossible to ignore the constant icy trickle down his back as the rain relentlessly found the small gaps in his armour.

The armour itself was one of the many sources of vexation. It was heavy and awkward, and it pinched and squeezed his ample flesh to the point of madness. He was a high priest…a *high priest*. He should not have been flouncing around on some battlefield at the whim of an idiot general wanting to play at war.

Again, he wiped irritably at the water on his face, flicking his fingers at the sodden ground. Unfortunately, he knew very well why he was expected to force himself into armour. A reminder lay on the ground at his feet, adding to the plethora of annoyances he was trying to digest. He sighed and turned his attention to the body.

He knew the young priest who lay in the mud. The boy's name escaped him, but he had seen him many times, bumbling around the temple. Not one of the brightest students, always seeming to rush from place to place with a perpetual look of surprise and confusion. Amonaki sighed. It seemed that even death couldn't rob him of that particular expression. A deep melancholy replaced the high priest's gnawing irritation. The boy's eyes were still wide open, and the rain was slowly washing away the blood that had burst from his nostrils. That fool, Erub, had tasked the boy with spying on the enemy lines. Amonaki had told him that the boy was not ready, but Erub was not one to heed any advice.

Erub… He scowled. He hated the man, an arrogant fool at the best of times. *If only arrogance was his main flaw.* He spat into the mud with disgust. But over the years, Amonaki had time and again found him to be dangerous, manipulative, and utterly consumed with his own self-interest. Amonaki had walked away in disgust, knowing full well that Erub would ignore his advice, and the foolish boy would try to impress and end up getting himself killed.

The imp that the boy had summoned was perfect for the task: small and deadly against a single man but most certainly not impervious to harm; a well-placed arrow or blade would kill the creature. Based on the evidence that lay in the mud at his feet, the boy had taken an imp too close; it had been seen and killed, and obviously, it had not been released

9

in time: Once the two were joined they shared each other's fate—kill either the summoner or the creature, and both would die.

Amonaki's frustration flooded back in full force. He suppressed an irrational urge to shout at the stupid, dead boy. He looked up at one of the soldiers nearby. "You. Take care of this," he growled, and with one last look at the dead boy, he stalked away, almost slapping the water angrily away from his jowls.

Damn this weather and damn this war and damn that fucking Erub! He stomped angrily through the thickening mud toward a phalanx of warriors. The men, together with the beasts and Nepyrim, had gathered beneath one of the red banners of his clan. The air fairly reeked of magic, powerful binding wards that held the larger demons in check. He could taste their malevolence, the coiled, insatiable violence just waiting to be unleashed.

Death walks this valley tonight, he thought sourly. *Death and lunacy.* The thunder grumbled as if in assent. He turned and looked over at the ranks. Close by, next to a group of miserable-looking foot soldiers, a particularly large demon squatted. The beast glared at him with baleful, glowing eyes. Its hate and hunger were palpable. Rain trickled along its blotchy, green hide , following the contours formed by the creature's massive muscles.

Amonaki could see the faint blue web of the ward he had cast over the beast. Its gossamer-thin flickering, stronger than bands of steel, was all that stopped the beast from killing everything around it. These creatures could be summoned, but they could not be controlled like the smaller imps. They were far too powerful.

Amonaki stared back at the creature, unafraid, even disinterested. Time had blunted the fascination and terror. They were just weapons— not one anyone could ever hope to control, but one that could be *unleashed.* The timing would need to be perfect, and they would need to be dismissed as soon as they ran out of enemies to feed upon. They certainly displayed no discernible bias when it came to prey. The creature growled, baring jagged, yellow fangs longer than the priest's fingers.

Amonaki found his hand stray to a pouch hanging from his belt. The stones felt warm to the touch. They always did this close to the creatures. *It will feed well tonight,* he thought, then turned his attention to the several towering Nepyrim. They stood like dark statues, the rain glistening on their iron-grey skin and black armour. He tugged at his own ill-fitting armour, and a sharp corner dug into the side of his ample belly. He shifted the offending sharp edge but then hissed as an icy trickle of rain snaked down between his shoulder-blades.

"I hate it when that happens," a low, gravelly voice said with a hint of humour. He turned to see a short, incredibly wide man walking closer. Ochibat Ochir always reminded Amonaki of a walking block of granite. The shock of grey hair plastered to his head and the sharp angles of his anvil-like jaw only emphasised the image. The general stopped next to him and tugged at the leather straps of his breast plate. "You really don't like this shit, do you, Amon? Here... loosen this up a notch." Ochibat deftly adjusted the strap and shifted the armour with a brief tug. It was immediately more comfortable. The general thumped a meaty fist into Amonaki's chest. "See. Better."

"Thanks, Ochi." Amonaki grimaced. "Now can you do something about the rain?"

"Unlikely. The gods don't listen to a gristly, old bastard like me." Ochibat's broad face split into a grin. He then cast a jaundiced eye up at the dark sky and grunted. "Jests aside... this isn't going to stop any time soon. And just in case you were wondering, the Kurg are on the move. Their main army should be close in a few hours."

Amonaki nodded and wiped a drop of water from his nose. "We outnumber them. The scouts estimate no more than one hundred thousand Kurg."

"Yes. And we have them." Ochibat pointed at the Nepyrim and the towering demon. "I'm not overly fond of those big grey bastards but they can fight."

"Well, if your brain was the size of a walnut, that's all you'd be interested in too. Come to think of it..." Amonaki drawled, cocking an eyebrow and making a show of appraising the squat general.

Ochibat barked out a laugh and sent Amonaki back a step as the palm of his hand clanged into his breastplate. "Point well taken Priest. Now enough of this idle banter. I need to make sure the men are ready. You go find a flagon to occupy yourself with until we need to you to point those monsters of yours at something."

Amonaki watched as Ochibat stomped away, his booming voice causing men to snap to attention or rush off on some errand. He looked back to where the demon squared in the mud. As terrifying as the creature was it was nothing compared to the beast they had first summoned. That had been an accident, before they had learned the nature of stones and how to wield them. That... *thing*... was no dull animal to be bound and used. He shivered at the memory of the uncontrollable power it had radiated, the rage, the insatiable hunger... the *intelligence.*

With effort, he turned from the smouldering glare of the creature and trudged through the thickening mud toward the large command tent. He was going to find that flagon that Ochi had suggested. In reality, he would prefer a piping-hot bath and a willing servant girl, but that was entirely out of the question. He allowed the heady thought of dumping his armour on the floor of his bath-house to persist for a moment, then shook it off as he neared the entrance.

The two guards snapped to attention as he approached. He dismissed them with a wave of his hand and flung aside the flap to step inside. The officers hardly seemed to notice his arrival, only briefly looking up from the charts strewn over the rough table in the middle of the tent. Amonaki paused and wrinkled his nose at the warm, damp stench that hung in the air. It was a noisome mix of wet canvas, burning oil and unwashed bodies. The men at the table were officers of middling rank.

As a high priest he outranked them all, yet they had chosen to ignore him. On most days he would not have cared. He left the military to their own devices as long as they didn't interfere with his plans. But today was not one of those days. He looked at a low table that held a few simple goblets and an earthenware jug filled with water. Not one to shout —he found the practice barbaric—he picked up the jug and dropped it. It shattered on the floor, sending shards flying. The low chattered stopped abruptly, and the officers at the table looked up at Amonaki who was standing, arms crossed, looking thoroughly annoyed.

"I'm looking for a bottle of wine," he said quietly. "I'm hoping one of you fine gentlemen can help with that." His eyes were dark and dangerous. "It will go a long way in preventing me from feeding the lot of you to that very large demon close to this tent."

The senior officer's eyes widened as he straightened. "Apologies my lord. I will attend to it at once." He waved at a younger officer, who all but bolted from the tent.

"Carry on," Amonaki grunted, then turned away from them, pushing the fragments of the broken jug to one side with the toe of his boot.

He did not have to wait long for the young officer to return. The man bowed low and swallowed nervously as he handed an unopened bottle to the scowling priest. Amonaki examined it. What hadn't been washed clean by the rain was coated in a fine layer of dust.

"This had better not be vinegar." he growled to the young officer, who stood rigidly at attention, a faint sheen of sweat on his face, watching as Amonaki broke the wax seal and withdrew the cork. The high priest sloshed the dark-red liquid into a goblet and paused as he lifted it to his mouth. He sipped tentatively, then closed his eyes and, careful not to smile, savoured the smooth, rich taste. *The demon will have to wait for its next meal, but no need for this fool to know that,* he thought with dark humour. He turned a black stare to the man and waited long seconds before he said, "Adequate. You may go." The officer practically jumped away.

"Ahh... you've managed to find wine Amonaki." a dry voice husked from the entrance to the tent. "Any good?" All the warm feelings that the wine provided evaporated instantly.

"Not anymore, Erub." Amonaki turned to the short, twisted troll of a man who had just entered the tent.

Erub basuri'Davaa laughed as he flattened the thin tendrils of wet hair clinging to his head and wiped away the water that dripped from patches of beard sprouting almost randomly from his sunken cheeks. Oblivious to the slight, he pointed at the bottle. "Find me a glass and I'll judge for myself."

"Find your own glass," Amonaki said quietly as he sipped deliberately at the wine. "Find your own bottle, for that matter." He pointed to the table of nervous officers who now seemed thoroughly unhappy now that a second high priest had entered the tent. "They are quite accommodating when threatened with death and dismemberment."

"Ahh, Amonaki... not still upset over the stupid boy, are you?" Erub chuckled dryly and looked to the officers. "Wine... I am in need of wine. You"—He gestured at the young officer who had procured the first bottle and was now trying ineffectually to blend in with the canvas behind him—"Find another one of those." He pointed at the bottle in Amonaki's hand.

"And I'd be quick about it, boy," Amonaki said dryly. "He's not as pleasant as I am. And make sure you don't forget the glass."

Amonaki sipped at the wine and studied the ugly, little troll over the rim of his glass. For a brief moment, he considered leaving the tent and standing out in the rain. He dismissed the thought. He despised the man but not enough to risk watering down this exquisite wine. Erub was a ruthless, abrasive, self-serving shit, and it took every ounce of self-control to maintain some level of civility. Amonaki breathed a sigh of relief as the officer returned with another bottle and glass in hand.

"Here. Come now, before I expire from thirst." Erub took the bottle dismissing the officer with a flap of his hand. "Mmm... a good vintage by the looks of it." Amonaki watched as the twisted little priest rubbed at the dust on the bottle with his thumb and bared his small yellow teeth in what Amonaki assumed was some sort of a smile. He turned away to refill his glass and took a long, slow breath. The rain and cold were swiftly becoming more inviting.

"Ahh, come now, Amonaki..." Erub had succeeded in peeling the seal off the bottle with his thumbnail and was now working the stubborn cork back and forth. "Are we really so different?" The cork popped from the bottle and the troll poured the red wine into his glass. He took a deep swallow and bared his teeth again. "You are not so far above this"—He waved his hand around—"as you think you are."

Amonaki simply cocked an eyebrow and sipped at his glass, not bothering to answer the man. He would not be baited into a senseless argument.

Erub chuckled and slurped at his wine. "Mmm... I can only imagine how irritated you were to be dragged away from your warm library and soft serving girls... to slop around here in the mud with the rest of the meat. What did you think would happen, Amonaki?" Erub quaffed the wine, some of it dribbling down his chin. "When your face wasn't between some girl's legs, it was buried in a book. It was just a matter of time before you found something *interesting*." The troll paused to fill his glass. "You're a digger, Amonaki and, given enough time, diggers happen upon things that have been hidden for an age. What you found had been carefully and deliberately hidden. How did you ever think it was going to stay *academic*?"

"People died, Erub," Amonaki said darkly. "You *know* what happened the first time. Or is your memory of it a little fragmented? If I remember correctly, you were too busy running away to see how five priests were

14

ripped to shreds by that thing that came through the portal. It was not those mindless beasts out there. It was something else."

Erub shrugged and took another mouthful of wine. "Yes. I ran away. Do I strike you as the heroic type, Amonaki? Or stupid, for that matter? We learned how to use the stones; we learned how to bind the creatures, and then how to turn them into weapons. Well worth the sacrifice, I'm inclined to think."

Amonaki's biting reply died on his lips as a horn blared. The officers rushed to leave the tent as the blast was swiftly followed by another, the third and fourth almost blended into a single braying plea.

Amonaki swore and looked at Erub who emptied his glass in one swallow. The troll stood rooted to the spot as he slowly turned towards the tent flap. "Try not to shit yourself running away, Erub," Amonaki snarled as he shouldered past the frightened little man.

He slapped the flap aside and stepped into madness. He blinked in surprise at the abject chaos that seemed to have just erupted in the camp; hooves drummed all around him and arrows hissed through the air from seemingly every direction. Orders were being shouted, only to be countermanded, and the troops milled around in confusion as they tried to react to everything and managed to do nothing.

An arrow flashed past Amonaki's head and punched into the shoulder of a guard to his left, almost spinning him around. The man stared at the shaft in shock. The next arrow hit him in the throat, and blood sprayed from his mouth. Amonaki stared wide-eyed as the man collapsed facedown into the mud, the arrow shaft snapping under his weight. And then Amonaki was running. He ran blindly, cutting between the tents, trying desperately to find any semblance of order.

His panicked flight came to a sudden halt as his foot caught on one of the tent stakes, sending him careening wildly into a soldier running in the opposite direction. The man's helmet smashed into his face, and Amonaki crashed heavily into the mud, badly winded and with blood trickling from his nose. The soldier scrambled to his feet and groped frantically around for his sword before disappearing between the tents.

Amonaki painfully picked himself up and tried to wipe the blood from his face, only succeeding in smearing it, along with mud, across his cheeks. He breathed deeply, trying to slow his hammering heart and fight off the debilitating panic that gripped him. He looked around, forcing himself to breath rhythmically. Gradually, his pounding heart slowed, and his head cleared. His nose still hurt and his eyes watered, but he was back in control.

Now much calmer, he noticed the riders flashing past. Foot soldiers ran in all directions through billowing smoke. Tents burned, and a mélange of shouts and screams mixed with bellows from demons and the sharp crack of spells being unleashed. It was a mess—and one he was unlikely to survive by standing around and watching how it all unfolded. Any action was better than doing nothing. He moved forward.

As he cleared the line of tents he saw a small detachment of soldiers. They milled around, obviously having no idea what to do but keeping away from a particularly large demon that sat on its haunches and hungrily watched their every move.

If there is a beast there must be… Amonaki scanned the group. *Yes!* A young priest, looking very scared and very alone, flitted around on the periphery of the group. He flinched at every shadow and shout. *It's a start.* Amonaki nodded and strode towards them, trying to exude a confidence he did not feel in the slightest.

"You!" he shouted at the young priest as he stomped closer.

The man turned wide-eyed. "My lord!" he stammered as he recognised the high priest.

"What the hell are you doing? And these men… Where is the commander?" Without waiting for a response, Amonaki pointed at the beast. "Is that yours?"

"I… yes…" The young man blinked and tried to answer everything at once. "The commander was killed… we… I was…"

Amonaki was about to raise a hand to stop the incoherent babble when he recoiled as the young priest's head suddenly snapped back as an arrow hit him in the eye. He dropped to the ground like a rag-doll. The demon bellowed in rage as the ward that held it shattered. Amonaki stared in horror as the massive creature slowly stood up until it towered over the men around it. It turned, bared teeth like daggers, and with a roar, it sprang into the detachment of soldiers, a nightmare of claws and fangs that ripped and tore through the hapless men in a frenzy of blood and limbs.

"Kill it! Kill it!" Amonaki screamed and the men hacked wildly at the creature while nearby archers sent shaft after shaft into its neck and chest with seemingly little effect. A soldier ran past Amonaki sword raised.

The demon's head snapped around to face this new threat; ragged flesh and cloth hung from its jaws.

The man swung his sword but was contemptuously batted aside. He flew through the air and landed in the mud in a crumpled heap. Amonaki watched in horror as the man tried valiantly to drag himself to his feet, only to for the creature to smash him into his the mud, driving dagger-like claws through his armour, deep into his back. The massive, hideous head dipped and its jaws closed around the body. Amonaki heard the squeal of tortured metal and the crunch of bones.

Amonaki stood transfixed, unable to even breathe. The creature looked up, its yellow eyes latching onto the priest. It bared those impossibly long fangs. Its muscles tensed as it prepared to leap forward. Amonaki fumbled at the pouch hanging from his belt. The draw-string was wet and stubbornly refused to pull apart. *The stones, I need the stones!* The demon hissed, and the high priest started to scream when an arrow slammed into the creature's head, buried halfway to the fletching. The creature spasmed and collapsed facedown in the mud.

Amonaki's legs felt like jelly, and he sank to his knees to take a deep, shuddering breath. His trembling fingers dropped from the pouch. He looked toward the path of the arrow. A horseman with a heavy recurved bow was busy nocking another arrow as his horse stamped and pawed at the ground. The rider sat with casual ease on the excited animal and was taking stock of the carnage around him. Three other horsemen burst into view. The first barked orders, gesturing with his bow.

More horsemen flashed past, some with swords, hacking retreating foot soldiers down before they could react; others galloped by, controlling their horses with their knees, and sending arrow after arrow with sickening accuracy into the milling, running mass.

Amonaki saw a Nepyrim collapse vainly tugging at the three arrows jutting from its throat; another's head careened to one side as a heavy shaft thudded into the creature's helmet. The riders were like ghosts, flashing in and out of the shadows, killing at will. The horseman with the recurve bow about to turn away when he noticed the pile of broken bodies surrounding the rogue demon he had killed.

"The priests!" the horseman shouted as he realised the importance of what he was looking at. "Kill the priests!"

His horse reared, its front hooves thumping into the ground, then snorted, tossing its head impatiently. Amonaki watched with dread fascination as the horseman finally noticed him. The man smiled and drew the arrow back to his cheek. Amonaki felt his blood turn to ice. He surged to his feet and turned to run. It was like a nightmare, each step being sucked into the soft, yielding mud, each movement agonisingly slow. He hadn't taken even a dozen steps when something punched into his back, causing him to stagger.

He could now hear the drumbeat of hooves behind him as death thundered closer. Against his will, he looked back, only to see the horse and rider upon him. A sword slashed down and Amonaki screamed. There was a flash of searing pain, followed by a bone-jarring impact. He crashed into the mud. He tried feebly to get up but found he could barely lift his head.

With supreme effort, Amonaki managed to roll over. There was a sharp pain as the arrow jutting from his back snapped. He lay staring up at the night sky. The dark clouds slid slowly past, and bright sparks danced upward from the spreading fires. They were strangely beautiful as they raced frantically upward into the roiling pool of darkness.

I'm going to die. The thought drifted slowly upward into his fading consciousness. His breathing was shallow, and oddly, the pain was not so bad any more. The drizzle felt cool and washed away some of the blood from his face. He blinked and marvelled as the noises from the chaos that surrounded him started to drift away. He felt the air ripple as more wards shattered. He heard he guttural roars of the creatures, mixed with terrified screams and the discordant clash of steel, as oblivion took him.

Amonaki groaned as the pain returned. He did not try to move and became slowly aware of the sensation of warmth on his face. There was a faint perception of light through his eyelids, and a hint of a cold northern breeze brushed his skin. He was not dead. He opened his eyes to see the vast, empty blue of the sky. He swallowed as a wave of nausea washed over him. The pain was much worse now.

He could hear the guttural croaks of crows nearby as they squabbled over the feast—the flapping of heavy wings, the sharp tearing of cloth, followed by the frantic, wet pecking of flesh. He tried to move his arm. It took a colossal effort to lift it only a few inches. He grunted as he allowed the limb to flop back into the mud. His face was stiff with dried blood, his right leg throbbed, and the arrow in his back felt as if it scraped against bone with every breath. Apart from the crows, there was no sign of life. He was alone, and the certainty that death would be slow and agonising started to settle in.

A bird landed on his chest. Amonaki sucked in a painful breath as terror surged through him. He stared at the large black crow as it ruffled its feathers. It cawed and turned its dark, empty gaze to him. The cruel beak poised to strike. *Not my eyes… not my eyes!* He turned his head away as a hand suddenly swept the bird aside. It took to the wing with an angry screech. Amonaki blinked in surprise and looked up at the dark-hooded man who crouched over him.

"Who?" was all he managed to whisper.

As the man knelt next to him, the hood shifted slightly. He could make out the line of the man's jaw and a hint of dark eyes that somehow reminded him of the crow. "Who… are you?" he asked, forcing out the words.

The man ignored the question, and Amonaki felt a tugging at the pouch that hung from his belt. *The stones! No!* Amonaki frantically tried to raised his head. The man pushed his head back into the mud and pulled the pouch free.

"No…please…" Amonaki groaned, clutching weakly at the man's robes. "Dangerous… you don't know…"

"Oh, but I do, Amonaki dorj'Baatar." the man purred as he swatted Amonaki's hand aside. He traced sharp nails down Amonaki's wounded cheek and smiled at the fresh flow of blood as they hooked into the ragged tear. Then he leaned close and grabbed the priest's flailing arm, holding it tightly. Amonaki's face twisted in agony as his flesh smoked and burned. "I know more than you could ever know," the man hissed.

Sarsini
The Twentieth day of 389, Night

Water dripped slowly from the ceiling of the chamber, forming dark puddles on the rough paving of the floor. Torches, set in metal sconces, spluttered and danced but did little to dispel the oppressive gloom. Apart from a massive stone altar at one end and a heavy, steel-braced wooden door at the other, the hall was empty and unadorned.

The altar was fashioned from a single, seamless piece of dark volcanic rock, polished smooth by the ministrations of thousands of forgotten hands over countless centuries. The silence, broken only by the soft splutter of the flames and the echoing drops of water, was thrust aside as hinges groaned under the great weight of a door as it swung ponderously open.

A tall, darkly cloaked man carrying a lantern stepped through. He pushed the door closed behind him, the low boom reverberating from the walls. The man slowly crossed the hall, carefully avoiding the shallow puddles that were illuminated by the small pool of light cast by the lantern.

He stopped half a dozen paces short of the altar, placed the lantern on the floor at his feet, and knelt. He reached under his cloak and withdrew three dark stones, then placed them down in front of him. They were flat, roughly square, and fashioned from a dark but translucent rock. Each had intricate runes etched into the face, their meaning lost to antiquity.

He stared at the stones. Their secret had evaded him for weeks. Each night he would come to this place and study the markings. He had turned them over and over. He had traced his finger-tips along the incomprehensible markings. At one point, he had even thrown them to the floor and shouted his anger and frustration to the shadows. Their power was unmistakable. He could feel it thrumming through his hands when he placed them close together, but what that power was capable of remained a mystery.

He took a deep breath and tried once again to focus his mind on the problem. He held a thin strand of black pearls in his left hand. Their soft click, click, click echoed faintly as he absently ran them through his fingers. *What is their secret? How do I unlock their power?* He could feel the anger rising once again as the thoughts flitted through his mind.

He closed his eyes and took several deep breaths to calm himself. He pictured the stranger who had given them to him. It was a chance meeting; he had been visiting Mittua and staying at the estate of a minor noble when this man had just walked up to him and smiled. The smile, quite predatory, never touched the man's eyes. *And those eyes,* he thought with a strange chill, *those jet-black, lifeless pools that seemed to slowly flay the flesh.*

"Well met," the deep voice had purred almost mockingly. "I have something for you."

"Do you know who I…" The reprimand had died on his lips when the man had smirked, baring sharp, white teeth. There was something very dangerous lurking behind the handsome face. Before he could collect his thoughts, the man had pressed a small black bag into his hands and, without another word, had turned and walked away. By the time he had recovered his composure, the man was gone, and oddly, no one could remember seeing anyone of his description.

The gift had proved to be extraordinary and frustrating in equal parts. There was no record of any artefacts that matched the stones. The etchings remained indecipherable. He had taken copies to a number of learned scholars in the city, and none of them had ever seen the like of the strange runes.

He shuffled the stones, absently feeling their warmth beneath his fingertips as the edges touched. The click, click, click of the beads in his left hand and the slow drip of water were oddly mesmerising. His eyes closed, and he allowed his thoughts to drift. All the while, he touched the stones, shifting them, feeling the edges of the markings, the rhythmical hum that emanated from their depths.

It wasn't long before strange images began to form in his mind. At first, they were vague and nebulous. He had the impression of being far underground, with immeasurable tons of dark stone pressing down around him. Then there was the hint of fire. Low flames sent shadows skittering around at the periphery of his vision. *What is this place?* he thought as he began to feel heat.

Slowly, he began to notice the voices, the low groans and distant screams. They were all around him, millions upon millions of voices. He suddenly became acutely aware of the crushing weight of their anguish and pain. The shadows now writhed and twisted in a grotesque dance of knotted limbs and bodies.

He tried desperately to open his eyes and found that he could not. The heat was now cloying and oppressive, and sweat ran down his face. The deafening ocean of voices crashed over him clogging the very air and sliding over his skin and face like obscene tongues, licking and probing, until he found he could not breathe. Panic surged though him, and his chest heaved as he tried to forced air into his starved lungs. He could not even cry out. His lungs screamed for air, and his body spasmed.

And then she was there. A monstrous presence that suddenly gripped him. His heart hammered uncontrollably as the being slid closer and the darkness coalesced into a female form that towered over him. Her body was covered in shining black scales, and her eyes where burning coals. She knelt down to look into his eyes. Her long hair billowed and dissolved like smoke as she leaned close enough for him to feel her breath fan his face.

"So weak, so frail," the goddess whispered. "Why would M'Lakh send this to me?" She touched his face almost lovingly. Then her nails, sharp as razors, split his flesh. She slowly traced a line down his cheek towards his chin. He gagged, his mouth filling with blood as the tips of her nails ground across his teeth and grated across bone.

"Always wheels within wheels," she hissed. "I do not see his plan… yet. But no matter. Wake and embrace your doom."

A sudden flare of pain surged up his arm, and his eyes snapped open; the stones were incandescent. He snatched his hand back and grabbed at his face expecting tatters of skin and blood. His face was unharmed. He drew a deep, shuddering breath and looked back to the almost blinding light emanating from the stones, and the air stirred.

It washed over him like cold, hidden fingers tugging at his cloak, a chilled, dry breath escaping from a tomb long sealed. This was followed by a weighted pause. It was time enough for him to look around in anticipation before he heard the first of them—the hiss of whispers, whispers within whispers.

They swirled around him, softly at first, at the very edge of his perception, yet heavy with malice and hate. Slowly, the sibilant maelstrom of rage built until it ebbed and flowed all around the expanse. Then, quite suddenly, they fell silent.

The black stone of the altar then burst into flame with a deep, throaty roar. Its surface rippled like oil, and a massive, horned creature slowly rose up from its surface until it squatted on the rock, towering above him.

The beast slowly opened its eyes and fixed its smouldering glare on him. Thin lips peeled back from long, yellow fangs, and thick, ropey saliva splattered to the floor. It gripped the edge of the altar with impossibly long claws and looked around.

"Where is this place?" It asked, the grating echoes of its voice reverberating off the walls. It looked back at the kneeling man. "You are not the summoner I know. The one who called my children."

The man forced himself to his feet, panic threatening to send him running for the door, away from this monster. He tried in vain to ignore the massive cords of muscle and sinew that rolled beneath the mottled grey skin of the creature as it shifted, waiting for his reply.

"Why have you summoned me?" the creature asked. It made no move to leave the stone altar and the priest felt a slow, tentative curiosity start to replace the rush of mindless terror. *Could this be a demon?* he wondered. He had read of tribes to the north that had found ways to summon incredibly powerful creatures, bending them to their will. He had always thought it was nothing more than the brute rantings of savages. And yet here it was, standing before him. He felt a surge of excitement, the fear of moments ago now slipping away quickly.

The man drew a deep breath and locked his eyes with the beast's. "I want much," he replied, his voice clear and steady. The click, click, click of the pearls filled the silence as he contemplated his next words. "And I don't care to leave those wants to time… or chance."

"Ahh… so there it is. It was such with the first summoner. But he soon came to learn the folly of his ways." The beast nodded slowly, its yellow eyes narrowing to slits. "The unfettered ambition of man is what we have come to know well. The lessons of the wise confined to the shadows of time." It paused, a grotesque smile splitting its features. "And what would you offer in return?"

The man thought briefly and then replied, "Anything."

"Anything?" The creature threw back its hideous head, and the rumblings of its laughter rolled through the empty expanse. "We doubt you even begin to fathom what that means."

"Do not presume to know what I can or cannot fathom, *demon!*" the man spat in a flash of anger, the terror now receding quickly.

"Mmm… truly, the arrogance of man is legend." The creature's grating laughter died away. "We are pleased by this. Tell us what you want."

He thought on this, momentarily surprised at the extent of what he truly wanted. He paused as he decided. It was obvious. "Adrastus Primatus must die," he said simply.

The beast nodded slowly. "This can be done. We can ensure that this Primatus meets his… God." It paused, its lips peeled back from the dagger-like fangs. "But… we know this is not all."

"No," the man replied softly. "It is not."

"Tell us," the creature growled.

"In time." The man smiled.

The beast nodded slowly. "Your second mistake, summoner. The belief that you have time." The great horned head tilted back, and once again, the beast's horrible laughter echoed through the chamber. "It is your nature to ignore the inevitability of your end even as the void gapes before you. What do you offer us in return?"

"What else could I offer but the flesh of innocents? An unwilling sacrifice of blood," the man replied. "Is that not what your kind expects?" He paused, considering for the first time what he would be willing to offer. "If need be, I will offer a legion of souls to be sundered and steeped in torment."

"Ahh! We recognise those words." The beast grinned, a rope of saliva dripping from its chin. "Reminiscent of the tenets of M'lakh. It is interesting how readily the Ascendant's words spring to your tongue. We have sensed his *meddling* in this." The creature fixed its smouldering glare on the man as it weighed his words. "Yes," it rumbled slowly, bowing its the hideous head to the man. "She has said it can be so."

*"As Darkness can never consume the
Light, revenge can never silence the
murmurs of the dead."*
—The First Book

The First Circle

*"'In sacrificing this flesh that is draped around me,' said the
Broken One, 'You shall be exalted above all.'*

*"Iudas, looking upon the ravages inflicted by his deceit,
wept.*

*"'You must believe this.' the Broken One implored. 'For each
man chooses for himself the weight of his shackles.
What you seek is too much to bare.'*

*"But Iudas chose not to see, and with a kiss to his master's
cheek, he turned away to embrace his ruin."*

—The Fall of Iudas

The night was cold and still. Dacian sat on his haunches in the bushes and watched as a guard walked slowly past the main gate of the estate. The man's boots crunched in the fine gravel, and his breath plumed softly in the chilly air. The guard looked bored, his gloved hand resting on the pommel of his sword as he idly scanned the edges of the shadows.

Well-manicured lawns lay beyond the black whirls of wrought iron. The wide, cobbled path leading up to the entrance of the house was lined with white stone pots that overflowed with purple creeping thyme. A warm orange glow spilled from lanterns silhouetting another guard, walking along the wide patio.

Dacian squashed a sudden surge of anger at the opulence. He needed to be cold, focused, unattached. He swallowed hard, looked down at his hands. They were still caked in soot and soil. They ached from the burns. Many of the blisters had burst and were now encrusted with dirt. He took a slow, deep breath and pushed the pain away. He looked up at the pacing guard, who had now stopped and was digging in his ear. *Move, you fool.* Dacian scowled at the man.

Finally, after a thorough examination of his finger, the guard resumed his slow amble. Dacian waited until the man had settled into his beat before he stood up into a low crouch. Keeping to the shadows of the brush, he moved quietly to his right, away from the gate. He followed the wall, looking for a place to scale the smooth stone. It was over twice his height, made from neatly aligned sandstone blocks, and offered little or no handholds.

He moved quickly, falling into the old habit of rolling his feet as he stepped to ensure he made almost no sound. There were three others patrolling the perimeter. Their paths overlapped, but the walls were vast enough to ensure some gaps for him to exploit. He paused. An old cork oak grew close to the far corner. It towered over the wall, and a few of its densely leafed branches hung into the estate.

Dacian waited for the guards. It wasn't long before the first rounded the corner. The guard sauntered past his hiding place, close enough for Dacian to smell tobacco and stale sweat. The leather of the guard's sword belt creaked as he stopped and stretched his back, grunting softly at the discomfort. He sniffed, rubbed at his nose, and then walked on.

A minute passed, and the second guard appeared. He stopped, looked around, then turned towards the tree. He stood fumbling at his leggings and then urinated noisily against the trunk. Dacian clenched his jaw in frustration. *Patience,* he chided himself. The man finished, adjusted his leggings, and after a cursory glance behind him, headed away.

Dacian waited for a few slow breaths and then moved swiftly. He crossed the open space to the wall quickly and pushed his back to the stone. Edging to the corner, he glanced around it. The guard was roughly twenty or so paces away, walking slowly to the far corner. He looked up at the tree. It was gnarled and offered an easy climb to the lower branches.

Ignoring the pain in his hands, he moved quickly and pulled himself onto the heavy overhanging branch within seconds. Hidden in the thick foliage, he listened once again for anyone approaching. There was nothing but the muted night sounds, the low buzz of insects, and the soft rustle of leaves.

Once again, he paused. He took deep, slow, deliberate breaths, breathing in through his nose and exhaling through his mouth. He felt his heart slow, and his mind cleared. He became acutely aware of his surroundings—the whisper of a breeze, a shifting shaft of moonlight, the dance of dappled shadows on the grass below him. He was ready.

He stood on the thick branch and, balancing easily, crossed over the wall, then dropped onto the soft lawn on the other side. He crouched, hidden in the deep shadows; without a doubt there were more guards on this side. Satisfied that none were close, he sprinted across the lawn to the shadow of the wall of the house.

He crept to his left, toward the back of the house. As he reached the corner, he noticed a low yellow light spilling across the ground. *An open door, perhaps, or a lantern?* he thought and then froze as he heard the creak of leather. *A guard! Very close...*

"Evening, Brin," came a low voice.

"Evening, sir," came a gravelly reply.

There are two. Dacian crouched low and eased his dagger from its sheath.

"Anything to report?" asked the first voice; the accent was refined, and the tone carried the edge of authority.

"Nothing, sir. All quiet. You expecting trouble?"

"No, Brin. But always best to be prepared."

Brin grunted his affirmation, then asked, "Anything to do with what happened this afternoon, sir? Some of the men in the barracks were talking about the young lord. They were on duty at the gate when he returned with Kratos."

"You'll ignore that if you know what's good for you," The officer said, his voice hardening. "Keep your head on swivel. Good night, Brin."

"Yes, sir. Night, sir."

Dacian listened to the crunch of gravel as the officer left. There was a creak of a door followed by a click.

"'Ignore that if you know what's good for you,'" Brin muttered. "Fuckin' hell. Head on a bloody swivel…getting too old for this shit."

Dacian heard the old guard clear his throat and adjust his sword belt before starting to walk. Pressing his back against the wall, he raised the dagger and waited. Brin rounded the corner, and Dacian struck. He grabbed the rim of Brin's helmet and slammed the dagger into his throat.

The blade severed Brin's carotid artery and crunched through the vertebrae of his neck, killing the old guard almost instantly. He slumped into Dacian, who immediately dragged the body into the shadows behind a low bush. He twisted the blade and pulled it free.

He looked down at Brin. It was a kind face, deeply etched by time, the jaw line covered by a neat salt-and-pepper beard. The tired, dark eyes, stared up sightlessly at the assassin.

"Sorry, Brin," Dacian whispered and then moved swiftly around the corner to the door.

Dacian tried the handle and pulled gently. The door opened, revealing a narrow staircase heading downward. He slipped inside and closed the door behind him. A dull orange light flickered below. He could see the edge of a rough wooden table and a simple chair. *The guard's room,* he thought as he descended quietly.

He paused on the last stair and glanced into the room. A man sat slumped on another chair, his feet crossed and extended toward a small iron brazier. His helmet and sword lay on the table, alongside a plate with the remnants of a meal of bread and cheese. Dacian listened to the guard's soft snores blending with the pops and crackles of the fire for a few moments. Satisfied that the man was fast asleep, he crossed the room to the door on the far side.

Keeping an eye on the snoring guard, he pressed his ear to the wood and strained to hear any sound on the other side. *Nothing.* He drew a deep breath, adjusted his grip on the dagger, and eased the door open revealing a dimly lit—and thankfully, empty—passage. Easing through the door, he carefully pulled it closed behind him and then moved swiftly down the corridor.

As he neared the junction at the end, he became aware of the smell of food and wood fire. *Must be getting close to the kitchens,* he thought. He paused once again at the junction. To his left was a heavy wooden door with a large silver handle. It was cool to the touch. *A cold-storage room,* Dacian surmised. *The large double doors to the right must lead to the kitchens.*

Once again, he pressed his ear to the door, this time hearing the sounds of water and the clinking of glass. *Scullery,* he thought as he placed his hand on the door handle. He hesitated. It was late, so it was unlikely that there more than one or two servants were working. *But if I'm wrong...* He crushed the thought and pushed the handle down.

A single scullion stood hunched over a large basin, his back to Dacian. A large stack of washed dishes and pots lay to his right, and an equally large unwashed pile lay to his left. Dacian quickly scanned the room for any other servants. The man was alone. He slid through the door, moving silently up behind the servant. In a fluid movement, he clamped his left hand over the man's mouth, jerked his head back, and pressed the point of the dagger to his throat.

"Be still," he hissed as the servant convulsed in fear. "Be still, damn you!" he repeated, adding pressure to the dagger to emphasise the point. The man froze, but his chest heaved as he sucked in panicked breaths through flared nostrils. His eyes were wide with terror.

"I'm going to ask you a question," Dacian whispered. "You will answer quietly or I'll kill you. Do you understand?"

The scullion nodded slowly.

Dacian slowly shifted his hand from the man's mouth, keeping the dagger pressed to his throat. "Where do I find Antoine d'Verana?" he asked quietly.

The servant swallowed. "East wing," he replied carefully. "His rooms are at the far end."

"How do I get there from here?" Dacian whispered.

"As you leave… the kitchens"—he pointed with a trembling hand to the far side of the scullery—"there are stairs… beyond them, the dining room… then the main portal." He swallowed. "There's a large staircase. Go up the stairs… then to the right. He's at the end of the passage."

Dacian clamped his hand over the man's mouth again. "You are sure? If I discover you've lied to me…" He increased the pressure of the dagger slightly. The man squirmed and shook his head slowly. Dacian removed his hand again.

"There are many guards," the man whispered. "You will not be able to climb the stairs without running into at least one."

"Not your concern," Dacian hissed.

"There's another way," the man whispered quickly. "You could climb to his balcony… far less likely to meet the guards. Leave through the service entrance." He lifted his right hand and pointed across the scullery to another passage. "It leads outside. There's a small courtyard. Turn left. Follow the wall. You will see the balcony. There are creepers you can climb."

"Why do you tell me this?" Dacian hissed.

The man blinked as he considered his words. "We servants…are not treated well. Your business with him is yours. I don't care."

Dacian paused. "What is your name?"

"Anouar."

"That's Akhbari," Dacian whispered. "You're a long way from home, Anouar."

"I have no home," the servant replied quietly.

"I'm sorry, Anouar." Dacian said softly, then slammed the hilt of his dagger against the side of the servant's skull. The scullion sagged immediately, and Dacian lowered him gently to the floor. There was a trickle of blood along Anouar's hairline, just behind his ear. His breathing was shallow, and Dacian had no doubt he would wake later with a beast of a headache, but he was alive.

He quickly fashioned a crude rope from dishcloths and bound the servant's hands and feet. He stuffed one cloth into Anouar's mouth and, satisfied that the man could still breathe, crossed the scullery, climbed the stairs, and carefully opened the service entrance door. The courtyard was quiet and dark, and hemmed by a low, stone wall. Tall shrubs grew outside the wall, shielding the yard from any guards who might have been patrolling the lawns.

Keeping to the shadows, Dacian crept along the wall of the main building, occasionally glancing up at the balconies overhead until he spotted the thick, intertwined branches of the creeper that Anouar had spoken of. Light streamed from the windows above, and Dacian could see thin, almost diaphanous curtains hanging in front of the open balcony doors. He moved quickly. The creeper was old, and its thick stems were heavy with broad leaves. He tugged at the plant. It would hold his weight.

Hot flames of rage suddenly ignited as he thought of the man in the room above. He had lost everything because of that man's greed. His hands had balled into fists, and his body trembled as the anger surged through him. He forced himself to take a long, deep breath. Slowly, he unclenched his hands, and an icy calm settled over him. *Death comes for you, Antoine d'Verana,* Dacian thought as he started to climb.

Dacian pulled himself up onto the balustrade and dropped silently onto the balcony. The silken curtains swayed slowly in the light breeze, causing muted shadows to writhe over the stone tiles beneath his feet. In the warm light of the room, he could see a man sitting on the edge of a large bed. He sat with his elbows on his knees and his hands over his face. A glass of wine rested on the floor between his feet.

Dacian stood and pulled the dagger from its sheath. He pushed aside the curtains with the back of his hand, leaving smears of black soot on the fabric as it slid down his arm and over the black leather of his jacket. Antoine had not moved, and Dacian glided silently across the marble floor until he stood in front of the man.

Dacian remained still for a moment, then pressed the point of the dagger softly into the man's cheek. D'Verana looked up suddenly, his eyes widening. Then he hissed in pain as the point punctured his skin.

"Shhhh…" Dacian held a finger to his lips and watched the thin thread of blood snake down the man's cheek.

D'Verana was not as he expected. The man was young, handsome; his eyes were dark but not unkind. There was not much of his father in that face. There were none of the hard angles and cruel lines he had seen in the face of Viktor d'Verana. He had been crying. But it mattered not…

"Antoine d'Verana?" Dacian asked quietly.

"Yes," the young man sobbed. "Yes. I…" His voice broke.

"I am Death," Dacian whispered.

Sarsini
The Twenty-Third Day of 389, Morning

The essence of Moloc drifted high above the great port city of Sarsini. To the south the Great Sea, green grey with flecks of burnished copper painted by the rising sun, stretched to the horizon. To the northeast, the great snow capped spine of the Arakura mountain range sprawled, separating the Sarsinian Kingdom from the endless grass ocean of the Kurgan steppes. Far below, the bay was filled with the billowing sails of ships, and the harbour writhed with activity.

There was a chill to the breeze that blew in from the sea, but this did not affect the idle Ascendant, for at this moment, he held no physical form and could not feel the cold. Even though it was early, the streets and avenues seemed to pulse as the thousands of people scurried this way and that, rushing from one trivial task to the next.

Much like ants, he thought, mildly amused. These mortals seemed utterly oblivious to how carelessly they spent their pitifully brief lives, throwing away each hour with such reckless abandon. The sun would rise, and the streets would fill, and they would run from one meaningless event to the next, chained to the past or groping for the future but never truly aware of the moment they were in. They would haggle, and eat, and fuck, and kill each other. And then the day would end, and the streets would empty. All of them rushing headlong toward their inevitable doom.

The immortal chuckled to himself. They were pathetic and deserving of their fate, so easily manipulated and moved, so blissfully unaware that they were mere pawns being shifted by one design or another, insects trapped in the webs woven by the Ascendants, the gods, or even their own inconsequential desires. To his great delight, Moloc had found that Sarsini presented more than a few choice flies for him to feed upon, and how they writhed in his webs! Their own insatiable ambitions, lusts, hate, and anger drew the strands ever tighter.

He drifted lower and floated past the towering black minarets of a temple. The dark basalt bricks had been sourced from a volcanic island off the coast of Verana at a staggering cost. Moloc doubted that Eresophi, the goddess of death, cared in the slightest. *Idiots,* the Ascendant thought scornfully, watching the grey-white smoke spiral up from the many chimneys as the bodies of the dead slowly burned away to ash.

On a whim, he darted downward, passing through the roof and hovering near the ceiling of the vast chamber. Wailing mourners were on their knees, gathered in groups around the stone cremation platforms. The red priests, their lips and eyes blackened with a mixture of charcoal and rendered human fat, droned and bowed to the beautifully carved obsidian statue of the goddess. The colossal statue, stretching up toward the ceiling, depicted a beautiful woman on her haunches, naked, arms extended, hands palms up and accepting. The eyes were closed; the face was tilted upward and serene. Moloc wondered what their reaction would be if they saw her true form.

He watched the antics of the clerics with mild contempt; their blind faith and empty claims of understanding the nature of the goddess were both irksome and helpful. The prayers and rituals were quite useless, but they did create powerful levers. Levers that his kind were quite open to using—but with sufficient care so as not to draw undue attention. As indifferent as they were, the gods were not to be trifled with. The Ascendants were powerful, but they were no match for an angry deity.

Koros would testify to this. Apparently, impersonating Hodan, the grim god of the Noordlandt, to seduce a priestess had been an exceptionally bad idea. At best, the war mongering Hodan was not known for his sense of humour. His doctrines—written in blood on human skin—promising eternal mead-induced brawls and battles for those who died in glorious combat should have been enough of a deterrent.

But not to Koros, and Hodan had made an example of him. Moloc had little doubt that being nailed to a rock and having your intestines ripped out was a decidedly unpleasant experience even for an immortal. He doubted the night with the priestess had been worth it.

Enough of this. Moloc dismissed the wailing temple mob and flew upward. High above the city, he looked to the north. There, the plans he had put into motion were coming to fruition. He felt the irresistible pull of blood and chaos and sped away. Forests and rivers flashed by beneath him. He flew over farmlands and the small hamlets, vaguely aware of the simple inhabitants as they ambled through their dull, meaningless lives. Onward he flew until he came to a hill overlooking a vast estate where he slowly descended to stand behind a man who sat slumped over on the grass.

This far north, the pale morning sun had done little as yet to dispel the cold of the night, and each of the man's long, slow breaths sent plumes of mist into the air. *Is he asleep?* Moloc mused as he moved closer. This one, who thought to fashion himself as a farmer, was a killer, an assassin, and supremely gifted at ending lives. How arrogant to think he could deny his true self. Oh, and how he had run. Run and run... only to be here, and now, he was little more than a broken and exhausted husk. *And so delightfully malleable,* the Ascendant thought.

Moloc looked down at the assassin's face. He was awake, but his gaze was empty. He was covered in dried blood. It crusted his hands and face, and matted his hair. The Ascendant grinned, exposing very white, almost predatory teeth as the man started to sob, his body heaving as the grief tore at him. Moloc had no small part in the affairs that led to this moment, and the man's pain was simply too beautiful not to savour to the fullest. The deaths of the wife and the child and the destruction of the assassin's home were all his doing.

He looked to the estate in the distance. The duke's man had been easy to sway. He was not complicated, a survivor by nature, and therefore required only the slightest of nudges. The duke's son had been more difficult to move, fighting each and every suggestion, but in the end, he had fallen, too. Bending the young noble to his will had been exquisite. The darkness, with its seductive whispers, always proved far too... *sweet...* for mortals to resist. That, and the taste of flesh and fear and power.

The Ascendant squatted down next to the assassin. The man's face was a mess: tears cutting through smears of soot and blood. How easy it had been to unleash the beast that was once so tightly shackled. He stroked the farmer's hair and crooned softly. This one could have served him so well for many years, but he had somehow managed to turn his back on that life.

Moloc chuckled. How did he ever manage to entertain such a fiction? How could he ever believe he had any control, any choice? All it took was the right leverage, and the years of will and resolve turned to nothing more than blood and piss and bile. And now, all was in motion. *Circles within circles with circles...*

His hand dropped away from the man's face, and he looked around suddenly, half expecting *her* to make an appearance. Of all the Ascendants, E'kia seemed the most fond of meddling in his plans. *E'kia, E'kia...* He rolled her name over and over in his mind, almost tasting her lips, her skin. She was known to men such as these, the assassin, as *Echo*, but he preferred her old name. There was a sharpness to it—a name much like his own, filled with edges and corners. *Echo*, he thought, his lip curling in disgust, was too soft.

Moloc scowled. As much as he tried, *her* agenda was always opaque to him. Her schemes were like billowing mist: just when he thought he could see the design of it all, everything shifted and dissolved before his eyes. How he loved her, *hated her,* but thankfully, on this morning, she seemed to be elsewhere. He didn't even want to contemplate what mischief she was engaged in.

With one final glance around, he leaned in close to the assassin to take pleasure in the smell of smoke and death. He ran his fingers through the man's matted hair, dug his sharp nails into the man's scalp. His agony thrummed through Moloc's fingertips, and the Ascendant shuddered with pleasure. His tongue flicked out over the man's cheek, tasting the salt and ash. Then, with lips almost touching his ear, Moloc whispered softly. "Kill them... kill them all. Drown them in an ocean of blood..."

The Smuggler

The Akhbari Coast
The Twenty-Second day of 389, Afternoon

The small stone house was perched almost precariously on a rocky head of land that jutted out into a windswept, grey-green sea. Tariq sat on a rough wooden bench under a bright sunshade that slapped and billowed in the late-afternoon breeze. He puffed quietly at his pipe and watched with mild interest as a dhow pitched and ploughed its way across the bay of restless whitecaps.

A trader, he guessed idly, *bound for Abuzara.* He scratched at the short grey stubble on his chin with the stem of his pipe. She looked low in the water, heavy with spices, cloth, or flesh. *Abuzara,* he mused with a half smile, *a man can buy or sell anything in that stinking cesspit.* As a younger man, he had almost lost his soul in dark places like that.

35

He reached for a small ceramic pot that shared the bench and filled a cup with a bitter, aromatic brew. The desert people called it khafja, and if he were completely honest with himself, he would have to admit that he was utterly addicted to the drink. It was one of his few remaining vices, introduced to him by a camel trader.

Feels like a lifetime ago... He frowned as he tried to remember the man's name. He could picture that dark, deeply lined face quite clearly, the broad, toothy smile, but not his name. He shrugged. *No matter.* It was a vice he was very grateful for acquiring and now bluntly refused to ever give up.

He sipped and allowed himself a small smile of satisfaction, then turned his attention back to the sea. The horizon was black with great masses of clouds stacked high that promised rain and heavy seas. The dhow was still a few hours out from Abuzara. If her luck held, she would be safely in the harbour before the worst of the storm hit. If not, she ran the risk of joining the hundreds of her kind that littered the rocky ocean bed of that treacherous coastline. Her fate was in the hands of the gods. Unfortunately, he could not think of a more capricious, self-obsessed and ultimately useless set of hands to have your fate consigned to.

He took another sip and chuckled at his terribly blasphemous train of thought. As a younger man, he had taken the utmost care to keep himself in the good graces of all the deities he encountered: the desert folk's stern god Elihaar, the fierce warrior-god Hodan of the Noordlanders, the Broken One of the white priests. He could not help but chuckle at the latter. If a god could be seen as broken, what hope had they? He even paid deference to the Ascendants—the elusive Echo, the dark Moloc, Koros, and the frivolous Panaii, to name a few.

He made the appropriate sacrifices, said the required prayers, visited the temples and shrines, and on occasion, even listened to their droning priests without yawning too much. He sipped the khafja. And thinking back, none of it had helped much at all. All he had ever achieved had been through his own strength and wits, though in some cases, he had to concede, success was due to nothing more than blind luck.

He could not remember a single moment where any one of these gods had taken the time to turn a blade, or even a deal, for that matter, in his favour. He remembered the countless times he had cried out to the empty skies, only to be flatly ignored. The choice had been simple: remain kneeling in the dust waiting on some fickle divinity, or simply get up and get it done.

Tariq's smile died away. The countless ignored petitions for himself he could forgive and brush aside. The night he spent on his knees begging for his wife's life as she burned away from the fever was not so easily forgotten. It had been more than ten years since her passing, and the pain was still as keen and sharp as a blade twisting in his chest.

He had felt immortal before Razia died. But now, in his fiftieth year, he found himself hoping there was an afterlife; he hoped he would see her one last time before being dragged off to whatever hell the gods had set aside for him for spitting in their divine faces.

He puffed at his pipe and tried to shake the sudden melancholy. A seabird screeched, and he looked up to watch as it glided past, riding the steady offshore wind. The dhow was making good headway. She bucked as a low wave smacked against her prow, sending a plume of spray over her decks.

He remembered the countless time he'd stood on the forecastle of a similar ship, the salt stinging his eyes, his hair plastered to his head, and gold heavy in his pockets. *So much gold,* he thought with a slight smile, *and such a burning impatience to get to port.* Abuzara, H'jah Karaam or Sarsini—it did not matter as long as he could sell, buy, and *spend.* And how he would spend. Thousands of coins spilling from his hands in glittering torrents: women, cards, wine and anything else that caught his attention.

He had even once bought a monkey on a whim: a silly-looking thing with green fur and huge brown eyes. He had haggled for hours with a Na'muud trader over a gourd of qymys, a vile, almost lethal concoction derived from fermented goat's milk. In the end, he had staggered from the man's tent with a monkey clinging to his head and a purse considerably lighter than anticipated.

He had hatched a cunning plan whereby he would use the creature as a distraction to his opponents while playing pahkur. A plan that had backfired horribly: not only did he fail to recoup the cost of the animal, but it had actively undermined his own ability to play when it constantly pissed all over his shoulders and tried to eat his cards. He chuckled to himself as he vaguely recalled giving the monkey to some cheap whore in lieu of payment.

He used the side of the bench to knock the last of the tobacco from his pipe and reached for a small leather bag. *It seems the khafja has a fair bit of company on my list of remaining vices.* He snorted, amused at the thought, and refilled the pipe with a lopsided grin on his face. There was a saying that the gods only took the most righteous young. If that were in any way true, he could safely assume that he was, for all intents and purposes, immortal.

His right knee protested as he stood. With the stem of the pipe clasped firmly between his teeth, he kneaded the muscles of his lower back; how he hated getting old. The dhow had by now disappeared behind a ragged head of rock, leaving the low, choppy waves to march uninterrupted across the bay. He pushed open the door to his house and stalked over to the small stove to find an ember to light his pipe. Within moments, he stepped outside again, puffing contentedly.

He turned from the sea to look down the narrow path of white stones and crushed shells that meandered up from the coast road to his house. He was surprised to see a young woman approaching, carrying a basket. The wind pressed her black cotton dress to the ample curves of her body and set her bright-red scarf whipping frantically behind her. He smiled. Even after all this time, watching Alia walk up the path was a most pleasing sight. He had not been expecting her for a few days yet.

Taking the pipe from his mouth, he yelled, "Alia!"

She looked up from the path and noticed him. She grinned broadly, waved, and called out a greeting that was whipped away by the strengthening gusts. She was flushed and breathless when she climbed the handful of stairs to the porch.

She pulled off scarf and shook out her jet-black hair. It fell in shining soft curls over her shoulders, and he felt his heart swell. She was beautiful, but if one had to be overly critical, one of her front teeth was slightly crooked, and the harshest of critics might have remarked that her nose was slightly too big. But the mischievous twinkle in her dark eyes and that damned disarming smile of hers made those imperfections disappear in a heartbeat. If only he was ten years younger. *Twenty years,* he corrected himself as she looked up at him.

"Hello, Tariq, you old rogue." Alia grinned and kissed him on the cheek.

"Old?" he growled, wrapping her in a bear hug. "Careful my dear. There's plenty of life left in this *old* dog."

"I have no doubt." She laughed as she pushed him away gently. "You need to shave," she chided, running her fingers across his grey stubble.

"Yes, yes. Tomorrow… maybe. I see you could not wait until next week." Tariq grinned. "Razia should have warned you of my deadly charm."

"She did! And that's not the only thing Razia warned me about." Alia smacked him playfully on the arm. "I brought bread, cheese, and olives. And this…" She removed a square bottle sealed with bright-orange wax from the basket.

"Oh, you did not!" Tariq's jaw dropped as he accepted the bottle, immediately recognising the small coat of arms that was pressed into the wax at the neck.

"Yes. I did." She grinned again.

"Sarsinian Royal Reserve." He gaped. "By the gods, how?"

"You know better than to ask that." She smiled slyly. "Close your mouth. Let's eat."

It was getting dark when they finished eating; only a handful of black olives, a small piece of creamy cheese, and crumbs remained on the plate resting on the bench between them. The clouds had finally rolled in, and the first drops of rain had begun to fall. The sea, now grey and angry, roared as heavy waves crashed wildly against the dark rocks below.

Alia gathered up the plate, and Tariq collected an armful of wood from his store before following her inside and closing the door. He pushed a few pieces of wood into the stove while Alia lit the oil lamps and several candles, and soon the room was well lit and pleasantly warm.

Tariq dropped the rest of the wood on the floor and then took two earthenware cups from a shelf in the kitchen before easing himself into a chair at the small wooden table in the centre of the room. Alia joined him, smiling as she watched him studying the bottle.

Tariq slid one of the cups over to Alia, then sat back, running a thumb over the silver royal insignia emblazoned on the front of the bottle. He picked idly at the bright wax seal.

"I miss her," he said suddenly.

"I know," Alia said sadly. "I do, too."

He looked up and smiled wanly. "Damn it to hell, but I can be a morose bastard when I'm sober."

"Then stop admiring that bottle and pour some wine."

He peeled the wax away with a thumbnail, pulled the cork with a soft pop, and filled both mugs.

"Really should use crystal." He sighed, lifting the mug to his nose. He closed his eyes and savoured the soft, wonderfully complex bouquet before taking a mouthful and rolling it around, then swallowing with a look of utter bliss on his weathered face. "How in the seven hells did you get this?" he asked again, shaking his head in wonder.

"I said don't ask." Alia lifted her mug and sipped delicately at the wine.

They drank in comfortable silence, listening to the low crackles of the fire in the stove and the hiss of the rain outside. He had known Alia for years. The young woman had simply walked up the path one morning carrying a basket of bread, olives, and cheese, and of course, wine. They were always the most extraordinary bottles of wine. And she had become a part of their lives, spending long, warm afternoons talking with them, listening to him tell wild tales, laughing with Razia at the obvious exaggerations and fabrications.

When Razia had fallen ill, Alia had been there to help: through each and every impossibly long night, until Razia died. And then she stayed to hold him close as his entire world threatened to fall to pieces. There were so many questions; he knew so little about her yet owed her so much. In so many ways, she was like the bottle of wine that rested on the table between them. He had no idea how something of such immense value could find its way into his life, but he knew enough to just accept that some of those questions would never be answered.

They sat in silence, enjoying the wine and the low hiss of the rain, until he was halfway through his third cup. He reached across the table and took her hand; he squeezed lightly before upending his cup.

"Thank you." He smiled as he pushed back his chair. "For everything." He stood up and swayed slightly before he steadied himself by holding on to the back of his chair. "I must be getting old. Look, three cups, and I fall all over the place."

"I'd wager you could still hold your own if the need arose." Alia laughed.

"Hold onto your coin, my dear." He grimaced, shaking his head. "I'm off to bed, and you're not leaving in that." He gestured toward the windows. "You'd drown before getting to the end of the path if the wind

didn't first blow you into the bay. The bed in the spare room is ready…
unless…" He winked.

"Rogue!" She feigned shock at his jest. He laughed and leaned over
the table to kiss her lightly on the cheek.

"Shave!" She crinkled her nose as his beard scratched her skin.

"Tomorrow!" he promised before shambling off to his room.

Alone, Alia picked up the bottle and smiled sadly as she ran her
thumb over the remnants of the orange sealing wax. *Tomorrow,* she
thought as she touched her cheek where he had kissed her. She looked
across the room to the traveling bag resting against the wall. Next to the
bag was a neatly rolled oilskin bundle. From the shape and size, she
guessed it held swords. Razor sharp Akhbari steel that would fetch the
old smuggler a handsome price in Sarsini.

He would be up before first light and on the road soon after. He
would have already secured passage from either Abuzara or H'jah
Karaam. Tariq could never say goodbye, not even to Razia. She would
just wake to find him gone. She learned that, similarly, she would wake
to find him back—tired, grubby, unshaven, with that roguish smile that
seemed to fend off all protest.

Outside, the storm raged as the woman named Alia poured the last of
the wine into her cup. She sighed and drained the cup in three quick
swallows. She would need to visit the royal cellars again. But this time
she resolved to steal *two* bottles.

The morning was cool and still when Tariq pulled the door to his house
closed. The skies were still dark but the worst of the rain seemed to have
passed. He paused for a moment, thinking of Alia asleep in the spare
room. Maybe he should wait for her to wake. She would no doubt have
much to say about this little, ill-planned adventure. And she would be
right.

He pushed the oilskin-wrapped bundle with the toe of his boot—
swords of the finest Akhbari steel. The taravari was a work of art, and he
had told old Sharif as much even while driving the price criminally low.
He flinched as he thought of the final price they had settled on. It was
almost embarrassing. He would make that back several times over on the
other side of the Great Sea.

He sighed. In truth, he had no need for the trip. He had amassed more
than enough wealth to see him comfortable for two lifetimes. He bent

down and shouldered the bundle. He then slung a small travel bag over his other shoulder and walked around the house to a small paddock, where a sturdy-looking donkey stood diligently cropping the tufts of coarse grass.

He opened the gate carefully, as the weight of the swords shifted, pressing into his shoulder. In a few weeks, the steel would be replaced by gold. *Far lighter but by no means easier to carry,* he thought with a wry smile. He stopped and watched as the donkey looked up and snorted softly. *More wealth than what I could spend in a lifetime... amassed by being away from the person who was my life.* He shook his head at the irony. He would give it all away in a heartbeat for one more day with Razia. *Why then, you old fool?* A hard edge dug into his neck, and he shifted the bundle slightly. He felt torn between ghosts. One that would have him sit and watch the sun dip below the horizon and another that would see him travel beyond it.

The donkey wandered closer and nudged him with a velvety nose. "Morning, girl." He smiled shaking off the melancholy. He patted the animal's neck. "Yes...we're going on a trip."

The Coast of Sarsini
The Thirty-Third day of 389, Morning

The dream always began the same way: He opened his eyes to see the desert, an endless ocean of rolling dunes that stretched to the horizon. It was early morning, and the night chill still hung in the air, yet to be banished by a rising sun. He raised a hand, shading his eyes from the blazing eastern skies and its lurid smears of orange and red.

A light breeze tugged softly at the coarse black wool of his to'ab as he stared at the city. As always, it lay to the east, with its towering minarets and mighty walls starkly silhouetted against the sky. It was an impressive sight from a distance, but he knew now that it was ancient and deserted, slowly losing its battle against the relentless march of time and sand.

Tariq, the dreamer, started to walk, never failing to be amazed at how swiftly he approached the city. The sun had barely moved, and already he was standing in the cool shadows of the wind-etched walls. Tufts of dry weeds had taken hold in the holes and cracks where the stone had split or the mortar had crumbled away.

Far above him, the wind hissed and sighed through the empty parapets. He stood for a moment and tried to imagine a time when there were once guards who walked there, guards who would look down and challenge this lonely traveler who had approached unannounced from the deep desert. Now they were only home to birds, small animals, and the shades of men long dead.

He knew now that a piece of the wall had fallen to the north. He had clambered over those wind-smoothened blocks a hundred times to enter the city. He had walked to the south the first time and found the massive gates, scoured and rusted, wrought from banded iron and dark wood, and resolutely shut.

He had walked almost right around the city that time before finding the breach. There was no need for that now, so he headed to the north, and within minutes, he was climbing over the fallen debris of broken stone. A blue-headed lizard watched his progress with keen interest before he got too close and sent it scurrying off to hide in a small crack.

The dreamer slipped and clattered down the other side, sending a small avalanche of pebbles and sand before him. At the bottom, he dusted himself off and once again looked up at the towering buildings, now empty and silent in their languid decay.

The avenue lay before him, weeds poking up through the shining, smooth cobbles. It was lined with long-dead trees, their trunks and branches burned bone white by the relentless sky. They seemed to claw at the silent blue emptiness above them.

"Have you no faith, Tariq?" came the sad whisper, so soft it was scarcely a breath, like the dry hiss of sand, but unmistakably Alia's. "Have you no *faith?*"

Faith? Alia? Tariq looked around in confusion, but before he could reply, a new voice bellowed, this one harsh and grating. "Smuggler! Wake up, damn you." The voice tore at the fragile fabric of the dream. Tariq frowned and, pulling his cloak tighter around his face, rolled away from the offending voice. The sharp kick to the ribs was far more difficult to ignore.

Tariq's eyes snapped open, and he found himself staring at a scuffed and dirty pair of sea-boots. He looked up at the squat, ugly sailor who glared down at him. The sailor had a jagged purple scar running down the side of his face and a scraggly, oily beard. Behind him stood a younger deckhand who was apparently enjoying the smuggler's discomfort. The boy's dirty blond hair was pulled back in a tight ponytail, and his pockmarked cheeks were covered with the adolescent wisps of a new beard. *He won't last long.* Tariq sighed inwardly.

"It's time to get up," the ugly one growled. "We've hove to, and Mareq don't like it much if anyone fucks with his timetable."

"Yes, Assak," Tariq groaned. "We wouldn't want to fuck with the timetable now, would we? I'll get my stuff."

He stood and stretched. It was hard sleeping on the deck, but faced with the prevailing stench of the lower decks, he'd rather endure the discomfort and breathe fresh air. It was one of the drawbacks of traveling on a slave ship. The advantages, though, were considerable. Seeing as they had no interest in visiting any legitimate port, he would face no customs, which meant no questions and, more importantly, no tax: this, of course, all translated directly into larger profits.

He heard an irritable bray of a donkey and the creak of ropes. He watched as the animal was winched up from the hold.

"Don't worry, girl!" Tariq called out. "We'll be ashore soon." The animal cast a baleful glare in his direction and brayed. Tariq smiled and ducked into a dark stairwell. Minutes later, he reemerged, dragging a large oilskin-wrapped bundle and his travel bag. He placed them on the deck and watched as the stricken donkey was carefully lowered into a waiting skiff. Tariq smiled at the beast as it stood stiffly, casting a glowering stare at the water surrounding it. No matter how many trips they made, she had never grown accustomed to sea travel.

Tariq stepped aside to allow two burly sailors to tie ropes around his bags and lower them down to the men in the skiff. He watched the men to ensure they made it into the boat without mishap and then climbed over the gunwale.

"Ho! Smuggler!" A voice boomed from the upper deck. Tariq looked up to see the captain leaning on the railing of the quarterdeck. Mareq always reminded him of a fat, oily, ill-tempered toad—all out of proportion, with a short heavyset upper body and long, thin legs. He was also so incredibly ugly that Tariq was amazed that his mother didn't drown him at birth. The captain looked down at him through heavy-lidded eyes; his fleshy lips seemed twisted in a cruel parody of a smile.

"Yes, Captain?" he called out, instantly wary. He had a long-standing agreement with the slaver, but he didn't trust the man as far as he could throw him.

"We'll be back in two days," Mareq growled, scratching idly at the stubble on his jowls. "We wait for one day. If you're not here in that time, you can fucking swim back to Akhbar."

"I'll be here," Tariq replied.

"And be sure to sell your pretty swords, smuggler." Mareq smirked. "With no gold, you can still look forward to that swim."

Standing on the lonely stretch of beach, Tariq watched the skiff knife through waves, the slavers hauling hard on the oars; the crew, onboard, were already preparing the sails to leave. Mareq would be raiding up the coast, north of Verana over the next two days. They would have more than two hundred unfortunate souls chained in the hold by the time he saw them again. He spat in disgust and tried to convince himself, with little success, that it was a necessary evil.

The donkey brayed, and he turned to the animal, shaking his head. "I know, girl," he said. "Last time. I promise."

He tied the packages to the animal, gathered the lead rope,   and started walking to the south. Sarsini was only a few hours away, and they would hopefully get there before dark. He gazed out over the grey sea to the west. The skies looked threatening, with heavy clouds gathering on the horizon, and he had little wish to spend the night outside in the rain.

The walk to the city had proved uneventful and the guards at the smaller western gates had seemed bored and disinterested. They were by far the best type of guards Tariq could have hoped for; he had little need to explain what he intended to do with his shipment of Akhbari steel. Any diligence on the guards' part usually required gold to blunt their interest. And he did not like parting with gold.

He smiled as he led the donkey slowly through the bustling streets of the market district. The orange stone of the buildings reared up on either side of the road, split by squat wooden warehouses and small shrines and temples. It was a glorious madness, and he revelled in the press of bodies and unceasing noise.

How he had missed Sarsini's wash of colours and smells. It was the largest of the Kingdom's seaports and home to almost a million people. Practically every valuable commodity flowed through this port and onto Verana, Romidus, the Noordlandt, and for those traders of stouter heart, even the Kurgan plains.

He turned left down a smaller street. The smell of sweat, hot metal, and burning coal filled the air, along with the cacophony of a multitude of metalworkers hammering at iron and steel. As he walked, plough shears and farming equipment gave way to pots and kettles and finally to knives and swords. He stopped at a small workshop where a massive troll of a man was busy working on what looked like the beginnings of a rapier.

"Kerrick," Tariq called out. "I'd wager that's a trifle large for a butter knife."

The man looked up from the blade, blinked, and then his face split into a wide, gap-toothed grin. "Tariq, you old bastard! I thought you'd be retired by now."

"I was." Tariq shrugged. "I got bored."

Kerrick lumbered forward, the heavy muscles of his broad, hairy shoulders bunching as he wiped his hands on a cloth. He grasped Tariq's hand and shook it vigorously. "Good to see you, my friend. It's been *years*! How is Razia? She not kicked you out yet?"

Tariq's smile died as the pain welled up, and Kerrick stopped putting a meaty hand over his eyes as the understanding settled on him. "Shit." He rumbled. "I am sorry, my friend."

"You didn't know." Tariq shrugged, forcing a smile. "But now you owe me a drink. You've still got a bottle or two of that Noordlandt emberwyne?"

"That I do." Kerrick forced a smile. "Take her around the back," he said, nodding at the donkey. "And bring *that* inside." He pointed at the oilskin package.

The remnants of lunch lay scattered across the table as Tariq pushed aside the empty pewter mug. He belched and smiled lopsidedly at the massive smith who sat opposite him.

"Gods, man. Where do you find that hell's brew?" Tariq frowned darkly at the half-empty bottle of emberwyne.

Kerrick grinned. "A mad Noordlander has taken a liking to my axes. Once a year, he commissions a great big double-bladed monstrosity and pays in gold."

Tariq nodded sagely. "Gold...always good."

The smith picked up the bottle and gave it a shake. "And more often than not, he gives me a bottle of this. It tastes good, kicks like a mule, and removes the rust from iron rather well, too." He grinned at the smuggler, who looked up in alarm. "I jest, Tariq. I jest." He held up a large hand, his deep chuckle sounding like rocks rolling down a hill.

"Good." Tariq scowled. "I have no need to spend coin on a visit to the apothecary to stop my guts from falling out. While you're about it"—the smuggler shifted his cup closer to the smith—"what is it with Noordlanders and axes?"

Kerrick slopped some more of the potent liquor into Tariq's mug and his own while pondering the question. "Well, it may have something to do with them being half-bear. A rapier, like one of those pretty blades you've just sold to me, looks a bit like a cheese knife in their hairy paws. They need something"—Tariq watched as the smith waved an equally large and hairy paw in the air—"something more *substantial*."

"And by substantial, you mean something that you could use to cleave, say, a dire wolf in two?"

"Exactly!" Kerrick grinned. "In *twain*." He made a chopping motion with his hand, almost knocking over his mug. "Fuck!" he swore causing Tariq to laugh, holding his own drink away from the flailing smith.

When order was restored, Tariq cocked an eye-brow. "Coming back to this *half-bear* assertion…"

Kerrick nodded. "Maybe a trifle *more* than half in some instances," he offered sagely, tapping the side of his nose.

Tariq frowned and scratched at his stubble. "I seem to recall you tumbling with a Noordlander tavern wench once. Thought you were quite taken with her."

"Aye. I did… and I was." Kerrick smiled, a faraway look of wistful affection in his eyes. "She was a wonder. And the cubs were beautiful."

Tariq snorted emberwyne over the table, and they both burst into uncontrollable laughter.

It was late in the afternoon when the smuggler left Kerrick's forge. The pouch of coin formed a pleasant and heavy lump under his shirt. The haggling had been almost as pleasant as the drinking. Kerrick was quite adept at feigning abject poverty, and his insults were subtle and amusing. Tariq, however, was a master. He had sold the twenty rapiers at a three hundred percent profit and the jewelled taravari at almost four hundred. He smiled. He truly loved the massive smith—a rich man who enjoyed what many perceived to be a simple craft.

He had left the bustle of the market district, and the streets were less busy now. He looked at the low clouds overhead; rain seemed imminent. He pulled his cloak a little tighter at a cold gust of wind. He needed to find a warm tavern with a stable.

"Come, girl." He tugged softly at the lead rope. "I know of a place close by."

The donkey brayed and made a show of hanging her head.

"Yes, girl, I know. It's cold." Tariq smiled at the animal. "But at least it's not raining yet."

A large raindrop hit his face. "Shit."

Tariq's eyes felt gritty and sore as he stared through the blue-grey haze of tobacco smoke that hung in the crowded tavern. As usual, the Priest, as it was known to the regular patrons, was filled to almost the bursting point with fishermen, travellers, and farmers from the rich vineyards that surrounded the city. The card game had not been hard to find, and the heavy purse and the promise of more had proved irresistible. He shared the pahkur table with four other men, and slowly but surely, as coin changed hand, the game had become increasingly intense. They had been locked in battle for over three hours, and the current hand was proving to be pivotal.

He stared idly over the top of his cards at the player to his right. He was a huge man named Sirvan dressed in a plain black leather jerkin and dark woollen trousers. He sat with his elbows on the table; his meaty forearms, crisscrossed with scars, spoke volumes of his life as a mercenary. He was glaring at his cards. He was a fair player but had proved not skilled enough to cause alarm. And now he was obviously of two minds, which was two more than he was accustomed to having, Tariq thought bleakly. *Gods, this might take a while.* He sighed to himself.

"Come, Sirvan," the smuggler chided. "Either bet or lay them down. Staring at them won't improve your hand in any way."

Sirvan glared at him. "Quiet," the big man growled. "I'm thinking."

"No doubt a new activity," Tariq mumbled irritably. "Hence the difficulty."

Tariq swallowed as Sirvan shot him a black glare. This was followed by a flood of relief as the big man returned his attention to his cards. Tariq shifted his gaze to the centre of the table, where an impressive pile of silver lay. He could hardly believe that no one had folded yet. He scowled at his own cards; a grinning knave and two plump dukes stared back at him vacantly. He would need more than a good share of luck to win. His hand was weak, and there was little chance he could bluff his way to victory. Sirvan was sitting on something powerful and would be difficult to dissuade.

Tariq shot a glance at the small stack of coins in front of the mercenary. The man was down to his last eighty drac and would be desperate to win this hand. And therein lay his downfall; card games and desperation were never good bedfellows. Inevitably, you chased something that just wasn't there, and that would cost you.

Scratching absently at the coarse stubble on his cheek, he pondered how to respond to the bet that would be sure to follow. The fat little man sitting to Sirvan's right was a clerk named Drigo who had raised a further five drac. Drigo's bet didn't concern Tariq at all. The poor fellow had been throwing away his money the whole evening. He was no card player, and everyone, including Sirvan, could read him like an open book. The poor man could not do worse if his cards were stuck to his forehead for all to see.

What concerned Tariq was the original bets. Not taking Sirvan's inevitable raise into account, he would still need to pay thirty-five drac just to stay in the hand. The risk was considerable, and he held nothing that resembled a winning set of cards. Sirvan's choice was a far more difficult one. Tariq gauged that the man possibly held a winning hand, but he would have to risk almost half his remaining coin. He watched as the big man hesitated for a second, then quickly stacked the required bet in front of him and pushed it toward the pile in the centre.

"Thirty-five," Sirvan grunted. "And"—he quickly counted out further coins and dropped them into the centre—"another thirty-five."

Tariq suppressed a smile as he watched Drigo's eyebrows shoot up involuntarily. This was followed by a look of consternation as the clerk frantically reexamined his cards. *Poor fellow should really find another game to pass the time,* Tariq thought. *His purse would be eternally grateful.*

Tariq's gaze flicked to the heavy Sarsinian who sat across the table from him. The man's face was like stone as he ran a large hand over his shaved scalp. His dark eyes betrayed nothing as he pondered the bet. Through the idle chatter of the evening, they had learned that he owned an apothecary close by. His accent was a bit different from those born to the city. There were strange inflections on some words that Tariq could not place. This irritated him, as his smuggling had taken him to many far-flung places, and he had an ear for language.

He pushed the thought aside and studied the man's face, wondering whether he would match the wager or not. He found his attention drawn back to the long, twisted scar that ran down the left side of the man's head, from the temple all the way down his cheek. He had noticed that almost immediately and wondered, not for the first time, how a dealer of medicines could be wounded like that. *There's an interesting history there*, Tariq mused.

Quite suddenly, the Sarsinian shook his head and tossed his cards onto the table. "No," the apothecary said softly. "This one is beyond me. My thanks, gentlemen." He nodded to each of them, then scooped up the remainder of his coins and dropped them into his pouch. He reached for the goblet of red wine he had kept faithfully full and tossed it back. His face twisted for an instant as he pushed his chair away from the table and stood up, using the table as support. "May the best man win." He bowed with a sardonic smile and turned to make his way to the exit.

Tariq noticed now that the man also favoured his left leg. *That and the scar... I wonder what his story is.*

"I think that apothecary fellow has a very good point," Tariq said absently, placing his cards on the table while waving for a barmaid. He smiled, sitting back. "This reminds me of another game. I had a monkey back then and—"

"Shut up," Sirvan growled without looking at him.

Tariq closed his mouth and decided to stack his coins into neat piles while he waited for his wine. He grinned broadly at the plump barmaid who placed a full cup of Sarsinian red on the table in front of him. He handed her a silver coin and winked roguishly. She smiled sweetly in a way that said both *thank you* and *no thank you* at exactly the same time. He sighed and sipped at the cup; with his cards folded, Tariq could now observe without reservation.

The brute, Sirvan, was glaring at the other remaining player to the right of Drigo. The man, who called himself Panos, stared back with steel-grey eyes, his manner cool and unflappable. Tariq liked the man for no particular reason. He had a certain style about him. He was well dressed but somehow managed to look a little scruffy. He was bearded, with dark, close-cropped hair, and a long-stemmed pipe hung at a rakish angle from his mouth. His most discernible flaw, in Tariq's estimation, was that he had proved to be a very accomplished card player.

Throughout the evening, Panos would habitually hold his cards fanned in his left hand while the right played idly with the steadily growing mountain of coins stacked neatly in front of him. Now and again, he would take an heroic pull from the heavy pewter mug of mead that rested to the right of the coins. Tariq noticed with grudging admiration that the swordsman generally drank as much as he won. A considerable amount on both points.

Tariq found himself once again strangely impressed by the man's nonchalant manner. But as relaxed as Panos seemed, the sword leaning against the edge of the table next to him looked as if it had seen more than a little action in its time. It served as a quiet suggestion not to take this man lightly.

"Mmm…" The swordsman pondered the bet, tapping the stem of the pipe against his chin. "What do you think, Drigo, old boy?" He looked to the very uncomfortable fat man. "Do you think our friend Sirvan is bluffing?

Tariq watched as Drigo shot a furtive glance at Sirvan and then back to the tall swordsman. Dabbing his upper lip with a small silk handkerchief, he cleared his throat. "I…er…I'm not sure," Drigo stammered, making a show of arranging the balance of his coins into neat stacks while continuing to mop his flabby jowls.

"Mmm…" Panos smiled easily. "Bluffing or carrying the whole royal family in that hand of his?" Tariq watched as the swordsman puffed at his pipe before transferring his gaze back to the glowering Sirvan. Free free of the constraints of the game, the smuggler knew instantly that Panos, too, carried a powerful hand. Perhaps even the winning one. *This is going to be interesting…*

"Well, my good Drigo," Panos continued. "I am quite intrigued as to what our large friend is holding over there. And for that reason, I am compelled to explore the boundaries of his enthusiasm: your thirty-five…" he said to Sirvan. "And another ten." The bet joined the pot in a silvery cascade.

Drigo's reaction to the bet was comically transparent. Tariq took a long pull of wine to disguise his amusement. Cards were fanned and closed, only to be fanned again. The poor man's jowls seemed to have a life of their own as he swallowed convulsively. He used his handkerchief to dab at the beads of sweat on his forehead. Tariq almost felt pity as he watched the poor man desperately try to find value in a hand that was now obviously hopeless and inadequate. Stuck between the stone-faced Sirvan and the ice-cool swordsman, he had only one possible action. With a deep sigh, Drigo placed his cards on the table.

"Hard luck, Drigo." Panos smiled. "I'll join you at the bar in a little while."

Drigo shook his head nervously. "Um... no thank you." He dabbed at his face, looking thoroughly wretched. "My wife is... er... expecting me." He quickly scratched his few remaining coins into his purse and scampered away from the table.

Tariq laughed and lifted his cup to salute the fast-disappearing Drigo. "Send my love to your wife!" Then he leaned over the table and grinned at the combatants. "Given the lightness of that purse, I think old Drigo's missus is going to be very angry indeed."

Tariq saw Sirvan's jaw clench as the large man fought to control his anger. "Yes, yes..." The smuggler slumped back into his chair, holding a hand up in surrender. "I'll shut the fuck up."

He glanced at Panos, who sat quietly puffing on his pipe, casually observing the seething anger across the table. *This man has no nerves,* Tariq thought. The bet had been coldly calculated. The swordsman had bet just enough to force Sirvan to commit everything to the game. That or fold. *This may just get messy.* Tariq casually shifted his chair a little further from the table to place a bit more distance between himself and what he gauged would be the arc of a swinging axe.

The Kurgan Steppes,
The Seventy-Fifth Day of 387, Morning

Panos sat in the saddle and studied the narrow canyon in front of them. His head throbbed mildly from the night before—too much emberwyne, too little sleep. He had made a small fortune, though, by winning the previous evening's impromptu sword tourney, betting on himself, and letting the coin ride to the finals. He had never favoured dice, which was the preferred form of gambling in the legions; cards was his game. So when Varden had suggested the tournament to keep the men sharp, Panos had jumped at the opportunity, knowing there were none within the ranks who could best him with a blade.

Unfortunately, the celebrations were now proving rather painful. The bottle of emberwyne passed around the tent he shared with three other officers had seemed like such a good idea at the time. He sighed and slid a finger under the leather strap of his helmet, seating it more comfortably. *What to do?* he thought and tugged at his beard as he looked at the jumble of rock that guarded the entrance to the canyon.

He knew the four men who sat in silence behind him were waiting for his decision, and he sensed their reluctance to enter the narrow confines of the defile. They were not wrong. They were tracking a large band of Kurgan tribesmen, and this would present an almost perfect opportunity for an ambush.

"What you thinking, sir?" Mace asked. The old sergeant's voice had an edge to it. He was a wily old veteran and not prone to being easily unnerved, but the emptiness of the Kurgan steppes had a way of scratching at the back of a soldier's mind. The vast open spaces seemed to pick at the scabs of long-forgotten fears and stir the dark waters of a man's soul. Even Mace, who seemed crafted from granite and old leather, was not immune.

And neither am I, Panos thought. He had felt the brush of icy fingers across the back of his neck and had caught himself listening to the whispers on the cold wind as it hissed through the ocean of grass.

"Sir?" Mace prompted.

Panos dismissed the question with a grunt and slight shake of his head. *They are in there somewhere... Or are they? How deep does the canyon go? Is it blind? Are there forks? Shit… all questions we need to answer.* He sighed and pulled his helmet from his head to allow the breeze to dry the sweat from his short dark hair.

This Kurgan raiding party had attacked a number of farms to the east of Verana, putting them to the torch and killing the families. The raid had been lightning fast, unanticipated, and brutal. More than likely, a result of young warriors trying to establish rank within their tribe. They had taken nothing of value, leaving only dead bodies and ruined homes in their wake. It was almost as if they wanted to be chased. The idea that they had been lured onto the steppes made him mildly nauseous.

They had found only one survivor, a girl of about six years. According to her, the band might number as many as twenty, maybe even thirty. She had shown them on her hands, being unable to count. The girl had been gathering berries in the woods when they fell upon the farmhouse, and she had watched her parents and brother get butchered from the edge of the trees. The girl was young and in shock, so the numbers may have been inflated, Panos mused, but he had seen the the tracks. *No less than twenty, maybe twenty-five horses…* He chewed on his lower lip as and he turned the problem over and over in his mind.

The duke had sent a detachment of five hundred men from the Eighth Legion to chase them down and bring them to justice. More than enough men to take care of the raiders. *Bring them to justice…* A wry smile split Panos' face as he thought of the duke's words. The duke's justice, perhaps—not that he didn't want to put an end to the raids. But there would be no trial, no justice. Revenge, perhaps, but a lasting lesson was unlikely. Nothing short of obliterating the entire nation would stop the tribesman from attacking the farms. The Kurg knew only one form of law, that of the sword and the bow. On the steppes, a strong arm and sharp blade were law.

And it's looking like we're going to chase these bastards all the way to Karakuran's royal ger to press that point. If we live to make it that far, Panos thought dryly. They were already a two-day ride from the top of Burned Man Pass and deep into the Kurgan lands. The Kurg were a violent and ruthless people, and there would be no casual encounter here on the steppes if the legionaries were discovered. They would be attacked on sight and butchered to a man.

So far, the tribesman had managed to stay one step ahead. They travelled light, their small ponies were known for their stamina, and the men were known to sleep in the saddle if need be. And now that they were in lands that they knew intimately, the prospect of finding them was looking increasingly hopeless.

Worse... the prospect of riding into a trap is looking more likely by the hour, he corrected himself. His hand strayed absently to the pommel of his sword. That gnawing feeling had started yesterday afternoon when the trail had just inexplicably disappeared. Varden d'Verana, the duke's nephew, who led the detachment, was at a loss yet again. Leading, in Panos' estimation, was a fair stretch above the man's abilities. He was not a bad man, just a poor officer. He simply could not make decisions, and on the steppes, that was a trait that tended to get men killed.

After an extended and painful deliberation, Varden had finally agreed to send three groups of scouts to find the trail. Panos had made a point of volunteering to lead one of the groups, even though, as a Centurion he would be in his rights to delegate the task to a lesser officer. He needed firsthand information if he was to help Varden and, more importantly, his men survive.

They had been searching for a day and half when they finally picked up the trail. He had chosen Taber as part of his group because the man had an uncanny knack for tracking. Renan and Oren were young but steady, and Mace was as tough as dried leather. It was not a surprise when Taber picked up the trail. It had led them to this narrow canyon that looked, for all intents and purposes, like a trap.

He heard one of the other men clear his throat. "What is it?" Panos asked without looking back.

"We going back, sir?" Renan asked. "You know, to get the rest of the men?"

"Mmm..." Panos waved a hand, ignoring the question. Varden was not a gifted leader. The man had no military mind and only held his rank because of his birth; he was the eldest son of Viktor's brother, Aryan. He needed to know more before returning and having Varden run headlong into a trap that would get the lot of them killed. He had no fear of death, but getting captured and slowly roasted by these Kurgan bastards would not be a pleasant, nor swift, transition to the afterlife.

"Sir?" one of the other men prompted.

"Wait," he snapped. "I'm thinking." *Is there a way up onto the plateau?* he thought tracing the jagged ridge of the rock on both sides of the canyon. The east ridge was almost vertical and strewn with broken scree. *But the west looks promising. If we could some men up there with bows, we could have cover.* He liked the look of a number of the narrow gullies carved into the rock face.

He turned to the gnarled, bearded sergeant. "Mace. Take Renan and Oren and follow the ridge to the west. See if there's a way up through one of those gullies. We meet back here in an hour. Be careful and be quiet. Whatever you find, do not engage the Kurg."

"Yes, sir." Mace nodded. "And you, sir?"

"I'll take Taber to scout the entrance to the canyon. We need to be sure they didn't double back." He turned to Mace. "If we're not here when you return, wait for an hour and then head back." He left the rest unsaid. If he and Taber didn't return, they had walked into a trap and were already dead. Mace would know what to tell d'Verana. With luck, the man would listen.

"Understood, sir." Mace nodded and turned to Renan and Oren. "With me, boys," he said, and the three moved off at a slow trot.

"Taber. Dismount and hobble the horses. We go in on foot," Panos said to the young soldier.

"Sir," Taber replied, immediately dropping from the saddle.

"Leave your sword. Bow and dagger only."

Panos loped behind Taber, his stride easy. The tracker ran quickly and quietly with a short recurve bow in his left hand. The tracks at this point were clear enough for even Panos to read, but it wasn't long before the grass and soft earth gave way to rock and stone. No matter how many times he had seen Taber at work, he remained in awe of the man's skill. The tracker had hardly slowed, pointing every now and again to a misplaced stone or a chip in the rock. *How, by the gods, does he do it?* Panos smiled to himself.

They were close to the entrance to the canyon and were now running in the shadows of the high cliffs that jutted upward into the cold blue sky. Taber had slowed, taking time to scan the crags and the jumble of stone that littered the entrance. They needed to be careful from here. There were too many places for archers to hide, and the Kurgan were famous for their uncanny ability with a bow.

They passed between the high walls of the canyon, and Panos felt his pulse quicken. The sense of danger was palpable as he loped alongside the tracker, mouth suddenly dry. He felt unseen eyes crawl over his skin.

Taber, though, was consumed with the hunt, all his senses bent to the task of following the all-but-invisible trail that drew them deeper into the narrow canyon.

Then Taber stopped and stooped to a crouch. Panos immediately dropped down next to him. The tracker was inspecting a patch of flat, hard stone in front of them. Panos took a moment to examine the high walls of rock on either side of them. It was quite cool in the shadows and, apart from the low hiss of the wind completely quiet.

"What do you see?" he asked quietly.

"Nothing," Taber replied. "The tracks are gone. They were heading deeper into the canyon…but they stop here." He tapped a knuckle on the stone at his feet. "Not even a scratch."

"We need to find those tracks," Panos whispered. "Keep to cover as much as possible. I'm not liking this."

Taber nodded and moved forward, crouching low, his eyes intense as he searched for the smallest clue in the unyielding stone. Panos followed closely behind him, probing every dark cranny and shadow for threats. He had nocked an arrow, holding the bow low but ready to use in an instant.

Taber stopped again, holding up a fist. He dropped to a knee. Panos froze and drew back on the arrow. "Here," Taber hissed, pointing to an almost invisible chip in the rock next to his foot. The tracker then pointed to the edge of a fallen boulder. A minute tuft of hair clung to the stone where a horse had brushed against it. He then slowly swept his arm forward, indicating the tracks led onward, deeper into the canyon. They took a few seconds to make sure the way was still clear and then moved forward, slowly keeping to the shadows and cover presented by fallen rocks.

Khulan sat on his haunches and played with the bone necklace that hung from his neck as he watched the two men below inch forward. The ledge he crouched on was deep in shadow and about fifty feet above the canyon floor, so he had little worry of being seen. The two Kingdom soldiers were very careful and very quiet. And the one in front was obviously a gifted tracker. Khulan smiled as the man pointed out the faint spoor to his companion, knowing that the clue was minuscule. He and his men had been meticulous in covering the trail.

He turned to Bortuun, who crouched next to him like a giant hairy boulder. The recurve bow looked like a toy in the man's huge hands. Bortuun's shock of blond hair had been carelessly tied back from his flat, square face with a thin strip of cloth; his long beard had been braided into a fork held by two simple silver rings. *A man of such exceptional ugliness, his own mother would have thrown him from her ger if it were not for his fierce loyalty,* Khulan thought with a ghost of a smile.

He leaned closer to the giant and whispered, "Allow them to come a little closer... twenty paces, no more. Then kill the tracker." Bortuun nodded without looking away from the soldiers.

Yamun and the others are already in place, Khulan thought as he watched the tracker paused to examine a patch of rock. The other was scanning the sides of the canyon, bow at the ready. Khulan smiled. *Your friends are already dead. You should not have sent them up the defile, and now there will be no escape for you, either.*

He ran his fingers over the bones, feeling the soft rounded ridges, worn by years of idle attention. The necklace was a gift from his mother after he had killed his first man. He was eight, and the man was a Guthur raider. The man had killed his father with the sword that he now carried on his back. It was a tulwar of exquisite beauty, a long curved blade of wickedly sharp Akhbari steel.

He could still remember the man's face, his shaved head, the dark stubble on his cheeks, the mad blood lust in his eyes. The raider had cut his father down, then charged at Khulan and his mother, sword raised, expecting an easy kill. But his mother had thrown a cast-iron pot at his face, and a moment later, he had sent raider to hell with an arrow to the throat. The man had taken a while to die, choking on his own blood. And after the battle, his mother had cut away the man's fingers and made the necklace for him from the knuckle bones.

He had killed many men since then, but with this raid he could finally be counted as a true warrior. He had led his men deep into the Kingdom lands, and they had laid waste to the eastern farms. But more importantly, they had drawn a great many soldiers deep onto the steppes. The deaths of the soft farmers meant nothing, but destroying the legionaries and burning the Kingdom officers in their fire pits would bring him and his men much standing.

They would kill them all and every man would have his share of bone and skin. They would be counted as men, and their names would be known by all. He smiled to himself when he heard the soft creak of the bow as Bortuun drew back the arrow. The big man slowly let out his breath, and then the string thrummed as he released the shaft.

Student

Verana
157th day of 366, Morning

Tanto watched as his student flowed through the kata. A fine golden dust hung in the cold air of the doh'ja, thrown up from the fighting circle when the boy landed from a spinning attack that saw the blade form a deadly, gleaming arc that would have neatly decapitated the imaginary enemy he fought. The boy's skin was already glistening with sweat and the lean, corded muscles of his upper body rippled as the sword hissed out its song of death.

Tanto toyed idly with the long grey plait that hung over his shoulder. His dark, hooded eyes were like chips of black glass, and his lean, deeply lined face was expressionless. Outwardly, he showed nothing of the pride he felt. The boy was, without any doubt, one of the very best students he had ever taught, effortlessly combining strength with almost preternatural speed and balance.

The only thing that kept this boy from being the wonderful weapon of destruction he could be was his impetuous and sometimes, mischievous nature, a source of great vexation for the old master.

Tanto permitted himself to sigh softly. The boy was anything but a fool. He had demonstrated time and again his ability to not only effortlessly grasp even the most complex of problems but also examine and expand upon the solutions. Tanto tugged at his braid. If he mastered his emotions, it would not be long before the student would far outstripped his master's own formidable martial abilities. *If...* Tanto's impassive mask hid the flash of frustration.

It had been years since the boy's father had first brought him to the doh'ja. Cranos was one of the duke's most celebrated captains, a man of iron will and fearsome reputation. Tanto smiled at the memory. The man had been shorter than expected. He had heard much of this captain and had almost expected a giant and, from the talk of his men, one possibly carrying a fistful of lightning bolts.

In reality, Cranos was lean and moved like a wolf; his face was all angles and lines—a stern face seemly chiseled from granite yet lacking any trace of cruelty. He was a hard man, but he was fair and deeply respected by his men.

When they had first met Tanto had bowed, deep and slow; he, too, would respect this Captain of men.

"Sword Master," the captain greeted simply, the hard angles of his face shifting into a ghost of a smile.

"Yes, Captain. I am Tanto."

"Tanto." the captain nodded. "A fitting name for a sword master." He then switched to Tanto's native tongue. "Your name means 'blade,' if I am not mistaken?"

Tanto blinked in surprise as he replied in the same language. "Yes, Captain. You are indeed correct. Forgive me for asking, but where did you learn to speak Geng'ho?"

"When I was a boy, my sword master, Hayato, thought it was essential to master the blade, but one also needed to learn to master a"—Cranos smiled slightly—"... a *civilised* language."

"One as lowly as myself would never dispute the wisdom of Hayato the Hawk." Tanto bowed deeply to hide his own smile.

"I have brought you a new student," the captain said without further preamble. "This is my son. He is young but has shown some promise with the blade. I would be pleased if you would explore the extent of his skill."

Tanto moved his attention to the small boy, who stood quietly at his father's side. He was no more than six years old, small for his age, but he had held his head high and had returned the sword master's gaze without flinching.

"If it pleases you, we will begin immediately, captain." Tanto bowed once more.

"It does." The captain nodded. "Regard him as steel. Temper him well."

Master and student watched as the captain turned on his heel and strode from the doh'ja without another word. The boy had then looked up to his new master.

"Do you see the goh'ji on that beam in the roof?" Tanto asked, pointing to a strange group of pictograms chiseled into the dark wood.

"Yes." The boy had nodded.

"It says, 'Gather each drop of rain without fail and soon you will have an ocean.' What do you think that means?"

"I am not sure." The boy shook his head.

"It speaks of humble beginnings and the fruit of unwavering resolve." The master had smiled. "Both of which you will experience in abundance in this doh'ja."

Tanto blinked and brought himself back to the present. The boy was flowing effortlessly through a leaping sequence of the kata designed to build on balance and spatial awareness.

"Stop!" Tanto's voice rang through the doh'ja. Instantly, the boy stopped and sheathed his sword before turning and bowing deeply. He knelt in the centre of the circle with his head lowered and waited for the master to approach.

"Have you considered the question I posed yesterday?" Tanto asked as he stepped into the circle.

"Yes, Master," the boy replied.

"When engaging an enemy, which opening attack is the most effective? Do you have an answer?"

"Yes, Master." He paused. "But it is difficult to explain adequately using words, Master."

Tanto considered this and then nodded slowly. "Very well." He moved to the edge of the training circle and drew his sword. The three feet of razor-sharp tempered steel gleamed in the dusty morning light. "Then show me."

The Kurgan Steppes
The Seventy-Fifth Day of 387, Morning

The canyon forked ahead. The path to the right was tight and headed steeply upward through broken rock. To the left, it also narrowed but not as much; the walls offered little cover. *Shit,* Panos swore quietly to himself. *Do we go further? This is madness...*

He touched Taber's arm. "Where?" he whispered. Taber traced an invisible line to the left with the blade of his hand. *We need to know.* Panos tapped the tracker lightly on the back, and Taber slid forward carefully. Panos followed a moment later, wondering if Mace and the others had found a way up to the plateau. They would be heading back already, but he and Taber had to follow the trail. It was still not clear if the Kurg had just ridden through or if they were lying in wait. It was a dangerous task, but it was worth the risk—the potential loss of two soldiers versus the entire detachment.

They had gone no more than a dozen steps when Panos heard the arrow hiss through the air. The shaft hit Taber in the throat, and the tracker crumpled to the ground. Without thinking, Panos grabbed the tracker's jerkin and dragged him behind a boulder.

"Taber?" He looked down at the tracker. The shaft protruded from his neck just above his right collarbone. The man's eyes were wide with fear, and blood burbled up past his lips as he struggled to breathe. *Shit, shit, shit,* Panos swore. He held Taber's hand; the man was dying. "It's all right. You did well," he said lamely, forcing a smile. "Mace will come get us. He's behind the bastards by now."

Blood dribbled down the doomed tracker's chin and he clung to Panos' hand with surprising strength.

"Hold on, Taber. Mace will—" he started to say when a voice called down from above.

"Hey, Kingdom." The accent was thick and guttural. "You are trapped. Throw down your weapons and come out."

Panos cradled the tracker's head in his lap. "Hold on, Taber. Hold on…" He stroked the dying man's hair. *Never thought it would end this way,* he thought. Somehow, he always imagined making it through to old age, a ridiculous assumption, given his present situation.

"Come now, Kingdom." the voice continued. "All your men are dead. We took care of those you sent up the defile. You are alone, so do not make it difficult for yourself. If we come and fetch you, it will not go well for you."

Panos looked down at Taber. The man lay still, his face oddly peaceful. Panos gently closed the tracker's eyes. "Sorry, Taber," he said softly as he lay the tracker's head down on the stone next to him. He looked at the bow and realised the futility of trying to fight. He picked up the weapon and tossed it into the open. His dagger followed.

"I'm coming out," he called to the unseen tribesman, then slowly stood with his hands raised. His skin crawled as he waited for an arrow to slam into him. Instead, he saw a stocky man step from the shadows to stand on the edge of a narrow ledge. A moment later, a huge bear of a man joined him, aiming an arrow at Panos' chest.

Panos heard movement behind him and turned slightly to see several tribesmen emerge from their hiding places, bows aimed at him.

"Well met, Kingdom." the stocky man called out. "I am Khulan."

Panos looked up at the man, anger burning hot in the pit of his stomach. Rough hands pulled his arms behind his back and bound his wrists tightly.

Verana
157th Day of 366, Morning

The boy stood and bowed, then drew his sword and dropped into his fighting stance. Tanto bowed in return and readied himself, his sword raised, his muscles relaxed and prepared. He noted with satisfaction that utter calmness seemed to cloak the boy. When the attack came, there would be nothing to warn him; each telling twitch or tensed muscle had been ruthlessly drilled from him through years of kata exercises, meditation, and painful lessons with the bukuto, the wooden practice swords.

The speed of the attack was terrifying and everything Tanto had grown to expect of his gifted pupil. It required all of the sword master's considerable skill to counter. Instead of attacking with the sword, the boy had opted for a sweeping kick, the blade following in a low, scything arc. It had come within a hair's breadth of succeeding.

A kick, far slower than any sword thrust, would never have been considered by his other students: only the boy's unnatural speed and balance had made this attack even remotely possible. Even now, having managed to evade the blow, Tanto still found himself being systematically backed up by a torrent of lightening-fast cuts and thrusts that would have killed a lesser swordsman in a matter of heartbeats.

The exchange lasted no more than a few seconds, a dazzling, jarring clash of metal, and the two fighters found themselves circling the ring in a momentary stalemate. Over a prolonged encounter, Tanto was still convinced he would prevail, but that advantage was being swiftly eroded by this brilliant student.

The master smiled and raised his hand.

"Enough," he said softly, and the boy sheathed his sword and bowed deeply.

Tanto returned the bow, lower than required to honour him.

"Your answer pleases me," Tanto said softly. "The most effective offence is that which the enemy least expects."

Panos rode slowly next to the tribesman, steering the horse with his knees. His body ached from the beating he had taken before they dragged him to his horse. The bodies of Mace, Oren, and Renan lay sprawled on the ground stripped of weapons and armour. The ears and fingers were missing, and broken arrow shafts jutted from their pale flesh. *Fuck these savages! Fuck them!*

The man, Khulan, sat comfortably in the saddle and played idly with a necklace of bones. There were some thirty-five tribesmen in his band. Most were openly hostile, only held at bay by the leader, who seemed to need Panos alive, for some reason. They had been riding steadily for a few hours, and by the angle of the sun, Panos gauged they were heading straight for the Kingdom camp.

Surely they don't intend to attack the camp with so few men? Panos thought. *Maybe they intend to bargain my life for some concession? But why? They could just kill me and ride away—they would never be found.* Panos turned the problem over and over in his head, but nothing made sense. *They would be outnumbered by more than ten to one. Why are they keeping me alive? Ransom? Leverage? Varden would never bargain with these savages.* For all his faults, Varden didn't lack courage.

"You know where we are going, don't you, Kingdom?" Khulan asked suddenly.

"Yes. They won't bargain with you," Panos replied bluntly.

"Bargain?" The tribesman laughed. "Oh, no bargain, Kingdom. We are going to kill them. All of them."

"In that case, if I were you, I would pray to whatever gods you have." Panos turned and smiled coldly at the leader. "You're going to need all the help you can get."

At this the Kurg laughed heartily and turned to the massive bear of a man riding behind him to his right. Through bouts of laughter, he said something in his own language while pointing to Panos. The big man guffawed and gave Panos a gap-toothed grin as he tapped his temple.

"You… are madman," he rumbled and then slapped his chest with a meaty paw. "I… Bortuun like."

Khulan turned back to Panos, obviously still amused. "Ahh, Kingdom, you are a funny man." He wiped tears away from his face with the edge of his jerkin. "We don't need the gods and neither do you. We would all be lost if we did." The Kurg smiled pleasantly before he continued, "You see, they don't give a shit about you or me or Bortuun." He nodded to the smiling giant. "They don't care whether we live or die. And they don't really want to be bothered with all this nonsense." He leaned forward to pat his horse's neck. "Think about it, Kingdom. I pray to my gods to defeat the your soldiers; you pray to your gods to kill my uncivilised savages. We leave it all to gods who don't care one way or the other. So we have a bit of a stalemate. This is the right word, is it not? Stalemate?"

"Yes," Panos grunted. "It's a term from a board game called *Sha'h.*"

"Yes! I have seen this!" Khulan exclaimed. "A trader once visited my tribe, and he taught me the game. Not as good as sho'gii mind you. If I remember correctly, you need to kill the other players' pieces by removing them from the board and trap the pasha, the prince." He leaned over to Panos with a puzzled look on his face. "I always thought it was strange that a game with no gods could end in stalemate. And why not just kill the pasha? Much easier than trapping him."

Panos ignored the question, and they rode in silence for a while before Khulan turned to him again.

"You have been a soldier for a long time, Kingdom?" The Kurg asked. "You are a leader, are you not?"

Panos nodded. *They are going to kill me in any case so what difference does it make?* he thought before replying. "Yes, I have been a soldier for almost my whole life. I am a centurion. I command a hundred men."

"A hundred men! So you are a man of some importance, are you not, Kingdom? A chief?"

"No." Panos shook his head, turning to the tribesman. "I am a middle officer. You understand this?"

Khulan frowned. "I lead these men, thirty-five. One day I will lead one hundred, then I will be a khan, a man of significant importance, and I will lead families and a tribe."

"The legions are different." Panos shook his head. "They are just fighting men; there is no tribe. There are ten thousand men in each legion. My legion is the Eighth. Each legion has ten cohorts of a thousand, each cohort has ten centuries of a hundred, and so on. So we need many officers, or chiefs, to command that many men."

Khulan grunted, his brow furrowing as he turned the information over in his mind. "With no tribe, why do you fight?"

"We fight where we are sent by the king or his dukes," Panos replied, tiring of the conversation, but the Kurg continued.

"And do the king and his dukes fight?"

"No," Panos said, and then turned to the Kurg with a wry smile. "Unfortunately not."

"Would you be here if your king had not sent you?"

"No. Probably not," Panos said after briefly pondering the question. "But if you had attacked my farm or that of my family or my friends, I would have hunted you to the ends of the earth."

Khulan grinned and nodded. "This I understand. Yes, I like you, Kingdom."

The Kurg attacked the camp in the early hours of the morning. Panos guessed it was between the second and third bell when the men were in their deepest sleep and the guards were cold and distracted. The men on the perimeter were dispatched with arrows to the throat so that no cries of alarm would be raised. Those who were not killed instantly were dispatched with knives. The men sitting around the fires were quickly dealt with, throats cut and their bodies dragged into the shadows.

Panos, gagged and tied and flanked by two tribesmen, had watched in horror as the Kurg had flowed into the silent camp like ghosts. Blades glinted in the moonlight, and when the killing began the cold efficiency of it all was horrifying. They split up, four tribesmen to a tent, and ruthlessly and silently cut the throats of the sleeping legionaries before moving on to the next.

They had gone through more than half the camp before the alarm was sounded. Then, as the men spilled from their beds they were met with volleys of arrows that scythed them down. Panos watched in mute rage as the Kurg obliterated the camp without the loss of a single man. When the slaughter was done, he was dragged to his feet and led into the centre of the camp.

The bodies of the legionaries who were not killed in their beds were piled up in a haphazard tangle of bloody limbs, the bodies bristled with arrows. *Poor bastards had no chance,* Panos thought as a rough hand pushed him forward. To his surprise, he saw four Kingdom soldiers on their knees, hands tied behind their backs. Two officers and a young legionary flanked Varden, who knelt, his head hanging forward, blood dribbling from his mouth.

Khulan stepped in front of him and pulled the wadded rag from his mouth. The Kurg's face and beard were speckled with blood, and in the flickering torchlight, he looked every inch the demon from the stories Panos had heard as a child. He turned from the tribesman to the legionaries on the ground.

"Sir!" Panos shouted to Varden.

The officer looked up with surprise. He blinked as if trying to make sense of what he saw. "Panos? That you? You're alive! How?" He paused, and when he realised that Panos was virtually unscathed, his face twisted. "Did you lead them here? Did you?" he shouted, awkwardly trying to get to his feet. "You led them here, you—" Varden grunted as a tribesman kicked him savagely in the ribs, driving him to the ground. He lay wheezing through clenched teeth. "Why? Why did you do it?"

"I didn't lead—" Panos started, shocked at the man's words.

"Shut your mouth!" one of the other officers snapped, cutting him short. "Burn in hell, you traitor! Burn in fucking hell! Coward!"

A Kurgan tribesman smashed his fist into the man's face, knocking him to the ground. Panos surged forward, only to be restrained by his two guards. A sharp blow to the stomach left him doubled over. He looked up to see the tribesman reached down and grab the officer him by the hair to pull him back to his knees. The officer hissed in pain. His breathing was shallow, and sweat beaded his face as he glared at Panos with undiluted loathing.

"Prepare them," Khulan barked.

Panos watched in horror as their hands were pulled downward and tied to their ankles with wet leather. Any protest or struggle from the men was met with savage blows to the head or a kick to the ribs. When the men were trussed up, they were each dragged to a shallow pit where they were made to kneel while stones were packed around them to keep them upright. Then came the wood, packed in neat bundles around each of the terrified men.

Panos saw how Varden somehow managed to keep himself composed. Sweat ran down his face, and he spat the blood from his mouth but otherwise remained silent. If nothing else, the man was brave.

"I'll see you in hell, traitor," he called out to Panos.

Panos shook his head before looking away towards the dark of the steppes. What could he say? He felt sick to his stomach. A rough hand pulled his face back to the horror about to unfold. The Kurgan leader grinned before slapping him on the side of the head.

"You will watch, Kingdom," Khulan said with a smile. His eyes glinted with a madness that chilled Panos to his core. "You will watch," the Kurg snarled as he grabbed a fistful of Panos' hair, "or I will have my men cut off your eyelids."

"Why not kill me as well, you fucking bastard?" Panos hissed through clenched teeth. "Why leave me alive?"

Khulan laughed, releasing Panos. "You live because you will tell the others what happens when you hunt the Kurg." He stepped in close, and Panos could smell the stink of his breath and the sour sweat that permeated from his leather jerkin. "You will tell them how we take bone and flesh from all who come here."

Khulan turned to the pit and waved two of his men forward. They carried burning torches. Almost casually, they walked among the bound legionaries and put flame to the wood stacked around them. It did not take long for the screams to start. Panos watched as they writhed and convulsed as their clothes caught alight. He flinched at the bestial shrieks as their hair flared and burnt away and their skin started to blacken and crisp.

"No!" The word tore from his throat, "No! *No! No!*" He shouted it over and over until his voice broke and his lungs burned from the acrid smoke. Then, as the stench of burning flesh washed over him, he fell to his knees, bent over, and vomited. The last thing he heard was the Kurgan tribesmen's cruel laughter mixing with the screams of the dying men; then something slammed into the side of his head, and all went mercifully black.

The boy was back on his feet in an instant. His eyes blazed as he angrily whipped the blood from his nose. He was bruised and battered, and every muscle of his body screamed in protest as he raised the bukuto, but he could not think of a single thing he wanted more than to feel the wooden practice sword crunch into the sword master's serene face.

Tanto shook his head. "Yet again, you do not hold onto the stillness. Even now, after all this, I can see the anger burning inside you. We will repeat the lesson... again."

"You punish me for my anger? We will see who tires of this game first," the boy snarled defiantly.

"I do not punish you for anything," Tanto said softly. "It is you who is punished by your own anger. Your rage makes you reckless. You do not think. You merely act, without being mindful of the consequences." The master paused to see if his words had penetrated the boy's rage. The boy's eyes blazed, and his nostrils flared. Tanto sighed and continued, "When you learn to detach yourself from your desires and emotions, you will see the path. Prepare yourself."

The boy barely waited for the sword master to take his position before he launched a furious attack. The bukuto hissed through the space where the master's head had been only a heartbeat before. The wild follow-through sent him spinning off-balance and the riposte—a short, cracking blow to the side of his head—flattened him once again. This time he took longer to find his feet. His head spun sickeningly, and this time, the trickle of blood from his nose went unheeded, a dark-red stream that dribbled down his chin and dropped to the matting of the practice circle.

"That was for not addressing me as master," Tanto said softly. "Prepare yourself."

The boy lurched forward, clumsily swinging the practice sword, and Tanto evaded the blow with ease, his response a lightening-quick tap to the ribs, just enough to sting. Enraged, the boy swung wildly at his teacher, who, each time, frustratingly just slipped out of reach and delivered a stinging reply that would land on his shoulders, legs, or arms. This continued until the boy was staggering with exhaustion. Sweat stung his eyes and mingled with blood, dripping freely from his face.

When Tanto decided to end the lesson, it was mercifully quick. He ducked effortlessly under a sweeping blow, then jabbed his bukuto into the boy's body, just below the rib cage. The breath punched from his lungs, and the boy folded over and crashed into the floor. Tanto stood back and watched dispassionately as his student writhed and fought to take a breath.

"Today you were punished by your anger," Tanto said, calmly waiting for the boy to recover. "Your desire to see me humbled was greater than your need to learn." The boy managed a ragged breath, and Tanto reached down to help him to his feet. "Think on this tonight," he said with a faint smile.

"Yes, Master," Panos said bowing deeply.

The Kurgan Steppes
76th day of 387, Morning

Panos floated in silence for what seemed like an eternity, drifting aimlessly in a warm, dark ocean. Above him, he watched as an endless expanse of stars wheeled with languid majesty, and he felt a deep peace that he had never felt before. But then, ever so slowly, he became aware of the pain. It grew and grew until it permeated his entire body, and when he finally opened his eyes, he found himself lying on his side in the grass.

He groaned. His hands were still tied firmly behind his back, and dried blood caked his hair. He could see snow capped mountains some way off, lit by the pale dawn light. His brow furrowed. He was near Burned Man Pass, as far he could tell. But how did he get there? He tried to piece together the horrors of the previous night. The last thing he remembered was Varden's blackened face and his last words that had cut through him like a blade.

He tried to roll to his knees and sit up but groaned as shards of white-hot pain lanced through his skull. He took a slow breath and then rolled carefully onto his back, where he lay, still trying to quiet the nightmarish images that continued to wash over him. A tear rolled down his cheek as he watched the clouds scudding across the boundless sky. But now the chilled wind that pushed them relentlessly to the east held no malevolence. The whispers that had plagued him before were now silent, held at bay by the horrors that were already inside.

Panos took a deep breath, and with great care, he rolled to his side and managed to sit up. He looked around and realised that he was only a few hours' ride from the pass. The Kurg must have ridden through the night to leave him here. His horse stood close by, quietly cropping grass, and a dagger hung from the saddle horn. He could not understand why he was not dead.

He struggled to his feet and walked to the horse, pulling the dagger free with his teeth. He dropped it to the ground and lay down, rolling to the blade. With considerable difficulty, he eventually managed to saw through his bonds, hissing in pain as the leather parted suddenly. He lay still for a moment and then rolled to his knees, where he rubbed at his hands and flexed his swollen, purple fingers to get the blood flowing once again.

Panos stood and walked to the horse. He reached down and removed the hobble from the animal's hooves, then pulled himself painfully into the saddle. He took up the reins and cast a long look back to the flowing grass of the steppes, remembering the ghosts of the men he was leaving behind. He had little doubt that their voices would follow him no matter where he went. He could never return to Verana; no one would believe him that the Kurg had spared him alone. The silent accusations of his fallen comrades would see him hanged for desertion and cowardice.

He sighed as he thought of the pain it would bring his father. It was better that he was thought to be among the dead, his bones lying somewhere on the steppes alongside his brothers. In truth, a piece of him had died, burned to ash. With a final look to the distant horizon, he pulled the horse's head toward the pass and put his heels to its flanks. With luck, he would be in Sarsini within a week. It was as good a place as any to start piecing together this new life.

Sarsini
The Thirty-Third Day of 389, Evening

It was bitterly cold, and rain filtered softly down from the night sky. The cart, drawn by a brace of oxen, creaked and clattered over the slick cobbles. Dacian sat hunched over, his sodden cloak clinging uncomfortably to his broad shoulders.

His elbows rested on the sword that lay across his knees as he scowled at the guttering streetlights of Sarsini from under his hood. The weather was truly as miserable as it could possibly be.

He cast a quick glance at the man who shared the bench with him him, an old farmer who sat with quiet acceptance, occasionally flicking the reins to keep the lumbering beasts moving. He had hardly strung two words together in the long, slow, bone-rattling hours they had shared travelling down the coast road.

Dacian's back ached, and he was tempted to see if his spine protruded from the top of his head from the constant jarring. *Still better than walking,* he admitted grudgingly.

Dacian returned his attention to the narrow street. It was getting late, and the city seemed all but deserted. The few people he had seen were either hurrying along, cloaks drawn tightly around themselves, or skulking in the shadows. The latter did not worry him in the slightest, and if they chose to test his patience on this particular evening, they would get far more sport than expected; in fact, that dark part of himself, which he had painstakingly buried from so many years, even dared them to try.

"Cursed weather," Dacian muttered half to himself, half to his companion as he transferred his glower to the swaying oxen. *Move your worthless carcasses,* he thought irritably as he brushed the water from his newly grown beard.

If I had been paying attention, I might still have my horse. His scowl deepened. He had been a week's ride south from Verana and following the lesser-traveled paths that skirted the broad western road. He had little doubt that the duke's animals would be tracking him, knowing that he had only one viable option.

The Vikingur to the north were not known for their hospitality, and the towns were far apart and small. There was nowhere to hide. The small port town of Prana to the west was crawling with Verana's agents, and the Kurgan plains over the eastern mountains would never enter any rational person's mind. That was simply a quick and horrible way to die. The Kurg were quite fond of roasting strangers over open fires for entertainment.

All that was left was the ride south to Sarsini; from there, he'd take a ship on to Akhbar. Once he was across the Great Sea, they would never find him. Verana's men would anticipate that, and Dacian had know doubt that they would have sent men riding hard for Sarsini, knowing that Dacian would take the quieter, more circuitous route. He would need to be cautious because they would likely be waiting for him.

He had kept an eye on the clouds as they steadily built and grew closer. He had figured that he would make it to the city before the rain set in, but a crossbow bolt had dashed those plans. He grimaced as he involuntarily touched the tender lump behind his left ear.

"Bastards," he growled to himself. The old man looked over at him and raised a bushy set of eyebrows in question. Dacian shook his head and waved off the unspoken question. The farmer shrugged and gave the reins a light flick that did little to coax more speed out of the disinterested oxen.

The road had been meandering through one of the many coastal forests when the crossbow bolt had slammed into his horse's chest. He had seen the silvery flash an instant before it killed the animal in mid-stride; the horse had just crumpled under him, throwing him over its head. He winced as he remembered hitting the road like a sack of wheat, the air exploding from his lungs.

Dacian's hands balled into fists as he stared blankly past the oxen. He had raised that horse from a foal, watched it take its first tottering steps on legs that seemed too long. The gelding had a white patch on his forehead that reminded Dacian of a throwing knife, and he had named him Shard. Yet another life, so close to his own, ripped away by a crossbow bolt from a thief...

Dacian staggered to his feet, head spinning and struggling for breath. His vision swam as he desperately tried to drag air into his lungs. He lurched backward and groped for his sword. The razor-sharp blade gleamed as it slid free of its scabbard. He turned unsteadily on legs that felt like jelly and scanned the tree line for any sign of the bowman.

The soft, sibilant hiss of the wind through the cool green darkness of the woods was all he could hear. His horse lay a few paces to his left, its lifeblood a dark, sticky pool on the dusty stone of the road.

He swore as he stumbled over to the gelding. "Not like this." He sank to one knee and touched the animal's neck. Its soft brown eyes stared lifelessly. "Not like this...not... like... this!"

He surged to his feet as his anger ignited.

"Come out, you gutless son of a whore!" he bellowed. "Show yourself!"

"Lay down the blade," said a voice from the shadows behind him. "All we want is your coin. No one need get hurt."

"Get hurt? You killed my horse! I almost broke my neck!" he shouted into the gloom. "Show yourself and I'll give you a lesson in getting hurt."

"Brave words for a man with a crossbow aimed at his heart." A dry chuckle drifted from the undergrowth. "Now lay down the blade or you'll join the horse."

His knuckles cracked as he wrung the pommel of his sword in frustration.

"Lay down the sword or die." Said the voice coming from the cover of the woods. This time, there was a cold edge to the words. "A simple enough choice, I would think. There's neither honour nor sense in dying needlessly."

Frustration and rage threatened to boil over within him as he glared into the trees. Years ago, in a different life, he would never have let his emotions run this wild. They clouded thought and hampered action. He took a long, deep breath. He had no choice. He opened his hand, and his sword clattered against the stone of the road.

"That's better," said the voice. "What's your name?"

"Fuck off," he snarled, scanning the undergrowth in the direction of the voice. He could see nothing, not the slightest movement, apart from that caused by the wind.

"Ah. I would have had a conversation with my parents if I were you," replied the voice with a chuckle. "No matter. I want you to lay your purse on the ground."

"Why don't you come and take it from me?" Dacian smiled coldly at the forest. "That is, if you have the spine for it."

A mocking laugh emanated from the trees. "I don't think so. A strapping lad such as yourself could probably put up far more than a fair fight. But this isn't a fair fight. Try to remember the crossbow and do as I say."

The rain was falling more steadily now as the cart trundled into an older part of Sarsini. The houses were jammed against each other, and dull, yellow light shone through the grubby windows. The rain and sea air did little to hide some of the more fetid smells that hung in the choking darkness of the alleyways that wound between the buildings.

The sound of raucous laughter and music reached his ears. A garish sign swung above the door of one of the buildings a little way up the road. In the poor light, he could barely make out the name of the establishment: THE PRIEST AND PARTRIDGE. It was a good enough place to start, and besides, he needed a place to sleep. As they drew closer, he noticed a rather sullen, miserable boy huddled next to a rickety gate.

"I'll leave you here," Dacian said to the old farmer. "I can't thank you enough." He reached for his purse and felt a hand grip his arm.

"No, lad, keep your coin. I would join you for a pint"—The old farmer smiled—"but I need to unload tonight."

Dacian gripped the farmer's hand and then jumped down to the road. He slung his sword over his shoulder before calling out, "Hey, boy! Open up." He pointed to the gates. It would be best if he didn't announce his arrival by walking through the front door. There would be an entrance that connected the stables to the main building.

"And who would you be?" the boy snapped, glaring up at him. "The bleedin' king of Sarsini?"

Dacian paused, swallowing down the flash of anger with difficulty. "Listen, boy… I'm cold, wet, and inclined to hand out a lesson in manners. Now open up before I make your night a bit more interesting."

The boy grimaced and pulled himself slowly to his feet. He slipped the latch and pushed the gates open. "My lord," he sneered with an overly elaborate bow.

A short, sharp backhand cracked against the side of the boy's head, sending him face-first into the mud.

"Don't say I didn't warn you, boy," Dacian grunted as he walked past the boy, who looked up at him, glassy-eyed, from the mud. Dacian then waved to the old farmer, who flicked the reins, urging the oxen to lurch forward. He watched as the wagon clattered slowly away before turning back to the small, grubby yard.

He noticed a stablehand standing under one of the eaves, puffing on a pipe, and watched as he approached. The man, short and grizzled, reeked of cheap tobacco and manure and looked as if he had not bathed in at least a year.

"Where's the master of the inn?" Dacian asked.

"That would be Master Varagus, sir," he replied.

"And where do I find Master Varagus?" Dacian asked.

"Oh, he'll be inside." The stablehand gestured to a small door at the side of the inn. "He's more than likely behind the bar. A large man with a black beard. Right fierce-lookin'. I'd be watchin' my step with him, I would."

"Thank you." Dacian nodded...

Dacian tore the purse from his belt and flung it to the ground. It landed with a heavy, metallic thud.

"Good. Now step away from the sword."

Dacian took three steps backward, his fists clenched so hard they ached. Every last coin he had to his name lay on the dusty road in front of him. Everything that he and Arianne had worked and bled for...He winced at the sliver of pain that lanced through his chest...Arianne and little Aron. They were both gone, too. Torn away from him by men much worse than these thieves.

A man rose slowly from the undergrowth. At first it looked as if the forest had suddenly grown limbs, so cunning was his disguise. Leaves and stems were tangled in his hair and clothes. His face and arms were stained a mottled green and brown, and he casually aimed a heavy crossbow at Dacian's chest.

Dacian watched as the thief walked slowly toward him, the weapon never straying. The man stopped at the small sack of coins. Dacian waited. If the thief looked down to retrieve the coin that would be his chance. He slowly shifted his weight to the balls of his feet and readied himself.

Then the man's eyes flicked to something behind Dacian. Another! Dacian had started to turn when something crashed into the side of his head. It was a glancing blow, but still, white-hot pain flashed through his skull and his legs buckled...

The common room was crowded, noisy, and filled with smoke. The stench of unwashed bodies, sour wine, and cheap ale hung in the air. He shouldered his way to the bar counter. A heavy, bearded man stood wiping his meaty hands on his apron.

"What'll it be, stranger?" he asked.

"I'm looking for Varagus?" Dacian replied.

"Aye, that's me. What'll you be needing?" Varagus nodded, lumbering over.

"I may need a room for the night."

"It will be a couple o' silvers for the room, three if you want a meal." The innkeeper grunted. "If you need the stables, that will cost you a total of five."

"No need for the stables," Dacian replied, leaning on the bar. Keeping his hood up, he quickly scanned the crowd. It was a rough mix of dockworkers, merchants, and a few darker characters. More importantly, no one looked out of place. Verana's men would be paying attention to the door and any newcomers.

There was, however, a particular group of five men that drew his attention. They clustered around a card table near the fire. One had the look of a local thug, two looked like merchants, the fourth was a fat little man who was probably being bled dry, but the fifth was a swordsman. The edge to the man was unmistakable. Despite his relaxed manner and a general shabbiness, there was a particular hardness that was difficult to miss. Dacian had spent a lifetime around that type of man.

He turned back to Varagus, "My thanks. Let me think on it... with an ale, if you please." He slapped a silver drac on the counter and turned back to watch the game.

Panos took another long drag from the pipe and glanced coolly at his cards: four paladins, resplendent in armour of iron, bronze, silver, and gold. It was a winning hand, beyond a shadow of a doubt. It had been a very lucrative evening. His opponents had ranged from predictable to downright transparent. And Sirvan's very evident frustration had betrayed him yet again. The man obviously held a powerful hand but was visibly torn, reluctant to play it as a winning hand but unwilling to lay it down.

Panos puffed at his pipe and blew a perfect smoke ring that floated out over the table to dissipate over the mound of coins in the centre. Idly, he tapped the pommel of his rapier and weighed up the man across from him. The huge muscles of Sirvan's chest, shoulders, and arms rippled and knotted as he moved. No doubt from wielding the heavy double-bladed axe that rested against the wall to his left. The man's dark eyes seemed to seethe under their heavy brows—a bad-tempered killer. Panos instinctively knew that he would have to be ready when the cards fell. He did not want to kill the man, but if Sirvan did not take this loss in his stride, there might not be another choice.

Sirvan was chewing on his bottom lip as he wrestled with the decision placed before him: fold and cut his losses or risk his last ten coins to see what Panos held in his hand.

"Damn you to the pit of hell!" Sirvan cursed, then shoved his remaining coins into the centre of the table. "I have a house of knaves and dukes. Now what are you holding?" he demanded slamming his cards down in front of him.

Panos glanced at his opponent's cards where they lay in disarray. As he'd thought, Sirvan had held a good hand, but his own four paladins beat the knaves and dukes easily.

"A house!" Panos feigned surprise. "Damnation! Sirvan, old man, I thought you were bluffing!"

Sirvan blinked in surprise, then grinned broadly and reached for the coin.

"Wait. A moment please." Panos smiled. "I said I thought you were bluffing. I did not say you have me beat." Slowly and quite deliberately, he dropped his cards one by one to the table. Sirvan stared incredulously as each of the paladins landed. Then his face twisted into a mask of rage.

"You cheating bastard!" he roared, hammering his fist onto the tabletop, scattering coins and cards. Sirvan's chair clattered to the floor as he stood. He grabbed for his dagger and froze as he found himself staring down the silvery blade of a rapier. The needle-sharp point hung motionless in the air in front of his left eye.

"Seeing that I not entirely sure of the marital state of my parents at the time of my birth"—Panos smiled calmly—"I can't take offence at being called a bastard. But no one calls me a cheat."

Dacian placed his tankard on the bar counter without taking his eyes off the two men. A coin rolled slowly from the table, and the metallic clink and rattle as it hit the floor was clearly heard in the silence that had descended over the tavern. The card table became the centre of attention.

The swordsman's reaction had been like lightning: his blade had cleared the scabbard in a silvery blur, the point stopping within a hair's breadth of the other man's face. The third man, the Akhbari trader, who had obviously anticipated this turn of events and quietly gathered his coin and shifted away from the table, now looked as if he was willing himself to be invisible.

"Stop this!" Dacian heard Varagus roar from behind the counter. "Ferenc! Over here! Now!"

Dacian turned and followed the innkeeper's glare over to a mountain of a man standing at the far side of the room. Ferenc was a head and shoulders taller than any other man in the common room. He stood with his arms crossed over his barrel chest glowering at all the patrons with small, close-set eyes that nestled under heavy ginger brows. His shaved head, covered with blue Noordlandt tattoos, gleamed in the light of the lanterns.

The giant looked up at the call and lumbered towards the card table, his menacing glower fixed on the two men. On an impulse, Dacian stepped in front of him. Ferenc stopped and looked down at him with irritation.

"No need to interfere here," Dacian said quietly. "Let them sort this out."

"Get out of my way, little man," Ferenc growled, reaching out with a melon-size fist to grab Dacian's shirt. Dacian's reaction was swift and instinctive: With his left hand, he seized Ferenc's arm, locking the man's fist against his chest. With the right, he grabbed the wrist and twisted it sharply up and over to the right, painfully locking the wrist and elbow. Ferenc instantly dropped to a knee with his arm twisted out straight behind him.

"If you struggle, I'll break it." Dacian warned, lifting the arm fractionally to emphasis the point. The large man groaned as the ligaments strained to the tearing point. "I said there was no need to interfere."

"Stop this!" Varagus roared again, slamming a short wooden cudgel against the bar counter. "You! Let him go!" He pointed the cudgel at Dacian. "And you two"—he shifted his glare to the pair at the card table —"take your money and get out!"

"I'm not sure that Sirvan here agrees with that solution." the swordsman replied calmly. His sword did not waver for an instant.

"Damn right, I don't," Sirvan's voice grated through clenched teeth.

"I thought you might not." Panos shrugged. "Pity... the courtyard to settle this, then? Oh... you'll need that." He gestured toward to the man's axe.

Sirvan nodded. The swordsman lowered the blade and looked to Dacian. "When you decide to let that one go, would you mind gathering up my money? I'll need it after I kill Sirvan."

Dacian nodded, then turned back to Ferenc. "I'm going to let you go, and I want you to behave. Otherwise, we'll do this again, but next time I'll rip your arm off. Do you understand?"

Ferenc hesitated for a second and then nodded. He winced as Dacian released his wrist. Ferenc grabbed his shoulder as his arm flopped down. He slowly got to his feet and looked down at Dacian for a long moment.

Dacian met his stare until the big man finally turned away and pushed his way through the crowd of patrons, who were jostling in an effort to get a good position in the courtyard. Dacian breathed out a sigh and went to gather the swordsman's coins.

Panos pushed through the press of bodies and stepped into the circle. Money was changing hands at an alarming rate, and odds were being shouted back and forth. At the other end of the circle, Sirvan shoved a few of the excited bettors aside, scattering coins, to their consternation. Panos watched with mild interest as the man swung his axe in lazy arcs, loosening the massive muscles of his shoulders.

"Quiet!" Varagus bellowed, and apart from a few hasty whispers and the almost frantic clink of coins as they passed hands, the crowd went silent almost instantly. "We are here to witness these men settle a dispute." An excited buzz started again.

"Silence, damn you!" he roared, waving his cudgel. "By law, they need to agree to the terms of honour! Gentlemen…" He paused and looked to Panos and then Sirvan. "To first blood?"

"He's a damn cheat," Sirvan growled. "I'll see him dead."

Panos just nodded.

Varagus nodded as well, irritated at the choice. "To the death, then," he announced. A duel to the death was legal, but with a match to first blood, there was less to explain to the city watch. At least he had the opportunity to make a few coins on the side to help ease the inconvenience.

"Whenever you are ready." Varagus stepped back.

Sirvan roared and sprang forward swinging, the axe in a murderous arc… and died. The crowd stared in stunned silence as Sirvan staggered, then stopped. His axe clattered to the ground. Blood spilled from his mouth as he sagged to his knees. Then he toppled to face-first into the mud of the courtyard.

"Fool," Panos said softly, hardly hearing the crowd bursting into a frenzied roar.

Dacian thumped the weighty leather purse into the swordsman's hand.

"My thanks." Panos offered his hand. Dacian gripped the man's wrist. The swordsman returned the grip. "You've seen service," he said.

"As have you." Dacian nodded. "I am Dacian."

"Panos," the swordsman replied. "I serve… *served* with the Eighth Legion."

Dacian paused, noticing the correction. "I served with the Tenth… in another lifetime."

"The Tenth? I think I would like to hear that story," Panos said. "A story best told over a drink, if I am not mistaken."

Dacian nodded slowly. "Yes, but I'm thinking we should find another inn for that drink." He gestured toward the fallen axeman. "No need to answer endless questions when the city guards arrive."

"Sound thinking, my friend." Panos agreed. "I know just the place. It's close to the waterfront. It's noisy and busy. The ale's not the best, but it is cheap. And most importantly, the serving girls are magnificent!"

Dacian smiled and followed the swordsman out through the gate. They walked in silence for a few minutes. The rain had stopped for the moment, but the cold wind that blew relentlessly in off the ocean would bring more before the night was out.

"You don't strike me as the walking type," Panos said suddenly.

"I'm not," Dacian replied. "I lost my horse."

"Lost?" Panos asked with a bemused expression.

"It was killed."

"Ahh... On the forest road, I take it?" the swordsman ventured.

"Yes."

Panos nodded, not at all disturbed by Dacian's abrupt answers. "I've also had a few... *altercations* with those who work that stretch."

"Altercations?"

"Well, they tried to rob me once... We turn here." He gestured towards a narrow road winding between looming warehouses. "I persuaded them it would be too expensive of an exercise."

The road curved slightly to the left, and at the end it opened onto a broad walkway that, despite the weather, was quite busy. Down one of the intersecting streets, Dacian could just make out the docks. The tall masts of trading ships stretched high into the night sky.

"Persuaded?" Dacian asked, looking at his companion.

"I killed three of them," Panos said casually.

"That tends to be a compelling sort of argument." Dacian nodded with a half smile.

"Yes. It certainly does!" The swordsman smiled broadly. "Here we are." Bright light spilled from the wide doorway of a busy tavern. The sounds of raucous laughter and the babble of voices marked it as a popular venue. "What do you say to a few gallons of ale and willing barmaid?"

"Just the ale for the moment," Dacian replied.

"For the moment?" Panos laughed and slapped him on the back. "My friend, rest assured, the moment is all we truly have."

Ascendant of Shadow

The Forest Road
The Thirty-Third Day of 389, Morning

The essence of Moloc drifted above the assassin as he tore the purse from his belt and flung it to the ground. The thieves had killed his horse, and now they wanted his gold. The Ascendant grinned at what was to be another small nudge down the path to chaos.

Moloc extended his hand and felt the life force of the first thief thrum between his fingers. *Rise.* The man stood up from the undergrowth and pointed his crossbow at the assassin's chest. *Take the gold.* The thief blinked, a look of confusion flashed across his face, and then he walked slowly forward, the weapon never straying.

The Ascendant glided over to the second thief, who was hidden in the thick brush. The first thief had stopped at the small sack of coins. The leather bag lay between his feet. *Wait.* The thief froze.

Moloc extended his hand to the hidden thief. This one was older, and his life force, though still warm, no longer pulsed liked the other's; it merely hummed. No matter. It would not no longer be his in a few seconds. The Ascendant flexed his fingers, nails piercing the warm glow between them. *Kill.*

The thief stopped with the bag of gold at his feet. Dacian took a deep, slow breath and readied himself. *Why is he waiting? Take the gold!* The man's eyes flicked to something behind him. *Another!* He whirled around, and something crashed into the side of his head. It was a glancing blow, but still, white-hot pain flashed through his skull, and his legs buckled...

"I got him, Jarek!" a voice yelled behind him. "I got *him*!" Another blow clipped the edge of his jaw, and Dacian's vision exploded into a flash of bright light as he pitched forward, desperately trying to hold on to consciousness. "*Kill him!*" shrieked the voice behind him. It was bestial, devoid of all reason.

The tottering steps took Dacian within a foot of the bowman, who jumped awkwardly aside, lifting the bow to avoid the collision. Dacian knew his life hung in the balance. He grabbed the weapon and twisted it savagely, hearing the snap of the man's trigger finger almost simultaneously with the crack of the bow. The bolt thumped into the other thief's shoulder, punching him to the ground.

Dacian tore the crossbow from the first thief's grasp, and in one swift movement, he smashed the butt into the man's face, crushing his nose. The man fell heavily to the road and lay still. Dacian shook his head as the effort sent him teetering on the brink of oblivion.

The second thief was trying to crawl away, his left arm dragging limply at his side. Dacian slowly walked over to his discarded sword. On rubbery legs, he carefully reached down to retrieve the weapon. His vision swam as he straightened, and a wave of nausea washed over him. He waited a few seconds for his sight to return, and then he turned to the crawling thief.

He walked over to the man and roughly kicked him over onto his back. The man's eyes went wide with terror as Dacian slapped the blade under his chin.

"Please…" the man whispered. "Don't."

Dacian stared down at him. His face was expressionless as he raised the sword…

Wait. Moloc glided down to stand beside the assassin. The sword was held high, frozen in the space between time. *It did not take this one long to remember his previous life… to remember his not-quite-forgotten skills.* The Ascendant grinned as he traced a finger along the razor-sharp edge of the blade. He leaned in close to the assassin. The thrumming of this one's life-force was *incandescent.* This *Dacian,* he found the name amusing, was very special. It was so rare that one with such an abundance of life would be so adept at dealing in death.

Moloc moved to the thief. The man's good arm was raised to ward off the coming blow. He knelt next to the man and tugged idly at the bolt jutting from the thief's shoulder. It was lodged quite tightly. Probably jammed in the socket of the joint, the Ascendant surmised. *Quite painful.* He bared his teeth and pushed at the bolt, feeling it grate against the bone. It mattered little; what remained of the man's life could be measured in the instant it would take the blade to drop to his neck.

He stood. It was pleasing that the assassin would be ready when the others came for him. Blood would be spilled in rivers before they took him. And even then, when he was dragged back to the old man, broken and subdued, the sport would continue. The old man would take his time killing this *Dacian.* The suffering would be almost endless, and when that blazing life was finally extinguished—he shuddered at the pleasure of the thought—it would be *exquisite.*

He leaned close to the assassin. This one's anger was truly beautiful, and with the right leverage, it would *burn. Kill them,* he purred as he stroked Dacian's face almost affectionately. Then the Ascendant stepped away to watch...

Dacian held the sword high for an instant before swinging it down viciously.

"No!" the thief screamed the instant before the flat of the blade smacked into the side of his head.

Dacian looked down at the unconscious thief. A large purple welt was already forming on the side of his face around the cheekbone. *Fool,* he thought as he sheathed the sword and retrieved his coin purse. Without looking back, he started to walk. With his horse, he would have made Sarsini before nightfall, now he would be lucky to make it by the morning.

Moloc seethed as he watched the Assassin walk away from the two unconscious thieves. *How?* he raged. *How could this mortal defy him? How? Was it her? Again?* He looked around, fists clenched.

"E'kia!" He shouted at the forest. "Is this you? Show yourself!"

He seethed as only the wind and trees answered. He stormed over to the thief Dacian had spared and, with a bestial growl, kicked the man in the face. The crack of his neck sounded before his head flopped back at an unnatural angle.

His rage insatiable, he crossed over to the other thief and reached down to grab him by the throat. He lifted the helpless man as if he were weightless and shook him violently like a rag doll, crushing his throat. Moloc held the lifeless body for a few seconds before tossing it aside with disdain.

He would *not* be defied again...

○

The Crow Inn, Sarsini
The Thirty-Third Day of 389, Evening

Panos stared blankly at the new frothy tankard that the barmaid had put down on the table. He blinked owlishly, trying to determine whether one more drink would further enhance *the moment* that he had touted to his new friend. It was proving to be quite difficult. His head felt full of wool, and any sentence, beyond the most rudimentary, required intense concentration.

"My manners!" he blurted suddenly. "Thank you… Jasmijn!" Panos turned and yelled with a broad grin. The girl turned and smiled, and then continued to weave her way through the crowded pub. Panos returned his attention to the tankard. *Fuck it,* he thought abruptly and took a mouthful of ale.

Dacian sat opposite him and seemed to be in far better shape. Panos studied the man over the brim of his tankard. He needed to drink faster—it wouldn't be sporting if only one of them turned into an incoherent cretin. That would give the other an unfair advantage with the ladies. He cast a jaundiced eye at his ale and placed the offending beverage down with exaggerated care.

They had found a nook tucked away near the back of the bustling Crow Inn, where the tables and benches surrounded a large circular fireplace built from rough stone. Most were occupied, and the air was filled with pipe smoke and the ebb and flow of conversation and occasional laughter. Low flames curled around the heavy logs in the fireplace, and the wispy smoke spiralled away up a brightly polished copper cowl that hung from the ceiling.

"I must admit"—the swordsman grinned lopsidedly—"I find that faint Noordlandt lilt quite alluring. Apparently, she's new here!"

Dacian just nodded and took a slow pull on his ale.

"A fine addition to a fine establishment!" Panos smacked his left hand onto the tabletop to emphasise his point and turned his attention back to the subject of his infatuation.

She was quite tall, and her long golden hair was drawn back from her face and held in place with a simple strip of leather. She wore a modestly cut white blouse that strained somewhat under the pressure of her ample breasts, paired with a long skirt that highlighted her narrow waist and the curve of her hips. *Not a classic beauty,* he conceded, *but very difficult to ignore, very difficult indeed.*

She glanced back with a mischievous twinkle in her emerald-green eyes and flashed a dazzling smile in their direction. Dacian, to Panos' disbelief, dropped his eyes to the table almost immediately.

"Are you feeling all right my friend?" Panos asked, suddenly worried. "Have you received any"—he waved his hands around, looking for some reason that his friend would ignore such a beauty—"particularly violent blows to the head?"

"Just the ale tonight," Dacian said softly.

"All right." Panos nodded sagely while trying desperately to make sense of Dacian's decision. "But then I think you should pay more attention to your drinking." He poked at Dacian's tankard before taking a slow mouthful of ale while frowning over the rim. He had heard that concussions affected the faculties rather badly. *Dangerous,* he thought as he tried to inconspicuously search for signs of lumps on Dacian's head.

"You wanted to hear of the Tenth," Dacian said suddenly.

Panos blinked in surprise and placed the tankard on the table. His friend looked up at him with red-rimmed eyes. "Yes," Panos said simply.

"There's an oasis on the eastern trade route," Dacian began. He lifted the tankard and drank deeply, then wiped the froth from his mouth. "The Wadi al S'hakh. The Well of the Sky. We were sent there to quell an uprising…"

It was late when Dacian's tale was told and Panos' head swam from the ale. He had watched his new friend stagger away to find a room without a word. What was there to say? The man was a hero, and he hated himself for it. The swordsman took another mouthful of ale and winced at the taste, which suddenly too bitter. There were parts of the tale that struck Panos hard, his own raw memories of fire and death surging back to the surface.

He pushed the tankard aside and leaned back in his chair. He had felt a flash of revulsion and rage at the story of the Akhbari pasha. It was brutal and savage, but he also knew it was not his tale. It was not something he would had done, but, then again, he had not lived through the battle at the Wadi. He had not lost what Dacian had lost.

Almost everyone knew a version of the story of the Tenth Legion. He had read many different accounts but had never heard a firsthand report. There were certainly parts that he knew, beyond a shadow of doubt, that Dacian had never told to another soul.

Panos cast a soured look around the common room. Many of the patrons had left, but there were a few tables still occupied. Most of these people who frequented the inn's pub would live their entire lives in relative safety and peace, a simple existence. They would feast on the heroic tales, never stopping to consider the darker side of each story. Flies and crows weren't half as exciting as invincible heroes in their shiny, unblemished armour.

It was so much better to hear about how the valiant legion stood against apparently insurmountable odds and somehow managed to prevail. No one would question why almost ten thousand men were butchered over a dry riverbed in a gods-forsaken desert half a world away.

Panos grimaced as the heady effects of the ale made the remaining patrons seem to mill around oddly, as if walking on the deck of a ship. It took a long moment for him to realise that he was swaying back and forth—not the entire room. He took a fresh grip on the table and steadied himself. He had served long enough to know that the written accounts of battles tended to vary from reality by differing degrees. The scope of that divergence was largely dependent on who wrote them and whose reputation they sought to protect or enhance.

He thumbed a wad of the aromatic tobacco into the bowl of his pipe and smiled bleakly before clamping his teeth down on the stem. *Enough of this, you melancholic fool,* he decided abruptly. He knew just the cure. After a heroic effort to get to his feet, he retrieved his sword from where it rested against the wall, hooked a thumb into his belt, and walked towards to fireplace with slow and deliberate steps.

He took a pair of metal tongs from a hook and grubbed around in the fire for a small ember. Holding it to the wad of tobacco he puffed contentedly on the pipe, drawing the smoke deep into his lungs. He missed on his first and second attempts to return the tongs to their hook, only succeeding on the third by grabbing the hook and leaning in so close to it that he had to squint.

"Melancholic," he said slowly to no-one in particular and then sniggering to himself. *Can't be that drunk,* he thought.

He swayed slowly as he surveyed the inn. *Now to find myself a soft lass and a willing bed,* he thought with an evil grin. *Wait...* He frowned before shaking his head; the idea was close enough.

The girl who had served them for most of the evening had been stunning. *What was her name again?* He examined the ceiling while scratching his forehead with the stem of his pipe as her tried to remember through the fog of ale. *Jemima, Jes... What in damnation? She was apparently new and had started that very night... Jasmijn!* He smiled. *Yes, Jasmijn.* He mouthed her name, oblivious to those close-by who looked at him with amusement. *Yes, quite beautiful.*

He frowned as he remembered that, for some inexplicable reason, she had seemed to prefer *Dacian.* He puffed and muttered to himself in disappointment at her obviously poor eyesight or very slow wits. After all, it was his coin that had paid for the ale. And if his memory served him correctly, he had always ensured that there was an extra coin or two. Evidently, this was not enough to overcome her very poor taste because she had not paid the slightest attention whatsoever to his razor wit and legendary charm.

He shook his head and then chuckled to himself as he a recalled the little trader telling a rather amusing story of a Noordlander and a bear earlier in the evening at the card table. He paused. *Or was the Noordlander the bear?* The details were all rather hazy. *Never mind...* He sent several frustrated puffs of smoke up from his pipe. The point was that there was no reason, logical or otherwise, that Jasmijn should choose Dacian over a fine specimen such as himself.

Panos shrugged and tapped the spent tobacco from his pipe into the fireplace. He was not one to dwell on misfortune; there were *always* other opportunities. He smiled as his gaze settled on a rather plump-looking serving girl with an abundance of very pleasant curves.

"And opportunities abound." Panos nodded sagely to himself. "You, my lovely, are the lucky girl tonight." He clamped his teeth down on the stem of his pipe and tried, with little success, to straighten his tunic. "Abound..." he slurred to himself with a silly grin, then staggered over to introduce himself.

Dacian stumbled into the room and lurched into a small wooden table, spilling the jug of water and knocking the ceramic washbasin to the floor, where it shattered. He cursed and kicked the jug into the corner;

the shards of the broken bowl crunched under his boots as he staggered to the narrow bed. He slumped down and rolled over onto his back to stare up at the ceiling. The room spun sickeningly, and he covered his eyes with his hands.

As the rain pattered softly against the glass of the window, Dacian slowly allowed the memories to surface: Arianne as she lay next to him in the long grass of the meadow; little Aron running as fast as his legs could carry him, his hair shining like burnished copper in the sun; their home; the smell of fresh bread in the kitchen. The unbearable pain of loss clawed at his chest, and he felt hot tears running down his face. He clenched his jaw so tightly it felt as if his teeth would shatter.

The next memory hit him like a fist. A hollow-eyed man stared up at him, the gaunt, haunted features of a man he had thought long dead. The memories, long suppressed, burst forth like pus from a suppurating wound. Even though he had told the swordsman everything, even the pieces of his story that he had told no one else before, not even Arianne, it did nothing to soften the blow. Somehow in the telling, it had felt like the other man's story, not his. Maybe that was why Panos had sat there without judgement or question, listening quietly to every bitter, blood-soaked word. Maybe Panos understood that it was not him; it was the other's soul that was steeped in blood and bone and burning flesh.

Dacian closed his eyes and fought down the nausea. Still, the images came, raw and unrelenting. He could almost feel the heat radiating off the sand. *Wadi al S'hakh*: a dry riverbed at the end of the earth that wound its way through a narrow canyon and bled out into the open desert. It would not have even warranted a line on a map had it not been for the Well of the Sky, a deep pothole filled with cold, clear water…

The hollow-eyed man stared up at him; crusted flecks of dried blood speckled his gaunt features. A warm breath of wind disturbed the surface of the pool, and the face rippled and distorted. He reached down and cupped water in his shaking hand. As he raised the water to his mouth, a drop rand down his arm, cutting through the dust that caked his skin. The coldness of the water never ceased to surprise him.

"Sir," a tired voice called behind him before he could drink. "They are here."

He paused, then nodded slowly without turning. It was too late. It was over. The man reflected in the dark pool stared down at the handful of water. He stood for a long moment before pouring it into the sand at his feet...

Dacian forced himself up from the bed and sat with his elbows on his knees, his face buried in his hands. On one side, blood and death tore into him, each memory cutting through him like jagged steel. On the other, the gaping abyss left by the loss of his family yawned before him, and he teetered on the edge.

I can't do this... I can't do this... I can't... With each shallow breath, the mantra seemed to get stronger. *I can't do this...* He reached for the dagger at his belt. The blade slid from the sheath, and he stared down at the beautiful weapon, remembering where and when he bought it.

His memory of the day was crystal clear, unblemished by the years that had passed. He turned the blade over and over in his hand, tracing a finger along its intricate etchings. Tears ran freely now, an indescribable sorrow mixed with an incandescent anger that he was powerless to control. He was a leaf caught in a storm that savaged his very being.

Meaningless, almost bestial sounds spilled from him as he sobbed. His knuckles were white as they tried, with impotent rage, to crush the hilt of the dagger. He would see the world burn and everyone in it for one more moment with her. He would kill them all. He would... He took a deep, shuddering breath and loosened his fingers.

He sighed. *No... she would never want that. That path belonged to the other. The one who stared into the abyss, the one she had helped to pull back from the edge.* A faint smile crossed his face as he nodded slowly and brushed the tears from his cheeks. He reversed the blade, holding the point downward. It was fitting that it would be this dagger that would bring an end to this... *hell.* He rested his left arm on his leg and pressed the point to his wrist. A sudden calm settled over him. He slowly started to apply pressure, and the point punctured the skin with ease. All he needed to do now was draw the blade upward.

There was a light knock on the door. He froze. He quickly placed the blade on the bed, wiped his face with the back of his hand, and cleared his throat. "Who is it?" he called out.

"It's Jasmijn." The reply came after a brief pause.

"What do you want?" he asked, his voice harsher than he had intended. When there was no answer, he dragged himself from the bed and staggered to the door. He pulled it opened. She stood in the narrow,

91

gloomy passage, her hands clasped in front of her, and ignored the question, her face expressionless. She tilted her head to one side, obviously examining him, almost looking *through* him. He swallowed, not knowing what to say.

"I don't need anything," he said awkwardly, the words feeling smashed together, incoherent. "Thank you," he blurted and tried to close the door, only for it to to meet the palm of her hand.

"Yes. You do," she replied abruptly, but her expression remained unreadable. *But those emerald eyes...* He found he could not break from their grip. They cut through him. He felt naked, almost transparent.

"They're dead," he said suddenly.

"I know," she said softly as she stepped past him into the room. She pushed the door closed. "There was nothing you could have done. You know that."

He ran his fingers through his hair, took a deep breath, and the tears began to flow. "Her name was Arianne... My son was Aron."

She reached out and touched his face. He could see his sorrow mirrored in her eyes.

"I killed him." Dacian held her gaze. "Slowly."

"I know," she replied.

His head dropped. "I thought the other one, the Dark One, was gone. I thought I was free."

"We are never truly free," she said sadly. "We are who we are. But sometimes we are lucky enough to share our moments with those who stand in the light."

He sighed, suddenly exhausted. His eyes were filled with the grit of grief and ale, and his heart was in tatters. As he looked up, she opened her arms. With that simple action, she suddenly seemed to radiate a power both beautiful and... *terrible.* He felt himself stagger forward into her embrace. Hesitantly at first, he put his arms around her, then clung to her as the sobs racked his body.

The woman named Jasmijn held him close and allowed his grief to pour out over her like a river. She could feel the roiling darkness within him. It was an inky blackness that had clawed itself up from the depths, with no light to hold it at bay. She looked at the dagger that lay on the bed knowing how close he had come to the abyss.

She led him to the bed and helped him to lie down on his back. She ran her fingers through his hair as his tears continued to flow unchecked.

Then she leaned close to his face and whispered, "Sleep." He drew a deep, ragged breath and closed his eyes. She waited until each breath was slow and steady before turning down the wick of the lantern. *They will come for him tomorrow,* she thought sadly. She stood for a moment in the dark and listened to the softly falling rain before leaving, quietly pulling the door closed behind her.

Ascendant of Light

Sarsini
The Thirty-Third Day of 389, Evening

The frigid wind swirled and moaned through the narrow cobbled lanes that ran down to the harbour. The drab stone of the buildings glistened with the recent rain and most of the windows were shuttered and dark. Three large traders occupied the main quays, and the rest of the docks were tight with ships of all sizes seeking refuge from the coming storm. The mass of masts and tangles of rigging swayed gently back and forth as the creaking ships strained against their ropes. Every now and again, the tortured squeal of wet wood could be heard above the wind as the looming hulls scraped past each other.

Echo watched the dock guards trudging miserably up and down the length of the quay. Apart from those forlorn figures, the district and the surrounding warehouses were deserted. Heavy swells, driven on relentlessly by the strengthening squalls, boomed in a frothed rage against the rocks of the breakwater. And from her vantage point, she could see the fires of the tall stone lighthouse as they flickered against the backdrop of an ink-black sky. The tall white stone of the building doggedly shrugged off each wave that thumped into its sides, hurling tons of foam and water into the air to hiss down in icy sheets.

A church bell rang through the night air, and she turned towards the solemn sound with a ghost of a smile. It was both a sad and oddly pleasing sound. She liked the white priests who served the Broken One —for the most part. Many of them were kindly and good, just unfortunately blinkered, refusing to recognise that their god was just one of many strange and fickle beings.

Most of the gods were carelessly indifferent, capricious, and contradictory. They would find the concepts of benevolence or evil, in the context expressed by those who served them, amusing. The awareness of the consequences of their actions could be likened to a man either stepping on or over an ant. While a matter of life or death to the ant, the man would be utterly oblivious to the outcome.

The Ascendants, on the other hand, were steeped in their game, prodding and poking for reasons that ranged from the frivolous to the terrifying. On the whole, they held each other in check. She sniffed and tucked an errant strand of hair behind her ear. *Some required more diligence than others.* She couldn't care less what Panaii got up to; her whimsical agenda hardly caused a ripple in the circles. To the north, Koros seemed to cause more trouble for himself than others. *But Moloc is a different story,* she thought with a twinge of sadness. She wiped a drop of water from the tip of her nose with the back of her hand. The city fairly reeked of his touch.

Circles within circles, she thought darkly. *Where others throw pebbles, Moloc tends to drop boulders...*

She shrugged off the bleak thought to stand, then run lightly along the ledge. At the corner, she jumped easily across the yawning gap between the buildings onto a lower roof. She was drawn to a place in the city where she could sense a convergence of his making. But there was something she needed to do first.

Moving from rooftop to rooftop, she ran and jumped towards the inner city. Below her, the streets slowly came to life, the flickering street-lamps starting to appear with more regularity, along with people moving from building to building, most of them bundled up against the weather. She finally stopped on a roof belonging to a jeweller, an old man named Barkus.

Barkus had, over many years, become quite famous for his work. His wealthy clientele hailed from every corner of the Kingdom, and his jewellery graced the bodies of the rich, the noble, and even royalty. Their appreciation had translated into gold that had swelled his pockets impressively.

The old man was, however, equally famous for his generosity. He and his wife had tirelessly helped those in poverty even before fortune had favoured them. And now that they had the means, they continued this work, even as they grew older, by funding programs that offered food and shelter to the many poor. He was a good man who was loved by many... and he was dying.

The old couple shared a comfortable but simple home that was conveniently situated above his workshop. He kept a sizeable reserve of gold and gemstones in an iron safe in their bedroom, and the key was kept in relative safety on a chain around his neck. *A very lucrative venture for any enterprising thief,* she thought with a half smile as she walked to the edge of the building.

For a moment she stood idly watching the bustling street below. Patrons milled around the entrance to a popular public house, keen to get inside to enjoy an ale and the warm fire-place. *Such simple lives with simple needs,* she thought with a sudden sadness, *all about to be caught like insects in a web they couldn't see...*

She skipped away from the brightly lit thoroughfare to the far edge of the building. Here, a dim, quiet alleyway snaked between the buildings. She dropped over the edge and climbed quickly down to a small barred window high above the narrow service lane. The window opened into the attic and the ornate buttresses and ledges offered a multitude of handholds and places to avoid detection from below. Once she was inside, access to the house and workshop would be easy.

The once formidable bars were weak with rust, and the mortar holding them into the frame was old and crumbling. Years of exposure to the salt-ladened air and weather had done their slow work. Echo pulled a small, heavy-bladed knife from its sheath and quickly chipped the mortar away from the base of the bars.

Making sure of her hand- and footholds, she grasped the first bar and tugged at it. On the third attempt, the bar popped loose from the frame along with a spray of mortar chips that fell softly into the darkness of the alley. Placing the dislodged bar carefully on a small ledge, she quickly repeated the process with the other bars and within less than a minute, she was able to force open the window.

A rat scurried frantically away into the shadows as she crawled into the dusty gloom of the attic. She crouched down, and though her eyes adjusted instantly to the low light, she waited motionless in the gloom. Almost every spare inch of the attic was filled with old, mouldy boxes and chests, their copper hinges and locks encrusted with mottled, green rust. Resting against one wall, bails of mildewed fabric leaned against each other in languid decay. A lifetime of belongings gathered and stored and ultimately forgotten.

She threaded her way through the jumble toward the trapdoor. The ancient hinges creaked noisily as she raised the trap. She winced and froze, listening intently for any sounds of movement below. Once she was satisfied that the old couple was still sound asleep she dropped quietly into the passage and crept towards their bedroom. The door was slightly ajar, and she could hear the sounds of soft snoring.

A stealthy movement near her feet drew her attention. A very plump cat was staring at her intently. It pushed through the gap in the doorway and rubbed its flank against her leg. She reached down and gently stroked the animal's back, smiling at the throaty purr.

She pushed the door open and walked quietly to the foot of the bed. The old man lay on his back, and his breathing was laboured. Thin wisps of snow-white hair capped his head. Quietly, she moved closer. The illness had ravaged his body. His flesh had wasted away to the point where his ashen skin seemed tightly stretched over the skeletal features of his face. His wife, a short, plump woman, lay close to him, her hand resting lightly on his arm. Short grey curls framed her round face. Even now, there was ample evidence of the beauty of her youth.

She drew her knife and walked around the bed to stand over the old man. A gleam of silver could be seen around his neck. Gently, she lifted a length of the chain and looped it around the blade. A small key hung from the chain. A quick tug with the knife and the soft links parted. She made sure the old man was still asleep before she took the key and crossed the room to the safe, where she knelt down and opened the heavy metal door.

There were three shelves. The bottom two shelves were filled with finger-size ingots of gold and silver. The top shelf was divided into small, velvet-lined compartments filled with precious stones of varying sizes. At the back of this shelf, there was a small wooden box. It was simply made from a dark-coloured wood. She removed the box and gently placed it on the top of the safe before opening it.

The inside of the box was lined with cloth. It contained a simple silver brooch, a pair of gold earrings, and a rough-looking copper ring with a childish pattern crudely engraved around its edge. They were among the first pieces of jewellery that Barkus had ever made, the simple ring being the very first. To all others, it was worthless, but to him, it marked the beginning of a special journey. She contemplated the contents for a while, then took the ring and slipped it onto her left thumb. She replaced the box and closed and locked the safe.

Returning to the bedside, she lay the key down on the bed next to the old man. He would think the chain parted by accident during the night. Barkus coughed and groaned in pain but did not wake. She stood over the old couple for a few moments, and then she reached out and gently touched Barkus on the cheek. The skin glowed where her fingers had touched him, and the old man drew a deep shuddering breath before drifting back into a deep, peaceful slumber. Then, on an impulse, she brushed a stray grey curl from his wife's face. The strands glowed in the dim light, and the old lady moaned softly and then smiled faintly.

Echo watched the couple sleep for a while, twisting and rolling the copper ring around her thumb. *Fickle and self-serving... benevolence or machination...* She did not care. She looked at the sleeping couple. They would have a few more happy years to share, and the world would be better for it. It was a tiny ripple in the circles, a minuscule scrap of light to be weighed against the dark. She was very careful where she chose to interfere.

If I choose to interfere, she thought as she turned and walked quietly from the room, pausing to stroke the fat cat once more. The cat flopped onto its side and batted at her hand with a paw. *But I have no choice when it comes to Moloc. There is a tinder box that needs to be contained. The sparks that could lead to hellfire must not be unleashed.* She tucked a strand of hair behind her ear and stood.

With a parting smile to the happy feline, she floated upward to the ceiling, then past the dusty memories and though the roof to hover above the house. There was one more thing she needed to do this evening. Something she could not allow to happen no matter what. Oddly enough, it was close to the ripples she sensed.

She flew over the houses and shops until she floated over a small inn. Below her, a miserable boy sat, wet and cold, hunched over by the rickety gate to the courtyard. An old stablehand puffed at his pipe and tried to stay out of the drizzle. She drifted slowly downward, passing through the roof and into the crowded common room.

Time stopped as her feet touched the grimy wooden floor. To her left, a bearded man tilted his head back in frozen laughter while his companion pointed a finger at the laughing man's face with a sardonic smile. The large barkeep stood stern-faced behind the counter, a tankard and a cloth in his hands, waiting for a patron to slowly grub through the coins in his purse.

Echo moved silently through the crowded bar, slipping between the bodies and shadows, moving towards the card table in the far corner. She passed a tall man leaning casually against the bar and stopped suddenly. She turned to him, feeling the seething pain and rage that radiated through the thinnest veneer of cool indifference. He was one part of the smouldering tinderbox. An inferno held tightly in check by years of discipline and love... *lost.* She touched his arm and felt the aching, inconsolable loss.

She turned back to the card table. The ripples fairly throbbed outward from the other man who sat at the table. This one also bore the scars of Moloc, older and more deeply buried but not forgotten and no less painful. *Such a dangerous pairing*, she thought sadly, *merely waiting for a well-placed breath to ignite them. Had they found each other by chance?*

She drew closer to the table. A smoke ring hung frozen above the table. The axeman's stoney, dark glare was fixed on the swordsman across the table. The swordsman sat at ease, pipe in one hand and a fan of cards in the other. His life-energy burned brightly, a strange mix of violence and sadness. *A dangerous man,* Echo thought, her fingers brushing the hilt of his sword as she slid past him.

The smuggler sat to the swordsman's right, a deep frown on his face as he studied his cards, scratching at the ever-present stubble on his cheek. She smiled as she moved over to him, running her fingers lightly over his shoulders as she moved to stand behind his chair. He held a powerful hand; the four paladins would handily beat the others. She looked up from the cards to the hulking Sirvan, whose black rage was about to erupt.

No... She tilted her head before quietly taking the cards from Tariq's hand and crossing to Panos. *Things to take and things to give away...* She slipped the swordsman's cards from his fingers and replaced them with the paladins. She moved back to Tariq and kissed him lightly on the cheek as she placed the useless duke and two knaves into his hand...

"Shave, you old rogue," she whispered, then disappeared.

The Docks District, Sarsini
The Thirty-Third Day of 389, Night

Drigo hurried along the narrow, winding lane. It was very late and the streets were all but devoid of life. The guttering street lamps cast lonely pools of flickering yellow light that reflected softly off the wet cobbles. He looked nervously around. Between each lamp, the buildings and alcoves were draped in stifling shrouds of deep shadow. His imagination conjured blades and beasts and far worse as he scampered desperately between each island of light.

He dragged in a deep breath as his heart hammered in his chest, in part from the exertion and in part from fear but mostly due to the anticipation of the tongue-lashing he was sure to receive from his wife. Kezizer was not a forgiving woman in the best of times, and tonight she would have his hide once she found out how much coin he had lost at the card table. *I'm dead, dead, dead,* he thought miserably.

He felt mildly nauseous from all the wine, and a cold sweat beaded his forehead. He dabbed at his face with his handkerchief. *What on earth possessed you to join that damned game? Why? You fool!* he chastised himself to the edge of tears. He had almost no idea how he was going to explain how he lost the better part of a month's wages.

The cheating bastards! He almost sobbed as he quickened his pace. The last hand had been the killer. He remembered fanning his cards and seeing nothing, but for some idiotic reason, he couldn't help himself. He kept dropping coins into the pile, hoping against hope that either the stone-faced Sirvan, or the ice-cool Panos would just... *fold.*

The lunacy of the idea was now apparent. The Akhbari had seen it; the smug bastard had sat back with his bloody goblet of wine and enjoyed the carnage. So had the apothecary, laying down his cards even earlier. *But not stupid, stupid Drigo,* he cursed. *No. Stupid Drigo could not just lay them down and walk away.* And now Kezizer would flay him for it. Maybe if he worked longer hours, he could recoup the shortfall. The mere thought of longer hours made him nauseous.

Drigo scurried on. He planned to cut through an alley that ran from the dock district to the marketplace. It would shorten the trip significantly even though it meant enduring the dark, and potentially dangerous, confines of the alley. The inevitability of Kezizer's rage went a long way toward blunting the fear of the shortcut. From there, it was only two blocks before he reached his home, a modest dwelling above a bookseller. He knew that Kezizer hated it. She nagged endlessly about moving to a more affluent area that was quieter and further from the bustle of market district—ideally, a house with a garden.

He had long given up trying to explain that this was never going to be more than a dream on the wages of a clerk. She would castigate him mercilessly for having no drive or ambition and would then spend hours carping about how she should never have married below her station. The nature of this station that she was referring to remained a mystery to Drigo. Being the daughter of a fishmonger was hardly a lofty designation in his estimation, a point of view he kept safely to himself. He had little wish to endure the verbal flensing that would ensue should he be stupid enough to voice that particular opinion.

Drigo was so lost in his thoughts that he almost walked straight past the alley. He turned and jerked suddenly to a halt as he was confronted with the terrifying inky blackness of the narrow passage. The night had transformed the gloomy alley between two looming dockyard buildings into what looked like a gaping maw. He baulked at the thought of stepping out of the feeble comfort of the street lantern and into that abyss.

I'll walk the long way around, he thought, taking a hesitant step backward. *But no, stupid Drigo, that will take so much longer. Will it be worth the tongue-lashing stupid, stupid Drigo?* The route following the dock would be far safer. There were guards along the quays—and more importantly, lanterns. *But it will take so much longer, stupid Drigo… and then Kezizer will flay you even more.*

He groaned. It was only the dark. Surely it wouldn't be that bad. He could walk with a hand against the wall, and he'd be through in no time. He clenched his jaw and took a tentative step toward the alley. He swallowed, his mouth felt dry. Then he forced himself forward and into the alley.

He had barely taken a dozen steps before he was swallowed by the darkness and a cold, dank stench. He forced himself forward. His fingertips ran lightly along the wall to his left, across coarse, cracked plaster and patches of smooth, wet brick. Patches of damp moss made him flinch as he imagined slimy, crawling things that would dart up his arm and—

He yelped suddenly as an icy drop of water struck his cheek.

Drigo froze, his heart hammering, as he quickly whipped his face with a shaking hand. *Gods, man! It's just water, you fool.* He took a deep, shuddering breath and was just about to continue when he heard it: a low, malevolent hiss. His breath caught in his throat. His legs refused to move. He stood paralysed, straining to hear where the sound came from. As wide as he tried to force his eyes open, the impenetrable, crushing blackness yielded nothing.

It's a cat... just a cat. What else could it be? he thought. *Now move you fool! Move!* But he found he couldn't. His bladder suddenly felt full, his heart thumped painfully in his chest, and he found that, much to his surprise, he was holding his breath. He moved his head cautiously from side to side, straining to hear the slightest sound, but apart from the soft dripping of water, the alley was now silent.

Just a bloody cat. Drigo released his breath in a long, relieved sigh. His heart still raced, and his chest ached, and from the throbbing at the tip of his index finger, he was certain he had lost a nail as he clawed at the wall in fright. *You are a prize idiot, Drigo old boy. You spend the day getting fleeced at the card-table and then half piss yourself in a bloody alley being frightened to death by a bloody cat!* He managed a smile and took a tentative step forward when suddenly, something heavy slammed into his back and smashed him into the wall.

Drigo screamed as pain seared through his chest, claws tearing through his clothing and flesh. He reeled backward, arms flailing, and dagger-like fangs clamped onto his shoulder. His terrified scream was cut short as he thumped into the cold mud and the air was brutally punched from his lungs. He rolled to his stomach and pushed himself to his hands and knees, only to be smashed downward again. All he could manage was a pitiful mewl as his face was forced into the yielding, stinking muck by the terrible weight pressing down on him. Then it was gone.

Drigo lifted his head from the clinging mud and gasped. He tried to lift himself, but the burning agony of his wounds drove him to the ground again. He sobbed. His shoulder throbbed horribly, and the wounds in his chest and side felt as if they were on fire. He rolled slowly onto his back, whimpering at the pain that even this simple movement induced. He inched over to the wall and dragged himself into a seated position. His breathing was ragged and shallow as he rested his head against the rough stone. A hot, fetid breath fanned his face.

Drigo shrieked and thrashed at the darkness. He clawed at cold, wet flesh, his left hand finding sharp and jagged teeth. The jaws snapped shut, shearing off three fingers in an explosion of agony. He screamed again, desperately trying to hold off the unseen creature that forced itself inexorably closer.

His hands, slippery with blood and muck, groped and slapped, unable to gain purchase on the creature until something warm and foul dripped into his eyes and over his cheeks.

"No, please! No, no," Drigo pleaded to the darkness, gagging at the cloying stench of its breath. "NNNNOOOOOOOO!" he howled as all reason fled. His scream was suddenly muffled as the hidden jaws tore into the soft flesh of his face. The inhuman, gargling cry was abruptly cut off as the teeth ripped out his throat in a hot spray of blood.

The Second Circle

"I am not these counted breaths.
I am not this crude flesh and bone
Nor am I thought or words.

"I am not the beating of this heart.
Not wayward, not lost.

"And in this... I am."

—Words of the Broken One

The sun blazed down, radiating off of the white stone and turning the Wadi al S'hakh into an oven. Dacra straightened up from the stone he had just placed and kneaded the muscles of his lower back. His skin glistened with sweat and plastered his short-cropped hair to his head. The wall was taking shape. It stretched all the way across the river bed and was already chest-high. It would never be much of a barrier when the fight came to them, but it would be enough to slow down the tribesmen. A young soldier approached with a bucket and ladle. *Gods, the boy hasn't even grown his first beard,* Dacra thought sourly.

"Water, sir." The boy grinned.

"Thank you." Dacra took the ladle and drank the cold water in three swallows. "It's Tirol, isn't it?" he asked.

"Yes, sir." The young soldier beamed, obviously happy that his commanding officer knew his name. Dacra made a point of learning every man's name. He found it made command easier for some reason. The men seemed to respond better when they felt they were not just bodies wrapped in armour.

"This is your first tour." Dacra smiled as the young soldier nodded vigorously. He handed the ladle back to the boy. "I have no doubt that you will make the cohort proud, son. Carry on."

He turned his attention back to the makeshift wall. He had the men working in shifts, his junior officers and sergeants alongside them. The Wadi was narrow, with steep sides of broken stone. It created a natural funnel. They could not be flanked, and by forcing the enemy's superior numbers into the tight confines, it would, to a point, nullify their advantage by forcing them to fight along a narrow, and hopefully, defendable front.

Dacra dusted his hands against his leggings as he ran his gaze over the steep walls of the Wadi. It was a double-edged sword; while restricting the enemy, it also effectively left the legion with only one passage for retreat: a narrow ravine. If they could not withdraw fast enough, it would be wholesale slaughter.

Dacra sighed. But he didn't have a legion. He had a single cohort, a mere thousand men. And if the estimates were correct, they were outnumbered by thirty to one. With an entire legion, he would have three cohorts manning the wall and a full seven cohorts in reserve, swapping them out for fresh men after every repulsed attack. Should the defence not fare well, they would be able to send a squad back through the ravine to request reinforcements.

"If a frog had wings," he muttered.

"It wouldn't fall on its arse, sir," came a gruff reply.

Dacra looked up to see a broad, grizzled face. "Syrio." He called out to the veteran soldier. The man had been promoted and bust down more times than he could remember. Insubordinate, undisciplined, and incorrigible—but he was a fighter through and through. "What do you need?"

"A runner has returned. He has news of Arrius."

"*Commander* Arrius," Dacra corrected the old fighter pointedly.

"Yes. Him." Syrio ignored the rebuke, rubbing at the thin scar that ran down the side of his face.

Dacra sighed. There was no point in pressing the issue. "Where is the runner?"

"At the well, sir. He's exhausted and dehydrated. He's run over twenty miles. The physician is seeing to him."

"Tell them I'm on my way. Then tell Centurion Alesio I want the wall on the right flank higher. I think we're in for a fight."

"Sir." Syrio thumped a meaty fist into his chest and stalked off.

Yes. Him... The old soldier's reply spoke volumes, Dacra thought darkly as he pulled on his shirt. Arrius had been given the command of the Tenth Legion by the king as a favour to his father. Poor, soft Arrius who, unlike his distinguished father, had never had any military training let alone seen battle. He had lived a sheltered, privileged life, accustomed to always having things go exactly as planned or as expected, qualities far removed from those of a successful military commander.

Predictably, Arrius had quickly surrounded himself with a staff of sycophants and inexperienced officers. He shunned the seasoned veterans whose iron discipline and collective experience both scared him and reminded him of his own plentiful shortcomings. Ironically, they would have negated many of those of faults, and Arrius would have been better for it.

Dacra grimaced. That herd had been far more inclined to fervently agree with Arrius' every suggestion no matter how idiotic or impractical. To do otherwise was to endure his unavoidable and irrational wrath.

Dacra's own path had been very different. He joined the legion as a boy, and through hard work and unmistakable talent, he was promoted from the ranks. He had climbed from common soldier to sergeant in less than three years, a feat not equalled by any other. Not long after, when his officer was killed in a skirmish against the Tahuti tribes in the cold north, he was given the century to command.

Once again, he had excelled as a leader, binding his men together with discipline and loyalty. Two years later, on the retirement of his commanding officer, he was given the command of the Seventh Cohort. A thousand men who didn't need to see the glowing references; he had earned their respect by standing shoulder to shoulder with them in battle. Three weeks later, Arrius had been given command of the Tenth Legion, and everything changed.

Dacra strode up the narrow path that threaded through the fallen scree leading up to the well. The deep pothole was nestled in the shadows of the high cliffs that rose steeply at this point of the Wadi. The path would be vital in the defence. He had already marked points where archers could lay down lethal cover as they retreated. It would cost the tribesmen dearly to take the well.

He stepped from the blazing sun into the cool shadows of the cliffs and could taste the hint of moisture in the air. The well was twenty paces wide and some thirty across, nestled under a heavy overhand of rock. He had asked that it be plumbed. The soldier had run out of rope at four hundred feet without finding the bottom.

The runner was sitting on a stone, elbows on his knees with his head hanging. Elias, the cohort's surgeon was wiping his skin with a damp cloth.

"A light run in the dessert has you broken like an old man, Nesta?" Dacra joked. The man ran like a hunting dog. He had no doubt twenty miles on the open sand at his pace would have killed most men.

"Sir!" The soldier tried to get to his feet.

"Sit." Dacra placed a hand on the exhausted scout's shoulder and sat down on his haunches. He was shocked at how shattered the man looked now that he was closer. He cast a worried look at Elias.

"He'll live," the surgeon growled sternly. "He needs to drink and rest and stay out of the sun. By tomorrow, he'll be able to swing a sword."

Dacra turned back to the runner. "What of Arrius?"

"He's gone," the man said softly. "The whole legion is gone."

Dacra kept his face impassive. "How?"

Nesta was the finest scout in the legion. Apart from his otherworldly stamina, he had a keen eye for detail and an extraordinary memory. Dacra had sent the man to follow the legion and stay undetected; when planning a near-impossible defence, the last thing any commanding officer needed was surprises. He needed to know what he would be facing. He had no faith in Arrius' ability. It was a matter of time before a serious tactical blunder would result in the deaths of many of the legionnaires under his command.

He had hoped the inevitable blunder would not prove to be catastrophic, but as Nesta's report unfolded, the inexperience and the arrogance of the man became crystal clear. The scout's report was direct and comprehensive, with no theatre or exaggeration. The legion had been obliterated, the enemy had suffered almost no losses, and the Seventh Cohort was in deep trouble, with no time or resources to prepare better than they already had.

"Get some rest, Nesta." He smiled as he smacked the man's cheek lightly.

Elias' face was like stone. The man was a veteran and knew what was coming.

"I'm ready," the surgeon said simply. Dacra had no doubt that the man would have drilled his stretcher bearers thoroughly and ensured the medical tent was stocked and prepared for the inevitable flood of wounded men.

"Good." Dacra nodded as he stood.

He walked down the path slowly, deep in thought. Arrius was gone, and strangely, he felt nothing. He had expected to feel some form of relief, having endured the commander's constant ire and irritation. In Arrius' eyes he had never been anything more than a common soldier, an upstart commoner, who had somehow connived and manipulated his way to becoming an officer. The fact that his men respected him deeply and were loyal to a fault was enough to set Arrius' blood boiling.

The commander had made no attempt to conceal his loathing. Arrius despised each successful skirmish, each victory, refusing to give any credit to the cohort or its leader. Oddly enough, turning the Seventh Cohort into pariahs had pushed the men closer, to the point where they would happily follow Dacra into the mouth of hell, trusting that if there was a single officer who would drag them back, it was he.

And Arrius put that to the test. How his men endured the worst and most dangerous assignments he would never know—their payment for their loyalty to their officer. The men he lost were replaced by those with the worst disciplinary records, some little more than criminals. Arrius had fumed as, against all reasoning, Dacra continued to mould this insubordinate band of thugs into a fearsome fighting machine.

Their fame grew with each victory, and paradoxically, so did the fame of the Tenth Legion and that of Arrius. Dacra grimaced. Ironically, it was probably the success of his Wolves, as they had come to be known, that had landed the Tenth at the arse end of the Akhbari desert, facing the entire might of the H'rutu army.

"Alesio!" he called out to a stocky officer as he reached the end of the path.

"Sir!" The man dropped the rock he was manhandling into place and thumped a fist into his hairy chest.

"That wall is good enough. Rest the men," he ordered. "Make ready. We are expecting unwelcome visitors."

"Yes, sir. I have two men on the west ridge, watching the desert."

"Good." Dacra nodded. The man was a solid officer who needed little guidance. "Sharp blades and oiled armour before nightfall."

He acknowledged the salute and followed the wall, repeating the message to the other officers. They were all ready. They knew what was coming. They knew why they had been left behind as a reserve.

Dacra had openly questioned the decision to march out to meet the enemy in the desert. Arrius had waited for him to finish and then simply exploded. The commander had made it excruciatingly clear that he would not entertain these cowardly, timid tactics. It was inconceivable to him that *uncivilised* savages could represent more than a passing annoyance to the might of the Tenth Legion. They would be swiftly crushed and brought to heel.

Dacra watched as a swirling dust devil danced and snaked across the dry bed of the Wadi. As a result of his obvious lack of backbone and inability to take the initiative, his Seventh Cohort would not take the field with the rest of the legion and would not share in the glory of the inevitable victory.

Dacra and his men had watched the column march out into the desert, the banners of the nine cohorts flapping lazily in the hot, dry breeze. In less than two hours, the nine thousand led by Arrius would meet an army of thirty thousand H'rutu in the open desert. Their king, Ingonyama, would not believe his luck.

Dacra sat down on the wall, his legs hanging over the edge, and stared out into the wasteland. The sun was high, rendering the Wadi stark and shadowless, just bleached sand and stone. Arrius' battle had been lost in less than an hour. In the open desert, Ingonyama had space to manoeuvre and use his overwhelming advantage of numbers.

According to Nesta's account, Arrius had attacked the H'rutu head-on. He had made it clear that he believed the H'rutu to be an unorganised rabble that could never withstand a cohesive frontal attack of nine cohorts. With two cohorts guarding each flank, he led the rest of the Tenth straight through the centre.

The aim was to cleave the massive army in two. In Arrius' mind, the collapse of the H'rutu centre could only result in the death of Ingonyama, who would obviously be cowering in the middle of his army.

The Tenth would then ride down the demoralised and leaderless mob and dispatch them at will. No other outcome even crossed his mind.

Dacra sighed. If Arrius had taken the time to read the historical accounts of battles between the Akhbari and H'rutu, he would have known that the H'rutu were far from mindless savages. He would have known that Ingonyama was a ruthless and keenly intelligent man who had grown tired of losing battles to smaller forces. He had discarded their traditional brute-force approach and devised battle tactics that, although rudimentary, were extremely effective, given their vast numbers and the natural ferocity of his men.

He replayed the scout's account of the battle in his mind. He could see each phase of the battle unfolding with sickening clarity. Nesta had watched from a hill...

At first the plan seems perfect. They hit the centre of the H'rutu ranks hard, and there is surprisingly little resistance. The entire centre almost immediately buckles and collapses.

Suddenly, the tribesmen are running from the reddened swords of the Tenth, who surge forward. Clouds of choking dust, thrown up by thousands of pounding feet, hide the flanks as Arrius and his legion are drawn deeper and deeper into the mass of warriors.

The first sign of danger becomes painfully apparent when the seemingly unorganised, swiftly retreating centre suddenly stops and inexplicably turns into an immovable wall of veteran warriors. This core comprises of the most experienced, battle-hardened men. They are the most difficult to kill and the most accomplished in their trade. The charge slows and eventually grinds to a halt, pressing against raw-hide shields and stabbing spears. The losses of men and horses begin to mount.

The billowing clouds of dust conceal the second sign of danger. The H'rutu flanks stream outward like vast horns. These horns are composed of thousands of young warriors, chosen for their speed and stamina. Within minutes, the two horns meets, cutting off all hope of escape.

At this point, Ingonyama, safe on his litter, surrounded by an honour guard of elite warriors, watches the thinly guarded flanks of the Tenth Legion get torn to pieces. With the Tenth surrounded and hopelessly outnumbered, the wholesale slaughter of the legion begins. Not a single man escapes...

Dacra sighed. A fool sent to the end of the world to protect the interests of other more powerful fools. Ten thousand men to protect a trade route from the H'rutu menace. Apparently, the safety of the merchants was of paramount importance to the king and his Akhbari counterpart, the shah, but Dacra had no doubt that the impact of the raids on their royal coffers was closer to the truth.

The pasha of Ras-al-Salah had not seemed enthusiastic at all about the presence of legion patrols along the eastern trade route. Dacra remembered the fat noble's notable disinterest in Arrius' plans to quell the raids. But then Dacra had also noticed the bustling port and wondered where the man's interests truly lay.

"Sir," a voice came from behind him.

Dacra turned. The young officer whose men were manning the east flank stood, holding his helmet under his arm. "What is it, Prota?"

"The watch on the east ridge reports all clear. I checked with Alesio. Same for the west. When do you think they'll come?"

Dacra turned back to the desert. "They have what's left of the Tenth Legion trapped like rats in a hole. They will come... soon."

Prota moved to stand beside Dacra. "Well, there's no point in letting us prepare properly." The young officer said with a half smile. "It wouldn't be fair at all. They don't have enough men."

Dacra grinned and thumped Prota's shoulder. "Get some rest, you young savage. Tomorrow may prove to be a long day."

"Sir!" Prota saluted with a broad grin and walked back to his squad.

Rats in a hole... Dacra frowned. He had been puzzled at the request to protect this single point on the trade route. It was defensible given enough men, but the terrain and difficulty in resupplying or bringing in relief made it easy to trap the defenders. With superior numbers, a legion could be whittled away and eventually destroyed.

A mere cohort, on the other hand, would stand no chance. The sheer weight of numbers would eventually push them back from the wall and into the ravine. There they would truly be rats in a hole. *Inconvenient rats,* Dacra thought with sudden clarity.

The Palace of the Pasha

Ras-al-Salah
The 114th Day of 380, Afternoon

The vast bulk of His Excellency, the pasha, Suleiman Ibn Ali Khalifa, lay sprawled over a small mountain of plush cushions. He idly stroked a slave girl's naked leg with his bejewelled fat fingers as he nursed a chilled glass of fruit juice. The pasha sighed inwardly as the Kingdom general, Arrius, droned on about how his legion was going to crush the H'rutu uprising and free up the eastern trade route.

He blinked his heavy-lidded eyes as he tried, with difficultly, to pay attention to the thread of the monologue. The problem was, the man was boring, and more importantly, Suleiman he wasn't entirely sure that he wanted the eastern trade route tinkered with at all—certainly not by Kingdom legionnaires. He was quite happy with its shoddy state of affairs. His port of Ras-al-Salah was doing very well indeed due to traders not wanting to risk the land route.

He sipped at the juice as he pondered the situation. Of course, His Royal Majesty, the shah, would see things differently. The taxes and goods that should have been flowing into his royal coffers and warehouses were now somewhere off in the Eastern Desert, gathering dust in a savage's grubby kraal. *Well, not all of those taxes and goods...* He smiled faintly to himself.

A slave girl quietly offered him a bowl of grapes. He removed a bunch and began nibbling at them while feigning interest by nodding now and again as the fool, Arrius, made a point or emphasised some military tactic they would employ. The man was an idiot. He sat there in his shining armour, yet it was patently obvious he had never seen battle. *Ingonyama will eat this primping fop alive.* Suleiman smiled faintly at the thought.

The fat pasha transferred his attention to another officer. This man sat the furthest away, the place reserved for the person of least importance. *Now this one is interesting.* The officer's armour, though immaculate and polished, carried the countless dents and nicks of battle. Suleiman noticed the keen dark eyes and how the man listened attentively, even to his fumbling moron of a general. *Why one such was this would be pushed aside, shunned?* Suleiman pondered.

He frowned at the empty stalks as he realised he had finished the grapes. He tossed the stems aside and reached for his glass. He sipped at the juice and held up a hand, cutting off the general mid-sentence. The pasha smiled slightly as he noticed the flash of irritation that crossed the general's face.

"Thank you, General," Suleiman purred, his voice oddly soft and effeminate for such a large man. "I think we have an understanding."

"I... uhm... I was trying to explain how..." Arrius stumbled over his words, obviously not used to being interrupted.

"Wadi al S'hakh." The Pasha said, cutting him off again again.

"Excuse me, Excellency?" Arrius' jaw clenched.

"The Wadi al S'hakh is an oasis on the eastern route." Suleiman said softly. "A strategic point on the route." He pointed a fat finger at the general to emphasise the point. "It is a perennial water-source. Whoever controls al S'hakh, controls the eastern trade route."

"Thank you, Excellency." Arrius puffed up, trying to reassert himself. "But as I was saying, this is a military affair and patrols along the—"

"The eastern trade route stretches over nine-hundred miles," the pasha interrupted, stopping the fumbling general's protest. "You don't know the desert. Those sands are brutal and the H'rutu would simply harry your men at will. The attacks on the caravans would continue wherever your men are not."

"I don't think you understand…" Arrius' face was flushed.

"I think you are forgetting yourself," Suleiman purred dangerously. He paused, enjoying the man's obvious frustration and discomfort.

"My apologies, Excellency," Arrius forced out before sitting back, tight-lipped.

"I will provide maps, water, provisions and guides. My man, Tamut, will see to it." Suleiman paused, then continued. "I am quite sure you and your men will put an end to the H'rutu… issue." He sipped at the juice before waving a fat hand to dismiss them. The pasha waited patiently for the Kingdom soldiers to leave and then called over his shoulder. "Come…"

There was a soft whisper of silk hangings parting, then the sound of bare feet on marble. A tall young man stood before him, he wore a simple loincloth. The only mark of his station was the leopard skin draped over the polished-ebony skin of his shoulders. *A beautiful specimen, this son of Ingonyama,* Suleiman mused as he studied the lean, hard muscle of the man's chest and legs.

"Baba." Ibhubesi, prince of the H'rutu, bowed slightly as he greeted the pasha with the tribal honorific. The fat pasha knew this word to mean *father.* He was oddly pleased by this. These tribesmen were like children —simple and, in many cases, wonderfully naive.

"Ibhu!" He replied, acknowledging the prince. "I take it you followed the conversation."

The young man nodded.

"I've sent the Kingdom legion to the oasis. They will interfere with our…arrangement," Suleiman purred, reaching into the ever-present bowl of grapes. He picked a grape from the bunch and chewed slowly. "The Wadi is a natural funnel," he continued. "They will have nowhere to run. Those who your father does not slaughter will die in the desert."

The pasha picked another grape and rolled it around between his fingers, studying the prince as he pondered the statement.

"These are not caravan guards." The prince spoke slowly in heavily accented Akhbari. "They are trained soldiers. The H'rutu will lose many men. I think we may need a new arrangement."

Suleiman smiled as he savoured the sweetness of the grape. "No," he said simply. "Your father will take his army and do as I say. There will be no new arrangement. Your father, and your people, are rich from what I have offered. I see no reason to change that."

"Then you go kill the legion soldiers." The prince shrugged. "The H'rutu are not your dogs."

The fat Pasha laughed, genuinely delighted at the young man's monumental naivety. He wiped his mouth with the back of his hand and stroked the pretty slave as he settled. Still smiling, he regarded the prince, who looked wonderfully confused at his sudden mirth. "Ah, my boy," he said, smiling broadly, "but you *are* my dogs. You are nothing more than a means to an end, and biting this hand will not end well for you. Tell me, how many men does your father have?"

The prince paused, searching for the Akhbari numbers. "Thirty thousand."

Suleiman pursed his lips. "Mmm... Do you know how many men my uncle, the shah, commands? Over one million." The pasha paused and allowed the prince to ponder this revelation. "Do you understand this number? For each of your father's men, the shah has more than thirty."

"I understand the number." Ibhubesi scowled at the thinly veiled threat. "But I also understand what that an army that size would cost to move. Why would the shah spend his precious gold to hunt the H'rutu? Your *dogs*?"

Suleiman smiled broadly. "The shah is a very pious man. He would be infuriated if his people on their h'jah pilgrimage were robbed and murdered. He would be compelled to call for a J'haad to honour his god, Elihaar be praised." He touched his lips and his forehead.

"We have never attacked the holy ones!" Ibhubesi snapped.

"I know," Suleiman purred. "There's not much profit in attacking penniless pilgrims. But word would reach my uncle very quickly if you decided otherwise."

The H'rutu prince remained quiet as the pasha's words drove home. "I will take your message to my father, Baba," he said simply.

"Ah, this is good, Ibhu." Suleiman smiled. He clapped his hands, and a male slave entered, carrying a wooden box. He bowed deeply to the pasha before placing the box at the prince's feet. Suleiman dismissed the slave with a wave. "Open it."

Ibhubesi eyes widened as he opened the box. It was filled to the brim with gems.

"You see, my boy?" Suleiman smiled. "I want our arrangement to continue, and I want the H'rutu to prosper." He sipped at the glass of juice. "But if you ever question me again, the next box I send to your father will contain your head."

"Sit still," the surgeon growled.

Dacra winced as Elias pulled the stitches in his scalp tight. He had lost his helmet at some point during the morning's battle. The chinstrap had snapped from a glancing blow. Not long after, he had ducked under a spear-thrust aimed at his face. He had been quick enough to avoid death, but the broad, rough-forged spearhead still opened a two-inch cut just above his hairline.

"Sit *still,* damn you!" Elias looked up from his bloody needle. "Unless you want this to look like it was done by some drunken wench more suited to darning socks ..."

"It's just a scratch." Dacra protested half-heartedly.

"It's just a scratch until it bleeds into your eyes when one of those H'rutu bastards is trying to ram his bloody spear down your throat." the surgeon retorted.

"Listen to him, sir," a tired-looking sergeant sitting to his left said. "The Wolves can't afford to lose you when there are so many more of the bastards left to kill."

"Aye," Syrio growled in agreement, sitting down heavily next to the fire. "Pity that other fucking idiot hadn't done his job. There may have been fewer of them H'rutu needing killing."

Dacra looked up at the leathery old soldier. "One more remark along those lines, and I'll have the skin flogged from your back."

"Sir," Syrio grunted and turned to stare into the flames.

He's right, though, Dacra grudgingly admitted. Arrius had paid the ultimate price for his incompetence. *And here we are still paying,* he thought darkly.

"Gods!" he swore at a flash of pain in his scalp. "Be careful, you ham-handed butcher!"

"Wear a helmet," came the curt reply.

Dacra grunted in disgust and returned to his thoughts. They hadn't needed to wait long, remembering Prota's question. The H'rutu host had marched into the Wadi that morning. Thankfully, the men had a full night's rest. How much difference that would make over the course of the battle was debatable.

The visceral, deep thump of the war drums rolled off the stone canyon walls like thunder. Dacra stood with the Seventh on their low wall, proud and confident, as the guttural, grunting war cry of tens of thousands of warriors joined the drums. HHUUU, HHUUU, HHUUU, HHUUU...

The tribesmen stopped just out of bowshot, filling the Wadi from edge to edge and stretching back as far as the eye could see. The mass of warriors surged and danced like some unimaginable beast, waiting to be unleashed by their king. Dacra was caught by surprise as the drumming suddenly stopped. Dust hung thick in the air and clung to the glistening ebony skin of the H'rutu as an eerie silence descended on the Wadi.

The front ranks opened and a tall, heavily muscled warrior walked forward. He wore a simple kilt of spotted fur, but to Dacra, he was unmistakable; Ingonyama, king of the H'rutu, moved to stand in front of his terrifying host like a god, a tasseled stabbing spear in this left hand and a severed head in his right.

Dacra rested his hand on the pommel of his sword and watched as the H'rutu king ran his gaze along the low wall and the thin line of defenders. Ingonyama's voice boomed out across the Wadi, and although no one understood the words, the message was thick with contempt and loathing. The mass behind him punctuated his words with an earth-shaking "HHUUU."

The H'rutu king had held up his grisly prize for all to see. Dacra sighed when he saw it was Arrius. With an almost casual flick, Ingonyama threw it towards the wall. Tens of thousands of spears stabbed the air and drums thundered as the head bounced twice, rolled, and stopped facedown in the dust roughly halfway across the divide.

"HHUUU! HHUUU!"

Rage ignited in Dacra, he would not let this go unanswered. He jumped over the wall and strode across towards the king, who seemed to watch with mild amusement. Dacra reached the head and tore his cloak from his shoulders. Using the cloak, he picked it up and quickly wrapped it in its folds. He stood and slowly drew his sword, levelling the point of the gleaming blade at the H'rutu king.

"You!" he bellowed. "I am Dacra! We are the Seventh Cohort of the Tenth Legion, you fucking son of whore!" He swept his blade back to follow the length of the low wall. "These are my Wolves." With that, he turned back to Ingonyama, his blade once more pointed at the face of the king. "And today, my Wolves will feast on your herd of sheep."

He spat into the dust and contemptuously turned his back on the enemy. "Dacra! Dacra! DACRA!" his men roared as he strode back to the wall.

Yet another sharp and painful tug on the stitches snapped Dacra back to the present. "Are you finished?" he asked the surgeon irritably.

"Finished?" Elias grunted. "I'm afraid I'm just hitting my stride."

Dacra touched the tender wound with its row of neat stitches. "Then get some rest." He looked at the tired surgeon. How the man was still functioning was beyond him. "Tomorrow will be busier."

Elias nodded and gathered his instruments. Dacra watched the surgeon spread out on a blanket and fall asleep within moments. He smiled. You could always tell the veterans by how quickly they managed to grab sleep. The longer the battle raged, the more exhaustion would play a role. The weakest would fall first, those who didn't know how to counter the gnawing fatigue, whittled away from the iron core that held the Seventh together.

Today, they had fought like men possessed, savagely repelling three attacks before the darkness of night. The H'rutu had fallen back to the mouth of the Wadi, taking their wounded and leaving their dead. Dacra had ordered that the bodies be dragged away from the wall and burned. He could not afford to risk sickness. They had done well and made the tribesmen pay dearly for each fallen legionnaire. But it was not nearly enough.

Dacra looked up at the breathtaking expanse of the sky. A thin sliver of a moon hung low on the horizon, and an immense ocean of stars hung above them. The H'rutu were close enough for the men of the Seventh to hear their drums and songs. Dacra listened to the muffled rhythms and tried to ignore the dull ache of the wound. He had no doubt the tribesmen had posted men to the north, ensuring the Seventh could not slip away in the night. They would make sure that the remainder of the legion would meet their fate here.

Dacra smiled grimly to himself. Tomorrow would indeed be busier. They had thankfully taken very few losses, and many of the wounded would be able to fight in the morning. But it was only a matter of time before the overwhelming numbers of the H'rutu army would start to grind them down. He had already briefed the officers and sergeants on the plan to fall back from the wall. It was inevitable. Eventually, they would not have enough men to hold it, and the retreat needed to be as controlled as possible; otherwise, they would be overrun and it would be a slaughter.

They could hold the path for a while. The H'rutu would only be able to send five or six men at a time. The archers in the fixed positions they had established would rain hell on them. Every step they won would cost them dearly. They could try to climb up the broken scree, but that would be very slow, and when scrambling up the steep incline of loose stone and rubble, they would be even easier pickings for the archers. At least on the path, they could use their shields.

The countless permutations milled through his mind. They needed to hang on as long as possible, forcing the H'rutu king to become reckless, even desperate. He could not know with certainty that the Seventh was alone. *If Ingonyama began to believe he could be trapped in the Wadi by another legion*... the thought trailed off.

"If frogs had fucking wings," he muttered. He lay back, but sleep was a long time in coming. And when Dacra finally drifted off, his dreams were filled with blood and steel... and a frog that was hopefully running like the wind toward the west.

Nesta waited motionless in the deep shadows, his back pressed to the cool rock of the ravine. A camp of thirty or so tribesmen lay below, the warriors sitting in small, quiet groups around their campfires. The commander had been right. There were enough H'rutu there to force back anyone trying to escape from the Wadi using the tight ravine.

The scout scanned the edges of the camp and followed the lines of the ledges, looking for the sentries. They would be close and attentive, and he could not afford to be spotted. The climb had been steep and difficult, compounded by the dark and the need for stealth.

He took a small mouthful of water from one of the water-skins he carried and continued his search. His hand strayed absently to the sealed scroll that the commander had pressed into his hands hours earlier.

"Get to Al Wahleed. Do not go near Ras-al-Salah, the pasha cannot be trusted. Give this to the commander of the garrison," he had said. The commander had then given him two water skins and a pack of food before gripping his hand hard. The scout remembered Dacra's parting words with a grim smile. "Go now. And, Nesta... don't die."

Nesta's smile faded as his eyes stopped on a particular shadow. He waited patiently, not shifting his gaze. A small movement revealed the hard line of a spear shaft. *Ahh...there you are,* he thought with satisfaction. *And if you're there...* He shifted his attention to the other side of the ravine. Quickly, he found the other sentry. The man sat on his haunches in a small hollow. From their vantage points, the H'rutu sentries could see the whole entrance to the ravine and the slope leading down to the open desert. Nesta would not be able to get past them without being seen.

The scout shifted his gaze back to the first sentry. He was slightly ahead of the second, meaning he would need to turn sharply to his right to see his counterpart. Nesta quietly pulled the water-skins and food pack from this shoulder and laid them on the ground. He had no idea when these men would be relieved. Hopefully, he would not need to wait too long.

An hour later, Nesta heard a low whistle, followed by another. The sentry to his left stood and waited as another H'rutu warrior climbed up to the small ledge. The scout checked the sentry on the right and spotted similar movement. He quickly gathered the water-skins and food pack and waited. Low voices and a soft chuckle carried to him in the still night air. He moved swiftly and quietly, keeping to the shadows, pausing only to listen to the soft banter between the sentries.

It took less than a minute to slip behind a fallen boulder that shielded him from their field of vision, but it had felt like an eternity. Nesta stopped and took a deep breath. The moon was low and waning, and the desert was filled with deep shadows. With luck, he would make Al Wahleed within two days. If the soldiers from the garrison rode hard, they would make it back within a day. As he started to run, Nesta sent a quick prayer to the gods that the Seventh could hold out that long.

On the morning of the fourth day, Dacra stood on the wall and tried to wipe the stinging sweat from his eyes but only succeeded in smearing blood and grit over his face. The first wave of the morning had been fought off, and the heat was already stifling, the blazing sun turning the dry riverbed into an oven. He squinted against the glare from the rounded white stones strewn throughout the powdery dust and tried to make sense of the carnage he saw before his eyes: blood and twisted bodies, broken shields and discarded weapons.

The fighting had been savage. The weak had died quickly, distilling the men on the wall to those who were like iron. Unbreakable killers who hacked and hewed at the seemingly endless waves of tribesmen throwing themselves at the wall with a primal ferocity that none of them had ever witnessed before. But even iron broke under enough pressure. They could not hold out much longer. Dacra wondered if Nesta had made it to Al Wahleed. It didn't matter. There would be no fifth morning, one way or the other.

"Aliso! Prota!" he roared. "Casualties?"

The officers shouted the counts back quickly. Fourteen dead and another twenty wounded; of the wounded, nine would not fight further.

"Get the wounded to the rear," he barked. "And be quick about it. Get water to the men. Alesio!" He pointed at the brawny, blood-smeared officer. "Watch that right flank. They have been testing the line for weakness, and they have not hit the right hard yet."

"Sir! None of those fucking bastards are getting through my wall." The man grinned and thumped his fist into his chest.

Dacra nodded. *Damn fine man...need to tell him that when this is over,* he thought. Turning away, he shouted "Prota! Prota!"

"Here!" the younger officer replied and strode closer.

"I need ten men. Is Syrio still alive?"

"Syrio?" Prota snorted, wiping the sweat from his eyes "I doubt even the Dark One could kill that old bastard," Prota replied with a broad grin.

"Nine men and Syrio if he lives," Dacra ordered. "Put Syrio in charge; he's a sergeant as of now. I need them to plug any breaks in the line. Tell him I will have his balls if he lets even one of those bastards through."

"Sir!" Prota thumped his chest, turned, and immediately roared out, "Syrio! Where the hell are you? Get your leathery arse out here, you skiving rat!"

Syrio looked up from a small patch of shade he had managed to find. "Here, sir." he called out. "No need for all that sweet talk. Not only am I cheap, but I also have very few moral values to speak of." A ripple of laughter ran through the small group of men sitting close to him.

"Good!" Prota yelled. "I have something for you that will really get you fucked." This was followed by more laughter and a few ribald comments directed at Syrio, who took them with a broad grin.

Dacra permitted himself a ghost of a smile before turning back toward the wide riverbed as the deafening boom of the war drums started again.

"Stand ready!" Dacra bellowed. "Bows!"

With a bestial roar, the H'rutu surged forward.

"Hold!" Dacra raised his sword. "Hold..."

The gap closed with terrifying speed. Dacra waited, having already marked the archers' maximum range. With luck, they could hit them with two volleys.

"Hold!" The tribesmen thundered past a jugged outcrop. "Loose!" Dacra dropped his sword, and over four hundred shafts scythed the front ranks of the screaming warriors down. The next volley came seconds after, and then bows were swiftly discarded for swords, as moments later, a howling, ebony wave of hate and destruction broke against the low wall of sand and stone.

Dacra killed the first with a clean thrust to the throat. The man sagged backward, swallowed by the dark, surging mass of H'rutu warriors. He quickly scanned the line to his left and right. Swords flashed in the morning sun. Blood sprayed as his men frantically hacked and slashed at the enemy.

A little way off to his left, the line of defenders suddenly buckled, and a small group of H'rutu broke through. Dacra smiled grimly as Syrio and his group of nine quickly blocked the breach. The H'rutu were swiftly chopped to pieces with brutal efficiency. Dacra turned his attention back to the wall.

The second man Dacra killed, he decapitated with a backhanded slash as the warrior clambered over the wall; the head bounced in the dust at his feet as the body crumpled in a fountain of bright arterial blood.

"Aliso! The right!" he shouted over the cacophony. The stout officer was standing in the middle of his men, dealing death. Dacra turned away satisfied that the man had the flank in order.

Dacra lost his sword killing the third. The warrior clawed his way over the growing mound of dead and dying, slipping and sliding on the bloody flesh. The sand in between the bodies, mixed with blood and excrement, had been churned into a clinging, greasy mud. None of this deterred the man as he was dragged along in the heaving, choking flood of his comrades.

The tribesman scrambled over the wall and hurled himself at Dacra. The blow from his short stabbing spear came hard and true. Dacra barely managed to knock aside the spear aimed at his chest. Still, he was driven back and collided heavily with another of his men, who tripped and fell and then died as an H'rutu spear slammed into his face.

Dacra leaped forward, his sword swinging downward in a brutal arc. The heavy blade smashed into the base of the warrior's neck, cutting through muscle and bone to bury itself midway down his chest. He fell away, twisting the sword from Dacra's grasp.

The fourth Dacra killed with his bare hands. The spear thrust, even though it was a glancing blow, punched the air from his lungs and left a deep score along the side of his armour. Pain flared in his chest, and Dacra desperately grabbed the H'rutu's spear arm. The warrior tried to rip his weapon free and died as Dacra smashed his fist into the man's throat, crushing the larynx; hot blood and spittle sprayed from the H'rutu's mouth, speckling Dacra's face.

Dacra could not remember the fifth or the multitude thereafter. He had a vague recollection of taking up two discarded stabbing spears and walking the line. He jumped to the wall wherever a man fell, stabbing at the heaving mass before him, a seemingly endless passage of carnage, until it abruptly ended.

He stood as sweat and blood dripped from his face. His arms felt like lead, and each breath rasped from his lungs. His forearms burned from the countless cuts and grazes. His head pounded from the heat and exhaustion, but they had beaten back another attack.

"Water!" he bellowed, throwing aside the short spears. "Alesio! Prota! To me! And someone bring me a sword!"

He watched as the wounded and dead were swiftly taken to the rear then looked up at the endless blue of the sky and sucked in a deep breath. The time had come. They had to fall back from the wall. They would not hold the next attack.

"Sir," came a tired voice. He turned to see Prota and one of Alesio's sergeants, an older man; his short dark hair was shot with silver, and his tanned face was lined and full of sharp angles. He was a veteran. A solid, dependable soldier whom the men respected.

"Prota." He nodded to the officer and turned to the sergeant, "Ganis. You're looking strong. This little skirmish is to your liking? Where's Alesio?"

"Sorry, sir. He's dead. Took a spear just before the attack broke off," the sergeant said simply. "I'm the senior man. Hope that's all right with you, sir."

Fuck... The news hit Dacra like a fist. He paused, then nodded, keeping the emotion from his face. "Of course, Ganis. Thank you. Consider yourself promoted."

"Thank you, sir." Ganis nodded. "Alesio was a... good man. I will do my best."

"I know." Dacra gripped the man's shoulder.

"Your orders, sir?" Prota prompted. "Are we falling back?"

"Yes. Move quickly. Archers to the platforms. Form groups of ten to hold the path. Set fire to the walls. That should give us time."

"Sir!" Prota and Ganis saluted and ran back to give the order. Both of them knew the plan, and more importantly, so did their men. Dacra had drilled it into the officers and sergeants, and they in turn had drilled it into the centuries. There would be no fifth morning. They all knew that. They had already laid out the oil jars and whatever wood they could gather along the wall in the early hours before daybreak.

Dacra sighed as he looked at the dried blood on his hands. He had never managed to speak to Alesio. He could only hope that the stocky, hairy man with the broad smile had found peace.

Dacra watched the as the flames roared along the length of the wall. Thick black smoke billowed into the sky, pushed away by an almost indiscernible breeze. The H'rutu had fallen back to wait for the flames to die down, and the soldiers of the Seventh were in place. Dozens of archers crouched on the four platforms to the right and left of the narrow path, each with hundreds of shafts. Two squads waited beside piles of rocks, ready to roll down the steep scree should any of the tribesmen attempt that route.

For better or worse, this was their final stand. There were less than four hundred men of the Seventh left, and most were wounded. The tight quarters of the path would funnel the H'rutu and allow the Seventh to rotate the defenders. But they were still hopelessly outnumbered. Fatigue was already taking its toll, and at best, the tactic would only slow the inevitable end.

Dacra chose to stand with the first squad of ten that would defend the path. Another squad stood behind them. They would drag any wounded free and plug the gap, and a third squad waited behind them as a reserve. His hand rested on the pommel of his sword as he checked the strap of his helmet. *Gods forbid, but Elias would be unimpressed if I manage to get myself killed from a head-blow,* he thought with a grim smile.

He felt a tug at his shoulder as the man next to him tested the buckle of his breastplate. He turned and nodded his thanks with a smile. The man grinned back. His face was unshaven and haggard, but his sword shone brightly, and his armour was oiled and polished. *These are good men. Such a waste...*

Dacra turned back to watch the flames. They were already dying down. There was not much to burn. The H'rutu would come soon, and this time, they would not stop until every man of the Seventh was dead. His mouth was dry, and he felt the familiar quickening of his breath. He closed his eyes and inhaled deeply. *There will be no fifth morning.* He found the thought oddly comforting.

Blood sprayed as Dacra tore the blade from the man's chest and kicked him away. The dying man was quickly swallowed up by the heaving mass of tribesmen that choked the narrow path. The attacks had been relentless. They had tried to rotate the defenders as much as possible but mounting casualties had slowly eroded any form of respite.

Dacra grunted as a spearhead thudded into his shoulder. The hardened, studded leather deflected the blow, but it still hurt. He thrust his sword into the frenzied mass before him, feeling the blade punch through flesh and grate against bone; a swift twist, and he pulled it free to stab again. There was no space to swing the weapon, just a mindless stab, twist, and rip.

The man to his left sagged as a spear lanced into his throat. He fell forward into the H'rutu who had killed him, blocking the warrior's spear arm. Dacra's sword plunged between his ribs, killing him instantly. He ripped the blade free just in time to fend off a thrust at his groin, the spear point leaving a shallow cut along his right thigh. Syrio, who was standing to his right, slammed his sword into the warrior's neck. Hot arterial blood fountained over Dacra's face.

He spat and wiped frantically at his eyes. "Oil!" He shouted, "Oil!" They had held two urns in reserve. *If we can buy even a few moments of rest,* Dacra thought as he heard the clay pots smash on the rocks among the H'rutu further down the path. A throaty roar followed as an archer sent a burning shaft to ignite the oil. The H'rutu screamed, as they were suddenly engulfed in the flames.

"Hold!" Dacra shouted. "Save the arrows! Let them burn!"

They quickly killed the tribesmen cut off by the inferno, then fell back from the blistering heat and choking stench of smoke and charred flesh.

Dacra turned to Syrio. The veteran stood blank-faced, watching the H'rutu burn. His sword dripped with blood and his face and armour were a gory mess.

"What?" Syrio shrugged, noticing Dacra's gaze. "I'm thinking there won't be an inspection tomorrow morning."

Dacra smiled despite the bone-deep exhaustion he felt. Every muscle screamed as he looked around to witness the last few moments of the all-but-broken remnant of the Seventh. Every man carried wounds; all were shattered and torn, and yet strangely serene. He watched as the men took the reprieve to walk around and grasp each other's hands or thump a fist into another's breastplate. Tired smiles and simple words were exchanged. The last few moments of brothers.

"Sir." Dacra turned at the call. Syrio stood with his hand outstretched. He took the veteran's hand, feeling the iron grip. "It has been an honour."

Dacra nodded. "Thank you, Syrio." he said simply, then smiled. "We could win, you know. Then this would be embarrassing."

"If a frog had fucking wings... sir." Syrio grinned broadly.

When the flames died, the H'rutu threw themselves on the blades of the Seventh with almost mindless ferocity, and the remnant of the Seventh Cohort made them pay dearly for every step they took. Blades flashed and blood flew, turning the dusty path into a sodden, treacherous slush.

Dacra blinked as a spear-point snaked past his jaw. Unable to swing his sword, he slammed his fist into the tribesman's face. The man's head snapped back, and Syrio plunged his sword into the man's stomach, his intestines spilling from the gaping wound.

Another of the enemy fell as Dacra managed to free his blade, swinging it downward to cleave through the H'rutu's skull. Dacra kicked the man away, twisting the blade free. The legionnaire to his left fell as a spear plunged into his groin, his lifeblood spurting from the gaping wound. The stricken man was quickly dragged away from the line, and another jumped in to take his place.

Dacra slashed his sword across a tribesman's throat, then suddenly slipped on the bloody mud, falling heavily to the ground. Chaos exploded around him as spears cut his arms and legs and clattered off his armour. He desperately stabbed and slashed, trying to find enough space to get to his feet. Suddenly he felt a hand grab the edge of his armour under his neck and roughly drag him to his feet.

"Get up, you bastard!" Syrio barked "Get up!" The old veteran almost fell himself as his sandals slid on the bloody mud. He swung his sword blindly, trying desperately to force a space between them and the tribesmen while Dacra regrouped.

Dacra staggered to his feet and then threw himself forward, his blade hewing with a beautiful, mindless savagery. He suddenly felt an insane laughter welling up inside him. Everything seemed to slow. Blows glanced off of his armour, and his blade scythed into flesh and bone. He felt like a god, immortal and terrible. Syrio stood beside him, and together they dealt death.

Then they heard it, the long mournful wail of a horn. The echoes reverberated around the canyon, and for an instant the significance of the call was lost to Dacra. On the second blast, the H'rutu suddenly broke off their attack, withdrawing swiftly down the path. On the third blast, Dacra blinked and took a deep, shuddering breath. *Nesta, you fucking glorious bastard. You made it!* He closed his eyes and his sword clattered to the ground... It was over.

Syrio wiped a bloody hand over his face and watched as the H'rutu ran. He looked down at his sword and then to Dacra who still stood in a trance. "Don't suppose you'll forget that bullshit we spoke about earlier?" he grunted.

Dacra stared at the hollow-eyed man reflected in the pool. He hardly recognised himself; crusted flecks of dried blood speckled his gaunt features, and dust caked the stubble on his cheeks. A breath of wind disturbed the surface of the pool, and he reached down to cup water in his shaking hand.

As he raised the water to his mouth, a drop rand down his arm, cutting through the blood and dust that caked his skin. The coldness of the water never ceased to surprise him.

"Sir." He heard Syrio's voice before he could drink. "It's the Fifth Legion from Al Wahleed. Nesta brought them back. The stupid fuck almost ran himself to death." The veteran chuckled tiredly.

124

Dacra paused, then nodded slowly without turning. "Thank you, Syrio." *Just in time or far too late?* he thought. They could help bury the dead and look out over the battlefield at the mounds of twisted corpses and somehow contrive to see glory. Dacra stared down at the handful of water. He stood quietly for a long moment before pouring it into the sand at his feet.

The Palace of the Pasha

Ras-al-Salah
The 127th Day of 380, Evening

It was early evening, and a light breeze blew in off the the sea, cooling the reception hall of the pasha. Suleiman Ibn Ali Khalifa ran a fat bejewelled finger down the blade of the dagger and belched softly. Dinner had been good, and he looked forward to a long bath, but there was a small item of business that needed to be concluded first.

The pasha pursed his lips as he regarded the young H'rutu prince with heavy-lidded eyes. The young man stood tall, flanked by two guards. Suleiman was a master at exuding an almost preternatural calm, no matter how he seethed inwardly. And how he seethed at these useless H'rutu dogs! They had all but opened the eastern trade route, and already, merchants were choosing caravans rather than paying the high port taxes. It would take years to reestablish trade dominance, and it would cost him a fortune.

"I am not happy, Ibhu," the pasha began softly while cleaning a manicured nail with the tip of the dagger. The prince started to reply, and Suleiman held up a finger. "Shh... Your father failed to get rid of the legionnaires even after I put their collective necks in a noose." He paused, then pointed the dagger at Ibhubesi. "Do you remember what I told you the last time you were here? Let me remind you." He flicked his fingers and a slave entered, placed a box at the feet of the H'rutu and opened it.

The prince's eye widened as he stared into the empty box. "Baba! My father will... No, *wait!*" It was all he managed before the guards kicked his legs out from under him, forcing him to his knees. The prince struggled to stand until a guard slammed a mailed fist into the side of his head. The H'rutu went limp and fell to the floor.

"Mmm... that will not do." Suleiman frowned. "Wake him. I want him to experience his passing to the fullest."

The guards swiftly bound the prince's hands behind his back and emptied a bucket of icy water over his head. Ibhu gasped and spluttered as he tried to rise on the slippery marble. A boot to the stomach folded him double. He lay still, his face contorted in agony as he tried to breathe.

"Don't make this difficult, Ibhu," The fat pasha said softly as the prince was dragged up to his knees. Bloody saliva dripped from his mouth, and his eyes were wide with fear. "I want you to know that I had grown quite fond of you. But I am far more fond of the gold that my port provides... I'm sorry... *provided*." He took a slow breath before continuing. "Your father has disappointed me, and I want him to know that. I want him to know the length and breadth of my anger before I wipe him and the remainder of his mangey tribe from the face of the earth."

The prince had started to blubber out apologies, and Suleiman sighed, shaking his head. "Quiet, Ibhu." His voice was silky. "You see, I have already sent a message to my uncle, the shah. Apparently, a group of pilgrims were slaughtered quite brutally. And the H'rutu spear recovered from the throat of an h'jadi elder was quite damning, I'm afraid. My uncle will be most displeased."

"Baba! Do not do this!" the prince pleaded.

"Come now, Ibhu. Begging is so... beneath one of your station," Suleiman said. "And besides, you should know by now that I am a man of my word." He nodded to the guards.

"Ba—" The word was cut off by a burbling gush of blood that erupted from the prince's mouth as the guard slashed a blade across his throat. The H'rutu's body convulsed, sending blood spraying across the arms and faces of the guards. Suleiman watched impassively as the dying prince thrashed on the floor. When the gargling slowed, the guards kicked him onto his back and began to saw through his neck. Suleiman was surprised at how long it took to sever the head from the twitching body.

"Send that to the father," the fat pasha ordered, pointing to the severed head. He pushed himself laboriously to his feet and straightened his robe; his lips curled in disgust as he noticed the speckled blood on the hem. "And ensure this is cleaned up."

Suleiman walked from the room without looking back. He needed that bath and something to eat. For some reason, he always felt hungry after concluding business such as that with the prince. The satisfaction he felt that the H'rutu would be obliterated—man, woman and child—paled in comparison to the frustration of losing his trade advantage. His years of careful planning and manipulation had been laid to waste in a matter of weeks. He would start putting that right in the morning.

Maybe a pact with the Tahuti in the north could bear fruit, he thought as he entered the bathroom. *Those painted savages would eat their own grandmothers for the right price...*

He paused and breathed in the subtle floral scent of the warm steam. Two of his prettier slave girls waited alongside the large sunken bath that lay in the centre of the room. Both were naked, one holding towels; the other, vials of massage oil. Suleiman allowed himself a moment to trace the smooth curves of their bodies with his eyes. Perhaps the day wasn't as bad as he first thought. But he was tired and distracted. They could join him later once he had put the stresses of the day behind him.

The fat pasha allowed the girls to undress him and then help him as he eased his large body into the steaming water. He sighed at the delightful warmth and leaned back against the marble edge, stretching out his legs. He reached for the glass of chilled fruit juice offered by one of the girls. The unpleasantness of the incident with Ibhu was already slipping away. He smiled with the knowledge that the rest of that flea-ridden tribe would be obliterated by the righteous fury of his uncle, the shah.

He took a small sip of the juice, then lay back and closed his eyes, surrendering to the drowsy bliss that slowly crept up on him. Tomorrow he would send Tamut, his emissary, to the Tahuti. He had no doubt that the way of things would be restored in short order. Suleiman was mildly surprised as a religious text he remembered from his boyhood flitted through his mind: *Fear not, you that are faithful. That which you lose, shall return tenfold.*

The irony was delightfully amusing. He smiled, floating in the warm embrace of the water. *Uncle would be so proud,* he thought just before sleep took him.

Suleiman jerked awake at the sharp sting in his neck. He raised his hand to investigate and had it roughly pushed away. Anger flared, and he started to protest as a gloved hand clamped over his mouth.

"Shut up, you fat pig." A voice hissed in his ear, and the first twinges of fear started to roil in his stomach. "I have a dagger pressed to your throat. If you so much as twitch, you will die. Do you understand?" The pasha nodded carefully, now acutely aware of the burning sting under his jaw. "Someone wants to have a word with you," the voice whispered. "And don't think of calling for the guards. They're dead." The gloved hand moved from his mouth, and Suleiman took a slow, careful breath. The point of the dagger still pressed into the soft folds of his neck.

A leather-clad man walked slowly into view. He was a Kingdom man, tall, dark-haired, and lean. His face was vaguely familiar. The man squatted down, and the pasha shivered as the dark eyes locked onto his. Time seemed to crawl as the dark man just stared, and Suleiman began to feel much like a mouse being watched by a snake.

"You don't remember me," the man said suddenly.

"No," Suleiman replied softly.

The man smiled. "I am not surprised." He paused and then looked up to someone behind Suleiman. "Prota."

Another man, much younger, walked into view. He carried an earthenware amphora, which he placed next to the first man. The burning hate in this one's eyes was palpable.

"This is Prota," the first man said softly. "He's the only surviving officer, apart from myself, of the Tenth Legion's Seventh Cohort. Syrio, who no doubt would love to drive that dagger into your neck, is one of the very few enlisted men to walk out from the Wadi al S'hakh."

Suleiman felt the first cold trickle of real terror as he remembered the nameless officer he'd noticed at the end of the table. These men meant to kill him.

The man smiled coldly. "You're probably wondering how we found out about your arrangement with the H'rutu," the man continued. "I had a suspicion, so I had one of my men ask your vizier, Tamut, a few questions. You may have noticed his absence." The man paused to take a deep breath. His voice remained calm, but his eyes blazed as he continued, "Your greed destroyed the Tenth Legion and cost the lives of most of my men. Syrio, gag him."

"Open your fucking mouth," the man behind Suleiman hissed. The pressure from the blade eased, and a wadded cloth was roughly pushed into his mouth and bound tightly in place. The one called Syrio stepped into view. He was an older man, solid like a block of granite. His short beard was shot through with grey. The leader stood slowly, lifted the amphora, and started to pour a clear, viscous liquid into the bath. The liquid spread quickly, and Suleiman's blood ran cold as the smell of oil reached him.

Panic surged through his body, and the fat pasha forced himself up, slipped, and fell forward under the water. He flailed around as he struggled upward. Finally he managed to stand, the oil coating his skin. He desperately wiped the water and clinging oil from his face and tried to get to the steps at the edge of the bath. The stairs were quite large, and he realised with dread that his servants usually helped him. He found that his legs could not push his fat body upward.

He was on his knees on the first step as he looked back at the three men. The leader now held a burning torch taken from a sconce on the wall. Terror flooded Suleiman, and he screamed into the choking muffle of cloth that filled his mouth.

"My name is Dacra," the man said softly, then dropped the torch.

Moloc watched as the oil ignited with a throaty roar. The flames instantly enveloped the fat pasha, crawling hungrily up his skin and over his face. The Ascendant smiled at the man's muffled shrieks as he clawed at his face and arms trying to wipe away the burning oil. He pitched forward with a great splash, only to surge upward into the floating flames, the burning oil once again clinging greedily to his body.

Moloc turned his attention to the the three men. All wore different expressions. The young one watched in horror, and the older man wore an expression of disgust, but the dark one in the centre—this one was *special*. Moloc grinned. The dark one, this *Dacra,* felt... *nothing.* His rage sated, he merely watched as the pasha's skin blackened and sloughed away. He stared impassively as his victim sucked burning oil into his lungs and then, finally, pitched forward into the flames to float facedown, twitching.

The Ascendant glided closer to the dark man and sensed the roiling violence that was held in check. This one would put the world to the sword if given the right motivation. Moloc ran his sharp fingernails softly across the man's cheek, then leaned in close to stare into those black eyes...

You are mine now, the Ascendant whispered. *Mine.*

Verana
The 157th Day of 380, Midday

Dacra walked slowly through the bustling marketplace, enjoying the warmth of the sun. The pleasant smells of food cooking and rich spices mixed with the more earthy odours of produce and livestock; it was a heady mélange that hung in the still morning air. He found himself smiling at the incredible cacophony of haggling traders, braying sheep, clucking chickens and rhythmic music.

It was pleasant to walk around and experience the frenetic bustle after two uneventful weeks of slow travel as he followed the coastal road northward. He had finally reached Verana, nestled between verdant forests to the south and the looming mountains to the north. It was close enough to the coast for the weather to be moderate and the trade to be brisk. The port of Prana lay only a few hours to the east, and a steady train of wagons plied the road between the two towns.

He stopped at a fruit stall and bought a large red apple for a copper coin. It crunched as he bit into the sweet fruit, and he chewed slowly as he continued to thread his way through the press of bodies. He had thought about what this new life of his could look like on the journey north, and horses seemed central to most of those plans. Unfortunately, all he had seen to this point were sheep and cows. He hoped he could find a horse trader; otherwise, those plans would need rethinking.

He was about to take another bite of the apple when an Akhbari man dressed in a dark, flowing to'ab jumped out in front of him, holding a dagger. His hand dropped instinctively to his sword but stopped as the man's scowling face broke into a broad grin.

"You have the look of a warrior about you." The trader poked the blade in the direction of Dacra's chest. "I've got blades that would slice the balls off the Dark One himself, rip the scales from a Metkuwhar!"

Dacra suppressed the urge to smile. "Mmm…I'm not sure I would want to get that close to the Dark One's balls. And Metkuwhari don't exist."

"Have you ever been into the deep desert? Some of those Na'muud women? Metkuwhari for sure…evil bitches! Kill you with a lash of their tongue!" The trader raised an eyebrow and knowingly tapped the side of his nose with the blade. "But no matter!" The man grinned. "Take a look at this dagger…" He flipped the blade around in his hand, offering the hilt to Dacra. "The finest of Akhbari steel, handcrafted by a master sword-smith. For you I will give the best price… only three hundred drac."

Dacra took the blade. The trader was right: it was superbly crafted. The blade bore exquisite and intricate etchings of entwined vines. The hilt was bound copper and polished dark wood, and the edge was keen enough to shave with. He flipped the blade up and caught it. The balance was perfect.

"Three hundred? I don't think so…" He shook his head. "It's pretty— I'll give you that. But the blade is heavy in the hilt, and if I am to meet one of those Na'muud women, I may need a blade that's a little… longer." He tapped the side of his nose and smiled at the trader.

The trader burst into delighted laughter and clapped his hands. "Ahh… today will be a good day." He wiped the tears from his eyes with the sleeve of his robe and composed himself. "Two hundred and seventy-five. My best price."

"Seventy-five." Dacra countered.

The Akhbari blinked. "Have you fallen on your head recently? That wouldn't even cover the cost I incurred smuggling it into the Kingdom! Two hundred and fifty. My best price."

"Ridiculous." Dacra shook his head. "That price makes you no more than a thief and a scoundrel."

"Guilty on both counts." The trader nodded sagely. "But if I were to accept that offer, I would be allowing you to steal the food from the mouths of my children."

"If you had children," Dacra countered.

"This is true, but I would make the best father."

They both burst into laughter.

"Come, my friend." The Akhbari grinned and tugged at Dacra's sleeve. "The battle lines are well drawn, and this business would be better concluded in my tent over a cup or two of wine. I have a bottle of superb red that a friend stole for me."

Dacra upended the cup and eased back in the chair. The trader sat staring quietly out at the people as they passed the open flaps of his tent. The wine was excellent, as promised. The dark, square bottle bore the red wax seal of some noble, so it was undoubtedly stolen. It had been a pleasant session of insults, lies, and laughter. They had eventually agreed to a price of one hundred and seventy-five drac—apparently his best price. Dacra smiled as he examined the beautiful blade once more.

"There's more." The trader nodded to the bottle with a grin. "Drink it before the duke of Mittua bursts in here and takes our heads."

"In that case…" Dacra leaned forward and picked up the bottle to refill his cup. He studied the intricate seal. "Your friend must be a very gifted thief to get his hands on bottles like this."

"*Her* hands," the trader corrected. "And I have no idea how she does it. While you're about it…" He pushed his cup closer.

They sat in comfortable silence for a while, Dacra with his legs outstretched, the trader puffing on a pipe he had produced from the folds of his robe. Dacra watched the lazy spiral of smoke and thought of the journey that had brought him to share a bottle of stolen wine with a sword smuggler.

The two-week crossing from Al Wahleed to Sarsini had been uneventful, with calm seas and favourable winds. Dacra had spent much of the trip working with the crew where he could, allowing the labour and the sun to burn away much of the brooding anger that seemed to coil around his insides whenever the memories of the Well of the Sky threatened to surface.

The news of the death of the pasha had not reached Al Wahleed by the time they had sailed. And they had left no witnesses, so Dacra was reasonably confident that there would be no repercussions to deal with once they reached Sarsini. He had no intention of ever returning to Akhbar.

After reaching Sarsini, he had reported to the garrison and resigned his commission, much to the disappointment of the commander. He collected his pension, a sizeable amount that he had no idea how to invest at the time. On a whim, he had decided to travel north in the hope that some opportunity would arise on the way. He had no wish to remain in Sarsini; he found the sprawling, crowded city to be too claustrophobic and manic for his taste. He had then bought a horse, a young and spirited grey stallion, and supplies, then left following the winding coastal road.

He had deliberately avoided the garrison, but before he left, he had heard that Prota had been promoted and was to join the Sixth Legion, leading their Fifth Cohort. Syrio had apparently deserted. The barracks guards had found his sword and armour discarded on the ground outside the gates. Dacra hoped the grizzled veteran would find some form of peace.

"Try not to think too much, my friend." The little man smiled through a cloud of smoke. "It's a bit like prayer… It doesn't help much and leaves you with a frightful headache."

Dacra nodded with a grin. "Sage advice." He upended his cup. "And with that, I will take my leave. Thank you for your hospitality." He stood and touched his lips and then his forehead with his fingertips in the Akhbari fashion.

The trader stood and offered his hand with a smile. "Travel well, Dacra. If, for your sins, you ever find yourself near *Abuzara,* take the road to the north. Find a small house overlooking a rocky shore. It is my home. You are most welcome to share another bottle of stolen wine with me."

Dacra left the trader's tent and tucked the dagger into his belt. The wine had left him pleasantly relaxed and he started to amble slowly towards the centre of the market. Maybe he could find someone who could help him with buying horses. He had not gone a dozen steps when he realised he had not asked the trader's name. He was turning back when he heard a shout of alarm.

"Stop him! Stop him!" A woman cried out as a small, ragged boy ran headlong into Dacra's legs. Instinctively, he grabbed the boy who struggled valiantly, raining a multitude of ineffectual punches on Dacra's chest and arms.

"Stop it," Dacra growled, giving the boy a swift shake.

A woman ran into view, and seeing Dacra holding on to the scowling boy, she came to a relieved halt. "Oh… thank you, thank you!" she exclaimed breathlessly. Her face clouded, and she stormed up to the boy to pry a small coin purse from his grubby fingers.

"You little thieving *rat!*" she shouted at the boy. "Give me one good reason why I shouldn't give you to the watch. Just one!"

The boy glared back, tight-lipped and defiant.

"Well, if it's not the watch what would you like me to do with him?" Dacra asked, keeping a tight grip on the sullen boy's shirt.

She looked up at him, and Dacra felt his breath catch. Her long dark hair framed the most beautiful face he had ever seen. She brushed a strand of hair aside and scowled at the boy. Then, with total exasperation, she looked back at Dacra and blurted "He's just hungry. I can't have him locked up for that. Can I?"

"No... I suppose not." Dacra shrugged. Then, on an impulse he fished out a small silver coin and knelt down next to the boy. He held the coin in front of the boy's face. "Apologise to the lady, and you get to eat."

"Sorry." the boy mumbled, his eyes flicking briefly from the bright shine of silver to the woman.

"Not good enough." Dacra shook him again.

"I'm sorry, m'lady," the boy said. "Won't happen again."

"Better." Dacra pressed the coin into the boy's hand and, with a light smack on the side of his head, released him. "Now get out of here."

"Thank you for your help." The woman smiled as Dacra watched the boy dart away through the press of the crowd.

"It was my pleasure." Dacra bowed slightly. "If I may be so bold as to ask a small favour in return. I am looking to buy horses, and this market is"—He looked about in exasperation—"very big."

She laughed. "Yes, it is. Of course I can help. Follow me." She took his arm. "Oh... I am Arianne."

"Thank you, Arianne." He smiled. "I am... Dacian."

The meadow lay shrouded by the early-morning mist. The ghosts of trees appeared, only to melt away as the soft, billowing clouds drifted slowly past. Arianne loved the quiet. She stood on the front porch of the small stone cottage, her rough woollen shawl held around her shoulders with one hand, a steaming cup of honeyed tea in the other.

She sipped the tea and smiled as she heard the rattling of a spoon in an empty bowl coming from the kitchen. Aron had no doubt wolfed down his porridge in anticipation of making an early escape, but she had little intention of letting the seven-year-old disappear before he had worked through his chores; there were chickens to be fed and a cow to be milked.

He was a notoriously slippery little devil, and if she didn't spell out her intentions in crystal-clear terms, he would slip the noose, and that would be the last she would see of him for the day. He would stumble home at sunset and attack supper like some ravenous beast before collapsing in a heap at the table to be carried to bed by his father.

She took a sip from the mug. Dacian had been gone less than two days, and already she missed him terribly. The house felt empty, and Aron seemed even busier. Dacian had a calming effect on the boy. The eight years they had spent together had been difficult but the best years of her life.

She remembered that day in the market as if it were yesterday and how lucky she had been to stumble across the enigma that was Dacian. She revelled in his edges and shadows—and his blazing light. There was so much still hidden even after so many years. *Luckily, I'm patient...very patient.*

She smiled to herself, then frowned. The kitchen had gone ominously quiet. *What is Aron up to?* She was just about to turn to call him when the soft snort of a horse drew her attention back to the field. *Who would be visiting at this time?* she thought. It was far too early for Dacian to return. The market in Verana was over a day's ride away, and he would take his time selling the horses. They needed the best price possible.

She placed her mug on a small wooden table and walked to the edge of the porch. *Maybe it was old Jesper coming to drop off wood?* She smiled as she strained to see through the thick mist. The old man was a gossip of note, and he would no doubt have a fresh batch of stories to share from the town over a pot of honeyed tea and a plate of biscuits.

She watched as a group of riders slowly emerged from the mist. There were ten of them. The leader was conspicuous in his appearance: tall, clean-shaven, dark shoulder-length hair, with a deep-red, woollen cloak. His black knee-high riding boots were buffed to a shine, and the rapier that hung at his side was trimmed in silver.

The others were rough-looking, mostly unshaven. All were armed. One in particular, on the leader's right, had a nasty air about him. His face was hawkish and full of sharp angles. He kept his long hair tied back tightly with a strip of leather. His brown riding boots were well used, but the scabbards of the sword and hunting knife that hung at his waist were spotless and well oiled. It was his eyes that filled her with dread. They were dark, almost black. They reminded her of a reptile, with no sign of warmth. Quite suddenly, she felt very much like prey.

"Good morning," Arianne greeted the tall, well-dressed man, forcing a smile. "How can I help you?"

"Where is your husband?" He ignored the greeting, looking to his left to the paddocks, where their horses were barely visible in the rolling mist. Arianne noticed small beads of sweat on the man's upper lip, and he blinked his eyes rapidly as if struggling to make sense of what he was seeing. "Your husband, where is he?" he barked.

"The market!" Arianne flinched and took a deep breath. "He's at the market in Verana." She paused. "May I ask what your business is with him?"

He turned back to her and wiped a gloved hand across his mouth. His eyes darkened. "Your rent," he almost purred, his voice soft and full of venom. "That is my business. I…" he broke off, then blinked rapidly again and looked at the house with a flash of confusion. He shook his head and kneaded his right eye with a knuckle. "It seems very convenient that he's not here."

"My apologies, my lord." She dropped her eyes, and for the first time, real fear gripped her. There was a roiling madness in the man's eyes. "I did not know… I—"

"Shut up." He cut her off with an abrupt wave of his hand, turning to the man on his right. "Kratos, have your men search the house and the barn. If you find him, bring him to me immediately. If he resists, beat him until he sees the error of his ways."

"My lord." The man nodded and waved two of his men toward the barn before turning his own horse toward the house.

Arianne swallowed as she realised who the man was… Antoine de Verana; his father, Viktor, owned the land they were living on. "He's not here, my lord." She stepped forward quickly, lowering her eyes and holding out her hands. "Please. He has gone to the market to sell three of the horses. What he makes there will cover the rent and more."

The man called Kratos paused and looked towards the young lord. De Verana stared down at her for a long moment, then swung his right leg over his horse's neck and dropped down from the saddle. He slowly pulled off his gloves, tugging at each finger. Once he had removed them both, he slapped them into his open palm. Arianne started at the sharp sound.

"I'm afraid it may be a little too late for that," he said softly; his eyes seemed glazed as they skittered over her breasts like hungry insects. He paused and shook his head as if struggling to think clearly. Then his eyes, filled with madness, returned to lock onto hers. "Carry on, Kratos." he said absently as he stepped towards her.

The sun was already low when Dacian pushed aside the brush and stepped into the clearing, leading his horse and a small donkey. The ride back from Verana had been uneventful, and he had taken time to gather some firewood along the way. He was lost in pleasant thoughts of gathering Arianne up in his arms and ruffling Aron's hair, so when his horse tugged at its reins and snorted sharply, he looked up and blinked as he tried to make sense of what he was seeing.

Smoke curled up lazily from the blackened ruins of his home. The roof had collapsed in parts, and the charred beams poked out like gnarled fingers. His blood ran cold, the reins and the donkey's rope dropping from his hand. The donkey brayed irritably and started to amble off with its load of firewood. He ignored it, taking a staggering step forward.

"Arianne!" he screamed as he broke into a run. "Arianne!" He looked frantically for any sign of his wife and son. "Aron!" *No, no... Arianne, where are you? Where?* He scanned the edge of the trees. *No, this is not happening!* His mind raced as he took a few halting steps towards the paddock, where only his horses nickered and pranced, skittish from the smoke.

He stopped and turned back to the house. "Arianne!" he shouted, striding towards the blackened door. He kicked at it, and it burst inward with a shower of sparks and ash. The heat was still intense, but the pain of it was buried deep beneath the terror that flooded his soul. Mindless of the agony that stabbed at his hands and arms, he started clawing at the smouldering beams and wreckage, flinging it aside.

"Arianne! Aron!" he screamed, the acrid smoke burning his lungs. "No... please no..."

He found his son first: the remains so pitifully tiny, curled up in the corner of his room. He knew then that he had also lost Arianne; no force

136

imaginable would have kept her from trying to save Aron, apart from death. He gathered up the little body and carried it to the grass, where he lay it gently down. Tears had cut lines through the soot and ash on his face.

"You wait here," he said quietly. "I'm going to fetch your mother."

The sun had set by the time he had buried them together at the bottom of Arianne's flower garden. He sat quietly on the grass, allowing the gloom of the coming night to settle over him. The wet soil had soothed the stabbing pain of his blistered hands. He had no idea how long he had been sitting there when a soft hand touched his shoulder. He turned and looked into an old, deeply lined face.

"Dacian," Jesper said sadly. The old woodsman wiped away the tears that filled his eyes as he looked past Dacian to the twin mounds of earth. "I am so sorry. So sorry…"

"What happened here?" Dacian asked quietly, looking up at the old man.

"Men came from d'Verana." Jesper answered, looking away. "I was on the edge of the woods," he said, gesturing with his hand. "I am sorry, Dacian; I did not do anything to help. I just stood there in the shadows and watched." Jesper stared at the young man. "There were too many of them. Too many…"

"You would not have been able to stop them, Jesper," Dacian said quietly as he got to his feet and placed a hand on the old man's shoulder. "You would be dead if you had tried." He looked back to the smouldering ruin that was his home. "Was d'Verana with them?"

"No. It was the son, Antoine, and the duke's man, Kratos. After they put fire to the house, Kratos wanted to round up your horses, but d'Verana stopped them." Jesper shook his head. "I don't know why. He shouted at Kratos that he'd kill any one of them if they so much as touched a horse."

Dacian turned back to the house.

"You had better leave." Jesper touched his arm. "They may come back. I have some coin if you need."

"I need to do something first, Jesper," he said, his voice so cold the old woodcutter shivered. "And thank you, my friend, but I have coin. I sold the grey stallion and two mares yesterday… to pay the rent."

Jesper watched as the younger man walked slowly back toward the house. A few moments later he returned with a bundle wrapped in waxed canvas. The edges were slightly brittle, but otherwise the package was unharmed. He watched as Dacian sat on his haunches to peel back the layers of thick cloth, revealing a military sword and a beautiful Akhbari dagger.

Both were untouched by the fire, having been stored under the stones of the bedroom floor. Jesper knew this, having helped Dacian lay the stone many years ago. He also knew they were the last remnants of a life the younger man had thought gone forever.

Jesper watched quietly as the young man lifted the dagger and slid the blade from its sheath. The silvery metal shone brightly in the sun. When he looked up, Jesper started at the change in his eyes—suddenly so bleak, so empty. The thin veneer of a quiet breeder of horses had been ripped away, and what lay exposed was something that had been carefully hidden for years. This man was darker and infinitely more deadly.

"Do what you must," Jesper said softly. Then on an impulse stepped forward and embraced the young man firmly. The smell of smoke and ash was almost overpowering. "Do what you must and then go away. Go far away."

Antoine d'Verana stood on the balcony of his room. The crystal glass filled with aged Sarsinian red wine stood untouched. To the west, the evening sky had been ablaze with fiery clouds, but he had not even seen them. The night had descended unnoticed, the rising moon and the glimmer of stars ignored. The wound to his shoulder had been stitched and treated by the physician, but it still ached fiercely as he stared blankly into the dark. The pain was nothing compared to the ache he felt deep within his soul.

His riding gloves lay at his feet where he had dropped them, the speckles of dried blood still visible on the leather. He closed his eyes and kneaded the muscles in his neck. He felt physically sick as the ragged images of what he had done came flooding back. He had done things he never thought himself capable of. He swallowed, pushing his hair back from his face. What had possessed him? How could he ever make it right?

He turned and brushed aside the soft silken curtains as he entered his room. He paused and looked to his left, where a full-length mirror stood in its polished wooden frame. The man who looked back at him should not have been capable of those horrific deeds. He stared into the dark, empty eyes. set in the handsome face of a killer. *No, so much worse than a killer*, he thought miserably.

He closed his eyes, and in his mind, he could still feel the heat of the fire. He could still hear the dry crackle of the flames and smell the acrid stench of burning thatch not quite masking the sickly sweet smell of...

He shook his head to try to clear the horror that welled up. But almost instantly, he saw the torch tumbling…

End over end… over…

…end until it hit the thatch of the roof in an explosion of sparks. The dry sedge caught fire almost immediately. He watched as bright flames leaped up, lapping eagerly at the roof of the small house. Kratos sat easily in his saddle and watched impassively while his men laughed and jested. But Antoine felt totally numb.

"You want us to wait for him, my lord?" Kratos asked simply.

Antoine ignored him and turned back to the burning house. How did it come to this? How did things get so out of control? Was there ever any control? His shoulder ached terribly where the woman had stabbed him. What was he thinking?

He could still smell her hair. It had reminded him of flowers. He had dragged her to the bedroom. Somehow her screams had meant nothing; her fists hammering against his chest and face as he had forced her down onto the bed didn't seem real.

Memories flashed though his mind: the taste of blood on his lips when she bit him, the sound of her dress tearing and her silken smooth skin under his hands. She had fought him the whole time, screaming as he tore away her underclothes, her nails clawing at his face.

He shuddered as he remembered slamming the back of his hand across her face. Her head whipped to one side; her eyes glazed. He remembered the mad, delirious frenzy: the strange, oily whispers that slipped and slithered through his mind, goading him on. Each word, each black and disturbing suggestion, was punctuated by the feeling of sharp nails digging painfully into his scalp. He had almost felt like a helpless puppet, just meat and bones being driven on by some malevolent mind.

"No, please, no…" She had pleaded, still stunned from the blow, but he paid her no heed. The fragments of what followed spun sickeningly through his head—hot, feverish; the salty taste of her fear as he buried his face in her neck; the softness of her flesh under his groping fingers. She fought him over and over, digging her nails into his face, sinking her teeth into his shoulder. But all her desperation, her horror, her loathing, was lost… swallowed by the tempest of lust that raged through him.

Where she had found the knife, he would never know, but the first he saw of it was when she rammed the blade to the hilt into his shoulder. The sudden flash of pain had been swallowed a black and horrible rage.

He had ripped the knife from his own flesh and slammed it downwards again and again.

The vivid picture of her blood splattered over the bed and his arms seemed engraved in his mind. He had staggered from the room, head spinning, as if all the rage had been suddenly stripped from him. He found the body of the little boy where it lay in the corner like some discarded doll.

"Oh gods, what have we done?" he said through clenched teeth.

"Nothing that cannot be taken care of," Kratos answered bluntly. "Do you want me to wait for him? I can get the boys to round up the horses in the meanwhile."

"No!" Antoine turned and shouted. "Leave the horses. They were late with the rent. The rent! Gods, what have we done?"

"Let me stay and take care of the man, my lord," Kratos said, not entirely able to hide the frustration in his voice. "This can end here, today. The boys and I can take care of it."

"No," Antoine d'Verana said as the watched as the roof collapse in a shower of bright sparks and smoke. The flames that burned around his soul blazed higher and higher as he watched the black smoke billowing into the clear blue sky...

Antoine sat wearily on the end of his bed. He could not imagine that this deep ache would ever leave him. Resting his elbows on his knees, he covered his face with his hands and wept. As the sobs racked his body, hot tears dripped through his fingers onto the marble floor. He did not hear the whisper of silk sliding over leather. Nor did he hear the soft footfalls. Not until the sharp point of the dagger pressed into his cheek did he react.

He hissed in pain as the blade punctured his skin. As he looked up, his breath caught. The shadows of dusk seemed to have melded into an apparition that chilled his blood. Through the tears, he could barely make out the blistered flesh of the hand pressing the point of the blade to his throat. The face was unrecognisable under the smears of soot and ash. The smell of smoke hung in the air. But worst of all were the eyes: black and hard as shards of obsidian and as cold and lifeless as ice.

"Antoine d'Verana?" the darkness asked quietly.

"Yes," he sobbed as a thin thread of blood snaked its way down from the wound to follow his jaw-line. "Yes. I am he."

"I am Death," the darkness whispered …

Sarsini
The Thirty-Third Day of 389, Evening

Willon stood in the shadows of the entrance to a warehouse and shivered. Her leather cap was pulled tightly over her head, leaving several thin, dirty strands of hair to whip around in the icy wind. She swore quietly to herself as the frigid air seemed to cut through her thin, patched cloak no matter how she tried to squeeze herself into the shallow doorway. She sighed, remembering a time long ago, before her beauty faded, when nights such as this would have been unimaginable.

She wiped her nose with her woollen glove and pulled her cloak tighter around her stick-thin frame. The gold that men had spent for her to share their warm beds was a distant memory. Now she had to make do with a handful of coppers earned in any way she could—like tonight, watching for a man she didn't know who was hunted by other men who scared her. She squeezed her eyes shut and prayed for the wind to die down, but knowing that the rain and cold would more than likely last through the night.

From the doorway, she could see the main quay of the docks to her left; there, three large merchant ships lay tugging at their moorings, waiting to be loaded. To her right, she had a clear view of a narrow street and the entrance to a busy pub. Every now and again, a group of people would arrive, and she would leave the scant sanctuary of the recess to look closely at their faces.

Willon sniffed and rubbed at her nose again. She took a folded piece of paper from her pocket and examined the drawing of a face in the guttering light of the street lantern. It didn't look like the face of a murderer, she thought, not for the first time. There were strong lines and an intensity to the eyes, but it didn't strike her as a cruel face. And she had years of experience in reading the faces of men. She had learned to see the monsters hiding behind the beautiful masks. And yet this one had apparently gutted the old duke of Verana's son.

She shuddered, recalling the story told by the duke's man, Kratos, as he had handed them the pictures before sending them out to watch the inns and taverns. Old Jerold had been one of the dozens there to earn what seemed like an easy coin or two. He had spoken with her as they left the warehouse.

"You be careful, love," he had said, patting her arm. "Don't want to hear 'bout anything happenin' to you." He had studied the picture before looking up with a strange intensity that the old man had never shown before. "Killin' a man is one thing. Gods know I've been there. But takin' the time to…" He had trailed off took a deep breath. "All I'm sayin' is there's more to this than's been told, Willon. You be careful. You promise?"

"Promise." She had smiled. "You too, you old fool." She had pointed a thin finger at the old man, to emphasise that he shouldn't go and do anything brash, either. They had parted with a brief hug, Jerold shambling off to watch an inn near the eastern gate.

Snapping back to the present, she looked up as a small group of men approached the inn. They were burly, with leather trews and heavy sea-boots. They laughed loudly at a muffled comment from their leader, a large man with a heroic red beard, before entering the establishment. *Dockhands out for an ale and a bit of trouble.* She dismissed them, pressing herself back into the doorway. None of them looked remotely like the face on the page she held.

She turned her attention back to the page. Apparently, the drawing was exceptionally accurate. She had overheard one of Kratos' men mentioning a man called Hanri, who had once sketched a picture of the man's wife from memory. The man had joked about whether it was a gift or a curse, having the image of his wife's face etched into his mind.

"Old Hanri drew her right and proper." The man had laughed. "Every damned angry wrinkle and line. Gave it to Dara for her birthday… She didn't speak to me for days."

The other had winced. "Gods. She got a temper, that Dara. Surprised she didn't kill you. How the hell did you manage to fix that?"

"Fix it?" The first man grinned. "Why the hell would I do that? Was the first bit of peace 'n' quiet I had in years!" They both laughed.

"So how'd he know this fellow, then?" The other asked, tapping the page.

"I heard he met him at the market. Don't take much for Hanri to remember a face. Kratos got him to draw all these for couple o'silver drac. I'm telling you , knowing ol' Hanri's work, this'll be damned close if not exactly right."

Willon yawned, then folded the paper and stuffed it back into her pants pocket. She looked up at the dark sky, again wondering whether the meagre reward was worth the discomfort. *Going to get soaked before this night's out.* She shivered again as her cloak shifted, allowing the icy air to briefly knife through against her flesh. There was a bonus of a silver drac for the one who found this man, and she mouthed another silent prayer that he would choose this inn. That would ensure she and Jerold would eat for at least a week. She worried about the old man. He would not see many more winters.

She pressed herself against the rough wood of the door, resigning herself to the prospect of a very long and uncomfortable night. The duke's man, Kratos, had spread the watchers all around the city. She knew the chances of earning the silver piece were small, but any chance was better than none. Kratos had said the man would try for a ship to Akhbar, so maybe being near the docks was a stroke of luck. Dozens of ships crossed the Great Sea every month, plying their trades between the Kingdom and the Akhbari Empire. Surely that meant he would want a place close by.

Willon sighed as she imagined sitting near the fire of the tavern with a bowl of hot soup. Jerold would be sitting opposite her, telling the wild stories of his distant youth, when he was a robber prince with more gold than the shah of Akhbar. She smiled. She didn't believe a word of it, but she still enjoyed the tales. She blew into her hands, trying in vain to warm them before tucking them back into her armpits with a mumbled oath. There would be no warm fire or soup—or anything, for that matter —unless one of them found the man. Until then, both of them would be standing outside in the rain, slowly freezing to death.

She was about to turn back to the docks when she noticed two men walk up to the entrance. The one on the right was well dressed, with an air of scruffy indifference, but he carried himself like a fighter. The one on the left was bearded, with a slightly heavier build. Willon pulled the drawing from her pocket and imagined the gaunt face with a fresh beard. She looked back and felt a surge of excitement. *Got you!* She waited for the two men to enter the inn and then set off at a run. She needed to get to Kratos.

"There is only now."
—The First Book

The Third Circle

"I am nothing
but ash and bone
Nothing but rain
over an ocean

"For without you
Love is the brief dance of an autumn leaf
before letting go."

—The Songs of E'kia

Sarsini
The Thirty-Third Day of 389, Evening

Tariq stared at the body of the axeman as it lay in the courtyard. Sirvan's face was paper-white, except for the dark smear of blood on his mouth and chin. The man's eyes stared blindly at the puddle of blood soaking slowly into the mud.

The fight, if it could be called such, had been sudden and shocking. He watched as two men laughed as another made a comical chopping motion before grabbing his throat. He sighed. A man had died, and to the crowd, it was a brief entertainment at best.

He shivered and pulled his cloak tighter. The entire evening had barrelled along to this bloody end. He had seen the frustration build throughout the card game, and he thanked the useless gods for the weakness of his last hand. He had been able to cut his losses and move from the path of the storm that was Sirvan's rage. He had little doubt that it would have been him that lay in the mud had he been facing that brute on a matter of honour.

On a brighter note he had more than tripled his money having wagered on the swordsman. More than a few fools had been taken in by the forbidding size and obvious strength of Sirvan. But the swordsman had one insurmountable gift: speed. The counter attack had been awesome to witness. The swordsman had simply dropped beneath the axe stroke and skewered the luckless Sirvan through the throat in one blindingly fast movement.

No playing to the crowd, no showmanship… just cold, deadly efficiency. Not terribly entertaining, but given the sudden and very welcome extra weight to his purse, Tariq was willing to forgive the man.

Once more, he tugged at his cloak, settling it tightly around his shoulders before looking up at the dark sky with disgust and spitting into the mud. He could not begin to describe how much he hated rain. Every fibre of his being craved the warm, flowing sands of Akhbar. The coin he earned smuggling Akhbari blades to these wetland kingdoms and the northern tribes had far outweighed any physical discomfort, but those days were now past. He wanted to go home.

He cast another bleak look skyward. This storm was wreaking havoc with that particular plan. The slavers would probably not risk sailing in this weather. If Mareq holed up somewhere to ride it out, he would not make their scheduled rendezvous in two days' time, and then it would be almost impossible to anticipate when he would arrive.

Tariq frowned deeply and turned to make his way to the stable. His donkey brayed irritably as he approached the stall. He smiled and rubbed the animal's velvety nose.

"Are you cold as well, my girl?" She twitched her ears and prodded him with her nose. "Ah..." Tariq grinned. "Cold and hungry!" He reached into his cloak and removed a rosy apple. He pulled a small knife from a pocket and cut the apple in two, offering the donkey a half, which she happily accepted. Tariq grinned and scratched her ear as she diligently chewed away at the fruit.

"Here, girl. Have the rest." Tariq shrugged. "I'm too cold to eat."

With another gentle rub on the nose, he left the animal and returned to his room, where a chambermaid had thankfully lit a fire, so it was almost warm enough to be comfortable. He added a few more pieces of wood to the stack, sending a flurry of bright-orange sparks upward. He drew up a chair and settled into it, stretching his legs out towards the fireplace.

He stared into the dancing flames and wondered how many trips he had made over the years. He had earned enough coin to retire comfortably to his home on the coast and never move again. *Why, then, are you here, you old fool?* he thought with a deep sigh. *Why are you not warm and comfortable on your porch, sipping Alia's stolen wine, watching the sun set over the sea? Because she's gone, Tariq... That's why. Who would you point out a pod of dolphins to? Or share a pot of khafja with, you old fool?* He took a deep breath. At least he would never need to see that insane bastard Mareq again. He remembered his very first trip. Flushed with success and a heavy purse, he had been so close to losing it all. That return voyage had skirted the edge of utter disaster.

He closed his eyes, feeling the warmth of the fire. He could still see the clear skies above, not a trace of cloud in that endless blue. He could feel the subtle ebb and tilt of the deck as they drifted on the glassy expanse of the ocean. As sleep settled over him, he could almost taste the salt in the air as he stood in the bow as a young man, full of fear and hope. Almost... but first, there was the dream...

The dreamer climbed the stairs and entered the cool interior of the temple. A startled bird flapped away noisily. He looked at the well as it lay in the illuminated in the finger of golden light. The dusty shadows seemed to stare back at him, silently disapproving of his intrusion.

As before, he walked to the well and paused to pick up the ancient bucket. A hint of a memory nagged at him as he bent down to pick up a small pebble. He rolled it around in his fingers, feeling the smooth surface, then raised his arm to throw the stone into the well...

"Have you no faith, Tariq?" Alia's voice whispered. "Have you no faith?"

With a sharp intake of breath, the dreamer stepped back, clutching the pebble tightly in his fist. "Alia?" he called out into the gloom. "Where are you?"

"No faith." came the echo, like the dry hiss of sand.

"Where are you Alia?" the dreamer again asked the shadows.

"With you…" the air seemed to sigh. "In you."

The dreamer took a deep breath as a strange feeling of sadness settled on him. "Alia? Why do you ask if I have no faith? What do you mean?"

"Lower the bucket, Tariq."

"What difference would it make?" The dreamer frowned, looking up from the small stone to search the dusty gloom. "Whether I throw a pebble or lower the bucket, I will know soon enough if there is water."

"This is true," Alia's voice sighed sadly from the shadows. "But should enough faithless men cast a pebble, the water will be lost forever."

The dreamer rolled the small pebble between his fingers without a word.

"Such is the nature of man," the voice whispered. "Always such a close examination of the path set before them that they forget to walk. And then always wondering why the destination remains out of reach, not realising there is no destination. Just the journey. Merely the setting of one foot in front of the other and trusting that the road will take you where you need to be."

"But if that road leads away from where I want to go?" the dreamer asked.

"Want? Need? Which do you think is more important?" the dry whisper retorted. "Open your hand, Tariq."

The dreamer opened his hand to find that the dull, rough stone had been replaced by a soft, yellow gleam. His eyes widened, and the shadows sighed. "You are in the middle of a desert, Tariq. And you cannot drink gold."

The Great Sea
The 153rd Day of 356, Afternoon

Tariq stood in the bow of the caravel and watched nervously as Mareq paced back and forth across the upper deck like a caged beast. They had been becalmed for almost two full days, and the captain's infamous lack of patience was strained to the limit. The squat and vile toad of a man was now looking for something or someone on which to vent his anger, a meaty paw resting ominously on the silver pommel of the taravari that hung at his side.

The young smuggler grimaced. He had learned quickly that Mareq, in this mood, was dangerous and unpredictable. He had seen the ugly captain kill a man for suggesting that the gods were angry with them. The man's head had bounced on the deck as his body fell over the side. "On this ship, *I am God!*" Mareq had raged, waving the bloody taravari around as if daring anyone to challenge that fact.

The crewmen were studiously avoiding eye contact with their angry captain, busying themselves with anything that would keep attention off them. Tariq wiped the sweat from his face with his sleeve and glanced, not for the first time, at the sails.

The vast yellowed span of square canvas on the fore- and mainmasts, and the triangular lateen-rigged mizzen hung limply in the hot and humid afternoon air. Every so often, they would flutter and slap fitfully in the fickle breeze, each time prompting Mareq to glare at these lethargic motions of the canvas with undiluted disgust and curse or spit over the side, or both.

Tariq turned away and allowed the salty tang of the occasional cool ocean breeze to wash over him. He breathed deeply. It was the only place on the whole ship where the sickly stench of human waste didn't permeate everything. He tried desperately not to think of the two hundred and fifty souls chained naked in the stifling heat below the decks.

All, except two of the prettier women, whom Mareq had locked in his cabin, were crushed together in the dark. When the weaker ones died, they were left to rot alongside the living. It was simply too much effort to unchain the corpses.

He rested his elbows on the gunwale and closed his eyes, enjoying the gentle roll of the deck beneath him and the soft sounds of the water lapping against the hull.

"Hey, smuggler," a gruff voice said behind him. "We want to talk to you."

Tariq turned slowly. Three crewmen stood a few feet away. The one who spoke was a stocky, pockmarked troll named Fahad. He had heavily muscled shoulders and arms. The sides of his head were shaved, leaving a narrow strip of hair that he wore in a topknot.

His two hulking companions stood sullenly behind him, one on either side. The one on the left tapped a short wooden-cudgel against the back of his leg, and the other rested his right hand on the pommel of a long, curved scimitar.

"What would you like to talk about?" Tariq replied more calmly than he felt. *Here's trouble!* he thought as he tried to lean nonchalantly on the rail.

Fahad paused. Despite the imminent danger, Tariq found himself enjoying the perplexed look that crossed the sailor's face. Apparently, his façade of nonchalance was better than he thought.

Fahad fingered the hilt of the slim-bladed dirk at his side. "We heard you made a fair amount of coin selling those pretty swords of yours."

"More than a fair amount," Tariq replied softly. "What of it?" He shot a glance over at Mareq, who was observing the exchange with great interest. *No chance of help from him,* Tariq mused.

"We feel we're entitled to a share." Fahad grinned menacingly, displaying an impressive array of brown-stained teeth.

"And how did you come to that conclusion?" Tariq asked. His mind raced to find a way out of what was swiftly becoming a very dangerous situation.

"This here's our ship, and it would be a shame if our one and only paying passenger were to have an accident." Fahad smiled at him. "But me and my associates here would be glad to take it upon ourselves to… protect you. For a fee."

"I see." Tariq nodded, pushed himself upright, and took a step towards his three antagonists. "Let me think on it…" Without the slightest warning, he smashed his fist into Fahad's face. The sailor's head snapped backward with a spray of blood, and he crashed to the deck.

The other two gaped at their unconscious leader, and Tariq took full advantage, thundering a left into the stomach of the one carrying the sword.

The man buckled over, the wind blasted from his lungs, and collapsed to the deck, his eyes bulging as he fought to take a breath.

The remaining thug roused himself from his shocked state and aimed a wicked cudgel blow at Tariq's head.

Tariq tried desperately to duck, but the weapon struck him a glancing blow on the side of the head knocking him to the deck. His head spun wickedly as he struggled to his knees, only to receive a heavy kick squarely in the chest that smashed him over backwards.

The man leaped forward with the cudgel held high, and Tariq kicked desperately at his leg. The blow landed solidly just below his knee snapping the joint with a sickening crack. He crashed into the deck screaming, with his leg folded up at an impossible angle underneath him.

Tariq dragged himself to his feet and then hammered a blow to the man's jaw, knocking him senseless. By this point, his second assailant had managed to struggle to his feet. Tariq brutally kicked him between the legs, and he folded into a heap.

Tariq's head throbbed, and each breath was agony. He looked up to the upper deck, where Mareq had been watching the proceedings with a smirk. *The fucking toad must have enjoyed that,* Tariq thought as he walked over to Fahad, who was still lying on the deck groaning. "Anything to break the fucking boredom," he snarled to himself.

Fahad was missing three teeth, and blood and spittle dribbled from his mouth. His eyes were glazed as he tried in vain to drag himself up from the deck. Tariq put a foot on his chest, shoving him back to the deck. He then knelt down beside the sailor, grabbed a handful of his hair, and pulled his head back. He could clearly see the tendons and veins against the taunt skin of his neck. Fahad squirmed and blubbered as he caught sight of the gleaming blade that Tariq now held in his hand.

"Now listen to me, goat brain," Tariq said softly, pressing the point of the hunting knife into the soft flesh under Fahad's right eye. "The next time you even think of threatening me, I'm going to slice off your face and feed it to the fish."

A bright bead of blood welled up around the point as it punctured the skin. "Are we clear on that point?" Tariq asked quietly, showing a calmness and confidence he didn't feel at all. He removed the knife, and Fahad nodded furiously.

Tariq released him, and his head thumped to the deck. He glanced up at Mareq as he slammed the knife back into its scabbard. The captain nodded slightly and turned back to the helm.

Sarsini
The Thirty-Third Day of 389, Night

Tariq woke with a start as the logs in the fire popped loudly. He rubbed his eyes as the memories flooded back, then settled back into the chair to enjoy the warmth radiating from the fire. He shook his head, a faint smile on his face. He had spent the remaining three days of that voyage in the cramped confines of his cabin, not daring to show his face on deck. When they finally docked in Al Wahleed, he had bolted ashore before they had even tied the ship to the dock. He vowed never to sail with Mareq again.

He had made over five thousand drac on that first trip, more money than he had made in the entire previous year. At the time, he had reasoned that his profits were more than enough to open a small business. He'd set himself up as a prominent purveyor of fine blades and get a small house on the outskirts of the town, where a devoted wife and children would wait for him to come home.

It had all been so clear that day as he stood on the bustling dock, resting a foot on a small chest heavy with coin. He remembered that particular moment so vividly. He could still smell the spices and sweat. He could hear the coarse cries of gulls overhead and the sharp crack of a whip as Mareq's men herded the surviving slaves from the bowels of the ship. It was impossible to forget those gaunt faces, dirty and confused, blinking in the bright morning sunlight.

Unfortunately, in less than three months, he was bankrupt, his profits squandered in smoke-filled, noisy khafja houses, drinking the thick, dark Akhbari brew and indulging himself with rich games of pahkur and even more expensive women. Not long after that, he had realised that *never* was a silly word and had embarked on his second trip. But this time he had done things a little differently.

First, he cut Mareq in on the profits, and that all but ensured his safety on board. Mareq was known to jealously protect his interests. Second, he acquired the services of a broker in Sarsini to manage his profits. Both choices had worked out superbly, and now, over thirty years later, he was, by most standards, a wealthy man. *Who should be happily retired,* he thought dryly.

"And yet, for some reason, here we are," he said softly to himself as he held out his hands toward the fire and soaked in the warmth. Now if only this damned storm would abate he could go to the rendezvous to see whether, by some quirk of fortune, that bastard Mareq was waiting for him.

Hunters

Sarsini
The Thirty-Third Day of 389, Night

Kratos jerked awake at the hammering on his door and swore as an empty wine jug fell from his pallet to shatter on the tiles of the floor. He groaned as he rolled out from under the blankets. He shivered and rubbed at his arms before casting a baleful glare at the broken ceramic shards at his feet. There was no fireplace in the small room at the back of the warehouse, and the wine had helped, but now he regretted it bitterly. *This had better be good,* he thought, trying to ignore the dull ache that seemed to permeate his skull.

The knock came again. "Wait damn you!" he shouted, wincing at the sudden, blinding flash of pain. It felt as if someone had just driven a nail through his forehead. He staggered over to the door and pulled it open to see the round, fat face of Abas and a small, painfully thin woman who held a leather cap in her hands. She looked almost blue from the cold.

"What is it?" Kratos growled, scratching absently at a flea bite on his ribs. He noticed a food stain on Abas' tunic. *Gods, the man is always stuffing his face,* he thought irritably.

"Willon over here"—Abas poked a thumb in the direction of the woman—"she says she's found the farmer."

Kratos straightened, his attention now fully on the woman. "Are you sure? Where?"

"Oh yes, sir." Willon nodded. "It's him, all right. He's grown a beard but he's the man in drawing that y'gave us. I saw him at the Crow— y'know the Inn down near the docks?" Willon wiped her nose. "Him and another man, got there not an hour ago. I came right away, sir."

"Good." Kratos nodded and went back into his room to retrieve his purse from the table. He fished out two silver pieces. He held them in front of her face. "This is your bonus... and another one." He closed his hand around them. "If you go back with Abas and make sure they don't leave. If they do... you'll follow them."

"Of course, sir." Willon nodded, excited at the prospect of the extra coin, yet disappointed in wasn't in her hands quite yet.

Kratos turned to Abas. "And you... just watch," he said pointedly. "If he gets away, I will personally skin your fat hide. You understand?"

Abas nodded with a petulant look on his face but said nothing.

"I'll be there in the morning with the others," Kratos continued. "With a bit of luck, we'll be heading back to Verana by tomorrow night with this bastard strapped to the back of a horse. Go." He dismissed them with a wave of his hand.

Kratos closed the door and crossed to the bed. He sat down and pulled the blanket over his shoulders. He knew of the tavern that Willon had mentioned. There was a stable entrance around the back that would serve them well. It was also quite close to the warehouse, so they could snatch the farmer and drag him back here quite quickly. He had no need to run into the city watch and try to explain why they had some man trussed up on the back of a horse. He had papers from the duke but he had no need to spend needless time at the watchhouse while some official decided the validity of the document.

Tomorrow morning, early, he would take Sciras and Cale to join Abas. He pondered taking another two of the younger men as well but dismissed the idea. The trick would be to take him alive and not too damaged. He didn't expect it to be overly difficult to take the farmer, but he couldn't shake the nagging thought that this man had managed to break into d'Verana's estate and butcher his son without being seen. There was obviously much more to the man than met the eye. Intuition and caution were skills that Kratos had honed over the years through bitter experience.

For someone with his obvious talent, he had left a telling loose end behind. They had found the dead guard's body in the brush and a slightly concussed kitchen servant tied up in the scullery. Kratos could not understand why he let the servant live. It hadn't taken long to confirm his identity. Maybe this *Dacian* just didn't care. Maybe he was even daring them to find him. *If only Antoine had heeded my advice,* Kratos thought, not for the first time. But no amount of irritation or wishful thinking was going to make this problem disappear. One way or the other, they needed to get this man back to the duke—alive.

He wondered now about the second man that the woman had seen. It would not be well if the farmer had friends in the city. They would probably need to kill that one. He wanted this clean and quiet, with no running pursuit back to Verana to worry about. D'Verana had promised a generous bonus if he brought the man back unharmed. And Kratos was willing to employ any means necessary to ensure he didn't lose a single coin of that bonus.

He thought idly of the revenge the duke would exact on the farmer once he got his hands on him. It would be slow and ugly; of that, he had little doubt. How slow and ugly would be up to the farmer. It would be better for him if he just died. He started reaching for his mug before realising it was empty. He swore softly to himself and contemplated fetching another jug of wine. He checked himself and filled the mug from a water pitcher. *I will need to be sharp tomorrow,* he thought sourly, remembering the morning at the estate.

The door burst open as Kratos was about to loosen the serving maid's blouse. The girl screamed, and he swung around with his fists balled, the curse on his lips dying as he saw the man's grim expression. Gods... something serious had happened. He dropped his hands. These men were well trained and not easily shaken.

"Lord d'Verana wants you in his son's room immediately."

"Why? Something has happened to Antoine?" Kratos asked.

"He's dead," the guard said simply.

"What? How?" Kratos grabbed his shirt, which was hanging over a chair, pulling it over his head as he pushed past the man.

"Murdered," the man replied, falling into step behind Kratos.

"What?" Kratos stopped so suddenly the guard almost walked into him. "My sword." He pushed past the man again and returned, clutching the weapon in his hand. "With me," he barked, breaking into a run.

He ran from the barracks, cutting across the lawns and burst through the main entrance of the house with the guard in tow, then ran up the staircase three stairs at a time with sword in hand, the scabbard discarded.

He reached the top of the stairs and pushed aside two servants who were milling around in stunned silence. He ran to his right down the wide passage. Two more guards stood outside the heavy wooden door to Antoine's chambers. The door stood slightly ajar. Kratos glared at the men before he threw it open and strode into the room with his sword ready.

"My lord!" he called out before staggering to a halt to stare in disbelief at what he saw. He walked slowly forward. Antoine was on his knees at the foot of the bed. He was gagged, and his wrists were bound above his head, the torn sheets tied to the tops of the bedposts. His body hung forward over the pale, bloody ropes of intestines that spilled from the gaping wound in his stomach. He had been gutted and left to die slowly in excruciating agony. Where are his eyes? *Kratos shook his head. He was no stranger to violence, but this... "My lord?" he said softly.*

Victor d'Verana said nothing as he sat on the floor in front of the body of his son. The duke's hands and clothes were bloodied. When he looked up, Kratos could see the burning madness in his eyes. "Find the creature who did this," the Duke said with an icy calm. "Find him and bring him to me. Alive."

Kratos sipped at the water and shook his head. They should have just waited for the bastard to come home. That way, they would have been done with it. They would have killed him, his wife, and the whelp all together. Kratos always found revenge to be a senseless, empty, and ultimately *reciprocal* business. There never seemed to be a satisfactory conclusion, ever. It was always best just to do it right the first time, a lesson he'd learned a long time ago. The dead don't climb to your balcony to gut you. The dead don't take your eyes, and the dead don't write curses on the wall using your blood.

He sat back, remembering the message and its unmistakable promise of violence. It was scrawled across the far wall of Antoine's bedroom, written in charcoal and blood. He hadn't noticed at first, but when he did, it felt like it was burned into his mind, along with the coarse, splintered rage in each word. This was no simple farmer, and no matter what

154

happened tomorrow, even if they managed to take him back to d'Verana, there would be no simple end to this business. Kratos felt it in his gut.

"*In the end, the earth embraces us all, kings and wretched alike.*" He had seen that inscription on a statue outside the temple of Eresophi, the goddess of death. He smiled bleakly to himself and sipped at the water. Even that dark, scaled bitch would know that you can't wash away blood with blood. *Revenge... senseless and empty,* he thought with a sigh.

The Port of Prana
The 215th Day of 360, Morning

The young boy ran along the crowded docks without looking back. His lungs burned, but terror drove him on. He could hear the other boys closing in, and his only hope was to lose them in the maze of alleyways between the warehouses. He vaulted over a stack of barrels, scattering a flock of seabirds that took wing with coarse shrieks of outrage. He sprinted past the gangplank of a large trader, ignoring the angry cry of a sailor who had to step back sharply to avoid a collision.

He flashed a look over his shoulder, and for an instant, caught a glimpse of one of his pursuers. He ducked to his left and slammed into the legs of a dockworker, who dropped the box of herring he was carrying, spilling the fish over the wooden boards of the wharf.

"Damn your eyes! Watch it boy!" the man barked, but the boy hardly paused as he darted into an alley to weave between the crates and discarded nets. A dozen or so steps later he stopped, dropped to his haunches behind a stack of boxes, and turned back to the entrance. His chest heaved as he sucked in air. With luck they would have lost sight of him before he left the pier.

Three boys flashed past, then another. He held his breath, and his heart hammered. A few moments later, a larger boy stumbled past, with three others in tow. They were chasing him for what he held in a white-knuckled grip in his left hand. That and the fact that Garen, the leader, wanted to beat the hell out of him for shaming him in front of the other boys. Almost reluctantly, he now opened his hand to look at the bright silver coin. It represented more than a month's wages, far more than his father could hope to earn selling skins and meat.

He had hoped to keep it for himself, but that was becoming more and more unlikely. Even if he managed to evade the others, Timos, his older brother, knew of his windfall and would take great delight in telling their father. He would probably fetch yet another beating for his troubles. Then the coin would be quickly spent on cheap wine and the painted women his father mixed with whenever he managed to earn anything of significance.

The boy's face darkened in anger at the thought of his older brother. Timos' lying and manipulation had made every day of his life hell, and he was powerless to stop it. Timos was older, stronger, and seemly capable of squirming his way out of almost every form of trouble. Or, like this morning, capable of turning any small success to his own advantage.

He leaned up against the brick wall of the customs house and looked around before carefully taking the coin from his pocket. It was larger than any coin he had ever seen and wonderfully shiny. He turned it over in his hand. There was an eagle in flight on one side and a man's head on the other, and he wondered if that was the duke of Verana or maybe even the king.

"What you got there, rat-face?" came a harsh voice, and his stomach lurched. He quickly placed the coin back in his pocket and looked up to see a fat redheaded boy striding towards him. Garen, the son of a wealthy fishmonger, was flanked by several other boys. At sixteen, Garen was four years older and more than a head taller than any of his pack. And where the boy was painfully thin, Garen's ample belly hung over the straining leather belt that held up his britches. He was a constant source of pain to any of the town boys who chose to disagree with him, and many had been beaten senseless more than once for failing to fawn appropriately in the fat bastard's presence.

"Hey, Kratos! Didn't you hear me, you little shit?" Garen yelled, his face face twisting into a nasty scowl.

"None of your business," he snapped back with far more confidence than he felt, but he was in no mood to give up his prize.

"It's a silver drac." Came another familiar voice, and his heart sank as he looked past the gang leader to his brother.

"Shut your face, Timos," Kratos shouted angrily knowing that now, there was very little chance he would be allowed to keep the coin. He had imagined all the things he could buy, but now, because his stupid brother wanted to gain favour with the town bully, it was going to be taken away.

"Oh! A silver drac is it?" Garen's fat face split with a nasty grin. "How'd a scrawny bilge rat like you get your paws on that? Think you'd be better off giving that to me, rat boy. For safe keeping."

"No," Kratos said defiantly before casting a final, desperate look to his brother, who stood behind the bigger boy with a smirk on his face. No help there, Kratos thought with an almost blinding flash of anger.

"Listen here, you little fuck," Garen growled. "Give it to me or I'll beat you within an inch of your worthless life."

"It's mine! I earned it," Kratos yelled, desperation creeping into his voice.

"Earned it?" He heard his brother laugh scornfully. "He lifted it from the dock boss' pocket, Garen. I saw him."

Garen stretched out his hand and glared at Kratos. "Thieving little rat boy," he sneered. "You'd better give it over before I drag your scrawny arse to the dock boss. I'm sure he'll wring that skinny rat neck of yours. And if he doesn't kill you, then your drunken, useless father certainly will." The fat boy's face again split with an ugly grin.

Kratos ground his teeth together in frustration. If he didn't give up the coin willingly, he would fetch a proper beating from this bunch and lose it anyway. He sighed and took the coin from his pocket.

"Give it to me, rat boy." Garen snarled, his small, piggy eyes glinting greedily.

"Fuck you," Kratos spat suddenly and kicked the fat boy hard between the legs. Garen's eyes bulged, and he collapsed to the ground, with his face twisted in agony. The other boys looked on in utter disbelief as their leader writhed, keening, on the cobbles. The consequences of what he had just done hit Kratos like a gut blow, and he took a tentative step backward. His back touched the wall. I'm dead... I'm so dead, he thought, frozen to the spot. He's going to kill me... Then as terror flooded through him, he turned and ran.

"Get him!" Garen shrieked. "Get him!"

Kratos slipped the coin back into his pocket. He kept an eye on the entrance to the alley. Apart from the dockhands and fisherman walking back and forth, he saw none of his pursuers. He began to feel a faint flickering of hope. It looked like they had not turned back, so there was a good chance they hadn't seen him leave the pier. With luck, they had left the docks already and were looking for him in the town. He waited for a moment longer and then stood slowly. The victorious smile died on his lips as Timos stepped into sight.

"Here!" his brother yelled, pointing into the alley. "He's here!"

Kratos grabbed at the boxes and pulled desperately with all his weight. His brother and two others were already running toward him as they started to topple. Timos, who was in the lead, had to throw himself backward as the boxes fell with a splintering crash. Kratos could hear the boys' angry curses as they scrambled over the debris, but he didn't look back as he ran. Then his foot caught in the loop of a net and he fell, hard.

He hit the ground, and the wind exploded from this lungs. He rolled and tried desperately to get to his feet when a kick landed on the small of his back, driving him down again. All of a sudden, he was in a storm of violence as blows landed all over his shoulders and ribs. He wrapped his arms around his head and tried to roll into a ball.

"Stop!" he heard Garen yell. "Get him up."

He felt himself being dragged to his feet, boy holding his arms tightly behind his back. Garen walked closer, his face the picture of rage. His brother stood to one side, and Kratos felt a white-hot flash of anger. If he managed to survive this, there would be a reckoning. Timos would pay.

Kratos turned back to the advancing gang leader and forced a smile. "How're the balls, you fat bastard?"

One of the other boys snorted a laugh, and Garen turned and punched him hard in the mouth. "Think it's funny, huh?" He grabbed the boy's shirt and glared at him before shoving him backward into a stack of crates. The boy shook his head as blood dribbled down his chin.

Garen turned back to Kratos. "And as for you... I'm going to fucking kill you now, rat boy," Garen hissed. His fist snaked out, and Kratos' head snapped back. The next punch landed in his stomach. The third broke his nose. His legs gave way at the fourth, and the boys who held him allowed him to fall to the muddy ground. A kick landed heavily in his ribs, driving the air from his lungs. Kratos hovered on the edge of consciousness, dimly aware of Timos kneeling down next to him. He felt a hand pulling at his pockets.

"Here," he heard his brother say.

"Stupid rat boy," he heard Garen growl before a kick smashed into his face and all went dark.

He had no idea how long he lay in the alley, but the shadows were long by the time he hauled himself to his feet. His body ached, and his head throbbed. His face was caked with dried blood and dirt. He tentatively explored the damage to his face. His left eye was almost swollen closed, and his lower lip was split. His nose seemed to be sitting at an odd angle, a bit off to the left. He hissed in pain as he tried to straighten it. He took a slow breath and made for the pier.

He held his ribs as he climbed slowly over the broken boxes and turned for home. No doubt Timos was already there, and who knew what story he would spin. Hopefully, his father would not be too drunk. That never ended well, and Kratos didn't want a fresh set of welts over the ones he had already accumulated.

The walk home was slow and painful as he wound his way up from the docks through the small town. The merchants were already closing for the day, and the streets were quiet. It gave him time to think about the earlier events. His anger at Timos had been replaced by an icy resolve. He would never allow Timos to betray him like that again. One way or the other, his brother would pay. Then that fat pig, Garen, would also be reckoned with. As he made his painful way to the outskirts of the town, a dark thought bloomed in his mind. *And if Father decides to beat me tonight, that, too, will be the last of it.* A smile crossed his swollen face.

Kratos crouched in the brush with the arrow nocked. The afternoon was warm and still, and the forest was filled with the buzz and hum of insects. They were hunting deer. His father was some forty paces to his left and slightly ahead of him. Timos was similarly off to his right. A small brook babbled over the rocks nearby. He waited, enjoying the warmth of the sun on his back. His father always said the hardest part of hunting was patience, waiting for the animals to come to you. But Kratos had little difficultly with this. He instinctively knew there was little point in running around in the forest, making noise. The animals needed to drink. Be quiet; be patient. Let them come to you.

He rubbed his damaged nose carefully. The bruises he had endured days before were beginning to fade, but the burning desire for retribution blazed. His father had taken a leather strap to him when he returned home late. Kratos hadn't even tried to explain. He remembered his father's calloused hand clamped around his neck, pressing his face into his pallet as the strap had fallen across his back and buttocks again and again. There was no point in trying to reason with the man. The reek of cheap liquor hung about him, and no doubt Timos had already had time to poison him.

No matter, Kratos thought. He looked to his left and listened. Apart from the soft sigh of the wind, there was nothing. He wouldn't be surprised if his father was asleep in the grass. The man had finished almost four pitchers of wine the night before. It was incredible that he was in the forest at all.

Kratos stood slowly and waited for a second before moving quietly to his right. He followed a low depression, taking care to keep out of sight. The long grass brushed softly against his legs, and he rolled each step to ensure he made no sound. The sound of the falling water grew louder as the brook dropped off a small waterfall ahead. There was a low overhang not far off that was in shadow at this time of the day. It gave a clear view of both banks of the stream. It was a perfect place to wait for the deer.

He inched forward, now taking even more care with each slow step. His breathing slowed as he became acutely aware of everything around him—the whisper of the breeze, the soft touch of the undergrowth, the feel of the ground beneath his feet. *There?* He froze and slowly dropped to a knee. He took a slow breath and raised the bow, pulling back smoothly on the shaft. He paused and allowed the breath to bleed from his lungs, and then, in the brief moment between heartbeats, he released the arrow.

The shaft hit Timos in the throat, and he collapsed into the undergrowth. Kratos rose smoothly and walked over to his brother to stand over him. Timos was not dead. Blood bubbled from his mouth, and he clawed weakly at the shaft that jutted from his neck. It had entered just under his jaw, the point protruding near the base of his skull. Kratos was quite surprised he was still alive. He knelt down and drew his knife. Timos's eyes were wide and pleading.

"Well, brother," Kratos said softly. "It comes to this. See it as a mercy." He grabbed Timos' hair and slammed the blade up under his jaw. Timos' body twitched and then lay still. Kratos twisted the blade and pulled it free.

The Forest Road, Verana
The Thirty-Ninth Day of 371, Afternoon

Viktor d'Verana sat astride his horse, his right hand resting easily on the pommel of his sword while he held the reins lightly in his left. They were moving slowing along the Forest Road to the south of Verana, having visited his cousin's estate. The lunch had been superb, and as always, the wine had flowed. The baron's red blend, made from the sweet purple grapes of his upper vineyard, was delightful. A few dusty bottles from the cellar had been a wonderful complement to the succulent venison.

But now the food and wine, coupled with the gentle sway of the walking horse, lulled the duke to the edge of sleep. He shook his head, sat straighter in the saddle, and took several deep breaths. *It wouldn't do to be sagging over my horse's neck, snoring,* the duke thought with a frown. Having just entered his fortieth year, Viktor was a striking man, lean and well proportioned, with cropped dark hair and a full, beard that had just begun to show flecks of silver on the chin. His nose was hawkish, and his eyes were a piercing blue.

He turned to Jorg, the captain of the guard, who rode to his left. "After the bridge, let us pick up the pace."

"My lord," the captain replied. A Noordlander by birth, Jorg Jorgenson was a bear of a man, towering over the duke, who himself stood over six feet tall. The captain was meticulous and disciplined, as evidenced in his pristine tunic and shining mail, which matched that of his men. *The duke's men... my men,* Viktor thought with a half smile as he looked ahead.

Willow Tree Bridge lay less than a hundred yards ahead. He could already heard the babble of the small river. Shortly after the crossing, the road turned North, and the forest grew denser and darker. Viktor enjoyed the tranquility of the Forest Road, so their pace up to this point had been purposely slow, but he knew that they would do well to clear the forest before nightfall. They were still a few hours from the estate, and even with the fifteen guards, he did not want to risk still travelling after dark. He had never quite managed to rid the forest of the thieves and brigands, though not for the lack of trying. The best fight, as far as he was concerned, was the one avoided.

The horse's hooves clopped hollowly over the wood of the bridge as Viktor took a final slow look around. He always found the the dappled shadows cast by the afternoon sun poking through the trees quite beautiful. Two old, twisted willows flanked the bridge, surrounded by ferns that grew thick on the banks of the stream, their drooping branches almost touching the swiftly running water as it tumbled over the moss-covered rocks.

Without a word Viktor tapped his horse into a trot, and his men took up the pace, coming into formation around him—five in the van and five to the rear. Jorg and four others took station around the duke. Viktor immediately sensed the heightened vigilance of the men. If there was to be trouble, it would be over this next stretch of the road where the forest was thickest. The closeness of the trees and the dense undergrowth would make any pursuit on horse very difficult. The duke, however, was not concerned. *No one in their right mind would attack a group of armed guards,* he thought. *To what gain? We carry no gold or goods.* The risk of death or capture far outweighed any possible bounty.

It was then that he spotted a slight movement to his left, but before he could point it out to the captain he heard a harsh cry of "Now!" There was a sharp snap, and then a hail of large stones tore into the leading riders, driving all five of the men and their horses to the ground in a tangle of bloody limbs. Viktor dragged his horse to a halt, the animal's hooves sliding on the gravel of the road. He looked in horror, trying desperately to make sense of what had happened.

"Captain! What—" he began to ask when thick ropes burst from the ground to the front and rear, blocking their escape.

"Protect the duke!" Jorg bellowed, drawing his sword. The duke's horse pranced nervously, and he fought to get the panicked gelding under control as his men formed up around him.

"Sir!" one of them called out. "Arvid is still alive!"

Viktor watched in horror as one of the fallen men staggered to his feet. His face was a gory mess, with a loose flap of skin hanging over one of his eyes where a rock had struck, tearing his helmet from his head. The guard tried weakly to draw his sword before collapsing to the ground.

"Watch the forest!" Jorg shouted, pulling his sword from its scabbard. "The forest!"

Suddenly, the forest seemed to come alive as men armed with a mix of wooden pikes, hammers, axes, and rusty swords burst from the thick brush on either side of the road. With a guttural cry, they surged forward. Viktor drew his sword and prepared to fight with his men even as the cold certainty dawned that they would die here on the road this day. They were outnumbered at least three to one.

And then the battle was joined and all thought was wiped away. Viktor found himself swallowed by the chaotic clash of metal and the screams of pain. He slashed down at the mass of bodies, feeling the blade bite into flesh and bone. A wooden spear thudded into the duke's left shoulder, almost unhorsing him. He grunted in pain and stabbed at a man who fell backward, bright blood spurting from the wound in his throat. The pain was excruciating. The mail had turned the point, but Viktor's arm felt as if it had been torn from its socket.

Hot blood sprayed across the duke's face as one of his men toppled from the saddle. Viktor slashed at the brigand who carried an old sabre. The man tried to parry the blow, but the rusted blade snapped at the blow. He swept his blade back, feeling it sink deep, cutting cleanly through the man's collarbone and sternum. Viktor kicked the man free from this blade and looked for the next brigand.

His horse shied to his left as a blade slashed across his leg. He hacked at his attacker, and the man fell away, to be trampled under hooves and feet. Viktor was lucky. Had his horse not moved, the sword would have bitten deeper, and he may have bled to death. Still the shallow wound burned like hell, and he could feel the blood running freely down his leg.

Ahead of him, the captain kicked an attacker in the face before steadying himself and sending his sword arcing downward to crunch through the man's helmet and into his skull, killing him instantly. Jorg pulled the blade free and slashed at another attacker, his blade tearing through the man's neck in a spray of blood. Then his horse collapsed as a bearded man with a blacksmith's hammer smashed the animal's front legs. Jorg hit the ground hard, with his right leg pinned under the stricken animal. Viktor watched in horror as the man jumped forward and swung the hammer downward, crushing the captain's skull.

"No!" Viktor bellowed and tried to kick his horse forward against the choking press of men. He raised his sword and hacked downward to cleave flesh and bone. A mindless, savage roar burst from his chest as he

163

dealt death. Another of his men died as a spear was rammed up under his chin. Viktor's rage was incandescent. His sword rose and fell with brutal efficiency. Around him, the remaining guards also fought with a similar desperate savagery. Nothing mattered to them now but survival.

Viktor had just managed to twist his blade free when he saw something flash toward him from the corner of his eye. The hammer glanced off his helmet but snapped his head back. He lurched backward and felt rough hands grab at him and pull him from the saddle. He screamed in pain as he landed heavily on his damaged shoulder. A boot crashed into his face, and his vision filled with bright pinwheels of colour. He tried to roll as the blows came thick and fast, boots crashing into his ribs, his stomach, and his shoulders.

"Kill him!" he heard someone shout. "Stick the bastard!"

Viktor desperately lashed out with his feet, feeling his boot make solid contact. Another blow snapped his head to the side, his mouth filled with the coppery taste of blood. He flailed feebly with his arms, trying to stave off the inevitable. He felt the weight of a man hitting his chest. He hissed in pain as a gloved hand took a fistful of hair and pulled his head back, exposing his throat. The man's bearded face was so close, he could smell the stink of rotten teeth and cheap wine.

"Now you die, you bastard," the man hissed. Viktor felt the cold metal of the blade touch his neck, and then his grip was suddenly released, and the man's weight fell away in a sticky, splash of blood.

"Get up, my lord!" one of his guards shouted, swinging his sword wildly as another extended a hand to the fallen duke. He grabbed the hand and had just forced himself to his knees when another boot slammed into the small of his back, knocking him to the ground again. Another brigand threw himself on top of the duke, but this time, Viktor managed to roll quickly and pinned the man beneath him. With a growl, he slammed his fist into the man's face, feeling the front teeth snap off at the gums. The second blow crushed the man's nose, and as he raised his fist again, he found himself being pulled roughly away and upward by the collar of his tunic.

One of his guards had hauled him off the ground and now pressed a sword into his hand. He looked at his remaining four men, now all bloodied and on foot. They had somehow managed to position themselves around him with their swords pointing outward. *Good men,* Viktor thought grimly as the brigands regrouped and surrounded them. It would not be long now. He took a firm grip on his sword and prepared for the end.

Calan dropped two more jagged, grapefruit-size stones into the sling of the trebuchet before checking the sighting one more time. He had lined up the machine with a small natural opening between the trees that gave a clear line of sight to the road. He had placed the trebuchet some twenty paces into the forest, where the dense foliage on either side screened them from the road. It was far smaller than the classic siege engines he had seen while fighting for the king, but they had built it for an entirely different purpose.

He and Baris, a former blacksmith, had taken months to perfect the machine. They had tested and refined the mechanism using straw mannequins until each shot tore the targets to pieces. He looked out to the road. At this range, the spread of the stones would be optimal, the speed would be lethal, and any horsemen would simply be obliterated.

"Baris," he called over his shoulder. "I want you to check the rope traps."

"By the gods, Calan," the blacksmith sighed. "I've checked the bloody things three times already. The counterweights are ready; the ropes are hidden unless you stand on them. It's all good."

"Check them again." Calan turned and glared at him. "We've got exactly one chance, you understand? And then check that the men are in place."

Baris hesitated for a second, then nodded curtly and stomped away through the thick undergrowth to attend to the tasks.

"You think this will work?" Calan heard a voice ask and turned to see the newcomer to their band standing with a hand on the arm of the trebuchet.

"Yes, Kratos." Calan sighed. "We tested it. It will work." The young man was tall and very thin and wore his long dark hair tied back from his face with a simple strip of leather. His clothes were little more than rags, but the wych elm longbow he carried was meticulously cared for, the wood polished and leather grip clean and oiled. "It must work," Calan said softly. "Most of us are here today because we've lost our land. That bastard d'Verana chased us away and reduced us to thieves. So many of us have watched our children taken by the fever or the cold or hunger." He shook his head. "It ends today."

Kratos shrugged. "Perhaps."

"What would you have us do?" Calan snapped. "Nothing? Grovel in the mud and die of starvation while that pig quaffs wine in front of a warm fire on his estate?"

165

"No, I don't think that. But killing the duke will not put bread on the table. I think you will just replace one tyrant with another."

"You're too young to have buried a child, Kratos. I will not rest until d'Verana pays for what he's done."

"Calan!" he heard a young voice call out. The boy skidded to a halt. "They're coming," he blurted before sucking in a few deep breaths, hands on knees.

"How many, boy?" Calan asked.

"Fifteen," the boy replied. "Five in the front, five at the back." He paused to suck in a breath and wipe the sweat from his face. "The captain and four others are with the duke. Look like they're bloody well out for an afternoon stroll, they are," he said with a gap-toothed grin.

Travelling slowly with only fifteen men. Arrogant bastard, Calan thought with a flash of anger. "Where are they now? Come now, tell me," he asked impatiently.

"Should be near Willow Tree Bridge by now."

"Good lad." Calan smiled and cuffed the boy lightly on the side of the head. "Now get out of here. We'll see you later."

The boy grinned and darted off into the trees.

"Baris! Janus! Get your men ready. They're coming!" Calan called out. "Olan, the trebuchet. Wait for my command." He turned to the thin archer. "Kratos, follow me. I want you and that bow here with me. If you get a clean shot, I want you to take it."

Kratos couched in the undergrowth with his bow across his knees and watched as the battle unfolded. Calan had placed him with a clear line of sight of the road. The hail of stones had been every bit as vicious as Calan had predicted, obliterating the first five riders. The fighting that followed had been chaotic and brutal. Kratos had watched the duke closely, even drawing a shaft at one point, but he never got a clear shot. The man fought well, but when he was pulled from his horse, Kratos thought it was over.

He was mildly surprised when the duke was dragged to his feet by one of his men. The man's face was bloodied and his tunic was torn, but he took the sword offered to him and made ready to fight. Maybe there was more to the man than he was led to believe. Kratos knew Calan had been disappointed by his questions, but he truly could see no material benefit in killing the Duke. *Well, not like this, at least,* he thought with a wry smile, remembering how a certain redheaded fat boy that had suddenly disappeared from Prana. A heavy rock tied to an ankle and dropped into an abandoned well took all unanswered questions with it.

No, killing this duke would not bring an end to anything, nor would it set anything right. It most certainly would not bring back the dead. It would probably only precipitate even more brutal reprisals when the new duke chose to make an example. Kratos was not overly fond of the hard life he had been dealt, but even living off scraps was better than being actively hunted and killed.

In the lull, he made out Calan as he pushed his way forward to the the edge of the circle that surrounded the duke and his remaining guards. The duke and his men had done well, but now there were only five of them facing Calan's band of over twenty. The end would come quickly.

"Today you die, you murdering bastard!" Calan shouted, pointing his axe at the duke. "The blood of countless families is on your hands." There was a rumble of agreement from the men around him.

"Be done with it, then," the duke growled back. "I haven't the time for your snivelling."

Kratos lifted his bow and nocked an arrow, then drew it back to his cheek. He sighted along the smooth shaft, aiming for the base of the duke's skull. At this range he could not miss if he tried. On the edge of his vision, he could see Calan raise his axe slowly. Kratos shifted his aim, and in a fluid motion, he released the arrow. It flew straight and true hitting, Calan in the left eye, killing him instantly. The axe toppled from his lifeless fingers.

Before the axe hit the ground, Kratos had nocked and loosed the second arrow. This one struck Baris in the throat. In less than a heartbeat, a third thudded into Janus' neck. The fourth and fifth arrows killed two more as fear and confusion rippled through the brigands' ranks. As the six and seventh arrows killed Olan and the man next to him, they turned and ran as one. Kratos coolly sent three more arrows after the fleeing thieves and three more men died with arrows jutting from their backs.

Kratos lowered his bow. He had learned quickly that if you didn't decide on a course of action, someone else would decide for you. *Sorry Calan,* he thought. *But that's never going to happen again.*

Viktor blinked in surprise at the leader's head jerked back from the impact of the arrow. As the axe toppled from the man's hand, he heard the hiss of the next shaft as it flashed past him to hit another brigand in the throat. Before anyone could react, yet another died. More arrows thudded into flesh, and suddenly the brigands were running. Three more died before the duke could turn to the trees that hid the archer.

"One of ours?" he asked the guard next to him as he scanned the thick brush.

"No, my lord." the man shook his head. "I'm sure of it. Captain Jorg would have briefed us."

"Come out! Show yourself!" Viktor called out.

A young man slowly rose from the undergrowth just beyond the tree line and started walking cautiously towards them. He was stick-thin, and his clothes were ragged. He held a long bow with an arrow loosely nocked. His men raised their swords.

The duke waved a hand at the guards to lower their swords. "Stop there. Where are the rest?" the duke asked.

"Just me," the man replied.

"Just you?" the duke asked, looking past the man to the woods.

"I know how to use a bow." The young man shrugged.

"I can see the evidence of that." Viktor nodded, looking at the fallen brigands. "You have my thanks. What is your name, bowman?"

"Kratos," the man replied simply.

"Well met, Kratos. I am the Duke Viktor d'Verana. How are you here at this time? It seems most fortuitous."

"I was hunting... my lord." The young man held up his bow as if that explained everything. When the duke made no reply, he continued, "There are many deer, fox, and badger in this part of the wood. I sell the meat and skins in Prana. I heard the sounds of a battle. What I saw didn't seem particularly fair, so I chose to even things out a bit."

"But why did you choose to help me, Kratos?" the duke asked. "I would would have thought that you'd have more in common with the brigands. Better to see me dead."

Kratos thought carefully about the question. There would be no fooling this duke. He shrugged. "Maybe I knew the man who lead that bunch and didn't agree with him. Maybe it was the honourable thing to do. Maybe I thought I could gain the favour of the duke if I saved his life... Maybe I am just tired of hunting deer, my lord."

"Indeed." The duke smiled.

Kratos stood in the dark, empty street in front of the tavern, holding the reins of his horse. Thankfully, the rain had passed, but the morning was icy cold. Abas and the woman, Willon, stood to his right, looking haggard from the sleepless night and thoroughly frozen. He couldn't care less about fat Abas, but he felt a twinge of sympathy for the thin woman, who was shivering uncontrollably.

The farmer had not left, according to the two of them, but neither had the man's companion. Kratos stared at the front door, unable to shake the uneasy feeling that there was more to this farmer than they were prepared for. Kratos hoped the four of them would be enough. They would need to be fast and quiet; waking up the entire inn would make things considerably more difficult and messy.

He fished the two silver coins from his pocket and handed them to the woman. "Go. You don't want to be here," he said. She nodded her thanks and then scampered away. He turned to his men. "Abas, Cale… with me. Sciras, you take the horses around the back to the courtyard and make ready for us. We will need to leave fast once we've got the farmer." He turned to them. "Questions?"

The men shook their heads.

"Good. We move." He handed the reins of his horse to Sciras and walked to the front door, pushed it open, and stepped into the common room. The space was already wonderfully warm from the large logs that blazed in the central fire place and almost empty, with only a handful of patrons, who seemed more interested in their oats and *khafja* than the new arrivals. Not one paid the three armed men more than passing attention.

A very large man with a shock of red hair and a long beard stood behind the bar counter, cleaning a tankard with a cloth. Kratos crossed the room quickly, and the big man looked up with a broad, friendly smile.

"Mornin' to you all," the innkeeper said as he continued wiping the tankard. "Jasuf's the name. How can I help?"

"Good morning, Jasuf." Kratos nodded and placed a drawing of Dacian on the counter. "Where is this man?"

"Uhm… what is it to you?" Jasuf frowned. "I'm not in the habit of giving out information on my guests. Bad for business, you know."

Kratos placed a silver drac on the counter and slid it towards Jasuf. "I understand completely. But we're here on the instruction of the duke of Verana, and this man is wanted for… questioning. Now if you could tell us where we can find him, we'll be done with our business with as little fuss as possible."

The barkeep put the tankard down on the counter and wiped his hands. He picked up the silver piece and dropped it into his pocket. "Up the stairs, down the passage, second door on the left."

"My thanks." Kratos nodded. "My man, Abas, will wait here… for your safety. Is there another way to the courtyard? I don't want to inconvenience your guests."

"Yes." Jasuf nodded. Kratos noticed the sudden look of concern that crossed the man's face. *No doubt wondering what that inconvenience might entail,* he thought. After the brief pause, the innkeeper continued, "Carry on with the passage and you'll find stairs. Take them down and turn to the right at the bottom. The door leads to the courtyard and stables."

"Wonderful." He turned to his men. "Cale, with me. Abas wait here until I call."

Kratos drew his sword at the top of the stairs, as did Cale. The passage was dimly lit by oil lamps on either side. He moved forward quietly until he came to the door indicated by the innkeeper. There, he waved Cale to take up position on his left as he crouched down and drew his dagger. Pressing the thin blade between the door and the frame, he slowly eased the latch upwards. He grimaced as the door popped open with a soft creak.

He stood up and pushed the door slowly open. "Wait here. Watch the passage," he whispered. Then, waiting for his eyes to adjust to the gloom, he stepped quietly into the room. He knew how to move without sound; years of hunting had honed the skill to almost preternatural levels. He glided closer, as silent as a ghost to the bed, carefully avoiding the broken ceramic of the wash basin. The farmer lay fully clothed on his back, with his left arm above his head.

Kratos slowly extended his sword and tapped the farmer under the chin. When the man didn't move, he jabbed the point into his neck drawing a pinprick of blood. The farmer hissed in pain and reached for his throat. Kratos slapped the hand aside with the blade and returned the point to the farmer's throat.

"Good morning," Kratos said softly. "Sleep well?"

Dacian swallowed carefully, acutely aware of the sharp point of the sword digging into the skin under his jaw. A thin man with dark eyes stared at him down the length of the blade. Dacian closed his eyes and tried to collect his thoughts. His head ached fearfully, and his mouth felt horribly dry.

"We've not met," the man continued softly. "So let me introduce myself. My name is Kratos and I am charged by the duke of Verana to return you, as unharmed as possible, to his estate. Now I feel I must emphasise as unharmed *as possible*... because rest assured, I will not hesitate to make this very painful, or even kill you, if you choose to resist. Am I clear?"

Dacian nodded slightly.

"Good." Kratos smiled.

"You were at the farm..." Dacian managed, his voice a dry croak. "You were with Antoine."

"Yes," Kratos said simply. "I was there. And not that it matters, but I did not kill your wife or your child."

"You were there," Dacian snarled through clenched teeth.

"Yes, I was. I burned your house to the ground, and I did nothing to stop the duke's son from killing your wife. I would have waited for you and killed you when you returned if I'd had my way. Then you wouldn't have spilled Antoine's guts over his bedroom floor, and we wouldn't be having this conversation. But none of that matters."

"It matters to me," Dacian spat.

"Then we may have something to settle on that point." Kratos shrugged. "But I'm afraid you will not have much of an opportunity in that regard. My men and I are going to take you back to the duke, alive or, failing that, in recognisable pieces, but one way or the other, you will go. Now, as delightful as I am finding this conversation, time is short." Dacian's vision exploded into a bright-white flash of pain as Kratos slammed the pommel of the sword into the side of his head; the world lurched and pinwheeled, and then darkness took him.

"Cale, bind him and get him to the stables," Kratos said as he stepped away from the unconscious Dacian and sheathed his sword. Cale roughly dragged Dacian from the bed onto the floor, and pulled his hands behind his back, and bound them tightly. He took an arm and was about to lift him when Kratos heard a woman's angry voice behind him.

"What's this? Let him go before I call the watch!"

Kratos turned to see a tall blonde woman standing in the doorway. Her eyes were emerald green, and she seemed totally unafraid.

"This is none of your business, girl," Kratos said softly, holding up a hand. "You should leave."

When she didn't so much as blink, Kratos sighed and reached into his pocket to withdraw a silver coin. He tossed the coin to her. "Here. Now go."

She snatched the coin from the air and slapped him hard across the cheek. "I'm no whore you can send on her way with a simple coin. Now let him go or I'll get the watch," she repeated, each word slow and controlled.

Kratos touched the tender spot on his cheek were she had struck him and smiled. He liked her spirit, but he didn't have time for complications. She would undoubtably run off and get the watch before they could leave the city. He stepped forward, and without another word hit her hard on the jaw. Her head snapped to the right, and she slumped to the floor, unconscious.

Why couldn't you just walk away? he thought with mild irritation as he knelt down next to her, looping a strand of her golden hair around his finger.

"What you want us to do with the wench?" he heard Cale ask.

Now you're a part of this. He sighed as he stood and turned to the man. "Tie her up," he replied after a moment. "I'll send up Abas up to help you carry them to the horses."

Panos opened his eyes and immediately wished he hadn't. His head throbbed hideously, and he was convinced that some small animal had crawled into his mouth and died. He groaned and rolled over into what seemed like two pale mounds of flesh. His eyes widened as he recognised that they were actually a pair of astonishingly large breasts.

Shit... He closed his eyes and lay very still, trying to piece together the night before. The girl snorted softly, stirred slightly, and then thankfully, remained asleep. She was pretty, in a plain sort of manner, and more than a trifle on the plump side. She was probably not the *last* woman on earth that he would bed, but Panos had to concede that the vast amounts of ale he consumed must have been a contributing factor to his current plight.

Strategic retreat, my son. He nodded to himself and then slid out from beneath the bedclothes with exaggerated care. He needed to leave the inn, and possibly the city, before she woke up. He looked around frantically for his clothes. He had managed to pull on his leggings and boots before he realised he was being watched. He turned slowly to see the girl propped up on an elbow, looking at him with an amused twinkle in her eye.

"Were you going to leave without saying goodbye?" she asked and pouted dramatically.

"Oh...No, no." He pulled his shirt over his head. *Damnation, why do I always do this to myself?* "No, of course not...I..." He trailed off and engaged in an elaborate but fruitless exercise to smooth the wrinkles

172

from his shirt. "You looked so peaceful... I chose not to wake you... quite yet." *Idiot.* He groaned inwardly.

"You're an idiot." She smiled sleepily and snuggled down under the blankets.

With a pained smile, Panos slumped before trying to unsuccessfully to flatten his unruly hair with his fingers. "I'm an idiot," he agreed.

"Yes." She laughed. "But a gifted idiot. Now go... before Jasuf finds you here."

"Jasuf?" Panos frowned. *Oh, things just keep getting better and better,* he thought darkly. "Who's Jasuf?"

"Oh, you will remember Jasuf, the big man with a red beard... the innkeeper? Served you an ale or twenty?" she asked with a mischievous little smile.

"By *big*, you are referring to the man who resembles a bear, the one who carried in a full keg of ale by himself? *That* is Jasuf?"

"Yes." She smiled sweetly.

"Oh gods, I'm dead." He groaned and bolted for the door.

"Only if he catches you." She laughed, "Oh! Don't forget your sword!"

Panos swore, grabbed the sword, and then hurtled down the passage with the sound of her laughter following him. He negotiated the handful of stairs at the end of the hall at breakneck speed. With a dose of luck that bordered on the miraculous, he made it to the bottom without inflicting serious bodily harm. There he stopped to draw a deep breath and take stock of the situation.

His heart hammered, his legs wobbled and his head ached. Things were about as terrible as they could get. *No, fool,* he corrected himself. *You bedded a barmaid in the servants' quarters. Jasuf's not likely to get all bent out of shape over a bit of a tumble with a barmaid? But what if he does? The man's big enough to snap you in half like a twig. No point in taking the chance!* Panos concluded and sucked in a deep breath, steadying himself as his vision exploded into pinwheels and bright lights. He blinked and shook his head carefully, not wanting to dislodge anything in his skull, and then headed for the courtyard. He needed a horse—and quickly. That would mean stealing one, but he could always arrange for the animal to be returned at some point.

Given the early hour, the inn itself was quiet, so when Panos pushed open the door of the servants' quarters and stepped into the small courtyard, he was surprised to see two men standing in the doorway to the stables. He stopped abruptly and tried to make sense of this unexpected development. The one on the left was short and ugly; the one on the right was fat, with a thick bull-like neck. He did not recognise either of them from the night before, and both were armed.

"And what's going on here?" Panos asked the ugly one with exaggerated casualness, as if he had every right to be emerging from the servants' quarters at the crack of dawn.

"None of your business," the man snapped, laying a hand on the hilt of his sword. "Now turn around and bugger off before you cause serious trouble for yourself."

"Trouble? No... I don't think so." Panos snorted, suddenly irritated. "Not from the likes of you, in any case. Now step aside. I need a horse."

"From the likes of us?" The ugly one turned to his companion. "Who's he think he is, Abas?"

The one called Abas ignored the question and growled, "Are you hard of hearing or bloody dimwitted?" He drew his sword and pointed at the door behind Panos. "Turn around before you get hurt."

Panos sighed and held up a hand. Maybe a different tack would yield better results. "Put the sword away. There's no need for this. I just want a horse and I'll be gone."

"You'll be dead." The fat one now pointed the blade at Panos' face. "Last chance. Fuck off."

Panos felt his irritation rise. "Right. So that's the way of it, then. To answer your previous question, I'm going to have to go with dimwitted because I can hear the shit that's coming out of your fat face quite clearly." He drew his sword and casually tossed the scabbard aside. The silvery blade hissed through the cool morning air as he whipped the sword back and forth to loosen up his shoulder.

"Now... coming back to that horse that I need. Which one of you stupid bastards do I need to gut first?" he asked with a scowl trying to ignore the dull throb that had started behind his eyes.

Jasmijn woke to the musty smell of horses and damp straw. She lay on the floor of the stable with her arms firmly tied behind her back. A cloth had been wadded into her mouth, and her jaw ached from the blow. She swallowed down the dark anger welling up inside her and carefully looked around.

A man was busy saddling a horse while the one who had hit her stood near the stable doors, talking with someone outside; she could not quite make out the conversation, but she heard *Verana* and *duke*. Dacian lay close to her. He was unconscious, and there was an ugly gash on the side of his forehead that ran up into his hairline. The congealed blood had transformed his face into a gory mask.

She tested the ropes that held her hands. The cords cut painfully into her flesh, but she bit down on the cloth in her mouth and struggled against the restraints. There was absolutely no give. The man who was busy with the saddle straightened from his task and started to turn towards her. She quickly lay back down and closed her eyes.

"Kratos. Come help me with this one," she heard the man say.

"Coming," came the reply, and she heard footsteps approach. "You take his feet," the first one said. She heard him grunt with the effort.

"Gods, Sciras, put your back into it."

"I'm fuckin' trying, Kratos," came the strained reply. "He weighs as much as an ox."

She stole a quick glance. Sciras, who was much smaller than Dacian, had managed to lift him but his face was bright red with the effort. The other one, Kratos, who had Dacian's feet, seemed unfazed. He was tall and lean, and his hard angular face showed no sign of effort. Together, they carried him to the packhorse and draped him over the back of the animal.

"Tie him in place," Kratos grunted, then moved back to the door. "I'll help you with the girl when you're done."

Once again, she tried desperately to free her hands. The pain of the skin around her wrists being rasped away by the coarse rope was almost unbearable, but she forced herself to continue. She snarled in frustration. She had to get loose. The man had already thrown Dacian across the back of a packhorse and was busy with the ropes. Soon they would come for her. Then she heard a voice from outside the stables.

"What's going on here?" the unseen man asked. She recognised the voice as that of Dacian's companion, Panos. *Will he be able to help? He'll be up against these two men and whoever is stationed outside in the courtyard.*

"None of your business," she heard another voice say, thick with menace. The voice was muffled, but she caught the last of the warning. "…serious trouble for yourself."

She heard Panos laugh, then lost most of his reply as he dropped his voice. "…don't think so… aside… need a horse."

"Are you hard of hearing or dimwitted?" A new voice growled. The two men inside the stable had now also drawn their swords but kept out of sight.

Panos' reply was once again soft and measured, much of it inaudible but Jasmijn made out "… no need for this."

The voices grew angry until she heard something clatter on the stones of the courtyard, followed by the sharp whip of a blade through the air.

"Now… coming back to that horse that I need. Which one of you stupid bastards do I need to gut first?" Panos said quite clearly.

Jasmijn watched as the two men inside the stable spoke quietly to each other, and then the one named Sciras moved to make sure he'd secured Dacian to the pack-horse. She struggled against the ropes, but there was no give. She could feel the blood trickle from her chafed wrists. She ground her teeth against the cloth in her mouth and fixed an ice-cold glare on her captors. *They will pay for this. They will pay!*

Kratos looked through a small knothole in the stable door. He watched as the man dropped into a classic swordsman's stance. *This one is dangerous,* he thought. *He looks a bit worse for wear but sill moves like a cat. And that sword is an extension of his arm.*

He turned to Sciras and whispered urgently, "This one is serious trouble. Get the woman onto a horse and be ready to make a run for it."

"What about Abas and Cale?" Sciras replied softly, nodding towards the door.

"They are already dead. They just don't know it yet," Kratos hissed. "You take the woman and I'll take the farmer. Head straight to the warehouse. We'll pick up the rest of the boys and be on our way." *We may need them if we have to deal with this one,* he thought to himself.

Sciras had started to drag the girl towards the other packhorse, and Kratos turned his attention back to the swordsman. Abas and Cale had moved apart and were slowly advancing on him. The man wore a lazy smile on his face as he watched his adversaries; he was speaking softly to them as his blade, held low, snaked left and right almost hypnotically.

There's no time. Abas and Cale will not hold this one long, Kratos thought and turned to walk swiftly to his horse. He had just swung into the saddle when the first harsh clash of steel emanated from the courtyard. Sciras dropped the girl and ran to the packhorse with the farmer, grabbed the reins, and handed them to Kratos, who looped them around his saddle horn. He needed to get the farmer out of there; before long, the whole inn would be in the courtyard, looking to find the source of the commotion.

"Get done with the girl, and be quick about it. We'll meet at the warehouse," he said, He whipped his head around at a grunt of pain from the courtyard. *Shit...* "Sciras! The door!" He waited for Sciras to push open the stable door before he kicked his horse into a run and clattered into the courtyard. The horse's hooves skidded on the slick cobbles as he pulled the animal's head toward the street gate. The horse whinnied in panic as it almost fell, and it took all of Kratos' skill to get the animal under control.

He quickly scanned the courtyard. Cale lay face down in a pool of blood, and Abas had been backed into a corner. The fat bastard was bleeding from a number of small flesh wounds, and his eyes were wide with fear. The swordsman had obviously been toying with him. *Useless to the fucking end.* Kratos glared at the man.

The swordsman's head flicked to the side; for a second his eyes locked with those of Kratos, and then he glanced at the packhorse. His eyes widened as he recognised the man draped over its back.

"Dacian!" the man shouted, leaping forward and grabbing the reins of the pack animal, tearing them from Kratos' saddle horn. Kratos swung his sword savagely, but the blow whistled harmlessly over the man's head as his horse reared again, almost dumping him from its back. Kratos threw his weight forward, relaxed his grip on the reins, and leaned into the animal's neck.

As he fought to get the nervous animal under control, Kratos saw Abas take advantage of the confusion, lunging forward and stabbing at the man's chest. The swordsman twisted at the last possible moment, and the blade sliced across his ribs, opening what looked like a shallow wound. The man grunted in pain and swayed back.

For a brief second, Kratos considered dismounting and helping Abas, but he knew he was at best an adequate swordsman. He had spent years honing his skills with a longbow and dagger, to the detriment of the long blade. The man would tear through his defences as if they were gossamer. He needed to get to the packhorse with the farmer, though. *If I can get the farmer back to the warehouse... Wait—where is it?* The animal had walked away from the fighting men and back towards the stable. *Stupid bloody animal!* Kratos swore.

He pulled his horse around as Abas lunged again desperately, only to have his blade deftly deflected. He watched as the lightning-fast riposte plunged into the base of Abas's throat. The swordsman ripped the blade free and immediately turned towards Kratos.

Damn it to hell! Kratos watched as Abas took two tottering steps backward, then sagged to his knees, blood jetting from the wound in his neck. Kratos desperately turned his horse to the open gate and kicked it into a gallop. He charged through and out into the street beyond, thundering away from the inn, mud flying from the horse's hooves as they tore at the road.

"Fuck!" Kratos shouted in frustration as he sped towards the warehouse.

Panos, nodded with approval as both men drew their swords and moved apart from each other; there was no sense in getting in each other's way. If the only way to the horse he needed was through them, he was more than happy to oblige. Balanced lightly on the balls of his feet, knees slightly bent, he raised the point of his rapier and moved slowly backward to create space. They would strike together in the hope that he would not be able to fend off both attacks. They would be wrong.

"I take it you boys believe quite strongly in the afterlife?" he asked with a faint smile, watching each of them closely for any sign that would give away the moment of the attack.

"What you on about?" the ugly one growled, his brow furrowing at the question.

Panos shrugged, and took another slow half step backward. "I have come to learn that this city has almost all the major temples…" He drew lazy circles with the point of his blade. "All the gods clustered within these walls. Quite convenient, I would think, if one were to have an unfortunate, fatal encounter with three feet of Akhbari steel. But I'm sure you boys know that already. Otherwise, you would have already pissed your pants and run away."

The ugly one hesitated, and then snarled, "Shut it. We'll see how much of a tongue you have when I'm carving my name into your liver."

Panos snorted a laugh. "A repulsive little lizard like you can't write, let alone find my liver."

The ugly one flushed with anger, and with teeth bared he launched his attack, slashing savagely at Panos' face. Panos swayed easily away from the gleaming arc of steel. He parried the vicious thrusts and cuts with almost arrogant ease, the ring of steel sharp in the still morning air. Then the man overextended, and Panos sent a lightning-fast riposte through the man's shoulder.

The man grunted with pain as the blade punched neatly through the muscle and sinew. His sword clattered to the cobbles. Panos' blade snaked out and ripped through the man's throat in a crimson spray of blood. The man stood for a second, his eyes wide with terror, blood burbling past his lips. Panos watched as he grabbed at the gaping wound, but the blood spurted through his fingers as he tried hopelessly to stem the flow. Without a sound, he toppled sideways and smacked into the cobbles.

Panos turned to the fat one, who had hung back during the exchange. "And now it's your turn," he said simply.

Abas backed away, his eyes flicking to where Cale lay in a pool of blood. The swordsman had disposed of the man with consummate ease, and now the cold certainty that this man was going to kill him, too, started to claw at his guts. He swallowed. His mouth was bone dry, and the hilt of his sword felt slippery from the sweat on his palm. He held up his sword and noticed that the blade trembled slightly.

The attack came like a bolt of lightning. The power and speed were terrifying. Abas stumbled backward, frantically trying to fend off the blistering attack. What would have been the killing stroke came low and hard, aimed at the pit of his stomach. Abas shrieked as his heel caught on the edge of a cobblestone. The point of the sword ripped through the soft flesh of his side as he twisted and fell backward.

Abas hit the ground with bone-jarring force, and his sword spun from his grasp, clattering on the cold stone. He scrambled desperately to his feet and watched with horror as the swordsman walked casually over to the discarded weapon. Sweat stung Abas' eyes and the warm trickle of blood from the burning flesh wound soaked into the waistband of his leggings.

Abas' eyes widened as the swordsman hooked the toe of his boot under the hand-guard and flicked the blade up towards him. He caught it awkwardly, swallowed hard, and raised the blade. *Oh gods I don't want to die!* He thought about flinging the blade down and running, but the thought of being stabbed in the back was somehow even more horrifying.

"Now where were we?" the man asked quietly.

With a desperate cry, Abas launched an ungainly attack, slashing wildly at the swordsman, who danced away from the undisciplined swings with contemptuous ease. His blade had just cleaved the air where the man's neck had been a split second before when something stung his cheek. Abas grabbed at his face. He stared in disbelief as his hand came away bloodied. He had not even seen the stroke.

Then the swordsman launched a searing attack, brushing aside the Abas's defence like mist. Abas screamed as the razor-sharp blade nicked his ear... jabbed into his shoulder... sliced across his forearm. He reeled backward, frantically trying to fend off the bewildering attack; then he slammed into the unyielding stone of the inn wall. Two tottering steps to the right, and his shoulder hit another wall. He was cornered.

"Wait!" He held up his hand and pleaded breathlessly. "Wait! Please!"

He could feel blood snaking down from the cuts, and he tried desperately to blink the burning sweat from his eyes. The swordsman shook his head slightly and raised his sword. Abas lowered his hand and waited for death. He was just about to raise his sword when suddenly, Kratos burst from the stable, leading the packhorse. The swordsman swung around sharply to face the source of the commotion. Kratos struggled to get his horse under control, the animal slipping on the cobbles.

Abas saw the man's eyes widen in surprise as he recognised the unconscious figure draped over the second horse.

"Dacian!" the swordsman yelled, leaping forward and ripping the reins of the pack animal from Kratos' saddle horn. Kratos swore and swung his sword wildly at the man as his horse reared almost dumping him from its back.

Abas saw his chance; he lunged forward, stabbing at the man's chest. The swordsman somehow twisted away, and the blade sliced across his ribs. The man grunted in pain and swayed back. *Shit!* Abas lunged again, desperate to land the killing blow only to have his blade deftly deflected. The riposte, blindingly fast, slammed through the base of his throat.

There was no pain as the swordsman ripped the sword from his flesh. Abas took two steps backward and then sagged to his knees. He tried to breathe and gagged as hot liquid filled his lungs. He coughed, and a gush of warm blood filled his mouth. For a moment, he stared at the face of the man who had killed him, then sagged backward into darkness.

Panos swore as he tentatively explored the shallow gash across his ribs with his fingers. It was messy but little else; a few stitches would be all that was needed. He walked over to the dead man and cleaned his blade on the man's cloak. He gathered his scabbard and slid the rapier back into it. He had just turned toward the packhorse carrying the unconscious Dacian when the back door of the inn burst open. The burly innkeeper strode into the courtyard, holding a stout wooden club. His face was flushed with anger.

"You! I want a word with…" The innkeeper stumbled to a halt and blinked at the two bloodied corpses lying on his cobbles. He looked up at Panos and then back to the bodies. "What the…" he stammered incredulously. "Who?" He stood in shock, shaking his head.

Panos shrugged, and walked towards to the nervous pack animal, and started working on the ropes that held Dacian. He had no inclination to engage in lengthy explanations. The man would either figure it out or not.

"Hey, you!" the innkeeper yelled, waving his cudgel at Panos' back. "Wait up! What happened here? I'll call for the watch!"

Panos turned, his irritation apparent on his face. "Look here… these charming gentlemen just attempted to abduct one of your guests. I managed to stop them. Unfortunately, that required more than a polite request and a bit of reasoning. Now if you wish to call the watch, go ahead and do it. But right now, I am going to assist this man." He hesitated, then dug a silver coin from his pocket and lobbed it to the stunned innkeeper. "For the inconvenience. Now go away."

In the stable, Sciras pressed his back against the wall next to the doors and eased a long hunting knife from its sheath. He would wait for the damned meddling swordsman to enter the stables, and then he would slit his throat from ear to ear. Kratos had made it out but without the farmer. He checked on the girl. She still lay where he had dropped her. Sciras spat and turned his attention back to the courtyard.

"All right, then," he heard the innkeeper say. "I'll send for the watch. Then you can give them the details of this… trouble. But after that, I want you, and him, out of here. And don't come back! Neither of you!"

Sciras risked a quick glance around the edge of the stable door. The swordsman had managed to untie the farmer and had laid him down on the ground. He took hold of the reins and began to lead the packhorse toward the stable. Sciras tensed and raised the heavy blade. He held his breath as the footsteps drew closer.

Suddenly, there was a clatter of metal. He swung around to see the woman kicking at a metal bucket. He looked back to the swordsman. The man had stopped and drawn his rapier.

"Damn you to hell," Sciras swore at the woman, who lay glaring at him. With the element of surprise gone, he slammed the knife back into its sheath and drew his sword. He stepped from his hiding place and walked out to meet his adversary.

"You'll find me more difficult to kill than the other two," he said simply and immediately attacked. His blade hissed through the air, his opening thrusts and cuts aimed at the swordsman's face and chest. The man's defence was impeccable. His blade seemed to weave an impenetrable net of steel as he neatly deflected each stroke.

Sciras broke off the attack. He circled slowly to his right, then attacked again. This time, he used feints, mixing horizontal slices with thrusts to the man's face and legs. Every attack was almost effortlessly turned aside. He danced back and circled to the right, away from the man. Sweat trickled down the centre of his back. This was like trying to pierce a wall, for all the effect it was having. His opponent, looking ridiculously calm, mirrored Sciras' movement, gliding smoothly to the left. There were simply no discernible gaps in the man's defence.

"Tell me where your friend is heading," the man said suddenly.

"Why should I?" Sciras asked.

The swordsman smiled. "I will let you live."

Sciras' blade dropped almost imperceivably.

"You do not need to die here. Tell me and then ride away." The man's voice was soft and compelling, yet his eyes were like steel.

"Kratos will kill me." Sciras shook his head. "You'll have me caught between the Dark One and his demons."

The swordsman shrugged. "Consider what you face now. Given a few days, any man can disappear."

"We found the farmer easily enough." Sciras said simply. He looked into the cold grey eyes of the swordsman, then attacked.

The swordsman slipped away from the thrust like mist. Sciras staggered as something punched into his groin. He looked down and gasped. Blood jetted from a deep and jagged cut.

"Fool," he heard the man say as he grabbed frantically at the wound. Blood spurted between his fingers. There was no way to stem the flow. Sciras looked up and watched as the man circled away without a trace of emotion. He sagged to his knees; he felt cold and weak as his life drained swiftly away to the cobbles of the courtyard.

"Where is he?" the man asked again.

"See you in hell!" Sciras hissed through clenched teeth.

"You may just." The swordsman nodded, then turned and walked away. Sciras toppled forward. He tried in vain to slow his fall, but his arms just buckled, and his head cracked into the cold stone. As he lay there, the first rays of sunlight cleared the roof of the inn, filling the courtyard with a soft, golden light, its frail warmth on his face in stark contrast to the chill of the stone beneath him. He smiled weakly and closed his eyes; he was suddenly so very tired…

Panos pushed the stable door open with the point of his sword. His morning had already been far more eventful than planned, and he had no desire to get killed by being careless. If there was another idiot needing to find out if there was an afterlife, he was more than happy to send them on their journey. He paused, his sword held ready, and scanned the interior of the stable. A horse cast a disinterested glance in his direction.

He took a careful step forward and immediately saw the girl. She lay on her side, her head resting on the stable floor. Her face was smeared with dirt, and straw clung to the sweat-sodden tendrils of her hair. Sheathing his sword, he ran over to kneel beside her.

"Are you hurt?" Panos asked as he gently removed the gag. She moved her jaw slowly from side to side, obviously in some pain. "Are you hurt?" he asked again.

"Fine... I'm fine," she managed to croak, waving irritably at him. "Dacian?"

"In the courtyard. They tried to take him," Panos replied with a half-smile. "I convinced them to leave him alone." He cut the bonds from her wrists and ankles. Quickly, he began to massage her hands, avoiding the scored flesh around her wrists as far as possible. She hissed in pain as the blood began to flow back into her hands and fingers.

"He must be a very good friend of yours," Jasmijn managed to say through clenched teeth.

Panos shrugged as he continued to work on her wrists. "I've known him for less than a day."

He smiled as Jasmijn cocked an eyebrow. "Yet you put your life in danger for him?"

They could never understand. Panos helped her to her feet. "This was not all for him. In fact, the altercation started when the first two would not let me steal a horse, and I'm not in a tolerant mood this morning. There's nothing particularly heroic or selfless about that."

"No. Not to begin with. But you could have let the last one take us both and still got your horse," Jasmijn retorted. "So why were you leaving?"

"It seemed like a prudent course of action… and my reasons are my own," he said, dismissing the question. "Besides, you seem to have endured a fair bit for a man you hardly know."

"Yes. But I, at least, understand my reasons."

"And those reasons would be?"

"My own," she snapped, her eyes blazing.

Panos shrugged. *There was definitely something… different… lurking behind those pretty eyes.* He could not put his finger on it and was not sure that he would want to find out.

"If you must know," he said suddenly. "He and I are similar animals…"

"Go on," Jasmijn prompted, plucking straw from her hair.

"Wolves recognise wolves. He would have done the same for me."

He took her hand and examined the angry scrapes around her wrist. "This will be sensitive for a while." He paused. "It is clear you have an… interest… in Dacian. But those men obviously wanted him badly enough to kill anyone who stood in their way. They will not hesitate to use you against him."

"I know," Jasmijn said simply. "They killed his family, and he took revenge."

"Revenge against who?" Panos asked.

"The duke of Verana's son."

"Shit," Panos groaned. "That old man has a long arm."

"You know him?" Jasmijn asked, her brow furrowing.

"Indirectly. I have had… dealings with the man," Panos said guardedly.

"And I suppose you have no wish to revisit those *dealings*?" the woman probed.

"Let's just say I've seen men on the receiving end of the duke's judgement. If he want's Dacian, he will get him. It's just a matter of time."

A retort was on Jasmijn's lips when a shadow filled the door. Panos' hand dropped to the hilt of his sword and he stepped in front of Jasmijn. The figure shuffled forward into the light.

"Wait. It's Dacian." Jasmijn pushed past the swordsman and strode over to Dacian. She grasped his chin and began to turn his head from side to side, inspecting the damage. His hair was matted with blood and dirt; the gash on the left side of his face was swollen and deeply bruised.

"Well, you're a mess," she said, letting go of his chin.

"I think that blow to the head has *improved* your features." Panos muttered, and Dacian smiled lopsidedly.

"Well, thanks for the concern. I've never felt better." Dacian grimaced before looking down at Jasmijn. "And you? Are you hurt?" he asked her softly. "I am so sorry. This is my fault. How did you get involved in this?"

She shook her head. "A few scrapes. Nothing of note. These apes couldn't rough up a kitten in a sack. And how exactly is this your fault?"

Dacian shrugged, looking thoroughly unconvinced, then turned to Panos. "Your handiwork in the courtyard I take it?"

Panos smiled and nodded. "Well, it did seem a bit rude, you rushing off with your friends like that. Without even saying goodbye."

"Apologies, but they presented a rather compelling case." Dacian smiled ruefully. "Thankfully, your powers of persuasion are quite impressive. I owe you one."

"Bear that in mind when they come back with reinforcements. One of them got away. Perhaps the leader. Goes by the name Kratos. Now they know you're here, and I have no doubt they will be back. And they don't strike me as being easily deterred."

The swordsman walked off towards the stable doors. *Leave, you fool! Don't get entangled with Verana; he has reason to see you dead, too...* He looked back at the man he hardly knew and the serving girl who was more than she seemed. *Why can't you just leave? It's not your business. But you've just made it your business by leaving a pile of bodies in the courtyard, didn't you, you fool?*

He sighed as he realised that wherever this led, he was now part of it, whether he liked it or not. "We can continue this discussion here or over breakfast," he called over to the two, who were watching him intently.

"And with luck, we can be done before the Watch get here. They really do interfere with my digestion."

Dacian nodded, but Jasmijn had cocked that eyebrow of her's again.

By Eresophi's black tits, what have I done now? Panos groaned inwardly.

"How can you even consider eating after... *that*?" She flapped a hand randomly in the direction of the courtyard.

Panos squinted at the woman. "How hard did they hit you?"

Jasmijn's mouth dropped open, and then her face flushed in anger. But before she could reply, Dacian grabbed her arm.

"I think he's hungry," Dacian said quickly, coming to the swordsman's rescue.

Her eyes blazed for a second and then she took a deep breath. She pulled her arm from Dacian's grip and walked toward the door ignoring the swordsman as she passed him.

"Men..." he heard her hiss as she shook her head in exasperation. "Complete and insufferable idiots."

*"There can be no harvest
until the rocks are tilled from
your soul."*
—The First Book

The Fourth Circle

*"Revel in your chains, for they are
of your own making.*

*"Rage against the death of days,
for the darkness that comes
comes from within you.*

*"Weep, lament, and curse the light
for you are mine."*

—The Tenets of M'lakh

Sarsini
The Thirty-Third Day of 389, Evening

Vasilios the Chosen pulled up the hood of his cloak before slipping the brass key into the lock of the heavy wooden door. The key turned easily, and he pulled the door open and stepped into a dimly lit alleyway. The slow drip, drop of water and the soft skittering of rats were the only sounds that reached his ears. To his left, the alley turned away into darkness; to his right, some twenty paces away, he could see the soft light of the street-lamps on the Avenue of Swallows.

The broad walkway ran all the way up from the harbour, past the temple grounds, and almost to the upper wall of the city, where it ended at the entrance to the palace. It was early evening, and the usually busy walkway was now quiet because of bad weather rolling in from the sea. It suited him well.

He locked the door, slipped the key into a pocket inside his cloak, and walked swiftly toward the avenue. Two guards in plain clothes stood on either side of the entrance to the alley. He ignored them; they were well compensated and knew better than to pay attention to anyone who left the temple precinct via this route.

Adjusting his hood, he made sure that his face was deep in shadow and started down toward the harbour. *Damnation, this wind has teeth,* he thought to himself. It was a night to be stretched out in front of the fireplace with a glass of wine, but there was much to be done. Idle lounging in his chambers would not accomplish anything. There would be time for that later.

Much to be done, indeed... He quickened his pace at the thought of the morning's meeting with the leader of his order, Adrastus Primatus. *Primatus...* he rolled the title around in his mind. *Primatus... the Prime. It had a much better ring to it than "the Chosen."* He slowed his stride to step around one of the larger puddles on the slick cobbles. Then again, he conceded, it wasn't that long ago that he had been named as one of the Chosen—the youngest in the history of the order, having just entered his fortieth year.

Old Dardinas' wrong step on a flight of stairs had paved the way for his accession. That ancient sack of dried skin and bone would just not die. So Vasilios had helped; brittle bones and marble stairs had proved to be a poor pairing for the old priest.

Vasilios smiled remembering Dardinas' husky prattling as he had walked him to evening prayer. He had fetched the old man under the pretence of getting guidance about a philosophical question regarding faith. Dardinas had clutched his arm with a gnarled claw of a hand as he shuffled slowly along. Vasilios could still see the hand, painfully thin, covered with liver spots and twisting purple veins. It disgusted him.

"Knowledge and faith cannot exist together," the old man had wheezed. "We spend our lives gathering one at the expense of the other..."

Vasilios had nodded, pretending to listen. *What a fool... What is faith but wishful thinking until a blade gets jammed between your ribs?* He preferred to be the one holding the knife rather than putting blind trust in some god that, at best, didn't even know you existed and, at worst, found your primitive grunts annoying.

"I have visited the great libraries, buildings filled with books and scrolls gathered from all the corners of the world over years and years," the old priest had rasped, squeezing Vasilios' arm. "And yet here we are, no closer to understanding the true nature of the God we serve... and we have no knowledge of when we will meet him. But..." He raised a bony finger and smiled. "Through dutiful prayer and meditation, we can build faith that one day, we will."

"Indeed." Vasilios had nodded, stopping at the top of the wide staircase that led down to the small chapel that Dardinas preferred for his evening devotions. "And oddly enough, that day is upon us." He paused as the old man blinked up at him with confused, rheumy eyes. "Well, for you at least..."

It had taken the slightest of nudges, and the old priest had clattered down the stairs in a flurry of limbs. Vasilios had followed at a more sedate pace to find that somehow, beyond belief, the fall hadn't killed the old man. He lay in a broken heap at the foot of the stairs, making the strangest mewling sound. But a quick twist of that stringy neck had sent him on his final journey.

Weeks later, the Council of the Chosen had voted for him to assume Dardinas' vacant seat almost unanimously. *Almost,* the priest thought with a flash of irritation. Of course, the proper and pious Adrastus had questioned the motivation behind his meteoric rise, pointing out that maybe a few years at his current station would do well to temper his *ambition.* The other voice of opposition had come from Edrard, one of the older Chosen. Vasilios had not missed the thinly veiled insinuation that not every step had been legitimate. The pompous pig stopped barely short of accusing him of murdering Dardinas. He would need to deal with that sack of dung at some point.

He turned from the broad avenue onto Quay Road, a narrow walkway that wound down towards the docks. Here, the windows were mostly shuttered, and the cobbles were not as polished. He slowed his pace as he neared the store of a copper smith. The man he was looking for would be waiting nearby. *Now where would he be?* He looked around and started as a tall man in a black hooded cloak stepped from the shadows of a doorway.

"Priest," the man said simply, his voice almost a whisper.

"She's close?" Vasilios asked. "And unharmed?"

"Yes." The man nodded, his face hidden in the shadows of the hood. "As you required. Now, my payment." He extended a hand.

Vasilios noticed how white the skin was as he handed over the small, leather bag of coins. *Like the belly of fish,* he thought with a strange trickle of fear. The man tucked the bag into a pocket under his cloak. "She's in the next alleyway. Look behind the wooden boxes." With that, he turned to walk away.

"You're not going to check your payment?" Vasilios asked.

The man turned back and the hood shifted slightly, revealing a predatory smile that sent a chill down his spine. "No," the man replied before turning and melting into the shadows.

Vasilios took a deep breath to try to dispel the crawling feeling of unease. Now he needed to get the girl; that was all that was important. He moved towards the entrance to the alleyway indicated by the man and walked carefully into the shadows.

Wooden boxes lay stacked up against the damp brick wall to his left. He bent down, trying to see into the darkness. As his eyes adjusted, he saw that they were stacked to create a space behind them. An oily brown tarpaulin that at first glance looked haphazardly discarded over the top of the boxes formed a simple roof. He looked closer and heard a soft intake of breath. He carefully moved a box aside and saw a small face surrounded by a tangle of dirty blonde hair. Large, terrified eyes looked up at him.

"Hello," he said softly as he knelt and pulled back his hood. He smiled warmly at the girl and held out his hand. "I'm here to help you."

Lidi chewed happily on the sweet given to her by the tall priest. The taste was so intense her eyes watered. It was the most delicious thing she had eaten in so long. She held his hand and chattered brightly as they walked. He didn't seem to mind; he would smile at her and nod as she laughed at some of the sillier things.

She was so excited at the prospect of not having to sleep on the streets tonight. Sometimes it was difficult to find a place that was dry and warm. She had built the little box house, but it was only a matter of time before the other children found it. They were mostly bigger than her and did not readily share. Or else they wanted... *things*... from her in return for offering shelter. She did not like that, but sometimes the nights were just too cold.

She had been alone for the past six months since her parents had been killed. She still missed them, but the memories were now nebulous and dreamlike. She could vaguely recollect the smell of baking bread in a kitchen that now seemed so unbelievably warm and bright. *No real place could be that beautiful,* she thought with a wane smile. The memories of her father were of a big man with a scratchy beard and enormously strong arms. She remembered how he would grab her in a giant bear hug and spin her around when he came home from the docks. Her mother had been very pretty and smelled like flowers. She used to plait her hair, and Lidi would fall asleep on her lap and somehow miraculously wake up in bed, all tucked up and warm.

In stark contrast to the memories of her parents, the memory of the man that killed them was a raw and lurid wound. She had woken to the sound of breaking pottery and a scream. There were noises of splintering wood and another loud crash, and when she heard her father cry out in pain, she scrambled from her bed. She tried to hide, but her room was so small, and all she could do was press herself into a corner.

She had not waited long when her door was pushed slowly open. He had stood there for what seemed like an eternity, dressed in black, the hood hiding his face. She had cowered in the corner, hoping against hope that he would just turn around and leave her alone. *But he had not...*

She had shut her eyes as tightly as she could, but she could not block out the sounds of his boots approaching and the soft creak of leather as he bent down. He grabbed her face and pulled her close. His hand were still wet and sticky with the blood of her parents. She opened her eyes then, and to this day, she wished she never had. The worst memory of all was of those cold black eyes.

He had just stared at her like a snake would at a rabbit while she trembled, too terrified to even scream. He had then leaned in close until his lips were almost touching her ear and she could feel the soft fan of his breath.

"Run, little dove," he had whispered. "Run..."

And she did. She bolted from the house into the night and ran until her feet bled. That first night had felt like an eternity. She had spent it hiding in a storm drain, half-frozen and terrified. What little sleep she had was fitful and broken by horrible nightmares. It had been very difficult for her in the beginning... before she learned to steal.

The nightmares were less frequent now, but every so often she would still be jerked from sleep by those whispered words—*"Run, little dove"*

—and a ghost of a breath on her cheek. She shuddered and thrust the dark thoughts aside. Her luck was changing. The nice priest had offered her warm food and a place to sleep out of the rain. She was so tired and so hungry.

Vasilios held the child's hand as they walked and endured her incessant prattle. He smiled warmly at her and answered her seemingly endless questions as pleasantly as he could. This moment had taken time and considerable coin. He had needed to be careful, ensuring that the parents were quietly taken care of to force the child onto the streets. The watch was always troublesome with the disappearances of children. They never abandoned the search when endlessly goaded by distraught parents. But this would not be the case with a waif who no one, apart from himself, even knew existed.

Further coin had ensured that he always knew of her whereabouts. These eyes were also to make certain that she was kept alive while enduring a life on the streets that was sufficiently hard to guarantee her compliance when the time was right. It was a costly and wearisome exercise that he would be most annoyed to see unravel at this point.

Luckily, their destination was not far, only a block or two from where he found her. He quickened his pace and almost immediately slowed as he realised he had was dragging the girl along behind him. *We're close; no need to hurry,* he thought and took a deep breath. They turned a corner, and he felt the tug at his hand as she stopped suddenly. Her eyes were wide with fear as she looked up and past him to the black stone of the abandoned church.

"I'm not going in there," she said softly. "There are bad things there."

"Hush, child." Vasilios knelt down next to her. "There's nothing there to be frightened of. I've made sure of that." He stroked her cheek.

"You promise?" she asked as her eyes started to tear.

"I promise." The priest smiled as he stood and led her to the door.

Vasilios checked the street and, finding it empty, unlocked the door and led the girl inside. He closed and locked the door behind them before finding a lantern and a small tinderbox on a dusty window shelf. He lit a thin taper and held it to the wick. A flickering orange light spilled from the lantern, sending dark shadows dancing across the empty church. Moss grew on the cracked, damp plaster of the walls and a thick layer of dust covered the floor.

He held up the lantern and looked at the girl. She stood with her back pressed against the door, with her eyes wide with terror. He held out his hand. She hesitated, then moved forward and placed her hand in his. He turned and walked to a small door. He pushed it open to reveal spiral stairs that dropped down into blackness.

"Nooo," she pleaded, pulling at his tightening grip.

Vasilios the Chosen ignored her and dragged her into the darkness. Her struggles hardly slowed him; her sobs echoed off the damp, stone walls. Gone was the façade; it was no longer needed now that they were descending far below, where her cries could not be heard. His hand strayed to the dagger tucked deep beneath his dark robes, and his thoughts turned to what lay ahead; the promised payment of blood for the life of the Primatus. He had asked for much, but this was only the beginning. There was so much more that he desired. *There was always more...*

The essence of Moloc the Ascendant drifted close to the ceiling of the chamber. Below him, the dark, wet stone of the altar glistened in the red-orange glow of the torches. The last of the sibilant whispers had finally subsided, to be replaced by echoes of water that reverberated softly as drops fell from the cold rock above him.

Moloc watched the priest as he stood in front of the altar with a long, curved dagger clasped in his bloody fist. He had stripped to the waist, and dark speckles of blood covered his pale face and chest. Moloc drifted closer. The priest's breathing was shallow and ragged, and he tentatively touched his mouth where he had inadvertently bitten his lip.

Behind the priest, the stones glowed brightly. He had used them to open a gateway, allowing him to consign the innocent's soul to the pit. The payment had been made, setting the wheel to turn... but it was but one wheel, a wheel with wheels within wheels. Nonetheless, the deed had been done, and it had been difficult for this one. *Even a killer has his limits,* the Ascendant thought with amusement as he floated above the man.

The priest ran a hand that still trembled through his close-cropped dark hair and looked once again at the small body that lay in a pathetic heap on the altar's cold stone. The pale-green eyes, still wide with shock, stared blankly at the dancing shadows. The dirty tangle of golden curls was glued together in places with congealing blood. On one of her pale cheeks, almost indistinguishable from the blood, was a smear of chocolate.

Moloc traced his fingers across the man's shoulders, smiling as the man shivered at the almost imperceptible touch. The man's hammering heart and shuddering breath spoke of the deep conflict of unbridled greed and self-loathing that raged through him.

With a final deep breath, the priest steeled himself to walk back to the altar. He quickly bundled the small body into a burlap sack and tied it closed. He lifted the bag with ease; the frail remains and two lead balls seemingly offered no significant test of his strength. Moloc followed as he walked to a low door set in the wall behind the altar, opened it, and crossed a the dimly lit passage to another door.

Here the priest struggled with the heavily rusted bolt. It groaned and squealed in protest as he worked to slide it back. When the bolt finally surrendered, he pulled the door open, only to be enveloped in a cloying stench. He hesitated and then, with a heave, threw the bag into the darkness beyond.

Moloc watched the sack splash into the slow-moving waters of the sewer to be dragged down immediately by the weight of the lead shot. Rats scattered as the door boomed closed, but then, as the silence settled, they once again ventured forth and chittered and scampered, oblivious to the few bubbles that drifted slowly to the oily surface.

Vasilios returned to the chamber and quickly washed his hands and face in a small bucket. He gasped as the cold water trickled down his chest and back. He dried himself and dressed before sluicing the blood from the altar with the remaining water. He then quickly picked up the glowing stones and returned them to their pouch. With a final look at the glistening altar, he turned and quickly made his way to the surface.

There was little need to hurry—the servants wouldn't return until just before dawn—but still, he felt a keen need to get back to the safety and warmth of the temple grounds. He locked the door, paused, and looked up at one of the buildings. He scanned the dark recesses and ledges. It had seemed, just for an instant, that he was being watched. *No matter...* He shrugged off the feeling and set off at a brisk pace, headed back to the temple.

A lithe figure crouched on an a small ledge far above the narrow, deserted street. Echo sat on her haunches, wreathed in shadow, her long legs folded up next to her. She was oblivious to the dizzying drop mere inches away. Far below, she watched the entrance to a deserted church, where a hooded man had stepped through the door and into the dimly lit street.

I see you, Priest... and I know what you've done, she thought as the priest looked furtively around before turning to lock the door. Her lip curled in disgust. He had set things in motion that would see the world burn. For the sake of his *ambition.* For the merest second, she imagined tearing him limb from limb. But then she remembered who was pulling his strings. She almost spat.

The priest had stopped and was looking upward. *Yes, I see you...* She glared down at the man, once again fighting the urge to intervene directly and decisively. But that would precipitate a war that would polarise the Ascendants. They could nudge, suggest, lure... *bait.* But no more. That was the rule by which they all played their games. They influenced the intricate circles within circles, the ebb and flow of life and death. Of course, they all bent the rules, and each had a collection of pawns that could be set against each other. But only a few had those they loved.

She watched the priest as he hurried away, pausing now and again to cast a glance at the rooftops. She reached out and felt the tendrils of unease and fear that had started to thread through him like a cancer. Her anger still glowed hot, and the impulse was strong to simply close her fist around the thrumming warmth of his life energy and obliterate it. *Feel it...* The Ascendant pulsed. *Feel the filth and the fear. See the things that hide in the dark...* Echo bared her teeth and released him. The priest staggered and clutched at his chest. She watched as he steadied himself with a hand against a wall before disappearing around a corner.

The Ascendant turned her attention back to the church. She felt the presence there, deep underground, a powerful essence like a roiling shadow wrapped in chaos. She floated down and slipped through the rough slate of the roof, downward through the dusty stone of the floor, then through the cold earth until she reached the chamber. There, hidden in the deep shadow, she stopped and looked below.

Moloc stood next to an altar. The flames from the sparely lit sconces sent shadows writhing across the walls and floor in the chamber, but she could see quite clearly. Blood smeared his mouth and dribbled from his bearded chin, and a pale, hairless creature sat on its haunches at his feet. It narrowed its large black eyes in pleasure as Moloc idly ran his long nails over its pallid scalp.

Sowing his seeds of chaos, she thought. The priest had no idea how he was being manipulated. She doubted that, even with his towering arrogance and ambition, he would have as much as touched the stones had he seen the consequences. Consequences that could very well cost him more than his life. Echo wondered idly how the man would have reacted if he had stayed to see the thing at Moloc's side claw its way into this world, the unfathomable fear he would have felt watching the gateway stretch and split like skin as the creature's face pressed upward. The terror as it spilled, much like a birth, onto the stone at his feet, all claws and teeth and insatiable hunger.

Her thoughts broke off as Moloc waved a hand over the altar, the oily surface bursting into flame. New shadows skittered over the vast dark walls.

"Arise," Moloc said. The rock distorted and stretched, and the creature at Moloc's feet mewled in terror as a towering horror rose from the flame. The beast turned to face Moloc, ropes of saliva dripping from its jaws.

"Will you do what the priest asked?" Moloc asked the beast.

"Yes. But not I," it rumbled. "She will send one of shadow. Such are better for the task at hand."

"I don't care who she sends." Moloc smiled coldly. "It must be done. The Primatus must die."

"Yes, and none will know of the manner of his passing. Such is the way of the shadows." The beast nodded. "But what of this, M'lakh?" It used his older name as it pressed a claw into the pliant rock beneath its feet. "This gateway"—the demon paused as its claw popped through the membrane quite easily—"is open."

Moloc pursed his lips and looked at the beast. "Yes. It is my doing. But none of your kind is to use it... yet."

"It is not for you to command us, M'lakh," the beast rumbled. "Do not over-reach, Ascendant. We answer only to *her*."

Moloc's hand shot out, fingers extended. He closed it slowly into a fist and watched as the demon's frame crumpled inward. The beast hissed in agony, and it struggled in vain against the immense power that threatened to crush it.

"I said *none* of your kind," Moloc said, his voice flat. "None, but these..." He gestured to the imp that cowered at his feet. "And the one of shadow that will do the priest's bidding."

"None of our kind," the beast agreed, bowing its great horned head.

Moloc released the demon, and it slumped to the altar. "Do you wish to feed?" the Ascendant asked softly.

"We do," the beast rumbled as it stood slowly.

"The flesh of the unwilling," Moloc said.

"As it is written in your tenets." The demon bowed, its yellow eyes never leaving those of the Ascendant.

"Then pay heed to my bidding and I will deliver on that promise a hundredfold."

The beast's eyes narrowed to baleful slits. It leaned forward, studying the Ascendant. "A bold promise. What do you ask of us in return?"

Moloc smiled and said nothing.

The beast remained silent for a long moment. "We think you overreach, M'lakh... but we will heed your instructions. For now."

The Ascendant grinned, baring his bloody teeth. "Prepare for a feast, the first of many. Now leave us." He dismissed the demon with a wave of his hand.

Echo drifted down. Moloc seemed unaware of her presence as he stood staring idly into the dying flames on the altar. He looked up when the creature at his feet hissed angrily and bared rows of wickedly sharp teeth. "E'kia. I was expecting you," he said simply.

She stepped out of the shadows. Her hair was still wet from the rain, and she tucked a strand of hair behind her ear.

"Why do you do that?" Moloc asked, pointing at her wet hair and clothes. "Why do you allow yourself the discomfort of flesh? Not to mention the danger that comes with it."

"So I can feel," she replied. "You should try it."

Moloc laughed. "I think not. A blade cannot kill what it cannot cut."

"I saw the priest," she said as she walked to the altar tracing her fingers over the pliant rock. "I know what he has done. Or rather what you have pushed him to do."

"And what is it to you?" Moloc cocked his head to one side. "Why is it of concern when these... *animals*... attempt to play their simple games?"

Echo turned to the dark Ascendant, and the creature at his side let out a low hiss. Its black eyes narrowed to hateful slits. She smiled coldly. "Careful, M'lakh... you are about to lose a pet."

Moloc dug his nails into the creature's scalp, and it whined in pain, dropping its eyes to the floor.

"I have no interest in *their* games," she continued. "But yours on the other hand... What are you looking for? Where do you think this will lead?"

Moloc let out a dry chuckle. "Ahh, always meddling. As if your games are more noble. And what of your *gifts,* E'kia, my love? Are they not part of the *game*? The jeweller and his wife, the swordsman, the smuggler... the *soldier*? I think my game and yours lead to the same place. We're just taking different paths."

Echo stepped in close. "Perhaps," she murmured. He was much taller than her, so she had to tilt her head back. She could smell the blood on his breath. She could see the madness coiling like black serpents behind his eyes. She reached up and gently stroked his cheek, then ran her fingers through his dark hair, a strand catching between her fingers. A sharp stab of sadness lanced through her as he flinched away from her touch.

196

"Not meddling. No," she whispered. "It's just things to take... and things to give away..."

Dockway Alley, The Lower City
The Thirty-Fourth Day of 389, Morning

Tibero hooked his thumbs into the thick belt that strained against his ample waistline. He tried with very little success to keep the annoyed expression from his face. His eyes felt gritty and sore, and he could not remember when he last had a decent night's sleep. Two days' stubble covered his considerable jowls, and his hair was an unruly ginger mop shot through with silver.

He sighed and scratched absently at his jawline. The sun had barely risen, and here they were dealing with yet another dead body in a cold, dank alley. It was irritating beyond belief. If it wasn't an alley, it was the harbour, and if not the harbour, then it would be some other dark, gods-forsaken cranny that a body could be stuffed into. He did not even want to think about what the sewers hid.

"Look at these bite marks," Nils was saying. "They are much too big for a dog."

Tibero took a cursory glance at the body, grunted, and pretended to be interested. *Nils... always so damned enthusiastic. Too big for a dog? What if it was a very big dog?* He tilted his shaggy head back and scratched under his chin, squinting at the sliver of sky visible between the buildings. It was obvious that this person was stabbed, robbed, and chewed on by some hungry stray. There was no need to investigate any further. It was all a colossal waste of time. *Every night someone finds some reason to stick a foot of cold steel into someone else... money, women, revenge...entertainment,* Tibero thought bleakly. There were simply dozens of reasons and even more methods. All he wanted to do was get back to the watchhouse, put his feet up on his desk, and get some sleep.

"He still has his purse," Nils continued. Tibero glanced down at the younger man who was now on his haunches, searching through the corpse's pockets. *Oh by Eresophi's knobbly tits, what's he doing now? The man is insufferable!* He turned away so Nils wouldn't see the flush of frustration on his face. *This cursed city and the stinking watch will be the death of me!* Tibero fumed. And he was damned sure it wouldn't be anything honourable or remotely glorious. He had long since given up on the heady dreams of youth, dreams of making any discernible difference. Ever since his wife had died some years back of a lung blight, everything had simply gone to piss and shit.

Tibero sighed again and picked absently at a patch of moss on the wall in front of him. The best he could hope for was probably a blade in the dark or possibly a stiff dose of poison from one of the many enemies he had accumulated over the years. In truth, he firmly believed that on some day, of no particular note, he would simply keel over and die in the cold mud of the Sarsinian streets. He looked back at Nils. And that bastard would probably be there to pick over his corpse and babble some nonsense about it being foul play. *Looks like poison, looks like a fucking robbery; looks like he was bitten by something... Oh, please, make it stop!*

"Sir... do you want to take a closer look? Surely this is not the work of a dog?"

"What the hell else could it be?" Tibero growled. "A bear, perhaps? How about an Akhbari lion? Not many of those wandering around the streets I'd wager. For the gods' sake, Nils, let it go."

He turned away and scratched irritably at his neck. He needed a shave, a bath, a bottle of red wine, and sleep. Most of all, he needed sleep, and until Nils gave up on his investigation, none of those things would likely to come to fruition.

"Sir!" A new voice called out.

Tibero groaned. He turned slowly and recognised one of the younger recruits. *What the hell is this boy's name? Melon... Mellis... He looks like a bloody melon with that great big head of his.* Tibero looked at the gangly youth with his ill-fitting uniform. "Who are you, and what do you want?" He snapped.

"It's Marol, sir. We've another incident, sir." The young watchman said. "Over at the Crow Inn, near the docks, sir. Apparently there's three dead."

Tibero sighed. "I know where the damn inn is, boy. Three dead? What else do you know?"

"Looks like it could be that Panos again. You know, the one that Varagus reported last night. Said he skewered Sirvan in a duel at the Priest." Marol paused, then continued, "Crow's innkeeper said one man sliced and diced the three of them quite nicely. Description matches the Panos fellow; the innkeeper says the man's waiting in the common room —apparently having breakfast, calm as a cucumber, with two others who seem to be involved."

"Cool," Tibero said, starting to correct the young watchman. "It's *cool* as a... gods, never mind." He shook his shaggy head before continuing, "Not terribly surprising about Sirvan... Stupid bastard was always going to get himself killed. Nasty piece of work, he was. It's just surprising it took so long for someone to poke a hole in him." Tibero paused to gather his thoughts. "Breakfast, you say? Sounds like a bloody fine plan. Nothing like a bit of egg and bacon after sticking a sword through some people."

Marol opened his mouth to say something and then closed it with a nervous smile. *Lad's learning,* Tibero thought as he scowled at the young man. *But otherwise, this day's got off to a superb start.* He tried with little success to shrug off the deep melancholy that had settled over him like a heavy blanket. He turned away from the young watchman and cursed through clenched teeth as he realised it was not simply going to go away. He'd have to deal with this himself. "By the Dark One's sagging balls, that man creates more work for us than the rest of this gods-forsaken city combined. Nils, finish up here. Melon! With me..."

"It's Marol, sir."

"Of course it is." Tibero turned away with an exasperated grunt.

He took a deep breath as he stomped from the claustrophobic confines of the alley. The streets were thankfully quiet, and the few people who were out stepped quickly from his path. He trudged towards the Crow Inn with the young recruit in tow.

Nils bit back a retort. *'Finish up here'... What the hell did he mean by that?* he thought irritably. He definitely didn't mean find out what really happened, or determine what actually killed this man, or ensure that this type of thing didn't happen again. No, Tibero meant get the meat wagon down here and have them lug this corpse away before if started to stink up the place. He turned back to the body and pushed the flash of anger aside. He needed to think clearly.

Tibero was getting too old for this job. He was too old to command the watch, too old to ruthlessly pursue justice, and just too damn worn out to give a damn. He cast a frustrated glare at the back of the lumbering captain before he could stop himself. *Bloody hell! Focus, Nils!* he chastised himself.

Now what am I looking at? What happened to you? The body was pressed up against the wall and lay on its back. Most of the face had been bitten away, the left eye was missing, and the throat had been torn out. Three fingers from the man's left hand looked to have been bitten off. But it was the wounds to the man's right shoulder that interested him the most.

He carefully lifted the ripped, blood-soaked material of the man's shirt. A ragged half moon of puncture wounds circled the shoulder. It simply didn't look like the bite of a dog. The shape was just... *wrong.*

He carefully lifted the shirt to expose the stomach and chest. There were two deep, almost perfectly round puncture wounds high on the left side. He paused, then slipped his hand under the body. He ran his hand over the cold flesh until his index finger slipped into a third matching hole in the man's back. Two deep gouges ran across the right side of the man's chest. The jagged flaps of pallid flesh hung open, exposing a layer of yellow fat, torn muscle and the pale bone of his ribs.

Next, Nils took the purse from the man's belt. He opened it and poured the contents into his hand: a few silver drac and a handful of coppers. Many had been robbed and killed for far less than what this man carried. He returned the coins to the pouch and examined each of the man's hands. The palms were soft, with no signs of callouses. *Not one for hard labour, not this one.* Judging from his clothes, the man was definitely not a beggar, but he was not particularly well off either. He probably worked in an office. *A clerk, perhaps,* Nils surmised.

"What more can you tell me?" Nils asked the dead man quietly as he stood up and took a small handkerchief from his pocket. His brow furrowed as he stared down at the ruined corpse while slowly wiping his hands. He then looked up and down the narrow alley. The dark walls of the buildings on either side were a patchwork of pockmarked, cracked plaster and old, weathered brick.

Near the ground, the walls were thick with dull-green moss and splattered with mud. Nils glanced upward. Water dripped slowly from the ledges far above his head, and only a thin strip of mostly blue sky could be seen between the rooftops. *What would a clerk be doing in this alley? Where were you going?* Even now the morning light only filtered dimly down to where he was standing. *In the dead of night, you would not have seen your hand in front of your face, my friend.* Nils pursed his lips as he turned the problem around in his mind.

He shook his head. It hardly made sense; this was not a man who would have been comfortable with this route. He must have been in a hurry and had little option but to risk this passage. *He would have been heading towards the market,* Nils thought, nodding slowly. This man was probably heading home and taking a shortcut. He could have walked past the docks, but this would have been quicker.

Nils nodded to himself as the picture started to make sense. He had entered the alley and had walked some twenty paces from the lane. At that point, he would have been well away from what little light there might have been from the street lanterns. Whatever had attacked him had waited until it was difficult, even impossible, to retreat. It had waited until he was at his most vulnerable.

Nils felt a creeping unease. It was obvious from the nature of the wounds that whatever had inflicted them was both fast and powerful. It was no dog. Nils found this disturbing but not half as disturbing as the cunning and stealth it had displayed in the timing of the attack.

A voice called out, breaking his train of thought. "Hey, mate. You call for the meat wagon?"

Nils looked up and saw a thin, bald man with a beak of a nose dressed in black standing at the entrance to the alley. "Yes. He's over here." He stepped back to allow them room as another man in black joined the first. They quickly picked up the body and started carrying it back to a small enclosed wagon.

"A moment," Nils called out. "This one's not to be buried. Tell Gethum I'll be bringing the apothecary to look at those wounds."

"Sure, mate," the thin man called over his shoulder. "We'll keep him on the slab for you."

Thorns and Roses

The Temple Precinct
The Thirty-Fourth Day of 389, Dawn

The morning sun had just spilled over the high walls of the cathedral's grounds. The soft golden light painted the long shadows of trees along the stone pathways and glistened in the puddles left by the rain of the night before. Brother Feris ambled down one of these paths, carrying his garden tools. He loved the early morning; the gardens were mostly deserted, meaning the need for him to pretend that he preferred the company of people over plants was blissfully absent.

His plan for the day was to tend to the roses in the eastern part of the garden. His slow, cyclical journey around the vast estate meant that it had been more than two weeks since he last visited the roses. He could only imagine the work the beds required, but it was work he loved. The old brother had already rolled up the sleeves of his grubby brown habit, exposing his thick, deeply tanned forearms. Countless pale, white scars crisscrossed the weathered skin.

Feris breathed in the cool morning air and smiled at the faint warmth of the sun on his face. He had finally found peace within the walls of the church. A peace he had never thought possible, given a life that had been filled with violence from his earliest memories. He had run away from home as a boy to find a brotherhood of blood serving in the legions. But it was not his blood that he had seen spilled more often than not. He had watched so many of his friends fall in battle, some of them dying in his arms. He could only look on as the light faded from their eyes, helpless to stop it and with no words of comfort to ease their passing.

So many of them were better men than he could ever hope to be. How the gods chose who lived and died was a mystery to him but one he had thankfully decided to try to unravel. Maybe in these twilight years, he would finally come to understand why he had been chosen to carry on.

Feris reached the rose garden and placed his tools in a tidy pile on the grass. He chose a small trowel and started to work on the dark, moist soil. He loved the feeling of the earth between his fingers, and he hummed softly to himself as he tugged at the small weeds around the base of the roses. Every now and then, a thorn would jab at his knuckles, but he would endure each scratch with a small smile.

"Without the thorns there would be no roses." He remembered the abbot's kind words in the early days. He wiped a small trickle of sweat from his deeply etched face, taking a moment to trace the thin scar that ran down from his forehead past his left eye, causing it to droop slightly. He had taken to the Brotherhood readily, though his fellow brothers had been doubtful of his motives at first. This changed as the years marched past. He had earned their respect but, apart from the abbot, had never forged any real friendships.

Feris always felt that it was because his beginning was so fundamentally different from theirs. His soul had been forged in fire and steeped in blood, and he had much to atone for. For him, absolution was a journey that, if he was lucky enough to attain it, would take the rest of his life.

He remembered his first day as if it were yesterday. He had woken in the barracks with the remnants of his legion, broken men shattered by the horrors of war. Each man plagued by the shades of those they had left behind. He remembered sitting on the edge of the bunk; his armour rested against the wall, a dusty, scarred heap of leather and iron. He had realised with sudden, cold clarity that he was looking at his soul. Without a word, he had walked out into the sun, through the gates, and past the guards. He had no idea where he was going; he just knew beyond a shade of doubt that he had to leave.

He found the abbey almost by accident. A street vendor had bumped into him, turning him around, and he had looked up at the wide-open gates that led to a beautiful garden. An old man stood in the entrance with his hands clasped, almost as if waiting for him alone. He had approached the priest, not knowing what to say.

"Greetings, my son," the old man had said pleasantly. "I am Father Silvanus, the abbot. How may we help?"

"I honestly don't know," he replied, feeling stupid. He was about to walk away when the priest laid a hand on his arm. Silvanus was as bald as an egg, a stick of a man with a broad smile and sparkling blue eyes that seemed to cut right through him.

"That is the first step, my son." The old man smiled. "The battle you are about to fight cannot be won with the weapons you have carried. And there is no armour that will protect you on your journey," he continued, his tone warm and filled with understanding. "You have rightfully left those things behind. Now you need to let go of this armour"—Silvanus pressed a bony finger into his chest just above his heart—"and follow me."

Feris had felt as if he had been suddenly stripped naked. A path away from the years of iron and blood finally lay before him. Tears welled in his eyes as he had stepped through the gates to follow the abbott into the cathedral grounds. He did not look back at the life he had just cast off like an old cloak.

He smiled at the memory, reached back for a small pair of pruning shears, and turned his attention to the rosebush, clipping at the wayward stalks. Not for the first time, he wondered at the stories these beautiful plants would tell if they could. It was only a few weeks ago that he had noticed one of the Chosen following a path through the trees close to the wall with a young woman at his side. Feris had seen her many times before—apparently, one of the daughters of a lesser duke. She visited the cathedral quite often, though he had thought on that day it had been very early for a visit.

Feris had watched as the Chosen, Vasilios, had ambled slowly, tracing his finger across the page of a copy of the One Book apparently instructing the young woman in the ways of the Broken One. The copy belonging to the high priest was far more ornate than Feris' own. Even from where he had knelt, he could see that the book was truly beautiful —soft, stitched leather trimmed with gold.

Feris smiled at how the lowly act of grubbing in the earth made one almost invisible to these people of power. He owned a battered, dog-eared copy, but as scuffed and old as it was, Feris had read it cover to cover too many times to recall.

He shook his head in amusement and tried to clear his mind and retune his attention to the rose. The words Vasilios' mouth had formed were not written on any page that Feris could remember. He had learned how to read lips in his life as a soldier. It was a handy skill in the chaos and noise of battle, but here, all it had done was expose the pretence and thin veneer of piety that covered vastly different lives than what the world around them was made to believe. *Power, greed... lust...*

Feris clipped at the plant. He did not know this man, or how he came to his high station, so who was he to judge? *"Let it go... It is not your journey."* The words of Silvanus echoed in his mind. Feris buried his fingers in the cool earth and bunched his hands into fists. The life of a man was nothing but dirt and the brief flitting of shadows. All he could hope for was to find some form of truth before falling into the deep night.

He recalled a conversation he's had with the old abbot.

"Just because the path was strewn with rocks and overgrown did not make the journey wrong," the abbot had said. "Your struggle is your own. Your vows are your own. Even if others chose to ignore theirs."

"But I am right in this, Father!" he had shouted indignantly, slamming his fist into the table.

"Mmm... right and wrong. If only things were that simple," Silvanus had said sadly. "It is true that they may have strayed, but that is their path. They may learn, or they may choose not to." He had looked into Feris' eyes. "Do not be too quick to judge. You have killed when they have not. You have destroyed; they have not. How right are you in these things, my son?"

Feris had opened his mouth to protest when Silvanus held up a hand. "Think only of your journey. The path you followed led you here, to this very moment. Without every misstep, every fall from grace, every swing of your sword, every life you took, you would not be who you are. Every ounce of despair, anger, fear, and hate brought you here. It is only because of the darkness within that you have become aware of the light. Always remember, my son, without the thorns, there can be no roses."

A thorn clawed at a knuckle as if to emphasise the old abbot's words. Feris flinched and held up his hand to look at the bright bead of blood. He frowned, but it quickly faded. He raised the wound to his lips and gently kissed it. He then leaned closer to the bright-red flower and gently drew in the sweet fragrance. Once again, peace settled over him, and he felt all the tension drain away.

He was about to move to the next plant when he heard someone approach. He stood to see a portly brother walking along the path, holding a small package. He sat back on his haunches and waved.

"Greetings, Brother!" Feris smiled. "How are you this morning?"

"Ahh... I am well, Feris." Antonio grinned. "And you? How are your children?" He pointed to the roses.

"Well, my friend. Though they seem quite inclined to give lessons this morning." He held up his bloodied hand with a wry smile.

Antonio laughed and handed him the package. "I brought this for your other rose. Bread and cheese from the kitchen. Some fruit as well. The berries are exceptional!"

"Thank you." Feris took the parcel and set it down next to his tools.

"Go, go... I'll return those to the shed." Antonio smiled pleasantly. "I know you enjoy seeing her."

Feris turned from the broad Avenue of Swallows onto the narrow confines of Quay Road and began to thread his way through the morning crowds. The small shops were busy making the best of the break in the weather, and the cobbled street bustled with merchants and patrons. He gently eased his way through the haggling throng, nodding greetings to those who recognised him. His rose hid in a small alleyway. He had found her by accident on one of his walks. *Well, not really found and not really by accident, either.* He smiled quietly to himself, though he was sure that at the time, she thought the chance meeting was a calamity of the highest order.

The girl had stolen an apple from one of the fruit vendors and was running away with her prize when she collided with the brother's legs and bounced off to land flat on the dirty cobbles. The apple had somehow, and quite comically, flown straight up into the air. Feris had caught it by instinct before reaching down to pull the small girl to her feet.

She had been terrified that he would drag her back to the fruit seller, a fate slightly worse than if he chose to keep the apple for himself. Her large green eyes flicked from Feris' to the apple and back again. She was a tiny, frail thing, half-starved and obviously frightened of everything.

Holding onto the girl's wrist, Feris had looked around for the fruit seller, half expecting to see the irate man pushing his way through the crowd to demand that the girl be thrown into the city dungeons for her crime. But thankfully, there was no pursuit and he knelt down next to the girl. She stared at him, trembling. He knew how frightening he must have looked to her; his scarred, stubbled face was hardly inviting. But he had smiled anyway and handed her the apple.

"Looks like you're in the clear, young lady," he said softly. "I am Brother Feris. I work in the gardens around the cathedral. What's your name?"

She had just looked at him, all eyes and tangled blonde hair.

"No matter." He had smiled. "I know you're hungry, but I want you to be careful. You promise? If you promise I'll bring you something to eat tomorrow."

She had nodded reluctantly, and he let go of her wrist. Following a brief hesitation, she darted away and disappeared into a nearby alleyway. Feris smiled at the memory. It had taken great patience and a veritable mountain of food for her to learn to trust him. But as with all delicate things, it was worth the time and care.

He pushed past a pair of men arguing loudly over the asking price of a bolt of silk. The two hardly noticed him as he gently made space for himself to enter the alley past the stall. A few steps in, he found the girl's hiding space and knelt down to peer under the stacked boxes.

"Lidi?" he called softly. "You there, girl? It's Feris. I brought you some food." He frowned when there was no reply. He stood up and called out a little louder. "Lidi! It's Feris. Where are you, girl?"

"She ain't here," came a gruff reply.

"Who's that? Show yourself!" Feris called out.

"I said she ain't here," a gangly youth repeated as he stepped out of the shadows. He was barefoot and wore a collection of torn canvas sacking tied with rope as clothes. His hair was dirty and matted, and his cheeks were hollow and pockmarked. His eyes were sunken and hard as flint.

"Where has she gone?" Feris asked, his voice lower and far less friendly. *If you've done something to her…* He let the dark thought trail away. "Speak, boy!"

The youth smirked and scratched at his armpit. "What's it worth to you, Priest?"

"I have no coin, if that's what you're hinting at," Feris growled as his anger started to burn.

"No matter. You have food." The youth pointed at the package.

"The food is not for you," Feris said flatly. "Now where is she?"

The youth's face twisted, and he pulled a knife from under the canvas sacking wrapped around his chest. "We'll see about that, old man." He spat and advanced on Feris, holding the blade in front of him.

The expression on Feris' face was thunderous as he waited for the thrust. When it came, it was slow and clumsy. The blow was aimed low, at Feris's stomach, and the monk stepped aside with ease and slammed his fist into the boy's jaw. The youth hit the ground in a heap. It took a long moment for him to push himself up, and when he did his eyes were still glazed. He shook his head before looking up at the brother.

"I'd stay down if I were you, boy," Feris growled. He felt a perverse surge of satisfaction as the youth struggled to his feet, his dirty face flushed with anger.

"I'll kill you for that, old man." The youth jumped forward, only to have his head snap backward as another sharp blow thudded painfully into his face. He sat down heavily, with blood dribbling from his broken nose. This time he took a bit longer to struggle to his feet and swayed on unsteady legs before raising the knife again.

Feris sighed. If nothing else, the boy had heart. If a different life they may have even fought together. The dazed youth staggered forward and slashed drunkenly at Feris, who caught the boy's wrist this time and twisted it sharply inward. The youth grunted in pain as his wrist locked, and the blade clattered to the ground. Feris' free hand gripped the boy's elbow, forcing the arm straight, and then drove him face-first to the ground.

"Enough, boy! Now I'm going to ask you for the last time," Feris said with an icy calm. "Where's the girl?" He applied pressure to the elbow for emphasis. The youth sucked in a sharp breath, gritting his teeth in pain.

"She went with another priest," he said quickly, in between sharp and shallow breaths. "Last night... he came for her."

"What?" Feris asked in surprise. "How do you know it was a priest? Did he wear a habit like mine?"

"No," the boy hissed through a clenched jaw. "Not like yours... Red. It was red and gold. He wore a black cloak..." He paused to suck in another breath, sweat cutting through the grime on his face. "But it hung open when he knelt down."

"Red and gold? Are you sure? What else did you see?" Feris twisted the boy's wrist.

"Yes! Yes! It was bloody red," he sobbed. "He was... tall. His face was smooth. And beads... he had black... beads... held them... in his hand." His face contorted with pain. "There was another... man... The priest paid him. He pointed out the place where the girl... hid."

"Who is this other man? Do you know him?" Feris asked.

"No. I don't know him." The boy said quickly. "But I've seen him... now and then... Bad things tend to happened... around him. Please..."

Who is this other man? Feris thought before releasing the pressure on the boy's wrist. "Where did he take her?" he asked.

"To the old church," the boy panted as the pain subsided. "It's close by... just further on, near the docks... I watched. He came out some time later... alone."

Feris let the boy's wrist go and stood up. "Leave," he said bluntly, dropping the parcel of food to the ground. The youth snatched it up and scrambled away into the shadows of the alley.

Feris' mind raced, and he felt a knot of fear in his stomach. This did not make sense... *Why would one of the Chosen come here and take the girl? Why would he take her to the abandoned church? This is wrong...* He turned and strode from the alley.

The crowds seemed to part for him as he walked, grim-faced, towards the docks. The church the boy spoke of was near the water. It had been closed and locked for years. *What would anyone want in that place? Why would one of the Chosen take someone there? Why not the temple?* The questions spilled over and over in his mind, and his fear grew.

He turned the corner and could see the dark stone of the spire jutting upward from between the buildings. As he approached he noticed the moss clinging to the mortar, the broken roof tiles, the slow decay. Feris climbed the stairs leading to the door and paused. *What will I find?* He reached for the iron door handle with a feeling of dark trepidation…and pulled.

Locked. He hit the door with his fist in frustration, oblivious to the skin he left behind on the weathered wood. He looked around and noticed a small, bony woman wrapped in a patched cloak, staring at him. She wore a leather cap and woollen gloves. She looked cold and hungry. Her dark eyes were sunken and dull with fatigue.

"I wouldn't go in there," she said suddenly. "Not at night, anyhow."

"Why, sister?" Feris asked, walking closer.

"I hear things." She looked past him to the dark stone of the building. "That's not a good place. Not anymore." She started to walk away.

"Wait. A priest took a young girl into this church. Possibly last night. Did you see anything?"

The woman turned and stared at him for a long moment. "That is not a good place," she said with a strange edge to her voice. "There are secrets that hide in the shadows." She paused, and when she looked up, her eyes were filled with a deep sadness. "You won't find the girl…I'm sorry."

Feris watched her thread her way through the people filling the narrow street. A sick, cold dread had settled in the pit of his stomach as he looked up at the decaying stone and mortar. *No… this will not stand,* he thought with iron resolve, then started walking with purpose back to the temple.

Knots between Threads

The Crow Inn, the Market District
The Thirty-Fourth Day of 389, Morning

The common room of the inn was empty except for their table. A remnant of the previous evening's fire still smouldered quietly in the central fireplace. Jasmijn watched in a strange mixture of horror and astonishment as Panos and Dacian methodically devoured platefuls of eggs and bacon. The innkeeper, Jasuf, had thankfully decided to make himself scarce, satisfied that the city watch was on the way and placated by another silver coin Panos had thrust into his hand with the promise of no further violence.

Then, after she had dressed their wounds, which were messy but not serious, they had launched into what could only be described as a single-minded attack on the food placed before them. Like starving wolves, they paused only to break off chunks of dark bread that they used to mop up egg yolk and grease.

"Gods above," she said finally. "If you don't stop soon, I'm convinced both of you will rupture something!"

Panos looked up briefly from his plate with a quizzical expression to grunt something incomprehensible around a mouthful of egg. Dacian continued to eat almost mechanically, needing the fuel but not showing any outward appreciation of the food. Jasmijn studied him, the bruising on his face, the blank stare at his plate. He had gone quiet since the courtyard. She shook her head. *There's something smouldering there,* she thought. *What will it take to ignite?*

"And what of the city watch?" she ventured again.

"What of them?" Panos shrugged, wiping his mouth on a napkin. "Those men tried to abduct you and Dacian, and I stopped them. Simple enough, I would think."

"There's nothing simple about it. The watch is on the way here, and with those men lying dead in the courtyard, there will be questions," she said slowly.

"All three tried to kill Panos first," Dacian replied, pushing food into his mouth. "He defended himself."

"Thank you. See… simple!" Panos pointed to Dacian. "And point of fact: They're not in the courtyard; the innkeeper moved them to the stable. It's bad for business having dead bodies strewn around the place." He winked at her. Jasmijn bit off a retort and glared darkly back at him.

"And what of d'Verana?" she countered. "What if he has informed the watch of the issue with his son? It is unlikely they'll take your word over that of a duke."

Panos sighed and carefully placed his knife and fork together on his plate. "In that case, let us hope he has not informed the watch." He produced his pipe and a small bag of tobacco as he sat back and stretched out his legs.

"Hope is not a plan!" Jasmijn smacked her hand hard into the tabletop, making the crockery jump. "Do we stay here and possibly await arrest on the mere hope that the watch is oblivious?"

"He has not informed the watch." Dacian looked up. His face was unreadable. "He wants me brought back alive, not arrested and rotting in some cell, waiting to be tried for murder. The fact that it was his men who tried to take me and not the watch confirms that fact." He pushed the food on in his plate around with his fork. "He wants revenge, not justice."

"That's sound reasoning, my friend." Panos nodded through a thick cloud of smoke as he lit his pipe. "And I must admit, I have a queasy feeling that I may have added myself to His Grace's list of people to kill horribly."

"I'm afraid you probably have." Dacian nodded ruefully. "Not exactly the finest repayment for saving my life."

"No matter." Panos puffed away at his pipe. "I was growing bored in any case. I've only been threatened with death a half dozen times in the last few weeks. Being hunted down to be tortured by a noble seems like a step up in the world. Far more exciting than simply being accosted by common thugs."

"You are an idiot," Jasmijn fumed. "You sit here joking about a man who will gladly gut the pair of you. What, if anything, do you plan to do about that?"

"Well, there's not much to do for the moment but wait for the watch." Panos smiled, pointing at her with the stem of his pipe. "I know most of them quite well."

Dacian nodded. "We wait for the watch, explain the events of this morning, and then I'm going to leave the city. No point in dragging the both of you further into this. With me gone, I doubt the duke will press the issue here."

"Then you'll be hunted by both Kratos *and* the watch." Jasmijn shook her head in exasperation.

Dacian shrugged. "Maybe not."

Jasmijn's hard stare bored into the man. He looked back at her, his face unreadable. *What are you planning?* she thought.

"Well, I, for one, am not inclined to wait with a parched mouth…" Panos smiled before she could respond. She shifted her attention to the swordsman, who sat grinning at her. Jasmijn smiled back coldly. *Oh, be careful where you go now, swordsman,* she thought darkly.

"And if I'm not mistaken, my dear," He continued, apparently oblivious to his plight, "you work here. So would you be so kind as to bring me an ale, if you please… and one for my friend."

Jasmijn clawed her nails into the tabletop and suppressed the urge to slam her fist into his face. She noticed that Dacian had the good graces to wince at the comment.

"More of that, and I don't think you'll need to worry about d'Verana killing you," Dacian said softly.

She snorted angrily and was about to stand up when two men walked into the common room. One was old and fat, with an unruly mop of ginger hair shot with grey; the other was young and nervous. Both wore the uniforms of the watch. They stopped just inside the entrance and looked around. The fat one's shaggy brows knitted together into a thunderous frown as his gaze settled on the reclining swordsman. He stomped over to the table with the gangly youth in tow. He hooked a finger into his belt as he glared at each of them.

"Dacian, Jasmijn, meet Tibero. Captain of the city watch." Panos smiled through a cloud of smoke. "And how are you fine gentlemen on this beautiful morning?"

"Indescribably wonderful," Tibero grunted and scratched absently at his stubbled jowls. "A little bird told me there's a small pile of dead people in the... where are they, Melon?" He glanced at the young man.

"In the courtyard, sir, and it's Ma—" the youngster replied.

Tibero held up a finger, halting the him mid-protest, before continuing with a tired voice, "Dead people. In the courtyard. Apparently, all three with your handiwork poked into them. That is a disturbing amount of bodies to rack up in the space of an evening, not to mention last night's business at the Priest, "

The swordsman pushed back his chair and continued to puff on his pipe. "Well, there are parts of that story that are not entirely true."

"Wonderful," Tibero grunted. "Which parts?"

"Well, for one, the three men you're referring to are not in the courtyard."

Jasmijn rapped her knuckles on the table and swore under her breath.

"Gods damn it, man," Tibero growled.

"And the incident at the Priest was a legal duel. There was quite a crowd that will attest to that," Panos continued before waving the stem of his pipe in the general direction of Dacian and Jasmijn. "And this morning was self-defence. I have two witnesses."

The captain of the watch ran his fingers through his messy mop of hair before laying both fists on the table top and leaning towards Panos. "Witnesses, maybe," he said evenly while glaring at the swordsman. "Accomplices more likely, seeing as both seem to be deeply involved."

Oh, this is too much, Jasmijn stood up from the table. "What do you need from us? The men in the stable tried to abduct us. Panos was good enough to stop them. And unfortunately, that involved a little more than friendly persuasion and a charming smile."

Panos grinned at her. She glared back at him; the annoying grin did not slip for an instant. *So infuriating!*

"And why did they want the two of you?" Tibero pushed . "Did you know them?"

Dacian opened his mouth to reply, but Jasmijn cut him off. "Yes," she said, nodding her head. Dacian blinked in surprise and let her continue. "One of them took a liking to me a few nights ago." She turned back to the captain. "He didn't take it well when I turned down his advances."

"All right. That explains you." Tibero frowned. "But what about him?" He pointed in Dacian's direction.

"He and I were together last night," Jasmijn lied, holding the watchman's gaze. Panos broke into a fit of coughing. She ignored him.

Tibero pursed his lips. "And this one"—he pointed at Panos—"just happened to come to your rescue?"

"Yes." Jasmijn smiled sweetly.

"He and I served together in the legions. We met last night, had a few ales, and…" Panos said holding the captain of the watch's gaze.

"Fine, fine." Tibero held up a hand, cutting him short. "This stinks to high heaven, and I'm sure there's far more to this affair than meets the eye. None of you are to leave the city until I have concluded my investigation. Make sure you stay put. If I have to find any of you I swear by the gods I'll have you in a cell." He turned to the young watchman. "Melon… get the meat wagon and have the bodies taken to the Dead House."

"It's Marol…" the young man started.

"Listen, Melon." The captain turned and raised a finger. "One more word. Just… one more word."

Tibero strode up the wide avenue towards the watchhouse with a thunderous expression painted across his face. He was oblivious to the people who seemed to part before him like reeds. All he wanted was for this business at the Crow to be taken care of so that he could get back to his office, shut the door, and let the world go to shit without involving him. Maybe he could get Nils to go over it with a fine-tooth comb. If anyone was going to get to the bottom of it, it would be him. As an added bonus, it would keep him occupied for a quite while and, more importantly, away from the watchhouse, where his bloody digging and scratching were a constant annoyance.

After his very large dog investigation, of course, Tibero thought sourly. *Who the hell knows how long that will take?*

The watchhouse was an imposing building of dark stone with high crenellated walls on the edge of the Market District. It commanded the top of a small hill at the end of the broad and lively Avenue of Trees, named for its stately oaks. The avenue was home to the established and wealthy merchants who sought to elevate themselves above the more visceral dealings of the market place. The added security due to the proximity to the watchhouse further enhanced the desirability of the location.

Tibero was, however, not convinced of its effectiveness as a deterrent. He had learned quickly during his years on the watch that given suitable motivation or reward, people were willing to commit almost any crime, regardless of the risk. He stomped up the stairs and pushed the door open. He ignored the chaos of the main room and walked straight to the day sergeant.

"Good mornin' to you, sir." The man straightened up from the desk.

"No, Rake, it's not," Tibero said bluntly. "Nils back yet?"

"Don't think so, sir." Rake looked into the main office to make sure.

"Well, when he's back, send him to me," Tibero said. "There's something I want him to look into. Oh, Rake…"

"Sir?"

"Send two men down to the Crow." Tibero scratched at his neck. "I want them to watch the place. Quietly. Need them to make sure no one gets killed. The meat wagon's been a bit too busy for my liking." He turned away without waiting for an answer. He stomped down a dark passage to a large iron-shod door. He pushed it open and stepped into the sanctuary of his office. Dim light filtered through the dusty, barred window, illuminating the sparsely furnished interior, which was dominated by two large book cases filled haphazardly with hundreds of leather-bound books. He took a moment to allow the noise of the morning to bleed away and then walked around the ornately carved desk to slump into his chair, the wood and leather squeaking as it bore his weight.

He sat back and took a deep breath, enjoying the quiet and the dry smell of the books. He was bone tired. He thought about the bottle of emberwyne in his top drawer but quickly dismissed the idea. He interlaced his fingers over his chest and closed his eyes. Maybe, just maybe, he could get a few minutes of rest before Nils burst in and turned his day upside down with fantastic tales of lions and foul play. The man was good, *very* good, he had to admit. *He's just too gods-damned enthusiastic,* Tibero thought before sleep took him.

Nils walked into the noise and bustle of the watchhouse and hung his blade and cloak on an open copper hook near the door. He cast a glance around and saw the usual morning clamour of people reporting crimes and watchmen dragging drunkards and lawbreakers to the cells to sleep it off or await trial, respectively.

Tibero was, as expected, nowhere to be seen—no doubt taking the opportunity to sink a tankard or two after interrogating the swordsman. It was a waste of time. Yes, on the surface, the bodies seemed to pile up around this Panos, but the man didn't strike him as a criminal. He had walked past the Priest on the way back and chatted briefly with Varagus, the innkeeper.

The duel was legal, and unfortunately for Sirvan, so was stupidity. He was a cantankerous bastard who'd had his fair share of run-ins with the watch. He had apparently taken exception to losing at cards and, as per usual, picked a fight. But if you pick fights with enough people, you're bound to chance upon one who's more adept at sending others into the afterlife than you are. And then you get loaded onto the meat wagon for your troubles.

After the visit to the Priest, Nils had taken his time walking back to the watchhouse. He had followed the path he thought the victim of the animal-attack might have taken, threading his way through the bustling marketplace. He had hoped for some further inspiration as to the identity of the victim and how he had met his fate. The wounds were not postmortem, nor had they been inflicted by a dog. Something had attacked the man, and he meant to find out what it was before it happened again. It was an investigation that he was determined to see through to the end, with or without Tibero's approval. And knowing Tibero, it would be the latter.

"Nils!" he heard the desk sergeant call.

"Morning, Rake. What you need?"

"The captain. Asked for you to go see him when you got back."

Nils sighed as he looked away. *What the hell does Tibero want now?* As he was pondering what to do, his gaze settled on a particular desk. Otho, a bloated pig of a watchman, whom Nils despised, sat opposite a young woman. She clutched her cloak around her slim shoulders and stared blankly at the scuffed wooden tabletop. She flinched as Otho barked at her in frustration and slammed a ham-size fist down onto the desk. He tossed aside the quill he was using to jot down the report and glared at the woman.

Otho at his empathetic best, Nils thought with disgust. "I'm not back yet," he called to the sergeant, who waved with a knowing smile, as he walked over to Otho's desk. "What's happening here?" he asked.

"Who the hell knows?" Otho growled. "She wandered in here just after sunup. Haven't managed to get a single word of sense from her. Shit about things in the bloody dark." He crumpled the sheet of paper into a tight ball and glared at Nils, almost daring him to say something.

"Let me talk to her," Nils suggested after a moment.

"Be my guest, and good luck finding out anything of use." Otho waved dismissively in the direction of the woman. He pushed his chair away from the desk and made to leave.

"Fine… but before you get down to idling away the rest of the day go and fetch the apothecary. You know the one. His name is Amon and he lives on Water's Edge Road near the dock."

"Why should I? Do it yourself."

"Because I need to ask his advice… because it's your job… and most importantly, if you don't, you'll need his advice on how to get my boot out of your fat useless arse!" Nils snarled.

Otho glared at Nils before turning away with a mumbled oath. He snatched his sword belt and cloak from a hook on the wall and stomped toward the door. Nils took a deep calming breath before he eased into the chair opposite the frightened woman. Her hair hung in wisps around her face. Her eyes, dark against the paleness of her skin, darted this way and that, flitting from the windows to the door, then back to his face… never settling on something for more than a heartbeat. Another tremor ran through her body. *She's not just frightened—she's terrified!* Nils thought. *And close to the point of collapse from fatigue and cold.*

"I'll be back in a moment," he said, touching her arm. She flinched but gave no other indication of whether she heard him or not. He gave her arm a gentle squeeze and then got up to retrieve a coarse woollen blanket from a chest, a small ceramic flask, and a rough pewter mug from a cupboard. He gently draped the blanket over her shoulders and then poured a generous amount of golden liquid into the mug, offering it to the woman.

"Drink this," he said softly. "It's emberwyne. Not the best, I'm afraid but it will help. Be careful—it's quite strong."

She took a tentative sip, wincing as the fiery Noordlandt liquor slid down her throat.

"Warned you," he said softly with a smile. "Let's start with your name." Nils asked.

"Emilia," she replied as she wiped her mouth with the back of her hand, her voice little more than a whisper.

"Thank you, Emilia." Nils smiled, the quill scratching at the paper as he recorded her name. "I am Nils. Where do you live?"

"Market Road. A little ways down from the Priest…" She paused, trembling.

"Thank you, Emilia." Nils smiled, his quill scratching at the paper. "You live on Market Road."

"No," she said softly. "Just off Market. I have a room on Dockway Alley. You know… between Market and Dock."

Nils looked up sharply from the page. "Did something happen to you last night?" he asked, trying to keep the urgency from his voice.

"Yes… no…I don't know what it was." She shook her head, pulling the blanket tightly around her neck.

"What happened Emilia?" Nils pressed gently. "Was anyone hurt?" He paused. *Or killed?* he thought as she looked up, her eyes wide. A shudder ran through her.

"You… won't believe me," she whispered.

"I want to help, Emilia," Nils said softly. "Please tell me."

A tear slid down her pale cheek. "I… work at night," she started quietly. "I was coming home when I heard… a scream." She paused and rubbed at her eyes as she started to cry. "A horrible scream. So much pain…"

"A woman?" Nils probed.

"No. It was a man." Emilia shook her head. "I just stood there, outside my door. I could hear…something moving… I just stood there listening. There were other sounds… horrible, horrible sounds."

Nils leaned forward, eyes intense. "Did you see what did this?"

"No." Emilia shook her head slowly. "But I heard it running toward me in the dark." She looked up at Nils, her eyes wide. "I barely got inside. It hit my door so hard! I could hear it clawing at the wood!" She said with an edge of hysteria, her voice rising.

Nils reached out and took her hands in his. "Shh… you're safe now. You've done a very brave thing coming here. Now I'm going to find out what happened, I promise."

She nodded, but her eyes still brimmed with tears.

"It was more than likely a large stray dog," he lied easily—no need to cause the poor girl more harm. "Strays can be quite dangerous when they get hungry."

"It didn't sound like a dog," she said, but took a shuddering breath, wanting to believe.

He shook his head slowly and gently squeezed her hands. "Look at me. Believe me. No harm will come to you. I'll make sure we send a few watchmen down to clear out all the strays." *You can't promise this you fool,* he thought as he forced himself to smile.

Emilia nodded, a faint smile on her lips.

Nils was about to jot down the particulars of her story when there was a loud crash. He looked up to see a large woman, obviously distraught, slam a meaty hand down on the front counter again, causing the duty sergeant to take a quick step backward.

"No! That is *not* acceptable," she barked pointing a finger at the wide-eyed watchman. "My *husband* is *missing,* and I need to know what *you* are going to do about it!"

"Emilia. I need to go and help that woman." Nils squeezed her hand. "Wait here. I will be back soon and then I will get someone to walk you home. That sound all right?"

The girl nodded and tried to smile.

Nils forced a smile, then stood and walked towards the upset woman. He had a sinking feeling he knew exactly where her missing husband was.

The Apothecary

Water's Edge, the Lower City
The Thirty-Fourth Day of 389, Morning

The shop's cold this morning, Amon thought irritably as he stacked wood in the small brazier. The long scar on his face always ached when it was cold. He rubbed absently at the puckered skin. His hip still protested from the walk home from the tavern the night before. But the occasional game of pahkur was one of the very few vices he had left, so he chose to ignore the pain.

The game had become quite intense, and he was certain it would have ended in some form of altercation between the swordsman who had sat to his right and the large, rough character across the table. Having spent more than a few hours observing them, he would wager one of them was on a slab in the Dead House this morning.

He pushed a handful of kindling between the logs and opened a small metal box. In contained a ceramic bottle and a number of slivers of wood tipped with a ruddy paste. The bottle held oil of vitriol, strong enough to melt the flesh from the bones if one was incautious. But, if nothing else, Amon was cautious.

He slowly removed the stopper and dipped one of the slivers into the clear liquid. It immediately started to smoke and then flared. He quickly dropped the burning stick into the bed of kindling. He pushed the stopper back into place and carefully replaced the bottle. Within a few minutes the fire was crackling and filling the small shop with its pleasant warmth.

He was just about to hang a small kettle over the fire when there was a knock at the door. He sighed. The tea would need to wait. He opened the door to see two men: one, a mountain of muscle, holding a bloody cloth to his face, the other a small, dark-skinned man whose broad grin displayed an astonishing array of crooked, yellow teeth.

"Greetings, Amon!" The small man slapped the apothecary on the arm. "I trust Yusi and I are not too early."

"No... but only by a hair's breadth, Ebrahim." Amon scowled at them. "Come in and I'll see what I can do."

They entered the shop, and Amon waved the large man to a wicker chair before disappearing into the back room. "Sit over there, Yusuf." His voice drifted out. "Did you at least win?"

"I always win." Yusuf's reply rumbled through the small shop.

"It doesn't always look that way," Amon replied as he returned holding a tray with a bottle of clear liquid, clean cloth, gauze, and a needle and gut. "This is why I always ask. Now let me see..." He removed the cloth. "Ahh... deep but clean. How are Yamila and the boys?"

Yusuf grinned, his broad angular face transforming from that of a brooding prizefighter to that of a proud husband and father. "They are very well, Amon. Usayd already hits like a mule; little Madhi runs like the wind... and given that his older brother wishes to practice on him, he needs to!"

"And Yamila still rules over your home with an iron fist." Amon allowed himself a ghost of a smile as he moistened a piece of white cloth with the clear liquid.

"Of course. We would not want it any other way," Yusuf agreed proudly.

"Good. It is always pleasing to hear that at least one parent has a bit of sense." The apothecary leaned in close. "Now hold still; this is going to burn like the fires of hell. Ebrahim... I was about to make a pot of spiced tea before you dragged this lout into my shop. Would you mind?"

Ebrahim nodded vigorously and set to work, arranging three small cups, then filling the kettle. "Tea, Amon?" He looked up with a yellow grin. "Where's the tea?"

"If you want the spiced tea, then the blue, square box; otherwise you will need to look," Amon replied, not turning away from his work on Yusuf's wound.

"Ahh!" Ebrahim's exclamation was followed by a flurry of busy sounds.

"And you say you *won*?" Amon asked as he pulled a stitch tight. Before Yusuf could growl his answer there was another knock on the door.

"Ebrahim." Amon sighed again. *A busy morning by the looks of it,* he thought, pushing the needle through the prize-fighter's skin. "Could you please see who that is?"

"Of course!" Came the little man's reply as Amon dabbed away a bead of blood. He heard the door open and caught parts of the muted conversation. *"Come to the Watchhouse now… body… the wounds are peculiar…"*

Amon frowned. It was likely Nils: very particular, very tenacious and probably rather annoying to whoever had to deal with the previous two attributes. Somebody must have died, and now he would want to know how and why. *Tibero's working on another ulcer,* the apothecary thought with a ghost of a smile.

"Let him in, Ebrahim!" Amon called out. "I'm almost finished stitching Yusi back together."

Amon glanced up at the large watchman who entered. *Otho… useless lout.* "Good morning to you Otho. How can I help?"

"Someone has died. Nils wants you at the watchhouse now," Otho grunted, not able to hide his annoyance.

"I'm just finishing up with Yusi. You've met Yusuf?" Amon looked back to the fighter and pierced the last flap of skin with the needle, then pulled the thread through.

"No," Otho said flatly. "Nils said now."

"I understand that, Otho," Amon replied calmly, not bothering to look up at the watchman. "But I am rather busy at this point in time. Now you can either wait a few minutes… or you can go back to the watch and inform Nils I will be there shortly. I won't require an escort, thank you."

Otho swore under his breath, flung open the front door, and stomped out into the road.

"Rather pleasant character, isn't he?" Amon murmured pulling the last stitch tight.

"For a troll," Ebrahim offered, and Yusuf grunted in agreement.

"There, it is done." Amon dabbed the neatly closed wound with the cloth, removing the last of the blood. "Ten days, then come back so that I can take out the stitches."

"Thank you, Amon," Yusuf rumbled as he stood up.

"And no fighting!" Amon pointed a finger up at the big man. "Ebrahim. If he fights and that gets ripped open, find someone else to patch him up!"

"No fighting." Ebrahim grinned, bobbing his head.

"Now where's that tea you were making? Or must I do that as well?"

The walk up the hill to the watchhouse was painful, but over the years, Amon had come to accept that. He chose to focus on the trees that lined the broad avenue and loved how the morning sun was diffused by the broad leaves. He was, however, breathing heavily and in dire need of a place to sit by the time he entered the building.

He looked around and saw Nils sitting in one of the corners of the main office. He had a large woman with him who was clearly distraught. Nils was holding her hand and speaking softly. The watchman then stood, gesturing to a young watchman, who listened intently as Nils gave him instructions. He pointed first to the woman he had been speaking with and then with a touch on the shoulder, drew the man's attention to a young woman who sat quietly at another desk. With a final soft word to the woman, he turned to walk toward the entrance.

Amon lifted a hand and waved. Nils saw him almost immediately and quickly crossed the bustling watch floor.

"Nils." Amon extended his hand. "A difficult start to the day, I take it?"

The watchman accepted his hand with a firm grip. "Thank you for coming, Amon." He nodded with a grim smile. "You could say that. All related, if I'm not mistaken. Come—I have something to show you. I'll warn you now: it's not pleasant, and I don't know what to make of it."

"Not pleasant..." Amon nodded. "I take it we have a visit to the Dead House ahead of us?"

"Yes." Nils looked towards the woman who was being gently helped to her feet by the young watchman. "Her husband was killed in an alleyway last night. And that young woman was almost attacked as well. I need you to look at the wounds so that I know what we're dealing with."

"Ahh... well, thankfully, I have not yet broken my fast," Amon said dryly. "Lead on."

The walk to the Dead House was thankfully short. A damp stone corridor opened into a gloomy courtyard, across from which there was a short flight of stairs that led down to large, dark wooden doors. *If hell had a gateway,* Amon thought.

Nils pushed open the door on the left and they entered a cold, high-ceilinged room. The room was sparsely lit with flickering torches and occupied by a single tall and painfully thin man who sat behind a scuffed, wooden desk. The man stood up and crossed the polished floor to greet them.

"Ahh... gentlemen... how can we... uhm... help?" He smiled bleakly. His voice was almost a whisper, and Amon noticed that he did not make eye contact, oddly choosing to focus on the centre of his subject's forehead.

"Gethum, this is Amon. We need to see the body that was brought in this morning," Nils replied. "The man who was attacked by a... dog."

"Ahh…" Gethum nodded, looking at the floor and then up to Nils' forehead. "Uhm…yes… of course. Ahhh… follow me." He turned and walked toward a long corridor.

Amon limped behind the two men. On a whim, he ran his fingers along the dark stone of the wall. It was cold and dry to the touch, the perfect place to store dead bodies, the low temperature and dry air slowing the putrefaction process.

Gethum stopped abruptly and stared once again at the polished floor. Then he opened a heavy metal door to his left. The walls of the room they entered were lined with metal racks. On each rack lay a shrouded body. Many of the white linen sheets bore dark reddish-brown stains.

"The… ahhh… third on the… left." Gethum said to Nils' forehead. "I'll wait… ahhh… outside."

"Thank you, Gethum." Nils nodded.

Amon crossed to the rack that Gethum had pointed out. The stains on this sheet were extensive. The soft round shapes under it spoke of a middle-aged, overweight man. He drew in a deep breath. The room smelled of cold and meat. He sighed and drew back the sheet.

His breath caught. *No… how is this possible?* The throat was torn out; deep puncture wounds penetrated the side… but that was not what caused the almost visceral reaction. Amon reached out to the semicircular bite wound around the right shoulder. He traced each hole and tear in the cold, pallid flesh with his finger. *This is not possible…* He felt the cold trickle of fear down his back.

"Amon?" Nils touched his arm.

The apothecary jumped at the touch. The watchman had been observing him closely. *Would you expect anything less from Nils?*

"What is it? What do you see?" Nils asked. "What animal did this?"

Amon slowly pulled the sheet over the body. He turned to the watchman feeling sick to his stomach.

"Amon?" Nils' stare was piercing. "What do you see?"

"I'm not entirely sure…" Amon swallowed hard. "I've not seen these types of wounds in many years."

"But you've seen something like this before haven't you, Amon? What animal did this?" Nils asked. "What are we dealing with here?"

"It's not an animal," Amon replied softly. "And if this is what I think it is"—He rubbed at the scar on his face while looking down at the broken body—"and pray it is not, we are in a great deal of trouble. You need to come with me. I have something to show you."

The apothecary had been quiet on the walk back to his home, limping alongside Nils, his eyes haunted. Nils had given up trying to get the man to talk before they reached his house. He only knew the situation was grave and likely to get worse. It was frustratingly slow, but at last, they turned the corner onto Water's Edge and walked up the short flight of stairs to Amon's house.

"Come in. Come in…" Amon held the door open and waved the watchman inside. Nils stepped into the cool interior and immediately smelled a soft mélange of herbs and poultices that formed the greater part of Amon's trade.

The apothecary stepped inside and slammed the door shut, quickly locking it and pushing a large brass bolt into place. Nils watched as Amon stood for a moment with his hand on the door as if in thought. His breathing looked laboured, and a there was a faint sheen of sweat on his forehead. Amon checked the bolt again before looking up. Nils could see the fear in the man's eyes as he forced a smile and gestured to a seat.

"My manners, forgive me." Amon shook his head. "Please sit. Can I offer you tea?"

"Perhaps you should first tell me what's going on, Amon," Nils said firmly. "You've not said a single word on the way here, and I need to know what I'm dealing with. A man is dead, and judging by your reaction, I can expect more like him."

Amon had walked over to the small stove, had filled the kettle, and put it on the plate. Nils watched as the apothecary reached for a blue box of what he presumed was tea…

"Amon!" he said sharply. Amon jolted, dropping the box and spilling the contents over the floor. He stood for a moment, as if trying to make sense of what he was seeing.

"Sorry… I'm sorry. I was going to offer you tea… but I seem to have dumped it all over the floor." He looked up. "I think we may need something a little stronger in any case. This is not an easy story."

Nils nodded and sagged into a chair, running his fingers through his hair. "We're in trouble, aren't we?"

"Trouble?" Amon grimaced. "Without being overly dramatic… unless we can get out of this city, we could all be dead."

Nils nodded slowly. "Well, in that case, I don't think tea would have been appropriate at all." He gestured at the splash of tea leaves on the floor.

"Agreed." Amon opened a cupboard and retrieved a bell-shaped bottle filled with a golden liquid and two earthenware cups. He poured a generous amount of the spirit into the two cups and offered one to Nils.

"I'd be careful if I were you," Amon warned. "That was distilled by Guthur monks. I'm not sure they had much to live for after taking their vows, so it's quite… potent."

Nils shrugged. "Apparently, we're already dead. How bad can it be?" He upended the cup and immediately broke into a fit of coughing. "Shit..." he wheezed.

"I did warn you." Amon sipped carefully at his own cup. He seemed a bit more composed. "More?"

Nils nodded and held out his cup.

"Brave man." Amon splashed more of the fiery liquid into the watchman's cup. "So... where to start?"

"The beginning seems fair." Nils took a cautious sip. "How do you know what's out there? Who were you before?"

Amon raised an eyebrow.

"I pay attention, Amon. The scar, the limp... not wounds you're likely to pick up around herbs and poultices." Nils pointed at his cup, "And now this charming brew distilled by a people who no longer exist."

Amon nodded slowly before taking a took a deep pull from his cup. Nils watched as he squeezed his eyes closed and bared his teeth at what must have been an explosion of heat in the pit of his stomach. Amon pulled up a chair and swirled the liquor around in the bottle as he collected his thoughts. "Where to begin?" He laughed dryly. "I was born to the wrong house at the wrong time in a kingdom ruled by the wrong king. But that doesn't really matter." He sighed. "If we hadn't found a way, someone else—someone just as ambitious, or *misguided*—would have, and you would be having a similar conversation with a different man." He looked up with a wry smile. "No doubt not as charming or hospitable as I... but..."

"Amon..." Nils frowned.

The Apothecary chuckled. "My apologies. The beginning..." He took a deep breath and ran a finger down the scar on his face before looking up at the young watchman. "So you have heard of the Guthur?"

"Yes. From books. I study great battles." Nils shrugged. "They were destroyed almost completely by the Kurgan army over twenty years ago."

"And what did the book say of that battle?"

"The usual—a normal, dry historical account. Numbers, places on a map that most people have never seen."

"Mmm... this story is anything but dry... or normal, for that matter..." Amon splashed more of the liquor into his mug and took another mouthful, squinting as the spirit burned all the way down. Nils flinched, he would be more than a little drunk if he had upended the cup like that, but it seemed like the apothecary needed a bit of help with dredging up memories long buried.

Amon touched the scar absently and got up painfully from his chair. He spoke as he walked over to a bookshelf. "The battle, as you know, took place on the flood plains of the Kukura River. The Guthur army gathered there, all its legions, men... Nepyrim... and..." He paused to take a thick leather-bound book from the shelf. He brushed the dust from the cover. "And *demons*."

"Demons?" Nils blinked. "Nepyrim? Amon, please."

"Nils..." The apothecary frowned as he limped back to his seat. He placed the book on the table between them and eased himself back into the chair. "If I said Nepyrim and demons, it is because I meant Nepyrim and demons," Amon continued with a slight edge to his voice.

Nils held up a hand in apology and waited for him to continue.

Amon sat quietly for a moment, staring at the book between them, then looked up at the young watchman and sighed. The flinty glare had softened. "I'm sorry. I just never thought I would ever be in need of telling this story within my lifetime." He leaned forward and topped up the watchman's mug. "Drink... you'll need it."

He opened the book, paging through the yellowed parchment until he came to a drawing of five stones. He turned the book to face Nils. Each stone had intricate markings; the opposite page had detailed notes in a flowing hand. "We had found ways to open portals using these stones. The portals—gateways if you will—opened to another dimension, a place...between, beneath... it's difficult to describe. The beings we discovered were... terrible beyond belief. But there were ways to contain them, to bind them... turn them into weapons. And we did." He lifted his mug to his lips and swallowed. "The most powerful were truly terrible," he continued. "The Demon Lords, if you will. They are indescribable. Massive, intelligent, insatiable. We summoned only one of those..."

Amon lifted his mug and gulped down another fiery mouthful. His eyes watered as he continued. "We lost many people before we managed to send that one back. Then there were the shadow beasts and the lesser demons. The shadows were violent and terrifying but controllable. The lesser demons were smaller creatures, like imps, that were far easier to control but still very dangerous. I think the first victim was attacked by one of the smaller creatures. The Nepyrim... they were different... somewhere between man and demon. We used them all... arrogant and foolish enough to believe we could bind chaos, control the uncontrollable."

Nils shifted forward to the edge of the chair. If this was even a fraction of the truth, they were in serious danger. How was he going to mobilise the watch? Would the watch even be enough to contain this?

Amon adjusted himself in his chair and grunted at the stab of pain in his hip.

"That battle should have been the end. The secrets should have been buried with my bones on that field, forgotten forever. But someone took a set of stones from me. A man in a dark cloak, not Kurgan. My only hope was that their secret would not be deciphered." He stared morosely at the bottle in his hand. "But quite obviously, that hope was misplaced."

"Why would someone do this, Amon?" Nils asked. "We're not at war, and this is a city—why would anyone take this risk?"

"Power, greed…" Amon shrugged, his expression was bleak. "What else is there? Imagine you could clear a path to whatever you wanted on a whim. Wouldn't this look like a way to do just that? You want someone dead? Command one of these creatures to do it. You want to be king? Command a legion to destroy the army opposing you."

"And if you lose control?" Nils asked.

Amon sat quietly for a moment, his face like stone, before letting out a slow breath. "Then you die."

The Temple Precinct, Sarsini
The Thirty-Fourth Day of 389, Morning

Resplendent in his robes of red and gold, Vasilios the Chosen sat upon the temple throne. He looked at the long line of supplicants and pilgrims and sighed inwardly. The sun had barely risen, and it was promising to be a long and taxing morning. Particularly given the fact that he had less than a handful of hours of sleep.

He knew that many had traveled for days and waited patiently throughout the cold night to present their cases to the head of the temple. *Misguided fools,* Vasilios thought vaguely while holding a benevolent smile in place. *But very useful misguided fools.* The smile did not slip for an instant as he ran a finger idly across a golden-threaded seam on the sleeve of his robe.

In the absence of the Primatus, the morning's duty had fallen to him, as the youngest and newest member of the Council of the Chosen. His eyes narrowed slightly as he thought of his fellow council members. *Outwardly pious, inwardly deeply political, self-serving, twisted old bastards one and all...* He squeezed the string of dark beads in his left hand, grinding them together, and forced his mind back to the present.

A woman had knelt humbly before him and was waiting patiently to present her petition. Her dress was simple, her frame was stocky, and her face was plump and ruddy. *A farmer's wife, no doubt,* Vasilios mused with little real interest. *Probably some family dispute. Or perhaps not enough rain. Or too much rain, for that matter.* He looked down at her with well-disguised indifference. *The gods don't care about you, or your village,* he wanted to say. *Why would they? You're utterly insignificant. Would you stop at an ant nest at the side of the road to ask about their well-being? Do you care about the animals you kill or displace when you burn the forest to plant more crops? No... because they are insignificant. So, my dear little ant, you need to realise that the gods didn't* allow *this or that to happen to you... That would imply they even knew of your existence. A trifle arrogant don't you think?* He smiled faintly and found his mind wandering to the succession once the Primatus had been dealt with.

Luckily, some of the Council members were pliable when it came to their vote. Two of them had mistresses, a fact that they would go to great lengths to keep from public knowledge. One owed a substantial amount of coin to a rather nasty book maker—a debt that, if not serviced, would result in rather unpleasant and possibly terminal consequences. Then there was fat Titus. That trough of lard would vote in any way that would ensure that his opulent lifestyle was least affected. Those four votes were all the leverage he required to seat him at the head of the order. There was just the small matter of Adrastus' demise that needed attention.

"Your Grace?" he heard a small voice say.

With a start, he suddenly realised that the woman had been speaking and was waiting patiently for him to answer. *Oh shit... what in the seven hells had she been going on about?* He pursed his lips and steepled his fingers as if pondering her request. *Now you've done it,* he chastised himself.

He quickly formulated a generic and hopefully sufficiently cryptic response and leaned forward, his expression beatific. A hand touched his arm. He turned to see a young acolyte standing quietly with his eyes downcast. *Oh thank the gods,* he thought, immediately appreciating the irony.

"Yes?" he asked.

"My humblest apologies, Your Grace. The Lady Desana has arrived, and she seeks an audience."

"The Lady Desana? She's here?" His heart tripped. As always, the excitement was almost immediately replaced with exasperation that her mere name could force such a reaction. These conflicting emotions were instantly pushed aside by the fear that she would simply leave and he that would never see her again. It was a maddening situation, that he both loved and hated. He was nothing more than a leaf in a hurricane.

He took a breath, trying to still the sudden rushes of heady exultation tempered with pangs of anxiety... *Of course she's here, you fool...* "Where can I find the Lady Desana?" he asked, forcing his voice to be steady.

"She is waiting in the private chapel of the Chosen, Your Grace."

Vasilios felt his stomach tighten and his breathing quicken. He had not been expecting her for at least another month. He took a deep breath and regained a semblance of composure.

"Tell her I will be there shortly," he replied more curtly than he wanted and waved the acolyte away. *Let her wait awhile... no need to go scampering after her.* And then, almost immediately, he swallowed hard, regretting the instruction. *What if she leaves?*

"My daughter..." Vasilios turned back to the peasant woman who had been waiting patiently, clutching her hands together. His smile was now wooden, and his insides churned. "I am sorry, but I have urgent business to attend to. Blessings be upon you and your house."

Vasilios swept down the corridor, his robes streaming behind him, scattering acolytes and priests in his wake. His steps echoed sharply on the polished white marble and he clutched his copy of the One Book to his chest like a shield. He had wasted far too much time with that idiotic gaggle. *She must still be here,* he thought, mildly queasy at the prospect that she may have gotten bored and left. *She must be!*

"Your Grace!" A young priest called out. "A moment, please!"

"Not now!" he snapped brusquely and swept past.

"Your Grace, my apologies… but it seems quite important." The acolyte almost ran alongside him to keep up. "There's apparently been an incident… at the old church… a monk,Brother Fe—"

"Shut up," Vasilios snapped, stopping and turning to the startled acolyte. "Make an appointment and have this Brother…" He waved a hand in the acolyte's face.

"Feris." The acolyte swallowed.

"The Brother Feris"—Vasilios poked a finger into the young man's chest—"can make an appointment and follow the correct channels. Understood?"

"Yes, Your Grace."

"Good." He turned and was turning from the shaken acolyte when the man's words struck him. "Wait!"

The acolyte froze. "Your Grace?"

"What did you say about an old church?" he asked slowly.

"The brother wanted to discuss an incident at the old church near the docks." The acolyte swallowed. "He didn't mention any… details…" He trailed off as Vasilios' eyes blazed.

Damn this all to hell! Vasilios swore silently as his mind raced. *What does this Feris know? Did he see something? Impossible… I was so careful. Whatever this is, it needs to be dealt with.* Vasilios pointed a finger at the young priest. "Tell him to wait in my office. Make him comfortable. I will be there as soon as I can. Post guards outside my door. They are to detain him if he tries to leave. Am I clear?"

"Yes, Your Grace." The acolyte nodded quickly.

Vasilios glared at him, seeing the faint sheen of sweat on the man's forehead and the wide, doe-like eyes. "Get it done," he snapped and turned to resume his headlong rush to the private chapel, trying with great difficulty not to break into a run. He would deal with this *Feris* shortly, but first, there was Desana.

They had met two months before at her father's estate in Mittua. He had been visiting one of the other Chosen, Cresus, a painfully righteous bore. It had been official temple business that he had normally managed to either avoid or delegate to one of his underlings. But this trip had been annoyingly unavoidable.

The dark and dismally boring day had been saved when the duke, a large man renowned for his equally large appetite, had been kind enough to extend an invitation for lunch. Naturally, Vasilios had accepted without hesitation, delivering himself from having to force down that bland slop those pious, sanctimonious peasant priests would have thrust upon him.

Gods how far is the bloody east wing? he raged, feeling slightly out of breath as he hurried along a blessedly quiet corridor. Even now, in his haste, he could recall that day clearly. The venison had been exquisite, served with a superb Sarsinian claret, a product of the duke's extensive vineyards. But everything had paled when compared to Desana.

Even now, his heart jumped when he recalled meeting her. He had offered his ring, unable to tear his eyes from hers. The jolt when her lips strayed from the ring and pressed against his fingers had been exquisite. He hardly remembered what inane blessing he had mumbled; all was lost as he drowned in her eyes. *What an utter fool!* he chastised himself even as he all but ran to meet her.

She had sat quietly at the end of the table on her mother's right. The priest had found her irresistibly beautiful, with her dark eyes and long jet-black hair. The battle to keep his eyes from straying to the front of her dress, where her ample bosom had strained heroically against the tight fabric, had been hell. But he could not imagine a more exquisite and agonising hell.

After lunch, they had found themselves at the edge of the crowd. Vasilios had smiled awkwardly and moved away to stand near of the verandah. Desana had followed and stood with her shoulder almost touching his arm. The soft scent of her, carried on the cool breeze blowing off the rolling fields, had been entirely intoxicating.

Later, he had made his escape without incident, but the coach ride back to the city had felt like an eternity. Nothing seemed to hold his interest for longer than a few moments before his mind would stray back to Desana. No woman had ever had this effect on him. He found himself equally angry, frustrated, and depressed, and with no inkling of an idea about how to quell the storm of emotions that raged within him.

The following weeks had been absolute misery. He had hatched plans to see her and then almost immediately dismissed them, further deepening his frustration and depression. He had stopped eating and drank little; everything seeming to taste like ash. The hell of it all had reached its zenith on a particular evening when he had stood on the balcony of his room, a glass of wine all but forgotten in his hand. The sunset had been truly a glorious blaze of colour, but to him, it seemed like the universe showing him everything he could never have.

Despair had settled on him like a dark, cloying blanket, and he had flung the glass out into the garden below, the blood-red arc of wine glittering with perverse beauty in the soft light of dusk. He had ground his fists into his eyes as he sobbed in impotent rage before slumping to the floor, tears dripping down his face onto the polished marble tiles.

He remembered angrily clawing at the tears, his misery and despair as complete and as deep as they could ever be. He could not have imagined an hour darker than that, so when the polite knock at his door had come, his anger had flared white-hot.

"What do you want?" he had shouted, scrambling to his feet and storming to the door to drag it open. A young acolyte, much like the one he had encountered today, had stood there with that same infuriating wide-eyed terror. "What do you *want*?" he had raged, his spittle causing the young priest to blink.

"My apologies, Your Grace," the young man had stammered. "The Lady Desana… has asked for an audience."

"What?" Vasilios blinked. He remembered his anger instantly being replaced by surprise… even fear... "Desana? She's here?"

"Yes, Your Grace. She's waiting in the audience chamber," the boy had stammered before scampering away.

The day was as clear as yesterday, and every visit since—and there were many—had not dulled the mess of emotions that tore through him; this was proved beyond a doubt as Vasilios quickened his step yet again, almost skipping down the corridors. He was now mindless of the fact that it would be decidedly inappropriate for one of the High Chosen to be seen running to an appointment. He was past caring, so great was his need to see her.

He turned the last corner, flung open the high doors of the chapel, and stopped suddenly. His breath caught as she turned and smiled. He never seemed to get used to her beauty.

"Your Grace," she said softly.

"My lady," Vasilios whispered.

"I thought we could walk in the garden again this morning. I enjoyed the roses and the shade of the trees on my last visit." Desana tilted her head to one side in that absolutely maddening way.

"Yes, my lady." Vasilios swallowed. "That would be… most pleasing."

Arrick shovelled oats into his mouth as the other two argued. Rork and Behn were at it again, and he did his best to ignore their endless arguments. All he wanted was for Kratos and the other's to return so that they could pack up and start the trek back to Verana. He didn't like Sarsini. Too big, too busy, and too easy to get yourself killed if you weren't careful. Back in Verana, he knew which card games to join without worrying too much about getting stuck if he landed the wrong hand. Back there he was one of the duke's men. Here he was just Arrick, nothing more than hired muscle.

"I'm telling you, Kratos said there'd be a bonus if we brought the farmer back unmarked," Behn was saying.

"Not for us, idiot." Rork shook his head. "We're not likely to see a single coin of that. Maybe Abas an' Cale an' Sciras will get a cut. They're there helpin' him. We ain't nothing but support if things get rough and the like."

"That's not what he said last night," Behn retorted. "It was my watch when I overheard him talking to Abas and the old woman. You know the one who spotted the farmer down by the Crow? Said there'd be extra coin in it if he were brought back here without any trouble."

"Gods, but you're bloody stupid." Rork slapped the table. "He offered the old hen an extra coin for finding the farmer and for waiting out there in the cold to see that he didn't run off. He said nothin' about all of us getting more money. Just be satisfied you're getting paid. It's been easy coin just waiting here for the job to be done. Even easier for a dim bastard like you."

"Easy coin? No, no, no!" Behn barked. "I'd rather be back…Did you just call me a dim bastard?"

"Gods. Enough," Arrick growled around a mouthful of oats. "Kratos'll do what he likes. Nothing you boys can do or say will make an ounce of difference. He's the duke's right hand, not either of you, not me, and not anyone else."

"Yeah… listen to Arrick. The duke wouldn't trust the likes of you to carry a bucket of piss across the yard," Rork quipped.

"Shut it, Rork," Arrick snapped. "I wouldn't trust either of you with the goddamned bucket."

He had just shovelled another spoonful of oats into his mouth when he heard a woman's voice call out.

"Good morning, gentlemen."

Arrick looked up from his breakfast and saw that a woman stood at the entrance of the warehouse. She wore a flowing, black Akhbari dress. "Who the 'ell are you?" He asked.

"That doesn't matter," the woman replied, walking confidently towards them. "You're Kratos' men, are you not?"

"What's it to you?" Arrick growled.

She ignored the question, stopping close enough for him to smell the subtle scent of flowers and spice. Her eyes scanned the warehouse before settling back on Arrick. "I need you all to leave. Now."

"What? Leave? Not bloody likely." Arrick laughed, leaning back in his chair. Rork and Behn looked at each other and laughed. Arrick wiped his mouth on this sleeve and pointed his spoon at her. "So why don't you fuck off... unless..." He shifted in his chair and looked her up and down. *The shape underneath all that cloth looks good enough.* "Unless you want to play with me and the rest of the boys while we wait for our boss."

"I'd rather play with a goat," she said evenly.

Arrick flushed with anger and dragged himself to his feet, his chair clattering to the ground. "We'll see about that, bitch." He was a large man, with a barrel chest, and he towered over her. "Come on, boys..." He nodded to Rork and Behn. "Let's teach this one a little lesson in manners."

He grabbed at the woman, but she spun away from his grasp, and he took a staggering step forward. Before he could recover, something struck him in the chest like a hammer. The air blasted from his lungs, and he felt a rib snap. Arrick's legs buckled and he collapsed to the floor, eyes bulging as he tried in vain to breathe.

"Hey! What you do that for?" he heard Behn shout. Through the waves of agony, he dimly saw Rork and Behn surge to their feet and rush forward. There was a blur of motion followed by a sound like the dry snapping of wood and a scream. Behn staggered back and dropped to a knee clutching an arm to his chest. Rork bulled in, fists balled, only to have his head snapped back with a spray of blood as the woman slipped under the clumsy punch and slammed the heel of her hand under his chin. The man crashed into the floor, unconscious.

What the hell? Arrick thought as he dragged himself to his knees and drew in a breath. The pain was excruciating. He saw several of the other men running toward the commotion, some with swords drawn, but the woman just scythed through them, like a flowing wave of destruction. Bones snapped, swords clattered to the floor, and blood sprayed. In no more than a handful of seconds, the carnage ceased. All of them were on the floor, either unconscious or groaning and writhing in pain.

Arrick watched as she walked over to him with terrifying purpose. He held up a hand. "No. No more!" he wheezed. "We'll go. We'll go!"

She smiled down at him, her ice-blue eyes blazing. "Good. Now there's something I need you to do. Listen carefully, because if you get this wrong, I will know. And then it will be more than your ribs that I break."

Kratos dropped from the saddle and savagely kicked at the doors to the warehouse. The large doors shuddered and creaked slowly open on their hinges. He tugged at the reins, pulling his horse forward. *How in the circles of hell did things go so wrong?* His anger about the morning debacle still burned brightly. Abas and Cale were dead, and based on what he had seen of the swordsman's ability, he had little doubt that Sciras had joined them in short order. *Who is this man? How does he know the swordsman?* Nothing apart from a gnawing hunch pointed to anything except a horse breeder. *The man had spent almost ten years on a small holding belonging to Verana!* Kratos fumed.

But now the time for subtlety was over. Failure was simply not an option. He had no desire to return to Verana to explain why they didn't have the man in tow. The duke was not a man prone to forgiveness. So now he had no choice but to take *all* the remaining men to the inn and—

He stopped and blinked. Apart from an annoyed snort from his horse, the warehouse was absolutely quiet.

Where the hell is everyone? He looked around. The other men were nowhere to be seen. He looked to the far end of the warehouse where they had stabled the horses and noticed that they, too, were missing. More worrying were the plates of food, half-eaten, on the table. That spoke of a hasty departure. A water jug lay on the floor and one of the chairs was upended.

"Fuck," he swore softly, dropping the reins in disbelief.

He heard a whisper of cloth and turned to see a woman standing in the doorway. She wore a flowing black *abaya* in the Akhbari fashion. She just stood with her arms folded, watching him without saying a word.

"Who the hell are you?" he snapped.

"You can call me Relic," she replied, walking into the warehouse.

"Relic." Kratos nodded. "Well met. Forgive my crass impatience, but I'm in the middle of something here. What do you want?"

"I see your men have left," she said, looking around, ignoring his question.

"Yes," Kratos said, unable to keep the frustration from his voice. "It would seem that way. And what, if I may ask"—he turned back to her with his eyes blazing—"would do you know about that?"

"They're riding back to Verana as we speak," she said as she stopped in front of him. She was a least a head shorter than him, so she had to tilt her head back to hold his gaze. "They'll be telling the duke that you failed. That several of your men are dead, killed by the man you hunted, and that you abandoned them and headed east to the mountains, hoping to find sanctuary with the Kurgan tribesmen."

"What?" he shouted and turned holding his head. He whirled back to her. "How? How do you know this? Speak, woman!"

"I told them to," she said simply.

"You told them to…" He blinked. "You told them to, and they just *fucking* listened?" he shouted into her face no longer able to hold back the rush of anger. *If this is true, Viktor will see me dead. By Eresophi's tits, I'm finished.* He glared at the woman, waiting for her reply.

"Yes," she said simply with a ghost of smile. "I can be rather… persuasive."

With that, something in him snapped. He pulled his dagger from its sheath and, grabbing her by the shoulder, pressed the point under her chin. "You will tell me everything," he hissed through clenched teeth. "Why did you do this? Who put you up to this? Was it the farmer? *Who is he?*" He pressed the point of the blade into her throat until a small bead of blood appeared as it pierced her skin. Apart from tilting her head slightly backward, she showed no sign of alarm or pain. Those piercing blue eyes simply held his, almost daring him to drive the blade home.

"Enough," she said and reached up, simply pushing the point away from her throat with the tip of her finger, and he found, to his amazement, that he could do nothing to stop her. He stood there with the dagger pointing stupidly to the empty space above her left shoulder, unable to move.

"Don't try again," she said plainly. "Or I will hurt you… and you're no good to me damaged. Now I want you to listen…*carefully*."

She spoke quietly as he stood frozen to the spot. When she had finished, she looked at him for a long moment. "Do you agree?" she asked.

He stared at her and realised how odd it was for an Akhbari woman to have such intensely blue eyes. What she told him was utter madness. And what she asked of him… he could scarcely believe it. But what choice did he have?

Choice? he thought bitterly. *None at all…* "Yes. I agree," he replied with a sigh.

"Good. Cross me on this and you'll wish the duke found you." Her lips curved into that half smile once again. She pressed something into his other hand and closed his fingers around it. It was the strap to a leather bag, and he could feel it's considerable weight.

"When this is done, you will leave by the western gate and follow the coastal road. There is a small cove between two jutting headlands that hides it quite well. You will need to look carefully for the path. You will not open this bag until you are there. I will know if you do. Do you understand?"

"Yes. And what am I to do once I get there?" he asked.

"You will open the bag," she said simply with a smile. Then she turned and walked from the warehouse.

The essence of Moloc drifted unnoticed above the man known as Kratos and the woman who called herself Relic. He held a fistful of her *abaya* with one hand and pressed a dagger into her throat with the other. The man's life energy blazed with raw anger threaded with fear. He wondered if the man would try to kill her. He watched with rapt interest. He had warned her of the dangers of the flesh, but she had not listened. Now she would truly *feel…*

Moloc drifted closer. *Ahh E'kia my love… One small thrust and this Relic of yours is ended,* he thought with an odd mixture of anticipation and fear. He could be rid of her, rid of her endless machinations. Her aura was incandescent, thrumming with the immense power of an Ascendant. But it would mean nothing if the man chose to sink the blade into her flesh. In that form, that disgusting mess of meat and blood, she was so vulnerable.

She had manipulated the hunter so easily, placing him in an impossible situation. There had been no subtly with his men, though. They were no match for her raw power. Those base beasts only understood lessons told in broken bones and blood, with the promise of worse. But this one needed to be backed into a corner, trapped, with no apparent hope of escape, and then given only one way out.

Should I allow this to play out? Moloc thought. This Kratos, could see his plans compromised, even destroyed. He could not allow this. Perhaps he should just kill the man. That would leave her plans in tatters. *Or would it?* he thought as a hint of doubt tugged at him. *Ah, E'kia, there is always a hidden barb to your machinations… Maybe you want me to kill this hunter.* He hesitated, he would need to think on this.

The woman who called herself Relic suddenly blazed, exuding a terrible and beautiful power. Effortlessly, she pushed the blade and held the man like an insect in the almost fathomless might of her will. Moloc listened as she instructed the man, leaving him with little choice but to accede to her wishes, giving him that single unavoidable path. She then passed him a leather bag, and with a few last instructions, she walked from the warehouse, leaving the hunter standing there staring dumbly at the wall, wondering how he had managed to be trapped so deftly. *Kill him now, you fool!* Moloc snarled to himself. *No…* He bared his teeth in frustration and then flew quickly after Relic.

She walked slowly towards the Docks, her abaya flowing softly behind her. *I see you E'kia, I see you…* He drifted closer using the full strength of his will to remain unnoticed. Relic blurred, and shifted, and the blue-eyed Akhbari woman was gone. In her place walked a tall Noordlander woman with flowing blonde hair, her striking green eyes, resolute and sure. And then, in the instant before she melted away Moloc noticed the small smear of blood on her cheek and it struck him. *Ah, E'kia, my love, I know what to do now,* the Ascendant thought with a surge of excitement. *Yes. It is perfect…* He drifted higher and higher until he floated far above the city. He then looked toward the spires of the temple. *Yes, my love. I know exactly what to do… but first, I have someone to unleash!*

Panos was well on his way to getting leglessly drunk. Dacian watched as the man tilted back the tankard, ale spilling down his chin to stain the front of his jerkin. The redheaded barmaid sitting on his knee laughed as he leaned close and whispered something into her ear. Dacian shook his head; the swordsman seemed to shrug off problems like old clothes. Jasmijn was nowhere to be seen. She had thumped the first two tankards Panos had ordered onto the table and stormed off without a word. *Probably for the best,* he thought grimly as he contemplated the rather vivid image of the girl stabbing Panos after some ribald comment.

"Drink up, my friend," Panos grinned at him, pointing at the half-full tankard. "There's really no point in worrying. It doesn't change anything and casts a bit of a wet rag over what is turning out to be a far better day than expected!"

Dacian forced a smile and waved off the suggestion. He needed a clear head. The beginnings of an almost unthinkable plan had been forming in his mind, and the fog of ale would not help.

"I'll see you in a while." He pushed back the chair and got to his feet. He slapped a hand onto the swordsman's shoulder and made his way to the courtyard door. He needed fresh air.

"I'll be here if you need me… perhaps out back. But you will need to knock!" he heard Panos' voice call out, followed by the muffled squeal of the barmaid. Dacian smiled despite the dark thoughts that swirled through his mind. This business with d'Verana needed to come to a head. And now the events of the morning had dragged both Jasmijn and Panos into the middle of it all. He would not allow anything to happen to either of them.

He pushed open the door and stepped into the courtyard. The blood had been washed away from the cobbles by one of the stablehands and there was no sign of the bloody events that had played out only hours before. The duke would never let this go. He would pursue them to the ends of the earth and he had the means to do it. There was only one resolution. He had to kill d'Verana.

"Yes," a cold voice murmured behind him. "That is the only way."

Dacian whirled around, his sword snaking from its scabbard. A man in a dark cloak stood a few steps away, his face almost hidden in the shadows of the hood. He was unarmed and seemed not to care in the slightest that Dacian had a sword levelled at his chest.

"Who are you?" Dacian snarled. "Are you one of his?"

The man snorted at that, the amusement apparent in his half smile. "No. But he and I have had... *dealings*." The man walked closer, and Dacian caught a glimpse of dark eyes and hard, angular features. "The duke's men are riding back to Verana. They left by way of the western gate not an hour ago." The man's voice was almost a purr. It seemed to have an hypnotic effect, and Dacian felt the point of his sword dip. "If you were to take a horse," he continued, stepping in close. "I am sure you could get ahead of them. The coastal road is quiet."

"Who are you? What is your business with the duke?" Dacian asked, unnerved by this stranger who was now standing uncomfortably close. There was something very dangerous about the man. It was like being next to a ravenous beast, not knowing what held it in check.

"That is of no consequence. As I said... the road is quiet," the stranger purred, ignoring the questions as he reached out and ran his finger down the gleaming blade. "And the wolves are hungry." The man's hand snaked out, and he grabbed Dacian by the throat, dragging him so close that he could see the roiling madness in the ink-black depths of the man's eyes. "Oh, and I want you to feast, my wolf. I want you to rend the flesh from their bones. I am growing very tired of waiting for you to cast off this...pathetic skin," the man hissed. "You are my killer. I have seen what you have done with steel and fire." The man leaned in so close Dacian could feel his breath fan against the skin of his cheek. "It is a trait that brought you here, and it is the one that will set you free. So destroy them. It is the only way."

Fear tore through Dacian as he tried desperately to pull himself free from the iron grip, but he was as helpless as a child. There was a mocking laugh, and then blinding flash of pain lanced through his skull. He staggered back, gulping in air. The man was gone.

Dacian stood for a moment, shivering as cold sweat beaded his forehead. He reached up and rubbed at his eyes with a trembling thumb and forefinger. He took a deep breath, blinked, and then reached down to retrieve his sword. He could not remember dropping it.

A horse nickered in the stable, and suddenly everything became crystal clear. The fear seemed to bleed away, and a strange calm settled around him, the debilitating helplessness replaced by an unyielding resolve. He sheathed his sword and strode toward the stables to saddle the horse.

Arrick rode slowly, holding the reins with his left hand. He cradled his cracked ribs with the right, trying desperately to minimise the sharp barbs of pain that flared at the horse's slightest sway. Rork and Behn rode next to him, and for once, they were quiet. He certainly didn't miss their endless bickering. He glanced over at the silent pair. Behn's face was as white as parchment, his broken arm in a makeshift sling; Rork's eyes were swollen and blue, and his nose sat at an odd angle to the left. It was an improvement Arrick had thought about providing on numerous occasions.

Arrick grimaced as he swallowed down the bile of being made to feel so utterly helpless. But if he were honest with himself, there was precious little he could have done; the woman had scythed through him and the men like they were nothing more than wheat blowing in the wind. He turned and took a painful look back at the rest of the group. The other six men all nursed injuries, from bruising to fractured bones.

Arrick shook his head and looked back to the road. He was in no hurry to get back to Verana. The duke would not be sympathetic in the slightest. But he had time to think about the message the woman had told him to deliver. Selling out Kratos didn't sit well with him, but it was damn side better than having his own skin peeled from his back—or worse. *I'll also have time to make sure none of these idiots contradict the story either,* he thought.

He was jerked to the left as the horse moved unexpectedly under him to climb a short rise in the road. He hissed in pain, clutching at his side with his gloved hand. *By the bloody gods who was that witch?* he thought for the umpteenth time and leaned forward, shifting carefully in the saddle to ease the ache of his ribs.

He was still leaning forward, his breathing shallow, when he heard Rork's voice, thick and nasal. "Arrick. Look." He looked up to see Rork pointing down the road. A man had stepped from the dark brush and now stood in their path. *What the hell is it now?* Arrick thought with a flash of irritation. If this was some attempt to rob them, they would teach this unfortunate arsehole the lesson of his life. It didn't matter how banged up they were; there were nine of them—more than enough to dole out one hell of a memorable beating. He drew rein and glared at the man.

"Get out of the way," he barked. The man simply stood there, arms hanging at his side. He looked eerily calm. "Get out of the fucking way unless you really want trouble." Once again, the man said nothing and Arrick felt his irritation rise. "Listen… We'd be more than happy to indulge you. It's been a shit morning, and beating you senseless would definitely make me feel better. Now get out of the way."

The man unsheathed his sword. Arrick drew in a breath and grimaced at the stab of pain from his ribs. "Ride him down," he growled drawing his sword as he kicked his horse into a run.

Dacian stood in the middle of the road, the faint warmth of the morning sun on his face. The ride from the city had been hard, but now the horse cropped sedately behind him. He watched the group of men draw rein with an odd indifference. He became aware of the light breeze that brushed his skin. It still had some of the teeth of the northern snow, and he breathed deeply, relishing the smell of pine and spruce mixed with that of the damp, earthy undergrowth.

"…make me feel better. Now get out of the way," one of them was shouting. Dacian, lost in his thoughts, had missed much of what the man had said. But it mattered little. These were Kratos' men, and they had to pay—for Arianne, for Aron, for their home that lay in ashes. He took a deep breath and drew his sword. The only pity was that he had noticed that Kratos was not with them. No matter—he would find him and kill him, too. He would find them all and drown them in an ocean of blood.

"Ride him down," he heard the big man on the right order, dragging his sword free from its scabbard and kicking his horse into a run. The others moved more slowly, swords flashing into view with muffled oaths. Dacian ignored them, focussing only on the leader as he galloped closer, his horse snorting as its hooves kicked out wads of earth, the man's bearded face contorted in what looked like pain.

Time seemed to bleed by slowly as he waited; his breathing slowed as he watched the man's sword swing upward. Still, he waited, his mind crystal clear, his eyes following the blade to the top of its arc and the beginning of its deadly descent. And then he was moving.

Dacian dropped under the swinging sword, his own flashing up like lightning. The point sliced deeply into the man's side just below the rib-cage, sending a spray of blood into the air. The horse ran on as the man toppled slowly from the saddle, his sword dropping from his hand to bounce and clatter on the road. But Dacian had already turned his attention away from the dying man.

His left hand dropped to the dagger at his belt. In one fluid movement, his arm swept upward and forward, releasing the perfectly balanced weapon in a silvery flash. It struck the next rider in the throat. The man slumped backward and fell from the horse. The animal veered to the left causing the next rider to draw back sharply on his reins, driving his horse down onto its hind-quarters, its sliding hooves gouging into the earth. The horse reared, ears pinned, and the man, whose left arm was in a sling, found himself thrown sharply backwards. He flew from the saddle, hitting the road hard. Dacian heard the man's neck snap. He twitched once, then lay still.

The other horses had slowed, and Dacian was quickly in among them, not waiting for them to get organised. His sword arced upward, ripping through a man's belly; the blade then darted forward, punching into another's groin. With a savage twist and gout of blood, the sword was free, ready to block a wild downward hack. The force of the blow shuddered down his arm. His stabbing riposte sent the point punching up under the man's ribs, through his lungs and heart.

As he tore the blade free, there was a sharp tug at his left shoulder and a white-hot burn. Instantly, he felt the warm flow of blood down his arm. He turned quickly, his sword flashing upward, barely managing to block the next blow. Steel rang sharply again steel, and he heard the man grunt from the effort. The rider swung the sword back at his head, but now instead of blocking, Dacian dropped under the blow, his own blade whipping upward as the other flashed past. He felt his sword tear through the man's flesh. Blood, hot and sticky, sprayed over his face.

There were two more. They had drawn rein and were frantically trying to turn their horses away from him. He could not let them escape. He threw his sword at the man closest to him. The pommel hit him in the face, snapping his head backward. Dacian didn't wait for him to topple from the saddle. He sprinted at the second man, who was dragging his horse's head around and trying desperately to kick the animal into a run.

Dacian launched himself upward, grabbing fistfuls of the man's jerkin and dragging him from the saddle. They hit the ground hard, and Dacian was on him in an instant. He drove his fist into the man's face, feeling teeth snap off at the gum-line. The next blow crushed his nose; the next smashed into his jaw, and then sanity fled. Dacian's fists rose and fell with mindless ferocity. Blood sprayed as the flesh pulped, and the sound that bellowed from his chest was raw and bestial.

His fists ached when he stopped. Blood dripped from his face, and his chest was heaving when he finally stood up. The rider who had taken the pommel of the sword to his face was slowly regaining consciousness. Dacian retrieved the weapon and walked over to the man. He slapped the point of the blade under the man's chin.

"Please don't," the man whispered, holding up his hands. His left eye was swollen shut, and there was a smear of blood under his nose. "Don't…"

"Where is Kratos?" Dacian asked impassively, ignoring the blubbering plea.

"I don't know," the man whimpered. "We left before he returned."

Dacian traced the point along the rider's jawline, across his cheek, and under the bruised eye. For an instant he thought about thrusting the blade into the man's skull. It would be so easy; he just needed to lean on the blade. He wiped the sweat and blood from his face with his sleeve.

"Tell d'Verana I'm coming for him," Dacian said softly. "Tell him I'm coming to burn his world to the ground." He slowly dragged the point of the sword down the man's face, pausing as the blade pulled at the skin near his chin. "Better yet," he snarled through bared teeth. "I'll tell him." The man's eyes widened as the cold realisation hit. Dacian's eyes blazed for an instant, and then he rammed the point of the sword through the man's neck.

Arrick lay on his side. He could not move; his limbs felt like lead. There was no pain, but he could feel his blood pooling under him. He was going to die, but he didn't care. He was tired. There was nothing left here for him anyway—he had no family, no land, no legacy. No one would miss him or stop to wonder what happened to him. He would be just another nameless body, apparently left by bandits, found by whoever might stumble across his corpse.

Each breath was now a short, shallow gasp. He remembered Rork's quip to Behn about this job being easy money. Those two stupid bastards were probably dead, wandering around in the afterlife, arguing about how they got there. He became dimly aware of the crunching of gravel under boots. The footsteps drew closer. *Coming to finish me off, you bastard?* Arrick thought, smiling weakly. It wasn't like he could do anything to prevent it. *Better than lying here waiting to bleed out…*

A dark figure sat down on its haunches, and Arrick heard a low, chuckle. He could not lift his head, and all he could see was the folds of a dark, woollen cloak bunched up around black leather boots. The figure reached forward and pushed back the strands of hair that hung over Arrick's cheek.

"Who?" It took almost all of his remaining strength to croak the question.

The fingers that stroked his hair tightened and he felt his head being twisted painfully upward. A face leaned in close to his, and Arrick became acutely aware of the figure's icy, jet-black eyes and white, predatory teeth. He felt a tongue flick across his cheek, tasting the blood that had congealed there. He felt the feather-like touch of breath on his ear.

"Do you wish to live?" Each whispered word seemed to slither into his skull like noisome serpents. "I can make it so…"

Arrick squeezed his eyes shut as sharp nails dragged down the side of his face. He drew a shuddering, painful breath and looked up into those cold, empty pools that regarded him like a dying insect. *Do I wish to live? And what would you want in return?* Arrick thought as a strange peace started to settle on him. It felt like warm arms, long forgotten, holding him close. He smiled then, and with a clear voice, he said, "No."

Moloc watched impassively as the life drained from the man. The eyes grew dull and glassy, the face becoming slack as the spark extinguished. *No matter.* He shrugged and stood up to look to the north. The assassin was riding hard along the coast road, his rage finally unleashed. It was so sweet, so incandescent that the Ascendant could feel the ripples of it thrumming through the very ground beneath his feet; he could taste it hanging in the air like the heavy silence before a storm.

Moloc suppressed a shiver of delight. By the time he reached his prey, he would be all but unstoppable, every vestige of that ridiculous façade stripped away, revealing the monster that had been so carefully hidden. It would be there for all to see… blood and wrath and hellfire. And how it would burn… it would burn through the duke's men and leave nothing but ash in its wake. But now he had to return to the priest. There were other circles to be put into motion. *Always circles within circles within circles…*

He drifted slowly into the air, where he hung for a moment arms outstretched. A large crow had landed on one of the bodies and started to peck at the exposed flesh. *Feast my friend—it is the first of many,* he thought, baring his sharp teeth, and then he turned and flew swiftly towards the city.

The Temple Precinct

Feris paced impatiently in the office of the Chosen. He had been waiting for hours, and there was still no trace of the man. If Lidi had come to harm at his hand, there would be hell to pay. Feris didn't care what the man's station was. He would see justice meted out if even if it meant the end of him. He stopped abruptly in the middle of the large room and glared at the closed door, willing it to open so that he could confront the man. It stayed frustratingly closed.

"Enough of this," he growled to himself and walked to the door, pulling it open. Immediately, the two guards stepped in front of him, barring his way. "What?" he barked at them.

"His Grace instructed that you are to wait in his office until he is able to see you," the one on the left said.

"Well, I've been waiting for half the morning, and I'm done with that." Feris glared at the guard. The guard laid a hand on his sword hilt, and the old monk shook his head slowly in disdain. *Boy, I had already spent half my life fighting when you were still hanging on your mother's*

244

tit… The old monk broke off the angry train of thought and took a slow, deep breath. "You won't be needing that, son," he said, regaining some of his composure. "I just need to know when I can expect His Grace. It is a matter of utmost importance."

"We don't know." The guard shrugged. "We were just told to keep you here until he came back."

Feris pursed his lips and folded his arms. He had no intention of being held prisoner in the man's office.

Before he could speak, the one on the right growled, "So why don't you get your arse back in there… before we put you back in there."

Feris turned a cold glare to the man, taking in the small, close-set eyes and the smirk on the fleshy lips. A weak thug of a man who inflicted pain to mask his vast inadequacies.

"I said—" the thug began raising a finger to poke into Feris' chest.

"I know what you said, boy," Feris said coldly, stopping the man before the offending digit came closer. "And I'm quite sure you've grown attached to that arm, so I am pleased you've revisited your train of action. Now I'm going to leave, with or without your permission. One way, you will be able to tell His Grace that the old brother has gone to the watch. The other way, he will need to visit the two of you in the infirmary."

The one on the right opened his mouth to reply when his companion stopped him abruptly with a hand on his arm. "What in the sevens hells?" the thug growled angrily. "You're just going to listen to this old man?"

"Yes," the first guard said simply, his eyes flicking down to the crisscrossed scars on the old monk's arms. "And so are you." He turned back to Feris. "My apologies. You can go, Brother."

"The hell he can!" the thug snarled, reaching for his sword, but before he could draw the blade, the old monk's hand snaked out and latched onto his wrist in a vicelike grip.

Feris dragged the guard in close. "Think very carefully, boy, about what you do next," he said softly. "I was not always a monk, and to my master's great disappointment, many of the teachings never took."

The thug's small eyes blazed with a brief defiance, and then he relaxed his hand on the hilt and looked away from the old man's piercing eyes.

"Sorry, Brother," he mumbled.

"No harm done, my son." The monk nodded, releasing the man's arm. The guards stood aside, and Feris strode down the wide passage without looking back.

Vasilios lay on his back, hands clasped behind his head, and allowed the cool morning breeze to evaporate the sweat from his skin. Sunlight spilled through the gap in the diaphanous curtains, their gentle sway sending soft shadows to caress the pale form of the sleeping woman next to him. He smiled as he idly ran a finger up the smooth curve of her hip. Desana stirred slightly, a ghost of a smile on her lips, but then she nuzzled the pillow and fell back into a deep sleep.

He smiled lazily to himself as he recalled the morning's deliciously fevered love-making. *How wonderfully uninhibited,* he thought as he looked down at the broken wine goblet and the upended side table, then chuckled to himself. He had barely been able to spirit her into his chambers before they had been clawing at each other's robes. Thankfully, they were far removed from any prying ears and eyes, and his guards at the doors were hand-picked and very well compensated; they were as good as blind and deaf when it came to his affairs, so the breaking of glass and any other commotion they may have become aware of would have been ignored.

He smiled to himself as he sat up and swung his legs over the side of the bed. The marble floor was cold under his bare feet, but he paid it no heed as he strolled over to the small table and set it right. He crossed to an open cabinet and took a bottle of wine and a crystal goblet from a shelf. Pushing aside the soft, translucent curtains, he walked through the open doors to the sunlit balcony.

The morning was cool and still after the night's rain, and the sea breeze had a faint bite to it. He leaned against the marble balcony and breathed deeply before pulling the cork from the bottle with his teeth and filling the glass. Far below him, beyond the high walls of the temple precinct, he could see the massive sprawl of the city. The broad avenues and thinner threads of roads and walkways seemed like the veins of some strange beast. To the south, the Great Sea gleamed, stretching away to the horizon; to the north, the rolling hills were bathed in the warm glow of the morning sun, and a scattering of small clouds drifted languidly across the sky.

It has been a good day, Vasilios thought happily as he sipped at the wine. Desana's visit had taken him by surprise. She always managed to fill him with such wild and conflicting emotions. As frustrating as it was, he knew beyond a doubt if he wanted her in his life, it was something he would need to learn to live with. The thought of never seeing her again was unthinkable. Imagining the loss of even these fleeting moments made him feel queasy.

Not even the gods themselves will drag me from her... He sighed contently at the blasphemy and swirled another mouthful of wine, tasting the cool sweetness. The walk through the temple gardens had been wonderful, filled with all the subtle innuendo that he had grown to love. Having her walk so close to his side and being unable to reach out and touch her had been both excruciating and intoxicating. She had been close enough for him to smell the subtle scent of her skin, to feel the occasional brush of her arm and the feather-light touch of her fingers. He was about to sip at the wine when a deep voice spoke behind him.

"Such transient beauty."

Vasilios whirled around almost dropping the glass. He ripped back the curtain to see the tall, black-robed man from standing next to the bed, looking down at the sleeping Desana.

"What the…" Vasilios spluttered, "What the hell are you doing here?" he shouted, grabbing his robe from the back of a chair and throwing it around his shoulders. "How did you get in?" He shot a glance at the door and then stopped abruptly, blinking in surprise as the man raised a hand, stopping him in his tracks.

"Quiet, priest," he said softly as he looked up, pushing back the hood of his cloak. He paused for a moment, his gaze seeming to claw across Vasilios' skin like jagged nails. Then he smiled coldly, revealing those white, strangely predatory teeth that Vasilios had caught a glimpse of on Quay Road. His close-cropped dark hair and rather prominent nose gave the handsome face a fierce, hawklike aspect. The eyes were jet black, and something very disturbing lurked in their inky depths.

Vasilios arranged his robe around him and shivered as the first icy fingers of fear traced lines down his back. *What does he want? Is this about the girl?* "Why are you here?" he asked carefully, now acutely aware that there could be far more at play than met the eye.

"Such fleeting beauty," the dark stranger repeated, ignoring the question as he traced a finger along Desana's side to her left breast, lingering over her nipple, which stiffened at his touch. When she moaned softly, he grinned, running his long fingernails lightly down to her stomach.

Vasilios reddened, and the beginnings of rage started to replace the trepidation. Now all he wanted was to reach out to tear the man away from her, hurl him to the floor, and smash his fist into his face again and again. He blinked, torn from the thought as the man spoke again, his voice soft, almost sibilant.

"Can you feel the glow of her life? No, I don't think so…" He looked up at Vasilios and then back to the sleeping woman. "So warm, so fragile and fleeting. A mere drop in the ocean of time." He traced a long nail down Desana's inner thigh before continuing. "I can feel your anger, Priest. Your ambition… your lust." He turned the ink-black eyes back to

Vasilios. The priest shuddered as they seemed to cut through him, laying bare everything he had taken such care to hide. The man laughed coldly then. "And yes… your fear."

"Who are you?" Vasilios grated through clenched teeth, fighting back the impotent rage. "Is this about the girl? You were well compensated."

"Your gold does not interest me, Priest." The dark man reached into his cloak and withdrew a small leather pouch. He dropped it to the floor, spilling the gold coins onto the marble. "Who I am is a far more interesting question." The man paused, as if pondering the answer. "I doubt you could ever comprehend," he said softly, shaking his head, then turned away from Vasilios to look down at Desana. "It will suffice that you know that I am the one who gave you the means to attain… all of this." He waved a hand to encompass the room and the sleeping woman. "And the means to attain a great deal more…" He smiled coldly at Vasilios before turning from the bed and walking to the billowing curtains. He pulled them aside and stood looking out over the city. "But now I want something in return. There is a woman who poses a great threat to your plans."

As the man talked, Vasilios walked slowly to the side of the bed and slid open the top drawer of the bedside table. *No, my friend,* he thought as he removed a long, slim dagger. *It is you who are the threat. You know about the girl, the stones… Desana…* He slid the blade noiselessly from the sheath and dropped it onto the bed.

"Unless she is dealt with," the man continued as Vasilios moved silently up behind him and raised the dagger.

"This is how I deal with threats," he said with a cold calm and plunged the dagger downward.

The blade shattered, and the jarring force of the blow slammed up his arm, twisting the hilt from his grasp and sending it flying. Vasilios staggered backward, clutching at his wrist. *What in the seven hells?* The thought was cut off abruptly as an immense force grabbed hold of him and flung him against the far wall.

Vasilios grunted as the air was slammed from his lungs. He hung there, crushed against the wall, unable to breathe, and watched in horror as the man he had tried to kill stood impassively looking out over the city, as if nothing had happened.

"No comprehension." He shook his head without turning. "And no… I am not a *god.*" He laughed scornfully at the unasked question on Vasilios' lips. The dark man turned and waved his hand. Vasilios dropped into a heap on the floor, where he lay gasping for breath. The priest watched as the man walked slowly over to him. "And I wouldn't bother praying to your god, either, if I were you. He's not listening…"

He reached down and grabbed Vasilios' arm. The priest shrieked as his flesh blistered and burned from the searing heat of the touch. "And even if he was… I think it might be too late."

Vasilios squeezed his eyes tightly shut and pulled in vain at the iron grip, gritting his teeth against the agony.

"Look at me," the man said softly. Vasilios sobbed. "Look at me!" the man snarled and shook him like a rag-doll.

Vasilios opened his eyes and then gaped in horror as the man's dark, handsome features seemed to slough away. His feet slipped on the smooth marble floor as he desperately tried to tear himself away from the black-scaled beast before him.

The creature's slavering jaws twisted into a hideous smile filled with ragged fangs. "Who am I?" the creature hissed as its claws closed around the priest's throat and dragged the Vasilios' face close to its own. "Who am I?" it whispered as its forked tongue flitted over the priest's face. "In the old books, I am M'lakh, the Ascendant of Shadow. I am despair… desolation… I am the Eater of Souls."

"Please," Vasilios blubbered, "don't kill me. I didn't know."

"Kill you?" The Ascendant sneered contemptuously and released the priest, allowing him to crumple to the floor. In an instant, the monster melted away, and once again, the darkly handsome man stood over him. "I have no wish to kill you, Priest. Besides, you should not fear death… rather, that what lies thereafter."

Vasilios clutched his arm to his chest and pushed himself frantically away from the Ascendant, stopping only when his back thumped into the wall. The Ascendant ignored him and walked to the foot of the bed in which Desana still lay, oblivious.

"You love this one," M'lakh said without looking at the cowering priest. "Or at least you think you do." The Ascendant turned those cold, black eyes to Vasilios. "It is the thing you tell yourself as you lie alone in the dark, hungering for her touch. You tell yourself that when you scheme and plot… and kill. That you elevate yourself for her. So that someday, you will be able to stand with her without the chains of those priestly robes." M'lakh paused, and Vasilios felt naked under those horrible burning eyes. "You think your ambition will be sated when you ascend to head of your order? I think not. Golden shackles are shackles nonetheless. No, Priest… you would be king. And you would see the blood of thousands shed to that end."

The Ascendant looked back to the sleeping Desana and then waved his hand at the wall above her head. The stone seemed to warp and tear, and a white-hot blast of air burst through the fissure. Vasilios threw up his hands to shield his face. Squinting against the searing heat, he looked through the gateway and saw a thin path of black rock that wound its way through a molten lake. At the end of the path, a massive dark form of a woman squatted on a flat plinth. Her jet-black, scaled skin gleamed in the flickering of the flames. Vasilios' blood ran cold as she looked up and her baleful eyes latched onto his. Her clawed hands closed on the edge of the stone at her feet, the crushing grip sending fragments of splintered rock falling into the burning lake, where uncountable bodies writhed in agony. Vasilios bit into his knuckles to stifle a scream.

The Ascendant turned to him and dropped his hand. The shrieks of the tormented and the dull roar of flames cut off abruptly, leaving only the cold stone of the wall. "That is your fate, Priest," he said, almost spitting the last word. "But first there is payment. You will find the woman named Jasmijn and take her to to the place of sacrifice. There, you will spill her blood... *tonight*."

Vasilios nodded, tears running down his cheeks, the taste of blood in his mouth having bitten through the skin of his knuckles.

"You will find her quite close to the old church," the Ascendent said softly as he crossed to the sleeping Desana. He brushed back a strand of hair from her face. "She masquerades as a tavern wench. But I warn you. Do not take her lightly, Priest. Also, there is a man with her. He is dangerous but of no value to me. He will kill you to protect her." M'lakh looked up, eyes blazing. "Fail me in this, Priest, and you will burn far sooner than you think."

Vasilios nodded again cradling his burned arm.

"And so you know who you serve..." He looked back to the sleeping Desana and paused for an instant. His face twisted, and his clawed hand plunged into her chest, splintering the ribs. Her eyes flew open and her body convulsed as the Ascendent tore out her heart. Blood sprayed from her mouth, speckling M'lakh's face, and then she slumped back and lay still.

"NOOOOOO!" Vasilios screamed. "NOOOO!"

"Do not fail me," M'lakh growled as he tossed the lump of ragged, bloody flesh aside. And then he disappeared.

Vasilios crawled to the edge of the bed, clutching his left arm to his chest. The blistered flesh around his wrist ached horribly. He had no recollection of how long he had lain in a crumpled heap on the floor, hardly able to breathe, but the blood on his knuckles was dry and crumbling. He flinched as a gust of wind sent the silken curtains billowing. Even the soft shadows seemed to crawl and slither across the smooth tiles of the floor. He almost expected them to coagulate into misshapen horrors that crouched in the corners, waiting to pounce.

He rested his back against the bed, unable to bring himself to look at her. Desana was gone. A small sob escaped his lips as he rocked back and forth. He knew he needed to face the nightmare that lay on the bed behind him. He needed to close those eyes, once warm, now dull and lifeless. He didn't know if he could take the glassy, blunt accusation.

Vasilios forced his eyes open. He took a deep breath, then another. He opened his hand and stared at it, willing the trembling to abate. It was early afternoon. He needed to take care of her... body. He flinched at the insanity of the thoughts that seemed to trip and stumble through his mind. *It isn't real... it can't be...* He swallowed and crushed the irrational flood of denial. The horror that lay on the bed was very real. And he needed to take care if it—now.

He stood up and waited for a moment for his legs to steady. Without looking at the bed, he walked over to his closet and pulled opened the doors. He walked past the rows of rich robes of silk and velvet that hung with impeccable neatness, the shoes of soft, polished leather and glass cabinets with rings of gold and glittering gems... He felt sick. This was the fruit of his unbounded ambition. *"Golden shackles are shackles nonetheless,"* the cold voice echoed in his mind.

At the back of the closet, he thrust the garments that hung there carelessly aside and thumbed a hidden catch in the wooden paneling. With an almost inaudible click, the panel swung noiselessly aside, revealing a small room. An oil lamp stood on a simple wooden table. On the other side of the room, there was a thick iron-braced door. It was locked, the key hanging on a brass hook next to it. Beyond the door lay a narrow spiral staircase that led to a number of passages, some that ran under the walls of the temple precinct and to the city, others that delved deeper, connecting to the sewers and a warren of dark tunnels.

He grabbed a leather bag from a shelf, quickly opened it, and removed several pieces of common, but well-made clothing and a pair of knee-high boots. He dressed swiftly, choosing trousers and a shirt in a dark wool. He winced as the coarse fabric tugged at the scorched flesh of his arm. Ignoring the discomfort as much as possible, he pulled on the boots and then removed a pair of black leather gloves from the bag. He slipped his hands into the soft, pliable leather and clenched his fists, steeling himself for what had to be done.

Vasilios turned slowly and looked past the clothes through the open doors of the closet. He could see Desana; she lay on her back, arms outspread, and her left leg hanging over the side of the bed. Even from where here stood, he could see the edges of the terrible wound beneath her ribs, the dried blood in stark contrast to her pale skin. He closed his eyes and sucked in a deep breath as a fresh bout of trembling shook his body.

When he looked up, he was surprised to find his vision blurred by tears, and he angrily wiped them away with the back of his hand. *No time for this... No time!* He gritted his teeth, trying with little success to stave off the crushing weight of the emotion. He felt as if someone had dropped a stone into his gut.

Move, you fool! He took a deep breath and forced himself forward towards the bed. He walked woodenly over to her, feeling like an unwilling puppet dragged along by the strings of an unseen master. He stopped, the tears falling unchecked now, and gently lifted her foot and placed it on the bed. Then he knelt and, with a shaking hand, reached over and closed her eyes. *I'm sorry... so sorry...* His fingers lingered on her cheek, the skin now cold.

Vasilios forced himself to his feet, and taking care not to focus on the gaping wound, he placed her hands on her chest and wrapped the quilt around her body, leaving only her face visible. For a long moment he stared down at her. Finally, he reached out and touched her cheek for the last time before covering her face.

Vasilios carried Desana's body down the narrow staircase. The dull orange light spilling from the small lamp was only sufficient to light four or five stairs in front of him. Shadows jumped and danced as he made his way carefully downward. His breath rasped and echoed as he strained under the weight.

The staircase descended steeply, twisting back on itself every twenty or so stairs in a maddening spiral that seemed to stretch on for an eternity, so when Vasilios stumbled into the chamber at the bottom, he grunted in surprise and relief. He stood breathing heavily, holding up the lamp. By its flickering light, he could see several doors. One to his left led to the cellar of a deserted house that he owned across the Avenue of Flowers. He and Desana had taken this passage so many times before. His heart heavy, Vasilios turned to his right.

With difficulty, he placed the small lamp on the floor and pushed open the door. Beyond it, the dry, pale dust that had covered the stairs to this point gave way to damp and moss. He wiped at the sweat that stung his eyes and tried to ignore the deep ache that hand settled into his arms and shoulders. Retrieving the lamp, he forced himself onward. Despite the chill of the passage, sweat now dripped from his chin.

Vasilios struggled on, his shoulders bumping and scraping against the glistening, mouldy walls. By the time the passage opened up into a large chamber, Vasilios was gasping for breath. His back ached, and the muscles of his arms and shoulders burned like fire. He needed to rest, so with great care, he placed Desana's body on the floor and set the lamp down next to her. Then he stood and stretched, grunting in pain as his tortured muscles protested.

Retrieving the lamp, he held it up to examine his surroundings. The air was cold and damp, and each breath echoed softly. The high vaulted ceiling was lost to the deep gloom, and to his left and right there were archways and pillars of dark stone barely visible in the feeble light. Beyond them, the darkness was complete so he had no idea of the extent of the chamber, nor could he guess its intended use. It was a long-forgotten place, now just decaying stone and shadow.

As he looked around, Vasilios slowly became aware of the feeble island of flickering light cast by the lamp. The small yellow flame seemed to strain against the oppressive weight of the surrounding murk, its pale shelter all that stood between him and unseen horrors. He forced down the rising claustrophobic panic. The river could not be far. The channel that ran under the city had to be close.

Placing the lamp on the floor, he stooped and, with difficulty, lifted Desana's body back to his shoulder. He groaned as pain seeped through every muscle. He steadied himself and then reached down to snatch up the lamp. He paused for a moment, his ragged breaths echoing back from the unseen walls, and then, holding up the lamp, forced himself forward. It was then that he felt the eyes upon him. A malevolent, feather-light touch of something unseen slithering across the back of his neck.

Vasilios froze. His breath caught, and he strained to hear beyond the slow, almost inaudible, drip-drop of water from the ceiling. In the silence, the beating of his heart was almost thunderous. *Nothing… it's nothing.* He let out the breath. *Gods, man… you need to get this done.* He was just about to start forward again when he heard the faint scratch, followed by a whisper of movement.

"Who's there?" he shouted, his voice echoing back from the shadows. "Show yourself, damn you!" He shuffled around, holding the lamp up high. The incomprehensibly small splash of light seesawed madly as it tried in vain to ward off the stifling, oozing weight of the darkness all around him.

"Show yourself, damn you!" Vasilios almost sobbed. "Show—"

There was a rush of footsteps, and something slammed into his back sending the small lamp flying. He hit the ground hard, Desana's limp form torn from his grasp. In a blind terror, he dragged himself to his knees. Desana lay a few feet from him. In the spluttering, dying light, he saw the quilt covering Desana had flopped open slightly. He could see the tangle of her hair and the smooth curve of her shoulder. He reached for her, and just before the light winked out, he saw clawed hands grab her body and drag her into the dark. The crushing blackness then descended, and Vasilios screamed.

The creature hung from the ceiling by its claws and sniffed at the cold air. Its prey was standing far below, wreathed in an almost unbearably bright light. It had appeared from the narrow passage moments before, carrying a dead thing over its shoulder. Now it had stopped; the dead thing was at its feet, and it was looking around. The creature slitted its black, bulbous eyes as the prey turned the light towards it. The warm, salty scent of flesh filled its nostrils and saliva spurted under its tongue in anticipation of the feast.

It bared small, razor-sharp teeth and hissed. It was hungry; it was always hungry. The gnawing emptiness in its gut was insatiable. It scurried silently along the ceiling to the far wall, where it hung in the deep shadow away from the painful light. It scratched at the pallid, hairless skin of its chest and waited.

The prey had picked up the dead thing once again. It would be vulnerable carrying that weight, slower. The creature crept a few feet down the wall before dropping to the floor. The prey stopped, rounding at the faint sound and holding up the light. The creature blinked rapidly and bared its teeth in irritation and pain. Its eyes closed to almost indiscernible slits, and it tried to avoid looking directly at the blazing object.

Moving rapidly to its right, it circled around behind the prey so now its body now silhouetted by the dazzling nimbus of light. Thin blue lips peeled back from its teeth in expectation. It would take the dead thing first, then it would feast on the hot quivering flesh. It crept forward, its belly scrapping the cold stone floor. The pungent reek of fear hung about the prey as it shouted into the darkness. The creature's lips curled back from its fangs, its muscles tensed, and it sprang…

Vasilios sobbed as he groped around in the smothering darkness. The muffled, wet sounds of feeding had thankfully stopped, but now he could feel the eyes upon him, he could hear the whispers of movement. He had to find the lamp. Nothing else mattered. He could not die in the crushing black stalked by some unseen horror. His hands flailed around the cold stone, nails hooking on the corners of the slabs. He cried out as his fingers struck metal, sending the lamp clattering over the floor, away from him.

"Noooo…" he wailed, crawling in the direction of the sound, fingers desperately clawing at the void in front of him. "No, no, no…"

The eyes lurking in the darkness felt like they were boring holes through his spine. *Not yet,* he pleaded silently. *Please not yet, not yet...* He groped blindly, cold sweat dripping from his face. He could feel the thing closing in on him, now closer than ever. Mindless terror tore at the fragile strands of his mind as he tried frantically tried to resist the useless urge to look back. *Not yet... not yet... NOT YET!*

His fingers closed around the metal ring of the lamp, and he almost sobbed in relief. With badly shaking hands, he reached into his pocket for the tinderbox. It was slippery in his clammy palm. Once again, he felt more than heard the faintest whisper of movement behind him. He forced himself to concentrate. He needed to light the lamp.

If I can just... The thought died with a sudden rush of footsteps. Vasilios whirled around and flung out his arms to try to stop the unseen thing that charged toward him. The lantern flew from his grasp and clattered once again to the stones. Vasilios screamed.

It hit him hard in his chest, knocking him onto his back. He felt claws sink into the flesh of his shoulders and back, and he shrieked in pain and terror, his fists striking wildly at the thing on top of him. Its hot breath fanned his face, and he felt what must be saliva drip onto his cheek.

Then, quite suddenly, he heard a sharp crack; it reminded him of a thick branch suddenly snapping. The ironlike grip relaxed, and then the weight was gone, and he heard something hit the floor, like a heavy, wet sack being thrown aside. He lay in the dark, his chest heaving.

When the lamp flickered to life, it was almost painfully bright. Very carefully, he pushed himself up from the floor and turned to the light. To his surprise, he saw a woman sitting on her haunches, the lantern hanging from her fingers. She wore dark leather that clung to her long limbs. She was beautiful, but there was a palpable air of danger hanging about her. He felt very much like a mouse being watched by a hawk as she absently tucked a strand of hair behind her ear.

"Who...who are..." he started to ask, and she raised a finger to silence him.

"That is of no importance," she said, rocking the lantern back and forth, sending the small pool of light skittering across the floor. "Where are the stones?"

"The stones?" Vasilios blinked in surprise.

Her face clouded. "You have one chance, Priest," she said softly, the tone somehow enhancing the threat. "Just one... if you want to leave this place alive. I know what you have done, and unfortunately, much of that cannot be stopped or undone." She paused, her piercing eyes glittering like ice. "Now I am asking for the last time. Where are the stones?"

Vasilios swallowed, acutely aware of the deep shadows that slithered on the edges of the swaying light. He sagged forward, his head hanging. "In my room. They are safe."

She laughed bitterly at that. "Safe? No, Priest. They are most certainly not." She stood and walked over to him, placing the lantern on the floor in front of him. "Get up."

Vasilios stood. His legs felt weak, and the wounds on his shoulders and back ached. He stared into her eyes, feeling very much like a fly trapped in a web. She reached down suddenly and then pushed the lantern into his hands.

"I know what he has asked of you. I know what he has shown you. Now if you have any hope of altering that fate, I want you to listen very closely…"

Echo opened her eyes. She stood in a valley. The moon, full and bright, hung in a clear night sky, casting long and twisted shadows over the dusty ground. There were no sounds, no movement... nothing. But it was always such in this place; a place in between the fabric of dream and reality. It was his place, where he would test the will of others.

She sniffed and tucked a strand of hair behind her ear. On an impulse, she bent down and picked up a small stone. She rolled in about between her fingers, feeling the tiny cracks and imperfections, and then tucked it away in a pocket. She looked around, finding the preternatural silence unsettling. It was always unsettling, but it was nothing compared to what was to come.

Echo brushed the dust from her hands and looked up at the hill that lay before her. The cave was near the top; at her feet were the beginnings of a path. It wound its way through the low bushes and stunted trees. She paused for a moment and then started to walk. The path was overgrown in many places, and she had to push the foliage aside. The dry rustle of leaves and the crunching of the loose stone beneath her feet were oddly loud. *A way not used to visitors,* she thought. *Of course, very few would be able to find it in the first place... and even fewer would want to.*

It was not long before she found herself on the wide, flat ledge. It was exactly as she remembered it: the long dead tree with twisted, bone-white branches that clawed at the sky, the massive, broken slab of stone still partially wrapped in rusted chain, the shattered links strewn around on the ground... and the entrance to the cave. She clenched her fists and took a deep breath, steeling herself for what lay beyond. She was about to start forward when she stopped. She reached into her pocket and pulled out the small pebble. She smiled as she rolled the pebble around in her fingers before tossing it aside and reaching down to pick up a broken link of the chain. *Things to take, and things to give away,* she thought as she walked to the cave and stepped into the darkness.

The essence of Moloc drifted through the busy, narrow streets of Sarsini. The Ascendant was only vaguely aware of the multitude of thrumming life forces that flowed around him. They meant nothing to him. Their brief lives were as meaningless as the base existence of insects. They played no part in the plans that were in motion, but they would all burn nevertheless—along with the priest, the assassin, and the woman. Everything they touched and loved would become ash. Everything that they clung to would be torn from their hands.

"A coin?" he heard a voice wheeze. "Spare a coin for an old blind man?"

He stopped and turned to drift toward the voice. An ancient man sat near the entrance to a dark alley, a battered wooden bowl holding a few copper coins at his feet. The man wore a filthy, threadbare cotton wrap, and his skin was like dark leather stretched tightly over bone. He looked cold and wasted. A morbid curiosity drew Moloc closer. He floated in front of the weathered face and looked into the rheumy eyes, milky white with cataracts.

Why don't you just let go? The Ascendant pulsed as he touched the feeble, flickering life force. A cancer ate at the man's lungs and pain wracked his frail body. *Why do you struggle? Why do you suffer?* Moloc stared into the sightless eyes set in the deep etchings of a long and hard life. The Ascendant drifted back slowly and was about to turn away when he noticed the old man smiling toothlessly.

"Because I do not to suffer," the old man rasped, each word like dry leaves skittering over stone.

What? Moloc pulsed, pulling back in surprise. *What did you say?*

"I have much left to learn," the old man wheezed. "So I choose not to suffer."

How do you see me? the Ascendant pulsed, drawing close again.

The weathered skin around the milky eyes crinkled, and the old man's shoulders shook with wheezing laughter that broke into a bout of coughing. He wiped bloody spittle from his chin with the back of his hand and pointed a boney finger in Moloc's direction. "I see you... because you burn."

The Ascendant hesitated and then settled next to the old man, willing himself to take form.

"Who are you?" Moloc hissed from under his hood. "Tell me! Or I promise you, you will regret it."

"What will you do, Ascendant?" The old man asked baring pink gums. "Hurt me? *Kill* me?" Again came the wheezing laughter. "Oh, I don't fear either anymore."

"Who are you?" Moloc grabbed the man's dirty robe.

"That is of no importance," he rasped, and then he smiled, baring his pink gums once more. "The far more interesting question is, Who are *you?*"

I am M'lakh... The Ascendant pulsed.

"No." the old man shook his head with a sad smile. "You are not."

Echo inched her way forward. The passage before her sloped gently downward, the floor covered in a coarse, black volcanic sand. The walls were cold to the touch as her fingers traced the fractured edges of obsidian to steady herself as the ground slipped and shifted beneath her feet.

She stared down into the depths, trying desperately to pierce the impenetrable blackness. The temperature dropped steeply as she went deeper until each breath plumed softly. Along with the cold, the darkness grew deeper as well, until it seemed to coalesce into something more palpable than the mere absence of light. It was thick and cloying, a smothering blackness that pressed itself into her mouth and slithered behind her eyes.

"What is your name?" the voice slammed into her from the darkness, each word rumbling and grinding like broken granite. They scoured her bones and drove the air from her lungs. Echo staggered backwards, her legs buckled and she fell to the floor. Her fingers raked at the course sand as she fought to take a breath, as the darkness clinging to her face. Waves of intense emotion coursed through her being—love, pain, crushing despair… ecstasy.

She slumped against the wall, feeling the sharp volcanic glass claw at the flesh of her back. She lay there fighting to breathe, her vision shattering into pinwheels and uncountable burning gems that flowed into and through each other. Memories of so many lives flashed through her mind, each as intense as the birth and death of stars, blindingly bright for an instant, only to fold into darkness.

She shuddered, her eyes wide as she was suddenly enveloped in the scent of desert flowers that clung to her mother's *abaya*… There was the pain of arthritic knuckles pressed into cool soft earth, along with the laughter of grandchildren… a stone striking her head… a mortar and pestle, the earthy smell of crushed herbs… the acrid stench of smoke, a flash of steel…

"Who are you?" the voice thundered and she groaned under the crushing weight of the words. "*WHO ARE YOU?*" Each word seemed to reverberate off the very edges of the universe to slam into her, threatening to tear her apart.

"E'kia…" she barely managed to croak. "I… am… E'kia."

Moloc drifted above the twisted, immolated ruin. The cobbles around the corpse had cracked from the heat. The small wooden bowl was now ash, and the handful of coins had fused together. But still, the old man's last words hissed through his mind… *No, you are not… No, you are not… No…*

The Ascendant felt another surge of anger at the nagging, elusive memories that flittered behind each word like moths in the night. He felt like he was looking down into the shadows of a deep well. Somewhere in the dark lay the answer, somewhere at the bottom of that terrifying plunge.

Who are you? the dry, husky words echoed in his mind. Moloc bared his teeth at the charred remains. *Who are you?* Once again, his anger flared white-hot, this time jarring loose fragments of memories: smoke spiralling up from a stone chimney... cold night air on his skin... rough hands and crushing fear... utter helplessness cut short by a searing flash of pain...

I am M'lakh... the Ascendant pulsed looking down at what was left of the old man. But this time he was not so sure...

Echo dragged in a deep, shuddering breath as the pain and the crushing weight disappeared. She opened her eyes to a float of pure, white light. Peace washed over her like a warm wave. She took in another deep breath and allowed the tears to run down her face, surrendering herself to the warm light. Then she felt strong arms gently fold around her. She felt the tips of fingers run down her forearms to her hands. She felt lips press gently against her cheek and a soft breath near her ear. She reached up and felt the scars, a crisscrossed legacy of pain and suffering.

"He cannot see," the voice whispered sadly. "He has chosen a darkness that was never meant to be his. He cannot see past the flame and death to the love that is still there."

"Is there no hope for him, then?" She blinked back sudden tears.

"There is always hope. Even death offers the hope of a new life," came the soft reply, tinged with sadness. "He was not ready. You know this."

Another tear slid down her face. "Yes." She whispered as she felt lips touch her eyes.

"It is just a circle within circles. Each a new beginning that requires an end," the voice whispered. "Open your eyes..."

She did and gasped. He stood before her, radiant and powerful.

"You know who he must see," the Broken One said gently. A sad smile settled on his beautiful face as he held up a small rusted link of chain. "And I cannot help with that. It is time for you to go...E'kia."

And the world fell away from beneath her feet...

Ostermeer, the Noordlandt
The Forty-First Day of 191, Evening

Mikha was so tired that he could feel it right down to his bones. His shoulders and back ached from a day spent loading grain sacks into the wagons. But despite this, he a wore a lazy smile on his bearded face as he trudged along the narrow, rutted road towards his home. The back-breaking work had taken most of the day because the harvest had been the best in years. He took in a deep breath and looked to the looming mountain range in the distance. The craggy, snowcapped peaks were golden in the setting sun. It was a good day.

He turned a bend, and the stone and thatch of his home appeared from between the yew and tall pines. A lazy spiral of smoke drifted up from the chimney, and he grinned broadly as he made out the large, shaggy pile of useless fur that was his dog. As usual, the hound was lying on the porch, soaking up the last of the late-afternoon sun.

Mikha quickened his pace and grunted as the strained muscles of his lower back protested. He looked at the wisps of smoke and started wondering what Signe had made for dinner. He had not eaten for most of the day, and his stomach grumbled. He could never avoid feeling a sudden tightness in his chest as he thought of his wife; she was the most gentle yet fierce, calm yet fiery woman he had ever met—a beautiful woman of staggering contradictions. And this was probably why he loved her with every fibre of his being.

He stepped onto the porch, and the dog roused itself to shamble over, with its tail wagging. Mikha knelt down to run his fingers through the animal's thick coat, enduring the bout of welcoming licking. "Not much of a guard dog, are you? Totally useless… I should skin you and turn you into a rug." The dog wagged its tail in happy agreement.

"Sig! I'm home!" he called out. "Feed me woman before I eat this foul animal."

"Eat it," he heard her answer from the kitchen. "I spent the day tumbling with the neighbour, so I've not had the chance to cook."

Mikha snorted. "So I need to rebuild the bed, then. Torsten is not the smallest of men." He heard her laugh. His neighbour was one of the very few men who had to both duck and turn sideways to enter their front door. Whenever he looked at the man, Mikha could not help but wonder if the god Hodan had, at some point, mated with a she-bear.

"Go wash," Signe ordered. "I'll not have you in my kitchen smelling like some wild animal."

"So you're saying you're not partial to wild animals, then, my love. Should I remember that after dinner?"

There was a pause. "That's different," she called back. "Go wash!"

Mikha laughed and made his way to the well. Signe had placed a bar of soap and a fresh set of clothes on a small wooden stool. He drew a bucket of water, stripped, and upended the basket over his head, gasping at the sudden cold. He then worked the soap into a lather and washed the day's grime from his body and hair. The cool evening air felt crisp and invigorating as he drew another bucket to wash off the soap. He smiled to himself. It was definitely a good day.

Freshly bathed and dressed, Mikha stepped into the warmth of the kitchen and felt his breath catch as Signe looked up from the pot and smiled. Her long straw-blonde hair was tied back with a strip of leather, and those blue eyes of hers—he drew a deep breath—so full of mischief and knowing.

"Finally," she chided, walking over to him while wiping her hands on a cloth. She tilted her head toward his neck and sniffed. "Acceptable." She dropped the cloth on the small table and drew his face down to hers to kiss him.

"Acceptable?" He grinned. "Gods, woman… I must have loaded ten wagons today."

"Only ten?" She sighed dramatically. "I'm sure Torsten would have loaded at least twenty."

"Torsten wouldn't need a wagon," Mikha retorted. "A sack of grain looks like a woman's purse in those meaty paws of his!"

Signe laughed and pointed to a chair. "Sit. Food is ready. If you were thinking about eating the dog, you must be starving."

Mikha pulled the chair back and sat with a sigh of pleasure. It felt good beyond belief just to be off his feet. "How was your day, Sig? Apart from tumbling Torsten, that is?"

"No one *tumbles* Torsten, my love." She laughed over her shoulder as she ladled the thick vegetable stew into a wooden bowl. "The man is a mountain… Sex with him must be like being caught in a landslide. I pity Tova. Poor woman must be perpetually bruised."

"They have six children." Mikha chuckled. "Can't be all that bad."

"Eat." Signe ignored the comment and placed the steaming bowl of food in front of Mikha.

"Your day?" he asked around a mouthful of stew.

Signe pulled up the chair next to him and sat. She watched him for a bit as he wolfed down the food before answering. "Hilda was here. She brought her daughter."

Mikha stopped eating and looked up. "What did she want?" he asked carefully.

Signe shrugged. "Help."

He frowned and placed the spoon back in the almost empty bowl. "We have spoken about this," he said softly. "It is not safe."

Signe held his gaze before reaching out and squeezing his hand. "I know. But they needed help, my love."

Mikha stared at his wife, not knowing what to say or how to articulate his fear. He could not lose her. "I know, Sig. But…" He sighed. They'd had this conversation so many times. "I just… just be careful," he finished awkwardly.

"I will." She smiled. "Now eat. There's more if you're still hungry."

He lay on his back, his muscles aching. His mind raced as he listened to the chirping of the crickets. As tired as he was, he could not find sleep. Signe was curled up under his arm, her head resting on his chest. He could smell her hair. It reminded him of sunshine and mountain meadows. Mikha smiled as he gently tucked a strand of it behind her ear and traced the line of her jaw with his fingers. She stirred, murmured something incomprehensible, and then fell back to sleep.

He stared up into the shadows of the thatched ceiling. No matter how he tried, his mind kept flitting back to the conversation at the table. He knew why Hilda had brought her daughter. The girl, small and sickly, had now developed a lung ailment. No one was expecting her to make it through the next winter. The priests had made their sacrifices and said their prayers and then left the matter in the hands of the gods.

Mikha had little time for any man that carelessly ceded his responsibility to the gods, especially when that very man would cling to power and station with a spiteful fervour. Mikha could see the hate and fear in some of them when they were confronted with that which they did not, *would not* understand. Trygve Ulfson was the epitome of such a man. Fat and proud and utterly wrapped up in his own importance—a dangerous fool.

Mikha sighed, thinking back to when they had first met Trygve over two years ago. He and Signe had been at the temple, offering thanks for the harvest, when a child was carried in. The boy's parents, distraught and desperate, having lost faith in the village healers, had brought him to the temple. He was stricken with some form of palsy. The poor child had gone blind and suffered from increasingly violent and painful seizures.

In the previous weeks, they had apparently come many times to the temple for Trygve to pray over the boy and make the necessary blood sacrifices. And each time, the priest had sent them on their way, assuring them that their pleas would be heard. They just needed to have faith. But on that day, their faith and Trygve's benevolence had run out.

"What do you mean?" Mikha remembered hearing the father ask Trygve. "The will of the gods? To have a child suffer like this? I don't believe that… I can't." The man wiped a trembling hand over his face and looked up with red-rimmed eyes at the stern priest. "This *cannot* be the will of the gods. To what end? Tell me, Priest."

"Who are you to question the gods?" Trygve had pulled his robes around his vast girth, almost like a shield, bristling at the man's apparent blasphemy.

"I am the father of a dying son!" the man had barked, pointing to the pale, unconscious boy. "I have every right to question them."

Trygve glared down at the man, not a shred of empathy or compassion evident. Then, with a slow nod and hooded eyes, he replied, "Yes. And perhaps now you know why." He waved a hand dismissively at them. "Take your son home and ease his passing as best you can. May you use this pain to learn humility."

At that, Signe had pulled her hand from his. "Sig. No!" Mikha hissed, but she ignored him and walked towards the small family. The boy was lying limp in his mother's arms. Signe had knelt down beside them and, without a word, reached out to the boy. Mikha had always known of her gift, but she had never used it so openly.

There were gasps as a blazing white light poured from her hands as she held the boy's head. The child's eyes flew open, and he groaned as the light seemed to flood into him. The grey parlour of his skin faded, his twisted muscles relaxed, and the pain etched around his eyes disappeared. Signe let out a shuddering breath, drained by the effort.

"By the gods!" the mother had cried stroking her son's hair. She looked up at the smiling Signe with a mix of gratitude and disbelief. "Thank you! Thank you!" she whispered over and over.

But Mikha had seen something deeply troubling. While others looked on in awe, Trygve had stood as if riveted to the floor, watching dumbfounded as the mother and father had sobbed their thanks to Signe. The look of disbelief and fear slowly melted away until all that was left was venom and hate. Mikha could never forget the poisonous glare Trygve had levelled at Signe or the trembling rage of his words. "Get out! Get out, all of you. And take that… *witch* with you." Mikha had stood to confront the priest, but Signe had laid a hand on his arm. "No. Just let it be, my love," she had said softly, pulling him away towards the door.

Mikha sighed as his thoughts returned to the present. Trygve was a small-minded man trapped in a world of dangerous absolutes. But he held sway in the village, and that frightened Mikha. He did not want Signe to draw attention to herself, no matter the perceived good. He listened to her soft breathing and suddenly felt keenly aware of how delicate this life was. How easily it could be torn away from him. He stroked her hair. *You are worth more to me than all the sick children in the world, my love,* he thought. He took a deep, slow breath and then finally drifted off to sleep.

Mikha woke suddenly as rough hands dragged him from the bed. He hit the floor hard, sending a small table clattering away from him. He heard Signe scream and tried desperately to get up, only to be slammed back down. Something hard cracked into the side of his head, and his vision exploded into bright white lights. He had just enough time to feel a trickle of blood down the side of his face before a rough sack came down over his head. He felt his hands being pulled behind his back and bound tightly.

"Signe!" he called out hoarsely, his voice muffled by the fabric. "Sig!"

"Mikha!" he heard her cry out. "What's ha—" The frantic question was cut short by the sound of a thudding blow and Signe's grunt of pain.

"Quiet, witch," Mikha heard a man growl. "Take them outside."

"Stop this!" Mikha shouted. "You don't—" A fist landed hard under his ribs, and his legs gave way as he fought to breathe. He felt himself being dragged across the floor towards the door. *Sig... Oh gods, what's happening to us?* he thought as his feet clattered down the stairs of the porch. The hands released him, allowing him to collapse onto the damp grass. He tried to roll to his knees, and a boot landed in the pit of his stomach. The pain was excruciating. "Signe," he groaned as he curled into a ball.

"Get him up," Mikha heard a voice command. He was dragged to his knees, and the sack was pulled from his head. He blinked as his eyes adjusted. A group of men stood in front of him; three held burning torches. Two held him by his shoulders, and another two held Signe. She sagged forward limply, strands of her hair poking out from under the sack over her head. The group before him parted, and a large man stepped forward. Mikha's heart sank as he saw that it was Trygve Ulfson.

The fat man walked forward and looked down at Mikha, his face split by an oily, satisfied smile. He reached down and grabbed a fistful of Mikha's hair, bending his face painfully upward.

"Tonight, you will see how we deal with witches," Trygve said softly, "and those who consort with them."

"Please...don't," Mikha managed to say through gritted teeth.

"Don't what?" Trygve asked with mock interest. "Oh... you want us to just go away? Leave this abomination unpunished?"

"She just... helped a... child," Mikha rasped. "Please..."

"No." Trygve growled, pulling Mikha's head back even further until the tendons stood taut against the skin of his throat. "She did not *help* a child. She *defied* the will of the gods." He leaned in close to Mikha. "Who does she think she is? Who are you to defend such... *heresy*!"

Trygve released his grip, and Mikha slumped forward. The fat priest looked with mild interest at the clump of hair that clung to his hand. He brushed it off and looked down at Mikha with disgust. "Watch, now, how we deal with witches." He turned to the two men who held Signe. "Tie her to the tree." He pointed to the old yew that stood near the fence. "And bring wood."

"No. You can't do this!" Mikha shouted as the horror of what Trygve intended to do struck him. "It was me... I told her to do it. It's my fault! Punish me!" Mikha watched in horror as Signe was dragged away to the tree. "Don't do this!" he screamed, trying to get to his feet. The man to his left smashed a fist into the side of Mikha's head, and he collapsed back to the ground, his vision swimming with pain and tears.

"Mikha! What's happening? What are they doing?" he heard Signe scream as they tied her hands. They looped the rope over a lower-hanging branch, and pulled her arms up above her head until her toes barely touched the ground. "Mikha!"

"What do we do with this one?" Mikha heard one of the men ask Trygve. He watched as Trygve walked closer and eased himself down onto a knee.

"You know how this is going to end," Trygve said softly. "But still you think you can change it somehow. You refuse to accept the inevitability of it all." Trygve smiled. "But I am going to show you the true meaning of finality. The true meaning of your place in this world." He looked up and pointed to Signe who struggled against the ropes as the others stacked wood around her legs. "I am going to show you how insignificant you are. How this deep *arrogance* has brought your downfall. I will show you that no matter what you think or feel, you cannot save her."

Mikha watched as Trygve pushed himself to his feet. "She will burn, and you can do nothing to save her. Nothing." The priest waved a hand, and one of the others threw a torch onto the wood surrounding Signe.

"No... no..." Mikha sobbed. "It was me... It was... my fault..."

"Kill him," Trygve said.

Mikha felt a rough hand under his chin drag his head back. *Signe... I'm sorry...* He felt the brief chill of steel, followed by a searing pain. He pitched forward. The hot, coppery taste of blood filled his mouth. He tried to breathe and his lungs filled with liquid. He felt, more than heard, the deep gurgling within his chest. He coughed convulsively, blood spurting from his mouth and the gapping wound in his neck. His muscles spasmed, and then all went black.

Down he sank into a crushing, cloying blackness that wrapped itself tightly around his body. He felt himself being dragged downward into the smothering dark. He could not move, could not breathe. He felt the darkness pour into his open mouth like thick tar.

"Who are you?" came a sibilant whisper.

Mikha… He felt the thought pulse feebly into the oily blackness.

"No, you are not that anymore," the voice hissed.

Anymore? But I am… He paused. *What am I?*

"What you have always been…" the voice hissed. "But now without the chains."

Who are you? he pulsed.

He felt a dry laugh scratch over his senses like shards of glass. "That is for you to discover."

Am I dead?

He felt, rather than heard the sibilant laugh. "Oh no. You have just shed the shackles of flesh. Who are you?"

I am… he pulsed, feeling a new and staggeringly power flow over him and through him, *M'lakh.*

The new Ascendant stood close to the low-burning fire. The flames no longer posed any threat to him. The blackened remains of a woman hung from a branch, and the flames curled around her legs and body. Fresh blood dripped from his hands, but it was of no consequence. Neither were the crushed bodies of the men lying strewn on the grass behind him.

He tried to remember why this woman was important. But the memory, though tantalisingly close, remained just out of reach, slipping away like the acrid smoke that billowed into the black night sky. Her head hung down, the hair burned away, the flesh black and charred. She was somehow *different* from the men.

He had wanted to destroy them, rend the limbs from their bodies. He had savoured their fear, their agony. He clenched his fists, feeling the sticky, congealing blood between his fingers. He had wanted to *feel* their terror.

Yet he flinched when the rope finally burned through and the woman's body fell into the fire with a shower of sparks.

"Can joy be harvested
from the seeds of sorrow?
Can darkness ever exist
without the light?"
—The Songs of E'kia

The Circle of Night

"There is no end to time,
no death of days;
Just doors to the light and shadow.

There is no unravelling thread.
There is naught to slip from errant fingers.

Just power or ruin, salt or loss.
Just doors hidden yet unguarded

So choose wisely;
for once you shed this mortal cloak,
Ascendency lies beyond."

—The Voice of the Ascendants

Feris pushed open the doors to the busy watchhouse and looked around. A small crowd clustered around the front desk, and a burly sergeant was doing his best to make sense of the noise and frustrated gesticulations. The old monk took a deep breath and clenched his jaw. He'd had ample time to think on the walk up from the temple precinct, but he still had little idea of what he would tell the watch. It sounded almost absurd in his mind that he believed a high priest, one of the Chosen, no less, had abducted and possibly killed a street urchin.

His brow furrowed, and he looked down at the floor. The story sounded utterly ridiculous. He had no proof, just the word of another homeless child who had apparently had seen the flash of red robe and caught a glimpse of a black-clothed stranger before the girl had been led to the old church. They were going to laugh at him. The old monk looked up and took a deep breath. He had to try; that was the only way. He had survived countless battles and couldn't back down on this one. He started to push his way through the crowd.

"Watch it!" a man growled as Feris eased past him with a hand on his shoulder.

"I'm sorry." Feris nodded but pressed forward nonetheless.

"Hey!" came a woman's voice.

"My apologies, sister." the old monk rasped as he moved her firmly but gently aside and pressed against the next man blocking the way.

"Who do you—" The voice cut off as the man noticed Feris' brown cassock and then the deeply lined face and piercing eyes. He moved aside.

"Thank you, brother." Feris nodded, and then he was at the counter. He paused and then bellowed, "Sergeant! A moment please." The other voices fell silent almost immediately. The large watchman blinked in surprise and looked around to see if there were any protests. Everyone was looking at the monk, quite stunned by the raw authority the old man's voice carried. The sergeant nodded to Feris.

"Yes? How can I help?" he asked simply as he laid a blank piece of paper on the counter and pulled an ink pot and quill closer.

"I need to report a missing child," Feris said abruptly. "I have reason to believe she has been abducted and that… she may be in mortal danger."

A low grumble of dissent started in the crowd around him as some of them began to realise that this might take longer than anticipated. Feris slammed a hand down on the counter with a sharp crack. "Enough!" he roared as he turned to them, daring them to argue. The crowd fell silent almost immediately. Not one seemed willing to incur the wrath of the iron-haired monk.

"Please…" The sergeant held up a hand to Feris "What is your name, Brother?"

"Feris." He turned back to the watchman. "I am Feris. I tend the temple gardens."

The watchman nodded. "Please, Brother Feris. A moment." He turned to the stunned crowd, and when no one protested, he lowered his hand. "Can I ask everyone to please be seated," he said quietly and gestured to the benches at either side of the entrance hall. "Please. We will attend to your needs shortly." The frustrated grumbles rose again but this time far more subdued, and then the others made their way to the benches. Some sat down, resigned to wait, while others stood and glared at Feris' back.

"Good. Now tell me about this child." The sergeant turned back to Feris preparing to take notes.

"She's an urchin," Feris began. "She lives on the streets near the waterfront…"

"She's homeless?" the watchman asked carefully.

"Yes." Feris felt his irritation rise. "Why would that matter?"

"Well…" The Sergeant frowned, not looking up from the blank sheet of paper on the desk. "The urchins and homeless people in the city are known to move around. Are you sure she has not just moved to another part of the city—someplace warmer or safer, perhaps?" He looked up into the monk's piercing glare. "How do you know she's been abducted?"

Feris chewed on his lip, collecting his thoughts. "I bring… I used to bring her food," he started, deliberately keeping his tone calm. "This morning, she was not there. I questioned another boy, and he had said she had been taken." He paused. "By a priest."

The sergeant pursed his lips and then placed the pen on the counter. He steepled his fingers on the blank page and then asked, "And there's no possibility that this priest could have merely given her sanctuary? What led you to believe she was abducted?"

Feris frowned and swallowed down his frustration. "The boy told me this priest took her to the old church—the one, near the docks, on Quay Road. It has been abandoned for years. I went there and found it to be locked, looking, for all intents and purposes, completely deserted. It does not make sense!" He gripped the counter, wanting nothing more than to reach across and shake the man into action. But that would achieve absolutely nothing. It would more than likely get him thrown out of the watchhouse. He relaxed his grip. "Something is just not right," he finished lamely.

The sergeant sighed. "I know you are concerned, Brother. Believe me, I do understand. We have hundreds of cases such as this, and the vast majority come to nothing." The watchman paused, then continued gently, "The boy could have been telling you this for a reward... a coin or some food."

"I know," Feris growled, looking down at the scuffed desk, feeling the helpless frustration wash over him. "I know!" He looked up at the burly watchman. "Nevertheless I want someone to investigate. I need to know."

"Brother..." The Sergeant sighed and looked away, unable to hold the piercing glare. "I really don't..." But before he could finish, the doors pushed open, and four temple guards walked in.

The leader was a tall, bearded man with close-cropped hair. His black leather armour gleamed, and his gloved hand rested almost casually on the silver pommel of his sword. He leaned closer to one of his men and spoke softly. The guard, his features blunt, with a fleshy, petulant twist to his mouth, nodded and then pointed toward the monk. The leader straightened and gestured his three men forward.

"That man is to come with us," he said, pointing a gloved finger at the old monk. His voice was hard and clear. "Immediately. He's wanted for questioning."

Rake watched as the temple guards stepped forward and roughly dragged the monk back from the counter. The old man cast a quick glance over his shoulder as they pushed him toward the door.

"Send someone!" he shouted, grunting as one of the guards thumped a gloved fist into his stomach causing his legs to buckle. "Send some—" His words were cut off as another blow landed, this one to his ribs.

"Shut it," the flat-faced guard growled as they dragged the monk through the doors.

The leader was turning away when Rake called out, "Wait." The man paused, turned back, and cocked his head to one side. "What's he done? The old monk?" Rake asked, ignoring the man's air of mild annoyance.

The tall leader of the temple guards paused as if considering whether to answer at all. "Sedition," he said finally. "He has been spreading unfounded and slanderous stories that drag his order into disrepute." With that, he turned on his heel and strode from the watchhouse.

Rake stood for a moment. Just as the old monk had said, he felt something was just not right. He didn't like the guard. He was one of those cold, arrogant pricks who thought themselves above the law. He nodded slowly to himself. *Bugger them… I'm going to find out if there's anything to the old man's story.* "Melon!" he called to a young watchman who stood nearby.

"It's Marol, Sergeant," the boy grumbled as he approached the desk.

"Yes, of course it is." Rake waved away the protest. "Find Nils. I need to talk with him." Rake paused, remembering Nils' altercation with Otho that morning. "He may be at the apothecary. It's just off Water's Edge Road in the lower city." He looked up from the papers on the desk, irritated to find the young watchman still standing in front of him.

"Now!" he barked, pointing at the door.

Marol bolted for the exit, and Rake sighed as he realised that the crowd of impatient citizens were once again jostling for position.

"Right. Who's next?" he asked and groaned as several hands flew up.

The Temple Precinct

The corridor was quiet and cold, the marble of the walls and floor holding little heat. Two guards stood side by side, hands resting on the pommels of their swords. One was bearded, his build broad and stocky; the other was tall and slim. Their black armour was polished and gleamed in the light spilling through the high arched windows to their left.

"One more bell, and I'm off for two days," Vitus said softly while staring blankly at the heavy door of dark wood that led to the Chosen's chambers.

The stocky, bearded guard grunted, swivelling his eyes towards his tall companion. "Lucky bastard. I got three more days." He shot a glance over his left shoulder and sighed softly. "Three more gods-awful borin' days. But at least the bloody pay's good."

Vitus suppressed a smile and whispered, "Damn right. A boring day or two in this quiet passage buys me a bottle of Veranian red and a wench for a night. Much better than walking the perimeter in the rain for a couple of coppers." He turned slightly to his fellow guard with a ghost of a smile. "Or sharing the barracks with some bastard who snores like a bear."

"Oh, you can bugger right off." Albar whispered. "You sound like you're fuckin' garglin' nails most nights." He paused and flashed a crooked smile. "Point taken though… I'd take guardin' his lordship's salacious cavortin' any day over the perimeter." Albar paused once again and then turned slightly to Vitus. "But I'd rather go for a glass or two of Mittuan claret over that Veranian slop."

Vitus grinned. "Fucking clueless barbarian," he whispered, shaking his head. "What you make of that bit of crumpet we caught a glance of earlier? Looked like nobility."

"Nothin'," Albar hissed, his face suddenly serious. "I thought nothin'. And you would do well to do the same." He looked quickly to his companion. "We didn't see a damn thing. I've no need to be found floating face down by the docks."

"Gods, Albar, that was Linus." Vitus shook his head. "I can think of a dozen reasons for someone to have poked a hole in that idiot's back."

"Me too," Albar whispered. "But that was not even a day after he told that story of his lordship and his"—he nodded slightly toward the door—"activities."

"Bollocks, man," Vitus scoffed.

"Not bollocks." The stocky guard shook his head. "Bariuz walked past, and I am certain he overheard." He shot another glance at Vitus. "The next mornin', Linus was gone, and the watch found him floatin' by the docks."

"He got pissed and got into a fight," Vitus said, dismissing the insinuation. "Nothing more."

"Believe what you like," Albar hissed. Then he softened his tone and added "Just be careful about what you say, mate... and to who. Would be a shame if you missed out on quaffin' that Veranian piss and a tumble or two."

Vitus nodded slightly with a faint smile. Albar was a good friend and meant well. He was about to say as much when the doors in front of them flew open suddenly and Vasilios the Chosen stormed into the passage.

Both guards froze instantly. *Gods, the bastard heard us!* Vitus thought with a sinking feeling in his gut, imagining his leave, his pay, and possibly his job suddenly disappearing. This bastard was known for being particularly ruthless with even the slightest transgression.

"Get Captain Bariuz," the Chosen snapped. "Now!" Vitus blinked, and then broke into a run. "You," he heard the man bark at Albar, "come with me."

Bloody hell! Vitus thought as he sprinted down the passage towards the guardroom. *What the hell happened?*

Albar followed in the wake of the flustered priest. He stopped abruptly as he entered the spacious room. At first, all he saw was the utter luxury of the chambers—the polished wood, the vaulted ceiling, the billowing curtains, and the doors opening onto the wide balcony. He had never seen such opulence. How could a single person have so much? And then he noticed the crumpled bedclothes stained with blood, the dark puddle on the polished stone of the floor, and the smear marks leading to what looked like a large closet.

Albar's blood ran cold. *Oh, by Eresophi's tits, what the fuck has happened here?* he thought as fear settled like a stone into the pit of his stomach. Did someone try to kill the Chosen? He could see no visible wounds. Besides, there was too much blood. It looked like someone had been gutted. He and Vitus had heard nothing, not that that would mean a gods-damned thing if Bariuz thought they were somehow negligent. The bastard had disposed of Linus for far less.

The priest strode around frantically. He was cradling his left arm to his chest; his eyes were wide and crazed. *Shit, he is wounded,* Albar realised with despair. *Still far too much blood, though. Shit, shit, shit!*

"Where is Bariuz? Where is he?" the high priest asked, rounding on Albar.

"I… He…" the stocky guard stammered, caught unaware by the sudden outburst. "More than likely in the barracks, Your Grace. He should be here shortly."

The priest swore and stormed to a large cabinet that stood against one of the walls. He pulled open a door and snatched out a bottle, pulling the cork before throwing it aside. He slopped the wine into a goblet and then drained it in three quick swallows. He hardly paused before refilling the glass. "Watch the door!" the priest snapped, his voice raw with panic. Albar drew his sword and stepped towards the open doors. "No! Not too far. Stay where I can see you!"

"Yes, Your Grace." Albar nodded slowly and took a step back, turning so that he could see both the entrance and the crazed priest. *Where the bloody hell is Bariuz?*

Vitus shot a glance at Albar, who stood stone-faced, watching Vasilios the Chosen pace up and down. The priest was cradling his left arm, but it was not clear how he had been injured. His face was black with rage, but thankfully, the objects of his anger were the two guards he had sent for shortly after Vitus had arrived with the captain. Both stood stiffly to attention. Both looked decidedly pale.

Vitus was not friendly with either of them but remembered them from brief conversations in and around the barracks. The flat-faced, stupid-looking one was Cletus, if he remembered correctly, and the taller of the two was Sergius. *No, Silvius.* He remembered sharing a very expensive bottle of claret with Albar after he had won almost a month's salary from the man in a game of dice.

Vitus shifted his attention to Captain Bariuz. He stood just behind the priest, tall, bearded, and heavily muscled. His dark eyes bored into Cletus and Silvius. Bariuz was not a forgiving man at the best of times. Vitus did not want to be on his bad side. His stomach had been in knots on the run back to the barracks. He knew full well there would be hell to pay if there was any form of negligence to be found on his and Albar's part.

The captain had reacted quickly to Vitus' message, instantly assembling a detachment of ten guards and leading them, at a run, back to the Chosen's chambers. They had found Albar standing, sword drawn, just inside the door. His friend had looked visibly relieved at the sight of them, and when Vitus saw the raving, frantic priest and the blood on the covers of the bed and the floor, he understood why.

Vasilios had sent for Cletus and Silvius almost immediately. They had apparently been asked to watch someone in the priest's office, and for some reason, the priest wanted that person here. No one seemed to know why, but it was obvious they had not performed that task particularly well when they had arrived alone. For that, Vitus was infinitely grateful.

The priest stopped his pacing suddenly and rounded on the flat-faced Cletus, whose small, close-set eyes shot wide with surprise. He reminded Vitus of the type of man who would kick small dogs when no one was looking. He glanced at Albar once again, who responded with an almost imperceivable shake of his head. He could almost hear Albar's voice… *Looks like we're all right mate, thank the bloody gods, but those two arseholes may be goin' for a swim…*

"What do you mean he's gone?" Vitus flinched as the priest shouted suddenly at Cletus, spittle causing the man to blink. "I told you to keep him in my office!"

"I… we…" Cletus started to reply, then hissed in pain as the priest grabbed a fistful of his hair, twisting his head down and dragging his face closer.

"He was supposed to be kept… in… my… OFFICE!" Vasilios shouted into Cletus' face before shoving the guard away from him. The priest shifted his attention to Silvius who seemed to visibly wilt under the black glare.

"My apologies, Your Grace," Silvius swallowed nervously. "But he… ahh…threatened us…"

Vasilios blinked and shook his head, as if not quite understanding the words.

At this, Cletus cleared his throat, his fleshy lips twisting in a petulant, almost wounded manner. "We did not want an... uh... incident in the temple," he mumbled.

"Incident?" Vasilios the Chosen said softly. "Threatened... threatened by a *monk*?" He threw the empty wine goblet he had been holding at the luckless Cletus. The man blinked as the glass missed his head by a hair's breadth to shatter on the wall behind him.

Vitus watched as the seething priest stepped back and closed his eyes, tilting his face upward toward the ceiling. Vasilios chewed on his lower lip and was visibly fighting for control. *Gods... he may kill them right here,* Vitus thought with sick fascination, wondering once again what this monk might be privy to. He caught himself as he imagined Albar's reaction to the question; *You don't want to know, mate. You really don't want to know...*

No, Vitus silently agreed with his friend as he imagined the sudden, sharp pain of cold steel punching into his back, followed by a short drop and the cold dark water of the docks closing around his body. *I really don't.*

Vasilios opened his eyes and stared at the vaulted ceiling of his chambers. He almost shivered with the blinding rage that coursed through him. The burns on his arm ached, and the loss of Desana seemed to claw at his chest. The monk had somehow known about the church. *But how much does he know? Does he know about the girl? What about the stones—does he know of them? Or worse... does the monk suspect what I intend to accomplish through the stones?* He took in a deep breath and tried to slow his racing mind. *Is he in league with the woman? Probable... she knew about the stones! And what of the other woman, Jasmijn?* It was unravelling, and he had to do something—now.

He opened his eyes and lowered his gaze to the two guards who stood like statues in front of him. The gods alone knew what, but the monk knew something. *But does he know enough to...* Vasilios' brow furrowed. *Enough to what? Extort money from me? Threaten to expose me? But to what end?* It was infuriating. And what made things infinitely worse was the fact that the idiot guards let him go!

"Bariuz," he said softly without turning. "I need you to find the monk. Take these two fools with you. They know what he looks like."

"Your Grace," Vasilios heard Bariuz's deep voice say, "should I bring him here once we've found him?"

Vasilios paused and then stepped in close to the captain. He turned his face away from the others and lowered his voice to barely a whisper.

"No. I don't want him here. I want you to make sure he doesn't... spread his lies... to anyone. Do you understand, Captain?"

"Yes, Your Grace."

"And once you have taken care of the monk, there's another task I need done." He paused, remembering what the woman in the dark had told him. "There's a tavern wench. A Noordlander who goes by the name of Jasmijn. You'll find her at the Crow Inn..." He stopped at the captain's expression. "I don't need you to understand. I need you to follow orders."

The Captain nodded, and Vasilios continued, "Get the woman, but do it quietly. I need her brought to the old church after dark." He pressed a finger into the captain's chest. "Use the warehouse. Hold her there until nightfall. And, Captain, I cannot emphasise enough how important this is." He turned his head and lowered his voice even further. "Once this is done, I will have no need for those two. I don't ever want to set eyes on either of them again."

Bariuz's eyes followed the Chosen's gaze to the two miserable guards. He nodded, his face hard and grim.

Vasilios stepped back and held the captain's eye for a long moment before he turned away. "Leave these two with me." He pointed to Albar and Vitus. "And send for the physician. I have need of him."

"The physician is out of the city, Your Grace... family business," Bariuz answered. "But I will send for an apothecary I have used many times when I've needed a man stitched up. He is very skilled."

Vasilios paused and then nodded. "Very well. Have him sent to my office within the hour."

The Watchhouse

As Feris was pushed roughly through the doors, he glanced at the guard to his right. He remembered the flat-faced, petulant pout from earlier that morning. The pout was now a twisted, ugly scowl. *No doubt the aftermath of letting me leave,* Feris thought with black humour.

"Move," the guard growled and shoved Feris hard enough to make him stagger forward. His foot caught the edge of the top step, and he fell heavily down the stone stairs and into the street. Feris rolled onto his back as pain flared in his shoulder and hip. *Should have expected that,* he thought as he started to push himself upward. He hadn't managed to get far when rough hands dragged him to his feet. He found himself staring into angry, close-set eyes.

"Did your mother drop you on your face as a child?" Feris grated through the pain, "Or were you born like that?" He grunted and doubled over as a fist slammed into his gut. Once again, the rough hands dragged him upright, and he braced himself for the next blow.

"Cletus!" barked a harsh voice. Feris turned his attention to the captain, who was striding down the steps. The captain glared at the guard who held Feris' robe in bunched fists. "Look around you, you fool," he hissed. Several people had stopped and were watching with keen interest. "Bring him," the captain commanded before turning on his heel and walking swiftly down the avenue.

Cletus paused for a second, his fleshy lips twisting in impotent anger, and then pushed Feris forward but with far less enthusiasm this time. "Move it," the man growled, grabbing a fistful of Feris' robe with a spiteful tug.

This is not going to end well, Feris thought, his body aching from the fall. He had no doubt now that the bastard Vasilios had been involved in the girl's disappearance. He felt a pang of sorrow as he thought of her little face, more often than not muddy and frightened. He sighed. She was such a delicate thing. She had deserved so much more, and he had not done enough.

With an effort he turned his attention back to the present. Where was he being taken? Back to the temple? He doubted that. He had a cold feeling that it would be a dark alley and a knife in the back. The watch would find him in the mud somewhere and write it off as a robbery gone wrong.

He hoped the sergeant would at least investigate. The man had seemed skeptical but reasonable. He must have thought that the temple guards arresting him was strange... *Even for a seditious old heathen like me,* Feris thought. Anger and frustration surged through him. If that bastard could kill Lidi, he would kill others. He needed to be stopped. The unanswered question, though, was why. It nagged at Feris. Why would he abduct a child? To what end?

The thought was cut short as he was shoved to his left. He hadn't noticed the captain turn from the main avenue onto a narrow, far quieter street. Old houses loomed on either side. In between them, dark warehouses seemed quiet and empty. There were far fewer people in the street now as well.

Not long now, Feris thought as he looked at the guards who surrounded him. Two flanked him; the flat-faced one still held a fistful of his robe at the shoulder. Not that it made a difference. He was never a runner, not even in his youth. One more was at his back, and the captain walked with another two more in front of them.

The captain struck him as a hard man. His eyes were cold, and his face had an arrogant twist to it. But he carried himself well. Definitely a career man-at-arms. *Definitely not one to trifle with,* Feris thought. The others looked the part, except for the flat-faced bastard who had thrown him down the stairs. That one had a weak, cowardly look about him. A cruel, stupid face and a soft body. If there was weakness in the group, it was there.

"Here," the captain said suddenly, pointing to the large weathered doors of a warehouse. He drew a brass key from a pouch on his sword belt. The lock was well oiled and turned easily. He swung the door open, and Feris found himself pushed inside the gloomy interior. The dull echo of the doors being closed reverberated through the vast empty room.

Feris turned to the guards, who moved to flank the captain. He looked at them with scorn and not a little disappointment. He was a veteran of Wadi al S'hakh and countless other battles. He had thought himself immortal at one point—when he was young and very stupid. But the years of tending the gardens at the temple had shown him another path. He was not afraid of death; he just never thought he would be here again, at the business end of a sharp blade.

He took a deep breath, knowing he would not make it out of this warehouse alive. Years ago, in a different life, there was a chance that he would have taken one or two of these bastards with him. *A slim chance, even then, old man,* he corrected himself.

An odd mix of heightened awareness and peace settled over him as he looked at his killers. He remembered waiting on the edges of battle with his senses sharpened to a keen edge. Even now, after so many years, the feeling had not dulled. He noticed the small movements of the men in front of him, how they stood, how their weapons hung from their belts. He could almost see how the fight would play out.

The flat-faced guard, Cletus, had a thumb hooked into his belt. It was his sword arm, and it would slow him down when he tried to draw the blade. The hilt of his dagger tilted forward, making it easier to grab. But most importantly, the man was still angry; his blunt, pig-like features were twisted in a black glare. It would affect his judgement, causing him to over compensate. Moving too fast was as dangerous as moving too slowly. It would provide openings.

Feris remembered the guard to the left of Cletus from the temple. He was taller, with a slighter build. He blinked nervously, and there was a faint sheen of sweat on his forehead. He fidgeted and seemed to be almost wringing the pommel of his sword with his gloved right hand. The sword hung on his right hip, and from the angle Feris had little doubt the man was left-handed. He would need to reach across his body to draw the sword. The movement would be slow, and the sword would be dragged away from Feris as it cleared the scabbard.

The remaining guards and the captain stood off to the left and a few steps behind behind the other two. They seemed to be almost deliberately creating space, but they looked ready. There was no weakness there. They would need to close the distance to strike, but Feris had no doubt they would be fast. *Fast enough?* He wondered. Ten years ago, he would have guessed not... but ten years ago, he was not Feris, a monk who tended gardens, replacing sword and armour with roses and books.

"What are you waiting for?" Feris growled. "Get it over with."

The captain opened his mouth, but before he could say anything Feris lunged forward. The flat-face guard's eyes flew open in surprise, and he grabbed for his sword. As Feris predicted, the movement was slow and clumsy. He caught the man's wrist and grabbed the guard's dagger from its sheath. In a swift, fluid movement, he slashed the blade upward cutting off the man's ear. The man squealed in pain and staggered backward, clutching at the side of his head.

"Get him!" Feris heard the captain roar.

The others surged forward, drawing their swords. Feris ignored them and hurled the dagger at the guard to his right. The man had just managed to drag his sword free of the scabbard when then blade struck him in the shoulder. The guard grunted in pain and staggered backward, his sword falling from his grasp.

Feris lunged for the falling blade, his hand closing around the leather of the hilt as the first blow struck. There was a sharp tearing sensation in his side. He hissed in pain and twisted toward the blow, feeling the blade snag in his cassock. He gripped the sword, the sharp steel slicing deep into his fingers. He ignored the pain and swung his own blade down hard as the guard staggered forward, off-balance. The flat of the blade struck the man solidly at the base of his skull. The steel rang from the blow, and the guard pitched forward, slamming face-first into the floor, unconscious.

Feris staggered backward as another ripping, burning explosion of pain erupted in his stomach. He grabbed the man's wrist, locking his sword thrust in place, and rammed the guard of the sword into the man's face, breaking his nose. The sword was ripped free from his stomach as the man staggered backward, followed by a warm gout of blood. Feris tottered on legs that suddenly felt weak. His sword slipped from his fingers and clattered to the floor. The world seemed to tilt wildly to one side, and he crashed into the stone of the warehouse floor.

The warm, metallic taste of blood filled his mouth as his face rested on the cold stone. Each breath was short and shallow. *Just winded by the fall,* he thought as he watched the dark boots of the captain draw closer.

Feris tried to raise his head but found, to his surprise, that he could not. There was a creak of leather as the man sat on his haunches.

"You are more than you seem, monk," the captain said without emotion. He tugged at Feris' sleeve where it had ridden up to expose the criss-crossed white scars on his forearm. "Soldier? A mercenary, perhaps?"

"Maybe... you should have...paid more... attention," Feris graded through the pain. "A few years... ago... would have... killed every one... of you poncing... bastards."

"No doubt." The captain smiled.

The old monk blinked. There was a light behind the captain. A small figure stood there, wreathed in the soft glow. He felt a gentle warmth flow into him and a hand touching his cheek. There was the scent of a rose. *Lidi?*

Come, Syrio, her voice pulsed. *It's time to go... Let go...*

*I've not gone by that name in years... I left that behind... My name is Feris...*He thought he heard a soft laugh at that.

Oh no, my dear Syrio. You cannot be what you are not. For all that is will rage against such a state until it is no more... The roses were part of you long before you learned to tend them. Come now... He felt a deep love settle over him and flow through him. *Let go...*

"I'll see you in hell, old man," he heard the captain's voice say, as if from a vast distance.

"No..." Syrio managed to croak with a bloody smile. "I don't think so..."

Water's Edge, the Lower City

"I'd better get back to the watch," Nils said, placing the cup on the table. "I have a bad feeling that we're going to be rather busy."

Amon paused before lifting his own cup to his mouth and swallowing down the fiery spirit. "Busy? Yes... I suppose that is one way to put it."

"How else would you like to put it?" Nils asked, the annoyance apparent in his voice. "There's not much else we can do until we find who has these stones of yours and what they intend to do with them." Nils paused and ran his hand over his face. When he looked up, his expression was bleak. "And no, we can't just leave. If what you say is true, people will die. I can't let that happen."

"People are going to die no matter what you decide to do." Amon grunted and reached for the liquor, then slopped a generous amount of it into his mug. He pushed the cork back into the bottle and paused. "I hope I am wrong. More than you could ever imagine." He took the mug and lifted it to his mouth, but before he could drink, there was a knock at the door.

Both men looked up, and then Nils looked at the apothecary. "A client?"

"More than likely," Amon replied. He placed the mug on the table and eased himself out of the chair, wincing at the sharp pain in his hip. Nils reached out a hand to offer support, but the apothecary stopped him with a wave. "No, no... I'm all right. The cold and rain just seem to get into this hip a little more each year." He forced a smile. "A small price to pay, my friend, for my many, many sins. Let me see who this is." He shuffled painfully to the door and pulled it open to see a young watchman standing outside. "Ahh... You'd be looking for Nils," Amon said, stepping back and motioning for him to enter.

The young man blinked in surprise and then blurted. "Yes... Um... thank you, sir."

"Who is it?" Nils asked, standing up.

"One of your fellows. Come now," Amon said, reaching out when the young man remained standing just inside the doorway and pulling him into the room by his collar. Nils smiled as he recognised Marol.

"It's Marol, sir."

"Yes. I know." Nils said, his smile broadening. "How can I help, Marol?"

The young man blinked, as if surprised by the sound of his own name. "Oh... I... Sergeant Rake sent me," the young man said, nervously straightening his shirt.

"Rake sent you? About what?" Nils asked; his expression grew serious.

"Um... he said it was about the old church, sir." Marol answered. "Apparently, a little girl went missing. There was this old priest... or a monk... I'm not sure. He came down to the watch with a story of a little girl who lived on the streets around there. Got pretty upset before these temple guards came along and dragged him off. Sergeant Rake thought it was rather strange and sent me to tell you right away."

Amon shot a glance at Nils and was about to comment when the watchman shook his head slightly before turning back to Marol. He forced a smile. "Thanks, son. Run back to the sergeant and tell him I'll look into it. Go on." He waved at the door.

"Thank you, sir." Marol smiled nervously and all but bolted out the door.

Amon slowly closed the door and turned to Nils. "The girl is dead," The Apothecary said gravely. "And it happened in or around that church. I'm sure of it."

"One of those creatures?" Nils asked.

"Perhaps," Amon said, tight-lipped. "Or... whoever is using the stones needed..." He paused.

"Needed what?" Nils asked quietly.

"Payment," Amon said softly, unable to meet the watchman's eyes.

"Oh, gods." Nils turned away, and when he turned back, his eyes were piercing. "You mean a sacrifice."

"Yes," Amon forced out the word and rubbed at the scar on his face. He saw the watchman's unspoken accusation in the cold glare. "And no... I have not." He looked down at the floor. "But I know of others who did... many times. My sin is that I did not stop them."

Nils stood frozen and then let out a slow breath. "I need to get back to the watch and speak with Tibero. We need to find this person—now." The watchman moved towards the door, and Amon reached for his arm.

"Yes. But we must also find the stones... and the gateway. It must be closed. You have no idea what this person can summon with a blood sacrifice."

Nils nodded slowly. "We find the person and we find the stones." He paused. "If this person is connected to the temple we may be dealing with someone very powerful. Not just anyone can send the temple guards to drag away a troublesome monk away from the watchhouse."

"That is going to make things very difficult," Amon said softly. "Are you sure about not leaving? I'm inclined to take a ship across the Great Sea and put as many miles between me and this city as possible."

Nils' face darkened, but before he could answer, there was another sharp knock on the door.

"Another customer?" the watchman asked icily, nodding towards the door.

"On any other day, I would say yes," Amon replied. "But as things stand..." He moved to the door and pulled it open. A temple guard in black and silver armour stood at the steps.

"How can I help?" Amon asked as he stepped forward, pulling the door closed slightly to hide Nils from the guard's view. He motioned with the hand that was hidden for Nils to move closer so that he could hear the guard's voice clearly.

"His Grace, Vasilios the Chosen, requests your presence," the temple guard said, his voice clipped and decidedly unfriendly. "Immediately."

"May I ask for what reason?" Amon asked.

The guard frowned, apparently annoyed that the apothecary had the audacity to ask a question. "To treat a wound," he said abruptly.

"And the nature of the wound?" Amon asked, ignoring the edge in the man's tone.

"Does that matter? His Grace is not one to be kept waiting," the guard bristled.

"Undoubtedly," Amon said dryly. "And it most certainly matters. I need to know what type of wound I am being asked to treat. How else can I pack the appropriate medicines?"

The guard flushed and opened his mouth, then bit back the angry retort with visible effort. "It's a burn. Circling his lower arm."

"Anything else?" Amon asked, outwardly ignoring the man's obvious frustration.

"I noticed blood on his shoulder," the guard said after a moment. "Possibly a cut… or a gouge."

"Thank you." Amon nodded. "Wait there. I'll be out shortly." He closed the door before the man could protest.

The apothecary rested his hand on the door and hung his head. He took a very slow, deep breath. He felt nauseated. *Say nothing… Just say nothing.* The desperate thought ran over and over in his mind, and then he sighed and turned to Nils. "I think we may have our man," he said softly.

"How do you know?" Nils asked. "Those injuries could have been caused by almost anything."

Amon moved past Nils to take a small bag from a shelf. He placed linen wraps and several small glass jars into the bag, then pulled the draw string tight and turned to the watchman. His face was grim, his eyes empty. "This girl-child goes missing. A monk or a priest reports this to the watch. But before anything can be done, he is taken away by temple guards. You said only a person of influence could arrange that. And now here we have another guard asking me to treat a burn on the arm of one of the Chosen."

"Why is the burn important?" Nils asked.

Amon reached down and pulled back his right sleeve. Pale, twisted scars wound around his lower arm. "The man… the creature… that stole the stones gave me these scars," he said softly.

The Temple Precinct

The walk to the temple precinct was slow and painful. The guard had remained stone-faced and taciturn, but that suited Amon. He had no want or need to talk to the man. His stomach churned, and he was desperately trying to crush the rising fear that threatened to overcome him. He had promised Nils he would examine the man's wounds. They needed to be sure before they acted, but what they could actually do if their fears were realised escaped him entirely.

284

The man was one of the most powerful people in the city. He had a small army at his disposal, and he had the stones. He could literally open the doors to hell and destroy anyone or anything that stood in his way. There was simply no way this man would simply surrender the stones. At best, he would have the two of them thrown into prison on the grounds that they were both completely and dangerously insane; contemplating the worst things that came to mind made him want to vomit.

He gripped the outside of his hip as he hobbled painfully up the stairs, through the archway of the main entrance flanked by massive iron doors, and into the cool interior of the temple complex. Their steps echoed on the polished marble as they made their way to a wide curved staircase.

Gods, more bloody stairs, Amon thought bitterly, the pain now stabbing into his hip. He struggled on but still somehow managed to be impressed by the incredible beauty of the building. He had only ever observed the massive structure, with its towering minarets, from outside on the street. Now he marvelled at the golden light streaming into the vast chamber from the massive arched windows high above them.

They walked past rich tapestries and paintings that hung from the walls, as well as a multitude of lush, flowering plants that spilled from massive pots of polished silver filling the air with their soft scent. *Such incredible wealth...* He shook his head thinking of the countless people who offered up almost everything they had to petition the gods. He was not sure the gods had much to do with how that wealth was spent or what else happened within these walls.

"Move it," the guard growled, cutting into his thoughts.

Amon started and realised that he had slowed to take in the breathtaking splendour. He winced at the stab of pain as he once again quickened his pace. The guard turned left into a wide corridor. Here, they walked past several priests, most dressed in flowing robes of purple and white, with two older priests in robes of red and gold. None paid them any attention. The guard walked on and eventually stopped in front of an ornate door of dark wood and iron. He paused to straighten his cloak and then knocked lightly.

"Enter," Amon heard a voice command.

The guard opened the door and pushed Amon into a richly adorned office. A pale man with dark hair sat behind a large desk, cradling his left arm to his chest. A glass of wine and a half-empty bottle sat in front of the priest. Splashes of the red liquid stained the wood of the desk, speaking of hasty or careless pouring. Sweat beaded on the man's forehead, and he looked to be in pain. His eyes darted around, almost as if he expected someone... *or something...* to appear.

He's absolutely terrified, Amon thought with a sinking feeling in his gut. He had never wanted to be more wrong in his entire life. But looking at the man, he knew. He had seen that look before—a burning, driving need to run, coupled with the blunt, cold horror of knowing there was simply nowhere to run to. The last time Amon had seen that look, it had been his reflection in the mirror. The time before that had been in the eyes of Erub basuri'Davaa before the coward ran away from the horror he had unleashed.

"The apothecary, Your Grace," the guard said simply, head bowed.

"Good. Leave," the Chosen said abruptly, waving his hand at the guard.

The door clicked behind the departing guard, and the priest looked up. "What is your name?" he asked, lifting the glass and draining it in three quick swallows.

"I am Amon, Your Grace. I am an apothecary with much skill in healing. How may I help you?" Amon said evenly. He was surprised at how steady his voice sounded, given the powerful mix of fear and anger that coursed through his body. This fool had put every soul in the city in peril… and for what? Power, position? It did not matter.

The priest hesitated and then pulled back his sleeve. Amon felt a chill as he looked at the angry, blistered flesh of the man's arm. He could make out the distinct pattern of fingers. Pain flashed through his own arm, and he drew a slow breath. He could feel a trickle of sweat run down his back. *Calm yourself.* He stepped closer to examine the wound. Then he looked up at the man's face. He could see the terror and the madness writhing behind those dark eyes. *How am I going to get the stones? Where have you hidden them, you bastard? Are they here? I know you would keep them close… very close…*

"Are there any other wounds, Your Grace?" he asked finally.

The priest eyed him suspiciously and then reached up and pulled his shirt away from his left shoulder, revealing a series of puncture wounds and deep scratches. Amon stood rooted to the floor. *And you've lost control. You used the stones, you dangerous fool… and you have no idea what you've done.* The thoughts roiled through his mind as he found himself being pulled between two almost uncontrollable urges: to run, and to get as far away from this mad man as possible, or kill him. He couldn't escape before; the web of power had wrapped itself so tightly around him that he had almost paid for it with his life. *I may yet still pay,* Amon thought coldly.

"Are you just going to stand there?" the priest asked bluntly as he tugged his shirt down and slopped more wine into his glass.

"My apologies, Your Grace," Amon said, snapping back to the present. He placed his bag on the desk, tugged at the drawstring, opened it, and removed a small glass jar and a roll of oiled gauze. "I will tend to the burn first. Then I will examine the wounds on your shoulder. I need to clean them, and I think some may need stitching."

Vasilios winced as the apothecary smeared a cold, green ointment onto the burns. The man worked carefully and methodically; but not once did he look up or try to engage in conversation. The priest took another gulp of wine and watched as the apothecary started to wrap the wound in oiled gauze. His arm felt much better already, but there was something about the man that bothered Vasilios. He looked almost angry… on edge. The was a palpable intensity about the man. *Like he wants to run from the room… or…* Vasilios cut the train of thought off, unwilling to plumb those darker depths. *Perhaps he has never tended to anyone of my station before. No, that's not it.* The thoughts roiled and spilled over each other. *How does Bariuz know this man? Oh, yes. He worked on some of the guards He must have done good work for the Captain to recommend him…*

The apothecary was now wrapping his arm in a dry bandage. Vasilios watched each precise movement, the concentration, the overlapping layers… the crooked scar that ran down his face. Vasilios blinked. *Why would an apothecary have such a wound?* It made the outside of the man's left eye droop slightly. *An accident, perhaps. But it looks like a blade cut. How well does Bariuz know this man? Should I have guards in here?* Vasilios stiffened at the thought. *Am I in danger?*

"My apologies, Your Grace," the man said, his voice even but devoid of any emotion. He stopped wrapping Vasilios' arm and looked up into his eyes. "Is the wrap too tight?"

"No," Vasilios snapped, breaking eye contact. "No. Carry on."

He watched as the man took a small scissors from the bag and split the end of the bandage to create two strands, which he then wrapped around Vasilios' arm and tied to hold the dressing in place. *What else do you have in that bag?* The dark thought slithered through Vasilios' mind as he reached for the wineglass. He watched the man closely as he upended the glass before placing it back on the desk. He wiped his chin. *How well do I know Bariuz?* he thought. *A resourceful man… lowborn, of course, but ambitious… and useful… but how ambitious?*

"Your Grace?"

Vasilios looked at the apothecary, who had apparently said something . "What?" he asked abruptly. The man was looking at him. His eyes were intense. The drooping eyelid gave him an almost manic look. Suddenly, Vasilios felt very much like a deer in the company of a wolf. Vasilios shifted slightly. He felt quite trapped in the chair.

"Could you please sit up, Your Grace?" the Apothecary asked. "I need to examine the wounds in your shoulder."

Vasilios eyed the man suspiciously and then sat up and allowed him to pull back his shirt. The man probed the edges of one of the puncture wounds. Vasilios hissed in pain. "Careful, you fool!" he snapped.

"My apologies, Your Grace," the man said evenly. "I need to make sure there's nothing trapped inside the wound. If anything is left in the wound and not removed, the wound can putrefy. This would poison your blood, which would result in fever… even death."

"Inside the wound? Poison?" Vasilios turned his head to look carefully at the man. "Like what?"

"Like a fragment of cloth, Your Grace," the man said carefully. "Or a chip of a…" The man hesitated.

"A chip of what?" Vasilios asked slowly. *What do you know? Why did you not continue speaking? Afraid perhaps that you'd give yourself away?* Vasilios' breath caught at the last thought. *Why are you really here? Why did the captain send you?*

"A chip of a claw… or a tooth," the man continued. His eyes were piercing. "I've seen many wounds inflicted by… wild animals… before, Your Grace."

Vasilios chewed on his bottom lip. *Should I call for the guard? What if the captain sent this man to find out about…* He paused. *Find out about what?* he thought as a cold feeling settled into his stomach… *The stones? How could he know of them? No one knows anything about them. There is no mention in any library, in any book… I searched for months and found nothing. It took ages to unlock their power. No… it cannot be the stones. Perhaps the blood on my bed and the floor of my chambers? The captain had asked nothing, but that doesn't mean he had no interest. How could he use the knowledge against me? What would he want? Gold? Leverage? Does he suspect my own ambitions… my intention for the Prime?* The thoughts ran like wildfire through his mind. *How well do I really know the captain? Why did he send you?*

"Your Grace? May I continue?" the Apothecary asked. "It will be… uncomfortable."

"Yes." Vasilios nodded, clenching his teeth. "Do it."

The Watchhouse

Tibero sat slumped back in his chair and stared blankly at the door. His left hand rested on his desk, a half-empty tumbler of emberwyne nestled between his fingers. Not for the first time, he wondered why he bothered to carry on. He had no time for the chaotic mess that lay beyond his office. The whole damn city seemed hellbent on stealing, raping, and killing, and there was very little he could do about it. It was like trying to empty the ocean with a bucket.

He sighed and lifted the glass, draining it in a single swallow. He grimaced at the sharp bite of the liquor while scratching at the ginger stubble under his chin. Dealing with this shit was better suited to some young idealist like Nils. The man was damn good and utterly relentless. *May the gods help you if he is on your trail,* Tibero thought. It wouldn't matter if you'd stolen a brass bean or murdered the king; he'd hunt you down either way with the same dogged, bloody-minded focus.

Tibero pulled open the drawer to his desk and retrieved the bottle of emberwyne. He drew the cork with his teeth and slopped a generous portion into his glass before returning the bottle and pushing the drawer shut with his finger. Hetta would tell him he was drinking too much if she were still here. *And I would be inclined to agree with you, my love,* he thought as he lifted the glass in a silent toast. *But if you were here to tell me that, I wouldn't be sitting here mildly pissed and alone like some morose, useless tosser now would I?* He lifted the glass to his mouth and swallowed half of its contents before slamming it back onto the desk, causing a fair bit of the liquid to splash over his hand.

"Bugger," he growled and sucked at his fingers. "Now look what you made me do," he grumbled to the empty office as he wiped away the spilled emberwyne from the surface of his desk with the palm of his hand. He dried his hand on his leggings and settled back into the chair. He felt completely trapped between the noise of a job he had come to hate and the silence of an empty home that he had come to dread. He sighed deeply and was about to reach for the drawer to refill the glass when there was a rap on the door. *What now?* he thought bleakly, shifting the half-empty tumbler out of sight.

"Enter," he barked, sitting up straighter and shifting his chair closer to the desk. Nils entered, and Tibero caught himself involuntarily running his fingers through his unruly mop of hair, as if in anticipation of the frustration to come. *By the gods, what have you dug up now?* he thought, immediately craving another drink.

"Nils. What is it?" he asked gruffly, not wanting to hear the answer.

"The body we found. I may have some information."

Tibero sighed deeply and pinched at his eyes with his thumb and forefinger. "What information?" He pointed at a chair and watched as Nils dragged it away from the desk and sat down. His eyes felt like they were filled with sand, and he became aware of a dull ache at the base of his skull. Nils seemed adept at creating these reactions.

"There may be a link between the victim and a missing person… that may involve a high-ranking temple official," Nils said, his voice annoyingly matter-of-fact.

Tibero struggled to keep his face blank as he fought off a sudden wave of nausea. It was like blandly announcing a death sentence. *Oh, and by the way, we're going to chop off your head.* He definitely didn't want to hear where this was going, and he knew Nils was determined enough to kick open that particular ant nest regardless of the consequences. He cleared his throat. "To be clear, this has to do with the body we found in the Dockway Alley?"

"Yes."

"The one that looked like it had been chewed on by a dog?"

Nils paused before nodding slowly.

Tibero blinked and then ran his fingers through his ginger mop. "All right…" He nodded slowly before taking a deep breath. "Continue."

"There was a report of a missing girl this morning. An old monk reported it to Sergeant Rake. Someone saw a man in a black cloak and red robes take the girl to the old church on Quay Road. She has not been seen since." Nils shifted, as if thinking about how to continue. "While this monk was talking to Rake, several temple guards came in and took him away." Nils paused before continuing carefully. "Not just anyone can just send a detachment of guards from the temple, so it was probably someone of *considerable* rank."

Tibero clamped his jaw shut and sagged back into his chair. *Red robes,* he thought sourly. That would be one of the Chosen. *Gods, this man will be the death of me.* Tibero stared at Nils without saying a word, his mind racing. Situations like this could end with someone floating in the harbour. The gods alone knew how many of those unlucky bastards he had fished out over the years. *Where, by Eresophi's scaly tits, does he see this going? The watch goes marching into the temple precinct to arrest one of the bloody Chosen? Interrogate the Prime? Gods, I should just cut my own throat and throw myself into the bloody harbour… save everyone the time.*

Tibero pursed his lips and stared at the younger man for a long moment. Nils was not one for high drama, no matter how wild a turn this particular story was taking. "And?" he forced himself to say.

"And nothing," Nils replied. "That's all I've got… at the moment."

"We can't just go traipsing into the Temple with some"—Tibero waved his hand in front of his face—"theory." Nils nodded, that infuriating calm not slipping for a second. "I need more," Tibero finally growled. There was no way that Nils would let this go. In some cases, it was just simpler to ride the bear rather than having it jump out unexpectedly.

"I know," Nils replied. "I may have that information within a few hours."

Tibero ground his teeth together. "And how would you… never mind. I don't want to know."

"I will need a few men," Nils said. "Two to look into the church. More than that if we need to… talk to someone at the temple."

"No one is talking to anyone at the temple until we have a lot more to work with, and at this point, we have nothing," Tibero groused. Then he sighed and continued, "We can look into the old church… see if we can find out anything about the missing girl."

Nils nodded.

"But we're thin on the ground with the morning and afternoon shifts." Tibero shook his head. "I already had to call Druk and Lem back from leave. They're watching the Crow, making sure the body count doesn't escalate."

Nils nodded again. "And Rake's at the desk. What about Sev? Otho?"

Tibero nodded slowly. "That could work. Sev'll be back later. And they could take Melon… The boy could use a bit of experience."

"Thank you." Nils pushed the chair back and stood.

Tibero waved him away, already thinking of the emberwyne in the drawer. By all the gods, he could do with a drink. "Nils," Tibero called to the younger man as he reached the door. "Tread lightly."

The Temple Precinct

Amon turned away from the priest and reached into his bag. He found a slim set of tweezers, a small bottle of clear spirits, and some wadding. His fingers strayed to another bottle. The cork stopper on this one was painted red. It was the distilled venom of a night adder. All he needed to do was dab this into one of the priest's open wounds, and the man would be dead within minutes. *Kill him.* Amon's fingers closed around the small bottle *Kill him and be done with it. But what of the stones? What if you can't find them, you fool? Then killing the priest will change nothing…* He pushed aside the poison, and picked up another bottle of clear spirits, and turned back to the priest, who was looking at him intently. Amon could almost see the black madness swimming behind the man's eyes. He stepped toward the priest.

"This will burn, Your Grace," Amon said as he dampened the wadding with the spirits. "I need to clean the wounds."

The priest stiffened as he started to apply the wadding to the first puncture. A slow dribble of blood started flowing down the man's chest, and Amon wiped it away to get a clear view of the wound. He took the tweezers in his right hand and held the wound open with the thumb and forefinger of his left. Carefully, he pushed the tips of the tweezers into the hole and started to probe.

"Gods! Damn it," the priest hissed as he stiffened with the pain.

After what seemed like an eternity, Amon felt the tips close around something hard. Carefully, he applied pressure. Then satisfied that he had a good grip on the fragment, he eased it from the wound. Amon held it up with strangely steady fingers. The small white fragment looked very much like the tip of a claw.

"What is it?" Amon heard the priest ask. "Tell me, man!"

Amon looked at the white-faced priest. The sweat of pain glistened on the man's forehead. Blood had run down his chest from the wound and joined the flecks of wine in staining his shirt. Amon stepped away from him and looked back to the tiny sliver of bone. *Where are the stones you fool? You used them, and now you've lost control. Reckless bastard! Nothing is worth what you've done…*

"I found the fragment, Your Grace," he heard himself say as his mind raced. "Now I need to stitch the wound." He moved to the desk and reached into his bag. *Needle and thread… stitch the wound, leave, and get to Nils.* His hand touched the red-stoppered bottle. *Or kill the dangerous bastard now. The stones must be here; he would never allow them out of his sight. They must be here…*

"What did you find?" he heard the priest ask. Amon ignored the question and closed his fingers around the small bottle of poison. *Kill him! Kill him now!*

"What did you find?" Amon heard the priest's chair scape against the floor as the man stood; his voice was now low and menacing. Amon started to turn when a hand closed sharply around his throat and he felt his head being dragged backward. He froze as something very sharp pressed into his back.

"Why are you here?" the priest's voice hissed into his ear. "Who sent you? Was it the captain? What do you know?"

Amon grunted in pain as the point of the blade punctured the skin of his back. He could feel the warm trickle of blood snake down. The pain in his hip flared white-hot as the priest dragged him away from the table. All the while, the hand stayed clamped on Amon's throat.

"Last chance," the priest snarled, twisting the blade point into Amon's flesh. "What do you know?"

The pain was excruciating, and Amon sucked in a breath through clenched teeth. "I know you... have the stones," he said and felt the priest stiffen. "You need to know... they will kill you... and many more." Amon groaned as the point of the blade dug deeper into his back. "I can... help you."

He felt the pressure of the dagger ease and the grip on his throat relax. "I can help," Amon said softly.

"No."

How can a single word be filled with such utter despair? Amon thought as the grip on his throat tightened.

"No... you can't."

Pain exploded in Amon's back. *Should have killed him, you fool,* Amon thought as the darkness crashed over him.

Vasilios dropped the bloody dagger to the floor and looked at the crumpled body of the apothecary. He lifted his trembling, bloody hands and tried to make sense of what he was seeing. He had just killed the man. But he had no choice. The apothecary would have exposed him, and he was so close. Just a little more time was all he needed, and this whole affair would be of no consequence. *A little more time...* He started pacing around the office. *I need just a little more time...*

He stopped and looked up at the door with a sudden chill. No, there were no guards posted outside; no one would have heard anything. *I should simply leave, lock the door, and take care of this afterwards.* He looked back to his bloody hands. There were stains on his shirt as well. *Shit... shit, shit, shit.* He balled his fists, and his body shook with the effort to suppress the urge to scream in impotent rage. He forced his hands open and dragged in a deep breath.

Leave... take care of this later. Vasilios stripped off the shirt and threw it onto the desk, which sent the Apothecary's bag flying off the side. He lunged forward but far too late to stop the bag and its contents from falling to the floor. He dropped to his knees and started scraping several small instruments, bandages, and a handful of glass bottles into a small pile. Thankfully, none of the bottles had broken, and he lifted one to examine it. It had a bright-red stopper and was filled with a clear liquid. He hesitated. *No, it wasn't this one.* The apothecary had used one with a white stopper. He dug through the pile and quickly found the bottle. He picked it up, pulled the stopper and sniffed carefully at the contents, pulling his nose away at the sharp smell of alcohol.

Quickly, he poured the liquid onto his hands, placed the bottle on the floor, and then rubbed his hands together. He then grabbed the bandages and wiped away the blood. Satisfied that his hands were now clean, he stuffed the bloody bandages, along with the medicines and instruments, back into the bag. He pulled on his shirt. There were blood stains on the front of it. *Gods damn it, this will not do.* His cloak lay over the arm of a couch. He snatched it up, swung it over his shoulders, and tied it at his neck. He could hold the cloak closed until he reached his chambers. *That shouldn't draw any attention.*

Yes… and then he could start to think about dealing with the woman. Hopefully, the captain had already dealt with the monk. Some many loose threads… so many. *I might need to deal with the captain as well,* he realised. *It was he who had suggested this apothecary.* Obviously, he could not trust the man. But for now he had to make use of him. He had no choice; he was too close.

With a final glance at the body, he walked to the door. Making sure his cloak was in place, he pulled open the door and stepped into a mercifully empty corridor. He dug a key from his pocket and locked his office. *A little more time . . . so close . . . must take care of the woman . . . so close . . .* The jumble of thoughts raged through his mind as he turned and walked quickly toward his chambers.

Albar pushed his hands into his lower back and leaned backward. He grunted at the pain. He had been on his feet for more than twelve hours. He looked to Vitus, who was staring blankly at the wall in front of him. He looked equally drained and more than a little pissed off. He should have been on leave already. Albar could not help a half smile as he imagined Vitus drunk as a lord, with a jug of Varanian slop in one hand and a large breast in the other.

"Bloody hell," his tall friend grunted as if on cue. "My feet are killing me."

"I hear you," Albar agreed. "Any idea when his bloody lord gracefulness is due back?"

Vitus shrugged. "Was meeting that apothecary to get that burn and those scratches looked at."

"What's that all about?" Albar asked, his dark brows furrowing as he looked around the Chosen's chambers. "What the hell d'you think happened here?"

"Gods if I know." Vitus shook his head. "Blood all over the floor, on the bed . . ." He turned to Albar. "Truth is . . . I don't want to know what that twisted bastard gets up to behind these doors. I just want that ponsey prick to get back here and tell us to bugger off so I can go on leave."

Albar nodded and stretched his back again. He was about to comment on the fact that they might have a very long wait when the doors slammed open. Vasilios the Chosen burst into the room, clutching his cloak to his chest. He slammed the doors shut and flung the cloak aside, storming over to the wine cabinet. He grabbed at an unopened bottle, carelessly knocking aside several glasses in the process. Muttering to himself, the priest pulled the cork and upended the bottle taking deep swallows before he finally lowered it.

Albar shot a glance at Vitus, who stood wide-eyed and riveted to the spot. There was blood on the man's shirt, and if he wasn't acting insane before, he certainly was now. *By the bloody Dark One's balls, please let this gods-awful day end,* Albar groaned inwardly as the priest turned, wine dribbling from his chin. He watched as the priest just stood there with the half-empty bottle in his hand, dark eyes blank and unseeing. For a long moment, the man just stared at the floor. *What the hell do we do?* Albar thought, more than a little concerned. *The man is crazed. And whose blood is that?*

Quite suddenly, the priest looked up and noticed Albar and Vitus. He took a half step backward in surprise. "What the fuck are you two doing here?" he asked, wiping at his face with his sleeve.

"You asked us to stay here, Your Grace," Albar replied, hoping the man remembered. "You wanted us to—"

"Yes. Yes." The priest waved a hand, cutting him short. Albar watched the man take another swallow from the bottle. The priest walked quickly closer, his dark eyes darting from Albar to Vitus as he seemed to study them. "Yes . . . I remember." He nodded as he chewed at his bottom lip. "I need you both to do something for me."

The East Quay, the Harbour District

Tariq scowled at the hulking captain of the Aqrab from over the rim of his goblet. The wine was as expected—exquisitely smooth, with subtle hints of spice and berry—but it did little to soothe the pang of irritation he was feeling. He sipped at the wine and examined the giant of a man sitting opposite him. The man's massive muscles rolled under skin of polished ebony as he lounged in his chair. He regarded Tariq with hooded, smoky-yellow eyes; the wineglass looked like a thimble in his ham-size left hand as he idly twisted the strands of his forked beard with his right.

"Gods, Iz," Tariq said finally as he placed his goblet on the table. "With that much silver, your bloody ship is likely to sink."

Izem Akale-Aki's rumbling laughter filled the cabin. "Gold, my friend. Not silver, gold."

"Gold?" Tariq's mouth dropped open. He looked at the captain as if he had suddenly grown an extra head. "That's obscene! I'm looking for passage to Akhbar. I don't want to *buy* Akhbar. How do you live with yourself?"

"Quite well, actually." Izem grinned, revealing a set of dazzlingly white teeth. "More wine?"

Tariq was still shaking his head as he pushed his glass closer with his index finger. "I think I may be in the wrong business," he grumbled, half to himself.

Izem chuckled again and filled the smuggler's glass. Tariq lifted the glass in a mocking salute and sat back. Iz was a man of numerous and interesting vices, which was probably why Tariq liked him in the first place, but unfortunately, he was also a shrewd trader—hence the rather hefty price tag for passage across the Great Sea. He knew Iz could sell the berth several times over and had absolutely no need to offer it at a discounted price.

Tariq swirled the wine around in his mouth before placing the glass on the table. It really was magnificent, but he had never known Izem to waste his time or coin on anything less than delightful. Having worked his way up from a deckhand to owning the Aqrab, the sleek caravel named for a deadly desert scorpion, Iz was a man with expensive tastes, and he had a keen eye for value.

"It's that time of the year," Izem offered by way of explanation for the exorbitant price of passage. "Shitty weather, strong currents, and the wind is all wrong. It's risky, my friend."

"Shitty weather?" Tariq retrieved his glass, looking doubtfully at the smiling mountain of a man. "That's the best you've got, Iz? Weather? As opposed to what? A time when there's *no* weather? When the ocean's a vast expanse of benign pudding?"

Izem's booming laugh filled the cabin once again. "I like you, Tariq." He wiped a tear away from his face as he calmed himself. "But you know what they say about beggars . . ."

"What?" Tariq took a sip of wine. "They smell horrible and dress badly?"

"No, my friend," Izem replied with a broad grin. "They can't be choosers. Why don't you try Praxion? His tub is moored at the end of the quay. I hear he's heading for H'jah Karaam within the next day or so."

"Prax? Look here... I love the man as much as any, but... seriously, how is he still alive?" Tariq pushed his now-empty glass toward Izem, who dutifully filled it.

"I truly have no idea." Izem smiled, his chair creaking under his weight as he leaned back. "But it is rather amazing, isn't it? For a man whose knowledge of sailing is so staggeringly sparse, I think he's done rather well."

"Sparse? Didn't he almost sink his ship by running it into a lighthouse?"

"I heard it was the harbour wall in Abuzara."

"Yes. That *and* the lighthouse!"

Izem blew out a breath. "A man definitely favoured by the gods, then."

"Mmm... I would say more likely ignored than favoured," Tariq grunted. "I wouldn't want the likes of that fickle bunch looking over my shoulder on the open ocean." He swirled his wine. "I don't think it would take much attention to sink the likes of Prax."

Izem smiled but touched his heart and lips at the comment. "And what of your arrangement with the... trader?"

"Trader? Oh, Mareq!" Tariq sipped at his wine. "Yes, that's still an option. But I didn't want to drag myself all the way up the coast to find out that the mangey bastard was holed up somewhere else. You know... to escape the weather." He waved his hand randomly above his head. "I thought if I could get a reasonable price with a reputable captain such as yourself, I could save myself some time and effort."

Izem grinned. "It is a reasonable price, my friend. You're just used to paying much less for a service that's much less than mine. And yes... I know about your need to avoid port customs. That's a strong point in our mangey friend's favour... but my ship smells far better."

Tariq winced as Izem crushed his hand with one meaty paw while pounding him on the back hard enough to shake his teeth loose. After three bottles of wine, Tariq felt decidedly unsteady, and the gangplank was definitely moving more than when he had arrived. *Possibly something to do with the tide,* he thought as he grinned at his friend.

"Safe travels, you bloody pirate." He slapped Izem's shoulder.

"You, too, smuggler," Izem rumbled with a broad grin. "And leave today..."

"Yes. Yes." Tariq waved dismissively before casting a jaundiced eye skyward. "Something about the weather holding . . . Oh, yes! I remember!" He staggered down the gangplank and then looked back with a rakish grin. "Pudding for the next day or three... so the... " He hiccuped. "The *trader* is... *should* be... waiting for me." He spread his arms in an elaborate bow, very pleased with what was obviously a very cunning turn of phrase.

"Bugger off!" Izem laughed.

Tariq bowed again, waved, and then started weaving his way up the crowded Dock Road. He was feeling absolutely wonderful, a bit off-balance, perhaps, but nothing to be alarmed about. *Iz has a point,* he thought. *The weather's good. Well, good is a stretch... better than it has been in days. So maybe that bastard Mareq will be there. And there's no way this side of the seven hells that the greasy toad would pass up easy coin.*

He glanced up at the sky. It was not yet noon. *Might just get a game of cards in and a flagon of the house red before I pack it in. The red's a bit young and nothing like Iz's, but a man could get worse for the silver or two. I wonder if that dark-eyed beauty's working today? She loves me... She just doesn't know it yet.* Tariq grinned and quickened his pace.

The Temple Precinct

Vasilios, dressed in fresh clothes, stared at the pale face in the mirror. The man was almost unrecognisable—the jaw tightly clenched, the dark eyes haunted. *Who are you?* he thought as he slowly turned his head from side to side and studied what seemed to be new lines etched into this strange man's face.

The face lowered, but the eyes stayed locked on to his. For an instant, the edges of the man's thin lips twitched upward into a half smile. But the smile never reached those eyes. There seemed to be something very disturbing swimming in those black depths.

"I am Vasilios," he said quietly. "Vasilios the Chosen."

The man with dark eyes just stared back at him. *I am... Vasilios the Chosen...* The thought rolled around his mind, soft and sibilant... *Are you really?* He shook his head and tore his eyes from the stranger's piercing gaze.

"I am... Vasilios," he muttered before looking back to the mirror. The gaunt man with black eyes just stood there looking back at him. *Who are you?* He forced himself to step closer to the mirror, closer to the stranger. He leaned until his face was almost touching the glass.

The forced smile was gone, and the eyes were like empty, oily black pools. *You are Vasilios the Summoner.* The words slithered through his mind like worms. He could almost feel them sliding around inside his skull, their fat, clammy bodies pressing against the back of his eyes. *The great summoner of shadows,* the cold voice in his mind mocked.

He flinched at the memory of the furnace-like heat and the horrifying black-scaled being. No, that couldn't be his fate. He had the stones, and with them, he had power. And he was convinced he had only scratched the surface of that power. *Yes...* He took a deep breath and ran his fingers through his hair. These... *problems...* were not insurmountable. After tonight, the Prime would be no more, and he already had support from the majority of the Council of the Chosen. He would be the next Prime. *Vasilios Primatus… and who knows what fortune that may bring.* For now, he needed to get rid of the woman. That was the first step. Then he could find a way to deal with that… creature.

He looked back at the mirror, and the tormented eyes stared back. *Summoner of shadows… wielder of power… Primatus or just a puppet about to burn?*

"I will not burn!" he shouted suddenly, flecks of spittle hitting the mirror. "I am . . . I am Vasilios the Chosen!" He smashed his fist into the mirror, sending shards of glass flying. Vasilios staggered back from the mirror, clutching his bleeding hand to his chest, and collapsed to the floor.

Gods, what's happening to me? He looked up at the shattered mirror, and now dozens of jet-black eyes stared back at him. *I know who I am… I know what must be done.* He dragged himself to his feet. I know what must be done… He stumbled to the closet and used a shirt to wipe the blood from his knuckles. He grabbed a black woollen cloak and threw it over his shoulders. Moving quickly to the back of the closet, he pulled open the secret door. He hesitated and then stepped into the small, dark room. Vasilios pushed the door closed behind him and heard the latch click into place and was suddenly struck by the weight of the darkness.

With trembling hands, he hurriedly lit an oil lamp and flinched as writhing shadows sprang up in the feeble orange light. He spun around, holding the lamp up high. His heart pounded as every murky corner seemed to hide the creature that had attacked him in the depths. *Gods, move, you fool,* he thought angrily and forced himself to step onto the narrow staircase that spiralled down into the darkness. *I know what must be done…*

The Crow Inn, the Market District
The Thirty-Fourth Day of 389, Afternoon

Panos groaned and opened his eyes. He lay on his back with his left arm slung above his head. His right was wrapped around the shoulder of a girl who lay nestled against his chest. An unruly mop of ginger curls hid her face, and she was snoring softly. He ran his left hand over his face and took a deep breath, wincing at the sudden flash of pain behind his eyes. *Gods . . . again. Not much of a learner, are you, Panos, my lad?* He groaned inwardly.

He had no recollection of this girl and the afternoon's antics. Clearly, there must have been ale involved. Probably heroic amounts, based on the thumping pain in his head. She moved and snuggled closer, her body soft and pleasantly warm against his. *Not all bad,* he admitted grudgingly as he sighed, closing his eyes.

He stroked her hair idly as he tried to piece the fragments of the day together. He remembered vaguely that Dacian had been rather serious after breakfast and then had gone off somewhere; the gods alone knew where he was or what he was up to. Panos had already been too drunk and too preoccupied to stop him or offer any sensible advice. There had been no sign of Jasmijn, either, for that matter. She had stormed off, apparently annoyed at what Panos had seen as a perfectly logical approach to the day. The city watch didn't want them running around, possibly getting killed or, worse, creating an even bigger pile of bodies for them to deal with.

Unfortunately, this had left him to his own devices, which had obviously resulted in a mess of ale and a midday frolic with one of the barmaids. He looked down at the girl. He gently reached around her head to tuck her hair behind her ear. Her face was freckled and pleasant enough. *Well, it's definitely not the worst way to pass the time,* he thought as he gently extracted his arm from under her head.

He rolled his feet from the bed and was about to stand when he froze. A woman was sitting on the lone chair in the small room. Her long legs were crossed; her hands rested in her lap. Her features were Akhbari, but her eyes were a piercing blue. Her flowing black abaya did little to hide the lean angles of her body, and she was looking at him intently.

"Who by the seven—" he started to ask.

"They will come for her," she said, cutting him short. "You must let them take her. If you try to stop them, you will die."

"Wait. Come for who?" Panos held up a hand, then, remembering the girl asleep behind him, turned quickly. She had not moved. He looked back to the woman. "What . . . Wait! Who are you?"

"Pay the girl no heed," the woman said, ignoring the question. "She will not wake."

"Who is coming? For who?" Panos stood and started to gather his clothes from the floor. He began dressing, suddenly acutely aware of the strange woman's gaze. Those ice-blue eyes made him feel oddly self-conscious.

"Who the hell are you? How did you get in here?" he asked as he pulled his shirt over his head, now more than a little annoyed.

She smiled. "If you need a name, you may call me Relic. And I go where I am needed."

"Ahh . . . good." Panos pulled on his leggings and sat back on the bed, then grabbed a boot. "Well met, Relic. Now if you could tell me why you feel you are needed . . . *here*, at this exact point in time, I would be eternally grateful."

Relic smiled; her gaze seemed to bore straight through him. There was something oddly familiar about her, but Panos could not seem to put his finger on it. There was something deeply unsettling about those piercing blue eyes—oceans of time obscured by the pleasant shape under the abaya. *A calculated distraction . . . somewhat like a well-executed feint before a fatal sword thrust,* he thought darkly.

"Listen carefully, swordsman. They will come, and they will take her. The one you know as Jasmijn. There is nothing you can do to stop them. If you try, they will kill you." She leaned forward. "And the others need you."

"Who needs me? Gods, woman, speak plainly!"

"You will know." Relic smiled.

Panos' eyes flew open at the sound of splintering wood. He lay on his back with his left arm slung above his head. His right was wrapped around the shoulder of a girl who lay nestled into his chest. *What in the seven hells?* He looked to the door as he pulled his arm out from under the girl. He heard a muffled cry from the passage, followed by another crash. He rolled quickly from the bed.

"Panos," he heard the girl mumble sleepily. "What's happening?"

"I don't know," he replied, grabbing for his clothes. "Stay here. I'll find out." He reached for his sword and then decided on the dagger. *Better for close work,* he thought, recalling the narrow passage outside the servants' quarters and pulling the small blade from its scabbard.

"Hold her," he heard a man's voice say, followed by a cry of pain. "Bitch!" the man shouted. There was a sharp crack of an open palm striking flesh, another cry of pain, and then the thump of a body hitting the wooden floor. Panos felt a surge of ragged anger as he moved to the door. He reached for the handle, ready to tear it open.

No, Panos! Let them take her! He heard the woman's voice in his head as clear as if she had been standing next to him. He ground his teeth together as he heard another blow land, then another. He balled his fist and then grabbed the handle.

Don't, her voice came again. *You cannot stop them. You will die. They will take her, stepping over your dead body.*

"How do you know this?" Panos grated, his jaw clenched so tightly it ached. "I can't just stand here and do nothing." Images of men burning to death in front of his eyes flashed though his mind. The same impotent, futile rage and shame roared inside him; every fibre of his being wanted to tear the door open, to hell with the consequences.

You will die, and they will take her anyway, the woman's voice echoed in his mind. *And if you die, they all die.*

"What is it? Panos?" the girl lying in bed asked, her voice now edged with fear.

"Nothing," Panos said quietly as he forced his fist open. He wiped the tears from his face angrily and, with great effort, turned from the door, trying desperately not to hear the sounds of Jasmijn being dragged from her room. He stood staring blankly at the floor, his hand trying to crush the hilt of the dagger.

Prepare now, came the voice again, this time with urgency. *The darkness is coming. And it is hungry.*

Dockway Alley, the Lower City

Cletus used the hem of the stained travel cloak to wipe the dagger clean of blood before sheathing it. He touched the sodden bandage on the side of his head gingerly. What remained of his right ear was a searing, aching mess. *Fuck that old man,* he thought bitterly scratching at his armpit, *and fuck Bariuz, too.*

He swore the plain clothes given to them by the captain were infested with lice or fleas. Considering what they were about to do, he understood that they could not be seen wearing temple armour, but surely the bastard could have done better than these rags. The fabric was coarse and scratched at his skin, and it smelled of stale sweat. The only thing that had stopped him from voicing his complaint was the ominous tear in the back of the shirt, a tear surrounded by a dark stain. Thankfully, Silvius was not so stupid to open his gods-damned cake hole, either.

Cletus looked down at the toe of a boot that was still visible in a mound of rubbish. He bent down and tugged at the edge of a dirty tarpaulin, dropping it over the boot. He inspected the result and, satisfied that the watchman's body was now completely hidden from sight, turned to Silvius. The man was busy throwing handfuls of refuse over the other corpse. He favoured his left shoulder, once again thanks to the gods-forsaken old monk. Luckily, the dagger the old bastard had thrown had not hit bone, just lodged in the muscle of Silvius's shoulder; it was still painful but not debilitating.

They had taken the two watchmen by surprise, luring them deeper into the alleyway with a cry for help and then dispatching them quickly and quietly with dagger thrusts. The stupid arseholes had practically run into their blades.

"Enough now," Cletus rasped. "Will be ages before anyone finds these two. Bariuz said we needed to get the woman to the warehouse before nightfall. You got the wagon?"

"Gods, Cletus. Yes," Silvius said, tossing aside the handful of rubbish. "For the bloody fiftieth time, it's in the lane near the entrance to the courtyard."

Cletus' fat face twitched with suppressed anger. With a great effort, he forced down a retort. Silvius was far too stupid to realise that Bariuz had asked them to do this because they were expendable. Abducting this woman in broad daylight was fraught with danger; any number of things could go very wrong. He glared at Silvius with small, close-set eyes. "Good. Let's get this over with."

The two men strode toward the exit of the alleyway and stepped onto the narrow cobbled road that ran past the entrance to the Crow Inn. Cletus casually looked up and down the thoroughfare. There were few people to be seen, and the late-afternoon sun cast half of the road into shadow. The gates to the courtyard stood open in front of them, and an old man sat on a low stool at the entrance, leaning against the gate post and puffing quietly on an equally ancient pipe.

Cletus shot a glance at Silvius and nodded. They crossed the road and walked up to the old man, who remained seated but looked them up and down. His face creased into a frown. "Entrance is 'round that way," he said dismissively, pointing up the lane. "You can't come through here."

Cletus pulled a silver coin from his pocket. "We need you to take a walk," he said simply.

The old man eyed the coin greedily. "Not sure I can do that," he said after pondering the offer. "Jasuf don't take lightly to his courtyard being left open and untended."

Cletus sighed and reached into his pocket to remove another coin, then deliberately placed his other hand on the pommel of his sword, a movement not lost on the old man.

The old man's eyes darted from the sword to the coins and back, but then he settled back into his seat. "What happened to your ear?" he asked, tilting his head to one side to get a closer look.

Cletus ground his teeth together and, with great reluctance moved his hand from his sword and fished out another coin. "You won't need to be gone long. Just long enough to take a piss," Cletus said with an edge of frustration in his voice.

The old man smiled, nodded slowly, and took the offered coins. "I'll be back in five minutes," he grunted as he dragged himself to his feet. "You'd both better be gone by then."

"We will be." Cletus' fleshy mouth twisted into a cold smile.

They watched the old man hobble away, and then they moved quickly towards the entrance to the servants' quarters. The blonde woman had entered less than an hour ago and had not left since. It would not be much trouble to find her room. Cletus pushed the door open and paused, allowing his eyes time to adjust to the low light. A narrow passage stretched in front of him, with four doors on either side. He gestured to Silvius, who stepped in through the door and pulled it closed after him.

Cletus pointed to the first door, removing his dagger from its sheath. Silvius nodded and did the same. He placed a gloved hand on the doorknob and turned it carefully. He opened the door. The small room was empty. Closing the door, he motioned to Cletus to move to the next room. Cletus stepped quietly to the door and twisted the knob. He pushed it open. A young woman lay asleep on a narrow cot. Her curly dark hair was an unruly mop. She lay on her side, her head resting on her arm. The two men slipped into the room and closed the door.

Cletus approached the bed, leaned over, and placed a gloved hand over the girl's mouth. He pressed down tightly as her eyes flew open with alarm. He held his index finger to his lips. "Shhh . . . quiet." Her nightdress had opened slightly, revealing the curve of a breast. Cletus felt a stirring of hot lust and licked his fat lips. It took him a moment to bring himself back to the reason they were there. "Where is the woman named Jasmijn?" he hissed. "Do you know which is her room?"

The girl nodded carefully. "Good. I'm going to let you speak, but if you scream, I'll kill you. Do you understand?" The girl stared at him, her eyes wide with terror. Then she nodded again, and Cletus lifted his hand from her mouth.

"Last room on the left," she whispered.

An oily smile split Cletus's face. He closed his hand around her throat, and with the other, he reached out to squeeze the girl's breast. Her face twisted in pain as he pulled cruelly at the nipple. A shiver of pleasure rushed through him. *If only I had more time,* he thought. He hesitated, then thought of what Bariuz would do to them if they failed to bring the woman to the warehouse. He imagined another rip or two in the back of the shirt he wore and the cold water of the docks closing around him. He stood up and moved toward the door. "Tie her hands and gag her," he said to Silvius.

The essence of Moloc drifted from the room as the flat-faced temple guard stepped quietly into the passage. The man had oozed such lust and cruelty that the Ascendant could taste it. The stupid ape wanted nothing more than to inflict pain upon the terrified girl, but Moloc would not allow it. No base creature's pawing salivations would sabotage his plans. He had been pathetically easy to manipulate because, as with many who resort to inflicting pain on the weak, he was a coward.

The other was making quick work of stuffing the gag into the girl's mouth and tying her wrists behind her back. She mewled in pain as the rough cord was pulled brutally tight, and then both men moved quietly to the room at the end of the passage. *How does she not know of their presence?* the Ascendant wondered. Yet again, he could not fathom why she would choose to take on these weak and incomprehensibly fragile forms. These pathetic fools would otherwise be moving swiftly toward their doom. He pushed aside the frustratingly obtuse conundrum. Everything she did seemed to be a mystery. *It matters not,* he decided as he floated closer. *All that matters is that they will take her.*

Cletus reached out and carefully tried the door. It was locked. His flat, cruel face contorted in frustration. He looked at Silvius, who just shrugged. *Gods, the man is astonishingly stupid,* he thought. *What was the fool thinking? That they could kick the door in quietly? They would need to be fast if they did... very fast... but there might be another way.* He took a breath and knocked softly.

"Who is it?" he heard a woman's voice ask. He said nothing, hoping that with a bit of luck, she would just open the door. "Who's there?" her voice came again, this time sounding a little closer, the tone a little harder. *Shit,* he fumed to himself. *The bitch is not going to open the door.* He took a step back and kicked hard at the door, his boot landing solidly next to the latch. The door flew open with a loud crash of splintering wood.

He was in through the door immediately. The woman stood in the middle of the small room with a water jug in her hand. She threw it at him, landing a glancing blow on the damaged side of his head. He staggered at the blinding flash of pain, righted himself, and then lashed out with his fist, hitting her hard in the face. She crashed into a small desk that stood against the far wall and fell heavily to the floor. Cletus leaped forward and swung his boot into her stomach. The wind burst from her lungs, and her face twisted in agony.

He touched the side of his head where the jug had struck him, feeling a painful lump beginning to rise just above the bandage. He growled an oath and reached down, roughly dragging her over onto her stomach before placing a knee between her shoulder blades. She cried out and struggled weakly as he pulled her arms behind her back.

"Hold her," he said to Silvius, who had entered the room behind him. Silvius moved quickly and grabbed her arms, pressing them down against her back as Cletus grabbed a fistful of hair to pull her head back. He took a wadded cloth from his pocket and reached around to stuff it into her mouth when her teeth clamped down hard on his thumb.

"Bitch!" he shouted in pain, tearing his hand from her mouth. Then he swung his open palm hard against the side of her face, driving her head into the wooden floor. She went limp.

"Gods damn you to hell," Cletus snarled though clenched teeth as he looked at the blood streaming from the semi-circular wound in his hand. He stood up and moved to the door. Sticking his head into the passage, he saw that it was still thankfully empty. By some unknown fortune, no one seemed to have heard anything. With another disgusted look at his injured hand, he turned back to Silvius. "Tie her up and let's get the hell out of here."

Moloc watched the two men drag the unconscious woman from the room. He could sense the swordsman standing behind the door. His anger and loathing blazed. There was nothing the man wanted more than to burst into the passage and lay waste to the two guards. But he remained in the room. Somehow, he managed to fight down the avalanche of guilt and the memories of ash and flame.

Of course, it suited Moloc that he remained trapped in that hellish torment, but if he chose otherwise and opened the door, he would die. Moloc would blind him for just long enough for one of those apes to stick a blade in his throat. He almost wanted the man to open the door. He willed it. He pulsed an ocean of pain and helplessness to the man.

He could sense the man's hand hovering above the knob of the door. *Open it... Open it. Don't abandon her like you abandoned your comrades. You can't allow her to burn...* Such delicious agony radiated from the swordsman, but somehow, he resisted. These low creatures never ceased to amaze him. Just when they seemed absolutely driven by their base instincts, they would do something... different, inexplicable.

The Ascendant turned his attention back to the two carrying the unconscious woman. No matter—there would be time enough for sport with this one. The levers he could pull were enough to move a world. But for now, all that mattered was that the woman named Jasmijn was taken. And after tonight, she would not meddle in his affairs ever again.

A Feast of Flesh

The Waterfront District
The Thirty-Fourth Day of 389, Nightfall

The sun had set, and the skies to the west were deepening from their blazing oranges and reds to blue and purple. The wind, blowing steadily off the sea, had a bite to it and a promise of more rain. The streets had started to empty as people hurried homeward to fireplaces and warmth.

The old church loomed dark and empty in the middle of Quay Road. Its silent spires used to be a favourite roost for the gulls and night larks, but now the loopholes and belfry were silent and deserted; only the remnants of old nests remained.

But not all was silent. Deep beneath the old church, in the vast chamber below, something moved. A low bestial breath burbled through the darkness as the ancient, pitted stone of the altar bulged and distorted like black, distended skin. As it bulged outward, a suggestion of large limbs could be seen pressing against the oily surface; there were horns, followed by the a broad face with angular features and full of ragged fangs.

The stone collapsed back with the wet sound of flesh on stone, only to bulge outward again, this time more violently. The glistening skin stretched slowly into the darkness. A massive clawed hand pressed against it and it burst, spilling a colossal beast and six smaller creatures onto the cold stone of the floor.

The lesser demons writhed in a mess of wet, pale limbs as they tried desperately to get away from the monstrous being that lay on the floor of the chamber. The beast pushed itself slowly upward, the great muscles of its arms and shoulders bunching. It paused there for a moment, feeling the cold air on its skin, sensing the intoxicating buzz of life all around.

It slowly drew itself upright until it towered in the darkness. The beast lifted its great horned head and shook the black tangled shock of fur on its shoulders; its great muscles trembled with the raw anticipation of the hunt. Then it turned its glowing red eyes to the door, and a low, guttural growl broke the silence.

Emilia stood in the deepening shadows near the entrance of Dockway Alley, just beyond the warm pool of light cast by a nearby streetlamp. *Like much of my life,* she though bleakly, *just beyond the pool of light.* She cast a nervous glance back to the swiftly darkening entrance to the alley behind her. The incident of the previous night still sat fresh in her memory, but she had no choice. She needed the money. The small room she rented was her only haven, and if she didn't keep up with the rent, she would be back on the streets. And if that meant enduring the pawing, frenzied attention of some drunken fool, so be it.

She tore her gaze away from the deep shadows and tried desperately to crush the crawling fear. *Gods, girl, pull yourself together . . . No one will want to tumble with a blubbering wreck,* she chastised herself as she pulled her bodice a little lower to emphasize her breasts. It was just past the seventh bell, so her first potential customers would be stumbling out of the pubs soon. They were mostly farmers or traders staying only briefly in the city. They would have concluded their business, and the extra coin in their purses made the ale a little more inviting. Luckily, none of them would last very long, which meant she could possibly earn a fair amount of coin in the evening.

As always, she hoped that none of them would turn nasty. Usually, the more hardened drinkers were rougher, the encounter more about power than sex, and she had learned through bitter experience which men to avoid. Some of her friends had not been so lucky. No amount of coin was worth getting beaten for—or worse. The city watch didn't seem to pay much attention to a prostitute ending up dead in a gutter.

Emilia cast a quick look down the avenue and watched as two men drew closer. They were talking loudly; a ribald comment from one had them both burst into raucous laughter. They slapped each other on the back. She smoothed out a few wrinkles in her dress and stepped forward into the light. The one on the right looked up and smiled drunkenly before leaning into his friend and passing some comment that she could not make out. They laughed and walked on without looking at her again. She frowned and stepped back into the darkness.

She shot a glance back at the alley. The shadows were deep, and she could only see a few feet into the depths. Who knew what was hidden there. She shivered, and the roiling fear bubbled up again. She tried desperately to fight it down, but all she could hear was the sound of claws gouging at her door as something tried to gain entrance . . . something *hungry*.

She shivered. The watchman had said it was just a stray dog. But it hadn't sounded like a dog at all. She took a deep, shuddering breath and dragged her eyes away from the dark to face the street; this time she stepped into the middle of the pool of yellow light cast by the streetlamp.

She didn't have to wait long before she noticed another man weaving his way down the street. He was short and plump and he was singing softly to himself. Every two or three steps he would pause and adjust his coat or his hat, only to smile to himself and resume his haphazard journey. He was quite close when she stepped out in front of him and smiled sweetly.

"Well, hello there," Emilia purred. "You look like someone in need of a little fun." She forced a broad smile. "Or by the looks of it . . . a little *more* fun."

He jerked to a halt and looked up in bewilderment. "Oh!" he exclaimed, blinking and trying to focus on the person who had just miraculously appeared out of nowhere.

He smiled slowly. "Oh, hello, pretty. I'm . . . always looking for . . . fun," he said, carefully over-articulating each word. "But"—he rummaged around in his pockets and retrieved a few silver coins—"this is all I have." He held out his hand to her and blinked expectantly.

Emilia took a step forward and looked at the man. He was obviously very drunk, but he had friendly blue eyes. The lines etched into his stubbled cheeks spoke of smiles and laughter and more than a little sadness. She summed him up quickly: he was a gentle man, and he would not hurt her. She took three of the silver coins and smiled. "That will get you a bit of tumble until the next bell."

The man smiled slowly. "Sounds . . . quite fine . . . to me," he said carefully. "And where would . . . we be . . . going?"

Emilia took his hand and smiled warmly. "Not far. Follow me."

In the darkness of the chamber, the great shadow beast dropped to all fours. An insatiable hunger filled it, and it shook its powerful shoulders as the nervous excitement of the hunt began to course through its veins. It looked with disdain at the pathetic, pale creatures that squirmed on the stone flagging in front of it. One of them looked up and hissed in fear and anger. The shadow beast's taloned hand snaked out to grab the creature in an iron grip. The beast paused to enjoy the creature's futile struggles and pain-filled shrieks. Then, with a sudden flex of its long fingers, it crushed the lesser demon, bones snapping like dry twigs. The creature went limp, and the great beast cast the broken carcass aside, watching as the others scattered into the darkness. It paid them no heed; its prey was elsewhere.

The beast flowed forward, sliding through the darkness much like a fish would glide through dark water. It found the door. Long talons grated down the dark wood and hooked into the iron ring. It pulled, and the door groaned on its hinges. The beast slid into the passage beyond, where it found stairs. It flowed upward, a shadow within shadows, following the cold spiral of stone. It floated past several other doors, but these it ignored. The way out was above.

The beast entered the belfry and felt the cold evening air on its skin. The mélange of heady scents hit the shadow demon like a fist: the dry, musty straw of old bird nests; the cold, salty tang of the ocean and flesh; and a pulsing, warm mass that clung to the very air all around. It shuddered and threw its hideous head backward, nostrils flaring to suck in the pungent smells. The beast stood transfixed, eyes slitted, jaws opening wide and then snapping shut like a steel trap. *Oh, how we will hunt! We will gorge to a bursting point!* But then it shook itself and broke the spell. First, there was the prey. *We must deal with the prey; then we can hunt.*

The great horned head lowered, and the bloodred eyes opened. It turned to look toward the tall minarets that stabbed up into the night sky. There it would find the prey. In the empty house of an old god. It moved quickly to the edge of the tower and slid over the side. It flowed like oil and shadow down the pockmarked stone to the overgrown courtyard below, where it dropped silently into the dark. There, it paused to suck deep breaths into its lungs. The smells were almost overpowering: damp earth, rotting plant matter, and the musky ammonia of tiny creatures that glowed hot in the darkness as they scurried around.

Suddenly, the small creatures darted away, disappearing into holes and burrows. The beast tilted its head and heard voices. The great muscles in its arms and shoulders tensed as the heady scent of meat and sweat washed over it. The beast shuddered with pleasure, thick saliva dribbling from its jaws. And then it moved with terrifying speed.

Quay Road, the Waterfront District

Albar lifted his helmet from his head and wiped a gloved hand through his short dark hair. He looked up at the bell tower of the old church and shook his head. *What, by the Dark One's balls, are we doing here? What the hell have we been dragged into?* He pushed the dark thoughts aside as he replaced the helm, pulling the strap under his chin and tugging at it irritably. *Bloody thing never sits right.* None of this made any sense—from the old monk to the bloody priest, to standing here for most of the day at the arse-end of the city, guarding a building that had been empty for decades.

"By the gods, what are we doing here, mate?" Vitus grunted, echoing Albar's thoughts. "I was going on bloody leave, and then everything goes tits-up." His friend stood in the middle of the narrow Quay Road with a pained expression on his face. "Tell me, why the bloody hell are we standing in the dark in front of this gods-forsaken pile of stone?"

"I dunno, Vit. Maybe 'cause His Royal Gracefulness said so, an' he's one of the bloody Chosen. An' from what I've seen, not a man to say no to." Albar sighed, sliding a finger under his helmet strap and tugging at it. *This gods-forsaken thing is choking me!* "Or maybe 'cause the gods don't particularly like us." He turned to his friend, a sardonic smile on his bearded face. "Or maybe we're just lucky."

"Fuck you," Vitus said with a snort, thumping a fist into Albar's shoulder. "Lucky? I was a few hours away from a bottle of red and a willing woman, only to find myself standing around in the dark with you."

"Could be worse." Albar smiled. "You could be standin' around in the dark with that witless idiot, Cletus."

"Eresophi's tits," Vitus swore. "How is that sack of dung not floating by the docks? Thought Bariuz was going to poke an air hole into him right outside the watchhouse after he hit the old man."

"Night's still young, my friend," Albar grunted. He reached into a pocket and pulled out a small silver flask. He unscrewed the cap and offered it Vitus. "It ain't your Varanian slop, but I'm sure a little emberwyne will go some way to easin' the pain of my company."

"Gods, Alb, you are a prince among men!" Vitus grinned, taking the flask and upending it to swallow a mouthful. "Damn it to hell," he wheezed, passing it back to Albar with watering eyes. "Only the good stuff for you, I see. Not sure I'll have any guts left after that."

"Puts hair on your chest. More for me if you're scared." Albar shrugged and put the flask to his lips. He tilted his head back and then winced as the fiery liquid slid down his throat to land like a warm stone in his belly. "Suppose we could take a look around the place. Don't rightly know what we'd be lookin' for, but a bit of walk is better than just standin' around here. There's a gate by the side." Albar pointed to his right. "About halfway up that lane. I remember it from when I was a boy. Used to play around here."

"You were a boy, Alb?" Vitus asked with a grin.

"Bugger off, whelp," Albar grunted and started walking toward the narrow lane.

Vitus snorted a laugh and held out his hand for the flask.

"Thought you didn't like it." Albar frowned, holding the flask away from his friend.

"I don't. Doesn't mean I won't drink it." Vitus motioned for Albar to pass the drink back.

"Bloody savage," Albar said, passing the flask to Vitus as they stepped into the deep shadows, the rough rock of the church's boundary wall to their right and the damp, windowless brick of the looming building to the left. "Priory Lane," he said almost absently.

"What?" Vitus handed back the flask.

"Was called Priory Lane back then. You could cut through here from Quay Road to Water's Edge." Albar took a sip from the flask before replacing the cap and returning it to his pocket.

"So what're we looking for?" he heard Vitus ask. The clouds had started to drift in from the sea, and each time one obscured the moon, his friend, only a pace or two in front of him, would be swallowed by the darkness.

"There's a gate comin' up. Just keep looking to your right," Albar said as he stepped in something soft and wet. He stopped and lifted his foot with disgust. "Ahh, by the gods! Hold up, Vit."

"A gate? I can't see my bloody hand in front of my face. Hang on— there's something up here," he heard Vitus say as he scraped his boot against the rough stone of the wall. "Did you hear th—" Vitus's words were cut short, and Albar heard something clatter to the ground, followed by a dull thud. Then silence.

"Vit?" Albar called into the dark. Suddenly, the lane seemed far too narrow and the shadows far too deep. He put a gloved hand on the handle of his sword. "Vitus! What's happenin'? You fall over, you clumsy bastard?" He took a tentative step forward. "Better not have tossed up any of that emberwyne . . ."

The clouds drifted apart, and a brief soft beam of moonlight pierced the blackness. Albar froze as the pale, silvery pool of light slid across Vitus' headless body lying in the middle of the lane. As the darkness descended once again, an icy fear gripped him. He stood rooted to the ground as he drew his sword. It felt woefully inadequate as he held the blade stiffly out in front of him. Somehow, he could not will himself to turn. The terror of having something run him down from behind seemed far worse than just standing there in the dark.

That changed as the shadows seemed to coalesce. Slowly, the darkness melded together to form an unspeakable horror that towered over him. Blood-red eyes set in a great horned head burned with an insatiable hunger. Albar opened his mouth to scream and it was upon him, its vast, crushing weight driving him hard into the ground. Pain seared though him as wickedly sharp talons punched through the lacquered leather of his armour like it was made of paper. The muscles of his chest and shoulders tore, and his ribs snapped. The claws then ripped through the soft flesh of his stomach with an explosion of pain. He gagged on the flood of warm blood that filled his mouth. A hot, foul breath fanned his face; something warm and wet slithered across his cheek. Then the massive jaws descended, and oblivion took him.

Dockway Alley, the Lower City

The pale creature sat in the darkness high above the narrow alleyway, its head cocked to one side. It sat absolutely motionless and listened to the low thrum of the city. Water dripped slowly from some of the balconies and the edges of the rooftops that jutted out above its perch. It hardly noticed when a cold drop would land on its pallid flesh, then snake down the contours of hard muscle. The discomfort was lost to the absolute rapture of the multitude of prey that surrounded it. So much warm flesh.

It shivered in excitement and let out a low, ecstatic hiss, saliva jetting under its tongue. It could feel the inexorable, burning need to hunt again. Not so much to feed, although that was important, but to kill, to feel lifeblood jet hot into its mouth, the fear-infused meat tearing beneath its claws.

These dark alleyways had proven to be such rich hunting grounds. They held scores of small animals: rats, mice, cats, a few mangey dogs. Some of these were quite difficult to catch, which only added to the sport. But none had come close to the human who had strayed into the shadows the night before. The fear that had radiated from that one had been exquisite—the palpable fear of the dark, twitching at sounds and imaginary nightmares that lurked on the edges of frail sanity. The soft flesh of that one had been infused with fear's pungent, sweaty smell.

The creature scratched idly at its pallid flesh, its thin lips peeling back from rows of razor-sharp teeth. It sniffed at the air again and, this time, caught a familiar scent. Its head snapped around, and again it sniffed, this time with more urgency. Humans... two of them, the rich scent of warm meat and blood, mixed with lust and disgust and blunt terror, wafting before them. It listened as their senseless monkey chattering drew closer.

It shuddered in delicious anticipation and leaned out into the darkness. Its claws scored deep grooves into the crumbling stone and mortar of the ledge as it filled its nostrils with each sapid wave of smells. And then it moved, silent and fluid. It dropped from its perch to land softly on the damp stone of the alley. It slid into the darkness to wait...

Emilia led the man into the alley. He held her hand softly and swayed gently as he bumped alternately into the wall and her shoulder. He rambled on drunkenly about his evening and how he used to be able to hold his ale far better when he was a younger man, not that he was that

314

old, mind you. The endless, mildly incoherent babble was broken by the occasional hiccup and blurt about how pretty she was. She nodded and smiled and pretended to listen, even laughing softly and touching his arm when he chuckled about some part of his story.

He did seem like a gentle soul, harmless but frustratingly slow. The cloying darkness around them terrified her. It seemed to lick at her skin, taste her growing unease. Every few steps, a small pool of light would splash down from a window or one of the sparse torches lit by the more conscientious tenants who had access to the walkway. But it did nothing to dispel the growing panic welling up inside her. She pulled at his arm, causing him to stagger slightly.

She tried to disguise her desperation with a forced laugh. "Oh, sorry, love! Come now—it's not far."

"Careful, pretty!" He laughed, grabbing her arm to steady himself, "My balance... it would seem... is a bit off. Felt like... an old mate of mine for a moment."

Emilia forced a smile and quickened her pace. They would be there in a minute or so. Then, hopefully, he would be quiet as he had his fun, and she would be a few coins to the better.

"Can't seem to remember his... name." He belched softly and continued, "Fell into the... harbour. Drowned, he did! Such a pity... he owed me a few... coins. If I remember... correctly. Are we close, love?" he slurred, staggering to his right, as he looked up at the thin sliver of night sky framed by the dark buildings.

"Yes. Very." She smiled sweetly and steadied him. "We're very close. So you can't be falling over. Not here." She touched his cheek, and he grinned happily.

Emilia turned and started forward when she felt his hand jerk suddenly from hers. She heard a grunt and flinched as a warm, sticky liquid splashed across her face. She blinked in surprise, reflexively wiping it away with the back of her hands. She could still feel some of it dribbling down her cheeks. *What the . . .* The thought died as her breath caught. Her hands were covered in blood; even in the dim light, it was unmistakable. *Oh gods, no!* Ice-cold fear coiled around her stomach.

"Hello?" she said softly to the shadows. Something moved in the deep darkness. She heard a dragging sound, followed by the ripping of cloth. "Hello?" Her mouth was suddenly bone dry. The ripping sounds stopped. She strained to see beyond the gloom. She was about to take a step forward when she heard a low, malevolent hiss. She turned and ran without looking back.

The patches of light flashed past. Terror thrummed through her veins, so when she tripped over some unseen object that sent her sprawling on

315

the cold ground of the alley, she dragged herself to her feet almost instantly, oblivious to the deep scrapes on her knees and hands. Her foot slipped on moss-covered stone, sending her careening into the rough stone walls of the alley. She cried out in pain as the sharp edges of broken mortar gouged into the soft skin of her shoulder.

She clawed at the stone, feeling a nail tear painfully away as she dragged her body forward with a desperate whimper. The darkness behind her, with its unseen horror, seemed to suck her back. Her feet felt like lead and the air as thick as treacle. *Run, run! Oh gods . . . run!* she cried over and over in her mind.

When she burst from the alley into the well-lit avenue, it happened so suddenly, she tripped and slammed heavily into the cobbles. She sobbed as she rolled to her knees, pushed herself upright, and staggered forward. The multitude of lamps that lined the avenue seemed impossibly bright. A man sat on the steps of a tavern, smoking a pipe. He looked around, noticing her as she forced herself forward. The man surged to his feet and ran toward her. Emilia drew a deep, shuddering breath and screamed, "Help me!"

The prey twitched under the creature's claws. The other human stood a few paces away, and the stench of its terror hung heavily in the air. It hissed angrily, fighting with the decision to kill this one, too, or to feed immediately. Then the human turned and ran, and the creature tensed to chase it down, but the hot, coppery smell of blood was too intoxicating.

It dipped its head and tore at the flesh of its prey. Blood dribbled down its chin, and it dug its claws deeply into the still-warm flesh at the pleasure of the taste. Its jaws worked the meat before it swallowed. It was about to rip another mouthful from the kill when it sensed the presence of another beast. It looked up with a low warning hiss, bearing bloody fangs. It dragged the kill closer and waited for the other to show itself. It did not need to wait long.

The other dropped from the shadows and landed lightly on its feet. This one was slightly smaller than itself, the skin a milky white with grey mottles over the shoulders and back. The large, round black eyes were pools of hate, and the small, razor-sharp teeth were bared in challenge. It hissed its fury as it sensed yet another pale form in the darkness behind this newcomer.

The Crow Inn, the Market District

Panos pushed aside the half-finished ale and stood up from the small table that occupied the furthest corner of the common room. He wore melancholy like a cloak and had no want for company. The pretty redhead was waiting tables, and she had made a point of regularly checking if his tankard needed refilling, but he was feeling too desolate to even get drunk.

He looked over to the girl. She laughed at something a bearded man said as she placed pints in front of him and his friend. *A sweet thing,* Panos thought as she turned to him and flashed a smile that suggested she was more than willing to repeat the afternoon's antics should he be interested. He forced a smile that slipped from his face the moment she turned away.

The swordsman sighed and poked at the tankard with his index finger, sliding it slowly away from him. The fragmented, drunken memories of the girl's boundless enthusiasm and pale, soft skin were replaced by the thought of standing in front of the closed door and doing absolutely nothing as Jasmijn was dragged away by unseen assailants. How in the seven hells could he let that happen? Surely, for all his faults, he was better than that. *Or maybe I just let all of my friends burn.*

Panos pushed his chair back and stood up. He ran a hand over his face, feeling tired and empty and so much older than his years. The room suddenly felt stiflingly hot, the walls too close. *Gods, I need some fresh air,* he thought, shaking his head. He made his way to the door, pushed it open, and stepped into the crisp night air. Pulling his cloak around him, he reached for his pipe. He clasped the stem between his teeth and dug about in his pockets for his tobacco pouch, finally finding it in the last one. *Always the bloody last pocket... always without bloody fail,* he thought as he stuffed the bowl with tobacco, his face creased with a deep scowl. *What did the woman mean by 'if you die they will all die'? Who would die? What about Jasmijn? Why did this woman have the power or right to choose, and why the hell did you listen to her?* He berated himself. Anger flared at the last thought, and Panos bit down hard on the stem of the pipe, trying to force down the sick feeling that he had failed Jasmijn.

But I did fail her... The sick feeling settled in his stomach. *You just stood there and let her be taken. And you know what? That's not the first time, Panos, my lad.* The dry, accusing voice in the back of his mind did not stop there. *You let the others burn as well, didn't you? You let them die.* Panos flinched at the sudden vivid images of burning men, their skin blackening and peeling away. He could hear their screams of agony as they writhed in the flames. Panos squeezed his eyes shut. *You let them burn...*

No! He shook his head. *I was a captive. Tied up, unarmed...* As true as it was, it somehow still sounded hollow and weak. He *had* watched them die. And then the Kurg had found a way to inflict an even more painful and cruel punishment on him. They had allowed him to live.

Panos moved to a small brazier that stood to the right of the door. He found a pair of tongs leaning up against the wall and fished out a small ember to light his pipe. He stared into the dancing flames as he dragged deeply on the stem. *If you die, they will all die.* He tilted his head back and blew the smoke at the dark sky. *What in the seven hells did she mean by that?*

He shook his head as he sat down on the top step and leaned back against the wall. He ignored the odd glances he received as patrons stepped past him to enter the common room. He smoked quietly, wrapped in his dark thoughts. He wondered where Dacian had gone. He hoped the man hadn't done something truly stupid. Dacian needed to put as much distance as possible between himself and the duke, but Panos didn't think he was one to run from a fight, particularly if he was backed into a corner.

Panos puffed at the pipe. What would Dacian have done if he were confronted with the choice of whether or not to help Jasmijn? Would he have listened or charged into the passage? He sighed and then leaned forward to tap the ash from the pipe. He noticed a movement to his left. He turned to see a woman running toward him. Her face was covered in blood. Panos stood suddenly and ran toward her. She stumbled as she threw a terrified glance over her shoulder. Somehow, she held her balance, eyes wide, then all but threw herself into his arms and screamed, "Help me!"

"I've got you." Panos grunted at the impact. "I've got you." He held her trembling body close and looked down the road, trying to see what she was running from. "What ha—" The word died in his throat as something stepped from the shadows of the alley some thirty paces away.

It moved low to the ground on all fours, pale, mottled skin stretched tight over sinuous muscle. The large eyes were pools of jet black, and thin blue lips peeled back from rows of razor-sharp teeth.

Panos reached reflexively for his sword and then remembered with sick dread that it was leaning against the table inside the tavern. *You fool,* he thought, then noticed movement behind the beast. Another creature moved into the light; this one was slightly larger, limbs longer. It, too, moved on all fours. The pallid, hairless skin in stark contrast to the black, oozing darkness it stepped from. The creature's face was covered in dark blood.

"Move!" he shouted as he grabbed a fistful of the girl's dress and pushed her toward the door of the inn. The creatures exploded into motion, moving low and with a frightening, fluid speed. *Oh gods!* Panos dived to the door, feeling as if he were moving in treacle. He yanked the door open and threw the woman into the common room. The things were close, horrifyingly close. He could hear their feet slapping on the cobbles of the street as he dragged himself inside. He just managed to slam the door shut and shove the bolt in place as one of the creatures rammed into the door with a loud crash.

"By the Dark One's balls, what are you doing?" Jasuf shouted angrily as he looked up from behind the bar.

"The shutters! Close the shutters!" Panos shouted at two men sitting near the window that looked out onto the road. They stared at him in mute astonishment. "Close the fucking—" The window exploded in a spray of glass and splintered wood. The man closest to the window shrieked as a pale-skinned nightmare burst through the open frame, sinking claws and teeth into his flesh.

The man shrieked and flailed around, desperately trying to grab anything to stop himself from being dragged back through the window into the night. Panos watched in sick horror as a clawed hand closed around the man's face; blood sprayed as long talons tore into his cheeks. There was a muffled scream, followed by a dry snap, and the man went limp. And then he was gone.

Jasuf blinked and then roared, "The shutters, gods damn you!"

The remaining man jolted into action, slamming the shutters closed and bolting them with trembling hands. The window secured, he moved quickly back and pulled a heavy-bladed hunting knife from its sheath. Fresh blood splattered the table and windowsill.

"What in the seven hells was that?" Jasuf asked quietly, running a hand through his shock of ginger hair.

The red-haired barmaid stood frozen, hands clasped over her mouth, her eyes filled with tears of terror. Next to her stood the woman Panos had just saved; she was trembling with shock.

"I have no idea. But if you have weapons, get them ready," Panos shouted. "Now! All of you!" Without looking down from the window, Jasuf reached under the counter and drew out a heavy cudgel; several men drew swords or knives.

Panos quickly retrieved his sword and moved to the two women, gently guiding them behind the line of armed men.

"Do you know what those things are?" he asked the girl from the street, touching her arm.

She recoiled from his hand and then shook her head. "No . . ." Her eyes were wild, and her lips were pressed into a thin line. "It . . . killed him," she whispered through clenched teeth. "It just came from the dark . . . and killed him."

Panos didn't know what to say to comfort her, so he turned to the red-haired barmaid. She was frightened but not on the verge of panic. "Stay with her. Stay together and stay back." She nodded and forced a brave smile.

Panos turned from the women and moved to the front of the defensive line. He noticed the white-knuckled grips and clenched jaws of the men. There were gasps as the door shook violently, the metal of the bolt clanging into that of the strike plate. Dust drifted down from the frame. *Oh gods, please hold!* Panos stared at the door.

"We need to brace the door," he said quickly. "The long table! Push it up against the door. Move!" Then he pointed to the window. "A bench . . . prop it up against the shutters!"

Five men moved quickly to drag the heavy table to the door. Jasuf and two others had just managed to grab a bench and wedge it tightly into the window when something heavy slammed into the shutters. They leaped back, wide-eyed. The bench stayed in place. Outside, there was a low hiss of anger, followed by the slow rake of claws on wood.

The Old Church, the Waterfront District

Quay Road, for the most part, was narrow and cobbled. During the day, it would be slow-going with the choke of merchants and customers, but after sunset, with the shops closed and little else to bring anyone to this part of the city, the two watchmen walked down the centre of the road side by side. It was that time of the evening when most people would be at home or visiting the taverns and inns found closer to the market square or in the upper city if they had the coin to spend on a more lavish establishment.

Sev walked slowly with the thumb of his left hand hooked into his belt, wanting nothing more than to enjoy the quiet, but there was a growing gnawing feeling in his gut that things were anything but peaceful. Nils had a nose for trouble, and when he asked someone to investigate, it was hardly ever an idle request. He was sure that there was some connection with the body that had been found in the Dockway Alley. Nils had been picking at that particular thread the whole day, but the gods be damned if Sev knew how it all hung together, and he didn't feel like running into some wild dog in the dark. Not alone, at least.

Well, you're not entirely alone, are you, my son? Sev thought as he shot a glance to the young watchman, Marol, walking next to him on his left. That particular little delight had been unveiled when he walked into the watchhouse for the night shift. He knew something was up the moment he saw both Nils and Tibero waiting for him at the front desk with Sergeant Rake. There would be no routine patrol this evening for Sev. All that needed to be settled was the matter of which hornet's nest he would be poking with a stick.

"We need you to look into the old church on Quay Road," they had said. "A street girl disappeared. She was last seen there. Might be related to the body we found in Dockway."

Sev had cocked an eyebrow at that. "How?" he asked. It wasn't like the girl would have been dragged off to an old abandoned church by some wild animal.

They weren't sure, they said. "But we need you to be careful," Tibero had added.

Careful... bleeding hell! Sev scowled. *Not like I've been doing this bloody job for half my life.* And that's when Tibero, damn the man's eyes, had dropped the pearler that he had to take the boy along. The great ginger arsehole had spouted the predictable bullshit about the lad needing the experience. As if he actually gave a shit.

But Sev's protests had fallen on deaf ears, with Tibero just glaring at him before sighing in that way of his that managed to sound both bone tired and pissed off at exactly the same time. Nils had said nothing, making Sev believe it was not a surprise to him, at least. He and Nils had watched without a word as Tibero had stalked off to his office, slamming the door on any further argument.

Needless to say, the walk to the lower city had been undertaken in stony silence, but that was now beginning to feel awkward. The boy looked pale and nervous. Sev doubted the lad would amount to much in a fight, but it was still better than trying to grow eyes in the back of his bloody head. Sev sighed heavily as he scanned the deep shadows on either side of the lane. Something was definitely afoot, and he was in no mood for surprises. Apparently, Otho was supposed to join them, but that useless lump of lard was nowhere to be seen. *Probably up to his ankles in cheap wine and whores,* Sev thought sourly, *head-first.*

Suppose I need to involve the lad if he's to learn anything, Sev thought, not really knowing how to break the silence. *Not like I didn't need someone to hold my hand when I first joined the watch.* Sev glanced again at the jittery youth. *I just don't bloody well remember ever being that young and that wet behind the ears.* It probably would have been better if he had been allowed to come alone, but he had to admit that maybe the boy could do with the experience. The gods alone knew when the lad would actually become useful, but a bit of a walk through the city at night might just speed that along.

Sev looked up and could see the weather-beaten bell tower of the old church poking above the buildings that loomed over the road. As they rounded the bend and the building came into view, Sev found himself hoping that Nil's nose would prove to be wrong for once. They'd walk around and rattle the doors before going back to the watchhouse to put their feet up with something warm to drink. His babysitting assignment would be over, and the lad would have racked up a smidgen of experience.

Sev drew in a deep, slow breath as they stopped in front of the church's heavy wooden doors. *Not bloody likely,* he thought glumly as he climbed the steps and turned the heavy iron of the door handle. He tugged at the door.

"Locked," Sev grunted, descending the steps and stepping into the middle of the road to look up at the pockmarked stone of the tower. "Looks quiet enough. What do you think, Melon?"

"It's Marol," the boy replied.

"Shut up," Sev growled, turning to glare at the boy. "Tibero said your name's Melon. So your name is *Melon* until he says otherwise. You got that?"

The boy frowned, then looked as if he were about to say something before nodding and choosing to remain silent.

Lad learns quickly. Sev turned away to hide his smile, then looked up at the belfry once again. *Odd that there are no birds.* Night larks frequented high places like that, but they apparently had no liking for this particular perch.

"Where are the guards?" Marol asked, looking up and down the narrow street. "Shouldn't there be temple guards?"

"Nah… place has been deserted for years." Sev shook his head. "Nothing in there to guard. Only locked to keep out the beggars."

"You'd think they'd leave it open, then," Marol said, shaking his head.

"What?" Sev frowned at the boy.

"I said that it's strange they don't leave it open, then. You know, to give the poor people a place to sleep, being a church and all." Marol shrugged. "They speak a lot about love and caring but don't seem to do much about it."

"Gods, Melon," Sev growled. "Have you seen the temple lately? You think they built that with love and caring? There are priests in there who live better than kings. Love and caring . . . bloody hell."

Marol opened his mouth to argue, but Sev turned away and pointed to the narrow lane to the left of the church. "Let's look around the back. Should be a gate and a courtyard. Let's check if there's any love and caring stored up there." Sev made a show of wiping his nose on his sleeve to hide his grin as the lad's face darkened.

"Lead on, lad." Sev hooked his thumb into his belt and nodded toward the alley. Marol sighed and tried to hide his frustration, with little success. He turned toward the alley with his hand on his sword. Sev was about to tell him to relax but caught himself. Something still gnawed at him. He looked around slowly. Moonlight had burst through the patchwork of clouds to cast long, dark shadows between the buildings. Nothing moved, not even the scurry of a rat, and the gods knew there were more than a few of them in this part of town. *It's just far too quiet,* Sev thought as the first pang of unease settled in.

"Hold up, Melon," he said softly, loosening his blade in its scabbard. "Be quiet and keep your eyes open."

Sev followed the young watchman into the shadows of the lane. They did not need to go far before they found the side gate; it was made of heavy black iron and topped with long, sharp spikes. He leaned in close to the gate until he felt the cold iron on his cheeks and looked into the overgrown courtyard; the wild tangle of plants and tall grass spoke of long neglect. *There's nothing here,* he thought with more than a little relief and was about to suggest they go back to the watchhouse when Marol gripped his arm tightly.

"Sev. There's something on the ground over there," the young watchman whispered, releasing Sev's arm and pointing into the darkness.

Sev stepped away from the gate and noticed the white-knuckled grip Marol had on the handle of his sword. "Where?" Sev asked softly.

"There. Near the far wall."

Sev strained to penetrate the inky darkness. "Got it," he whispered as he made out a set of booted legs. He paused. It was an unlikely place for a drunk to fall and sleep things off, and that gnawing unease had not relented one little bit. "Draw your sword… quietly," he hissed as he carefully drew his own blade from its scabbard. He shot a glance at Marol. Sweat glistened on his smooth, boyish face. "And *breathe,* Melon." Sev forced a smile. "You won't be much help if you pass out on me."

He slipped past the boy and allowed his eyes to adjust. He glided forward into the deep gloom, scanning the alley for any signs of movement. He could now make out the soft glint of a sword on the ground. The boots were black polished leather, the leggings dark wool. He stopped and held up a hand to Marol. Sev inched forward, and the pale-purple ropes of intestines and dark pools of blood came into view.

The gods damn that Nils, Sev thought. Lying a few feet beyond the first body, he could make out another against the wall. Even in the dim light, he could see clearly that it had no head.

"Oh gods…" he heard Marol say behind him.

"Quiet!" Sev hissed, carefully stepping forward. Black and silver armour came into view. *Temple guards… What the hell were they doing here?* He looked at the horrific wounds. It looked as if they had been torn apart by a wild animal. *What could have done this? Not a bloody dog. Isn't one big enough to do that…* He gripped his sword tighter and looked back to see the white-faced Marol rooted in place.

"Melon!" Sev whispered with a sharp gesture. "Move, damn you!" Sev spat through grated teeth. The boy finally jerked forward, sword raised.

Gods, what to do? Sev thought, looking down at the mutilated bodies. Then he turned and grabbed the boy's jerkin and dragged him close. "Listen. I need you to get to Nils. He's more than likely at his home, a small house with a green door in the upper city on Willow Road." He waited for Marol to nod before continuing. "Tell him about these guards. Tell him to bring whoever he can and I'll meet him at the temple. We need to find out why these men were here. It makes no sense." Marol nodded again, wide-eyed, with a tightly clenched jaw.

"What about them?" the boy asked stiffly.

"I'll get the wagon for them once we're sure it's safe," Sev replied softly and forced a smile. "Relax, Melon. Have a stiff drink after you speak with Nils. Ask him for some of that gods-awful emberwyne of his. If that doesn't kill you, you should be all right." He slapped the boy's cheek lightly. "Now go!"

He watched Marol bolt from the lane and disappear up Quay Road before turning back to the dead temple guard. He looked at the deep gouges across the man's chest and stomach. He remembered seeing a man after he'd been attacked by a white bear in the Noordlandt. *Even those horrific wounds were nothing compared to this,* he thought with a sick feeling. Gripping his sword tighter, he moved deeper into the dark. He would cut up Water's Edge toward the temple. He hoped to the gods that he would not encounter whatever had killed these men.

Willow Road, the Upper City

Nils paused before knocking on the green wooden door of his home. He was bone tired and had not been able to shake the feeling that the night had only begun. The fact that Amon had not returned from the temple worried him. He had waited at the watchhouse for most of the afternoon before walking to the apothecary's home, only to find it locked. Had the man run away? Had something happened to him? But he had no way to find out. He could hardly walk into the office of one of the Chosen and demand answers. The questions gnawed at him as he rapped his knuckles lightly on the door.

Hopefully, Sev and Marol would cast some light on the matter when they returned from Quay Road. According to Rake, the old monk had been adamant that the girl had been taken to the old church. If there was anything out of place, Sev was the man to spot it. He was steady and seasoned, with a keen eye. The lad Marol would learn a lot from a man like him.

If Amon was right, the thread that tied it all together was wound around one of the most powerful men in the city. He would need irrefutable evidence if the watch was to move against Vasilios. Nils had no idea what would be enough. Men—like the old monk—disappeared for simply suggesting wrongdoing. The girl, the church, the stones, and the body in the alley… there had to be something that led back to the priest. He sighed. Amon was convinced, but until he returned, they were just picking at a tangled web, hoping there would be no more visits to the Dead House before dawn.

His bleak thoughts were interrupted as he heard the bolt slide back. Warm light and the delicious smell of cooking food spilled through the opening door. Cilla stood in the doorway with a white kitchen cloth in her hands. She took a look at him and cocked an eyebrow with a soft smile. It was not the first time he'd brought an unresolved problem home, and she could read him like a book.

"There's a problem in the city." Nils shrugged.

"And an ugly one, by the look of it." Cilla reached out and tugged at the front of his shirt. He stepped into her embrace and kissed her softly. Nils felt her melt into him, and he took a moment to enjoy the warmth of her and the soft smell of flowers that seemed to hang around her before he gently disengaged. He took a quick look up and down the road before pushing her inside, closing the door, and sliding the bolt home.

"What is it, my love?" she asked as her smile slipped. She knew him so well. "This is bad, isn't it?"

"Yes," he said simply and touched her cheek. "And it's going to get worse if I can't figure it out."

Cilla nodded slowly and then said, "Food. We can't think on empty stomachs." She squeezed his arm and walked to the kitchen.

Nils stood for a moment, then turned and checked the bolt on the door. If Amon was right, it probably wouldn't be enough, but the thought of a stout, locked door between Cilla and the night made him feel better nonetheless.

He stepped into their simple living room, feeling the warmth from the hearth, where a small fire lapped at a stack of wood. The only furniture was a low table, a wooden rocking chair, and a couch strewn with earthy-coloured cushions. He could hear Cilla setting the table in the kitchen. He ran his hand over his face and leaned down to drop another log on the fire. He considered his words carefully. He hated being away from her. He sighed again.

"Cilla," he called out, not turning from the flames. "I may need you to leave the city for a while. Perhaps you could visit your uncle and aunt until this matter is sorted."

The sounds in the kitchen stopped, and Nils turned to see Cilla standing in the doorway, wiping her hands. Her expression was serious. "Why?" she asked.

Nils sighed. "I'm not sure. I don't know what's going on. There are a number of things that are... that *seem* connected. There was a man killed last night. It looked like an... animal attack. But I'm not sure." He shook his head. "Something was not right about the wounds, so I asked Amon to look at the body." He paused and looked deeply into her eyes before he continued, "I've never seen Amon react like that. He was shaken. He knows something. He's seen this before... and I think that that attack and other events are connected. And it's all just the start of something far worse."

Cilla nodded slowly and then gestured to the kitchen. "Come eat. It's going to be a long night." She turned and then stopped to look over her shoulder. "And no. I'm not leaving. Not as long as you're here."

Nils knew better than to argue. He had seen that expression before. Once Cilla had made up her mind, it stayed that way, and nothing in this world or the next would sway her in another direction. He followed her to the kitchen and pulled back a chair, sitting down wearily.

"Tea?" Cilla asked as she placed a hand on his shoulder and squeezed softly.

Nils nodded, the chair creaking as he leaned backward and rested his arm on the table. "I sent Sev and one of the new men to investigate the old church. You know... the one on Quay Road, near the docks. Rake told me about an odd incident this morning. An old monk came into the watchhouse with a story of a missing street girl." He paused and ran a hand over his face. "They should be back within the hour."

Cilla placed the steaming cup in front of him and gently touched his cheek. "You're worrying about what they'll find. And you're more worried that they might not make it back?"

Nils looked deeply into his wife's eyes. "Yes. If I'm right, they may be in great danger. I should have sent more men." He forced a smile and slurped at the tea. "It's good... too much honey."

"I know. Just the way you like it." Cilla smiled. She looked into his eyes. "You have a gift, Nils. You see things others miss. I trust your feelings. And so does Sev. They will be careful, my love."

Nils nodded slowly as he set the cup down on the table. "Let's hope it's nothing. I'd like nothing more than to be wrong." He reached out and took her hand. "Sev and Marol will come here first. No point in reporting to Tibero. You know that he takes forever to make any sort of decision. We'll know then."

Cilla smiled and squeezed his hand. "Food. You must eat. It's going to be a long night," she said as she pushed back her chair.

Nils grinned suddenly. "I love you."

"I know." Cilla smiled. "I—" She was cut short by hammering on the door.

Nils stood immediately and strode to the front of the house. "Sev? Marol?" he called out.

"It's Marol, sir," came the breathless reply.

Nils pulled back the latch and opened the door to see the young watchman doubled over with his hands on his knees. His chest was heaving, and sweat plastered his hair to his head. *Gods, he must have run all the way from the lower city,* Nils thought. "Come in, come in!" He stepped aside to allow the young man to stagger into the house. "Where's Sev?"

"On his way... to the temple," Marol said between ragged breaths. "We found... two bodies... temple guards. Gods, they looked like they... were killed by... a bear!" The young man looked up and saw Cilla, and his eyes widened. "Shit... sorry, ma'am."

Cilla dismissed his breathless apology with a smile and turned to Nils, who stood woodenly before her. "I need to go," he said. "Latch the door. Don't open it for anyone. I'll be back as soon as I can."

"Be careful," she said softly as he pulled his sword from the peg and strapped it around his waist. "I will see you in the morning. Bring young Marol here; I'll feed you both."

He held her gaze for a long moment and then turned to Marol and gripped the young man's arm. "With me, Marol. We need to get to the watchhouse and gather up a few more men."

The young watchman looked up at him and then nodded slowly. Nils could see the beginnings of a new strength in the young man. His eyes were less wide, the set of his jaw a bit firmer. "Good man. Let's go," he said with a grim smile. With a final look to Cilla, he turned and strode from the house.

"Are they gone?" asked a bearded man. He held a docker's hook stiffly out in front of him. He was staring fixedly at the door, as if expecting it to come crashing in at any moment.

"Don't think so, mate," the man next to him said softly. "But one way or the other, I ain't goin' out into the dark."

"Me neither." The bearded man shook his head. "Not bloody ever again."

"Stay calm, my lads," Panos said softly as he walked over to the burly innkeeper. He turned away from the others and leaned close. "Jasuf. The door to the courtyard?" Panos asked quietly.

Jasuf swallowed and flicked a glance over his left shoulder to the passage that led away to the back of the inn. "It's closed and locked." The big barkeep grunted after a brief pause. He wiped at the sheet of sweat on his forehead. "And it's iron braced, lad. Should hold against almost anything."

"You sure?" Panos asked.

Jasuf cast another quick look to the dimly lit passage. "Yes. I'm sure."

"Good." The swordsman nodded. "What about upstairs? Or outside in the servants' quarters?"

Jasuf shook his shaggy head. "No. Everyone's in here. Kitchen staff, too." He pointed to the plump cook and her two scullery maids, who were huddled together in a corner. "What are those things? You or that girl might have got a better look at them when you were outside."

"I don't know," Panos said quietly. "I asked the girl. Whatever they are, they killed whoever she was with, and they did it quickly. We can't —"

His words were cut short by the crash of shattering glass. Both he and Jasuf looked up at the stairs. "Oh gods," Panos swore as the realisation hit him. "The bedroom windows—one of the shutters must have been open." Not taking his eyes from the top of the stairs, he pushed Jasuf toward the others, who were now huddled even closer together. One of the women started sobbing quietly. He looked into the pinched faces. The wide-eyed, bowel-loosening fear gripping them was palpable.

"Get them into the corner away from the stairs," he said to Jasuf. "And get the women behind you. Anyone with a weapon to the front." Panos waved them back and stepped toward the staircase, raising his sword. He could just make out the flickering yellow lamp of the upstairs passage as he placed his foot on the first step. He was about to take the next step when a shadow moved, and then another, and another. There was a glimpse of pale, mottled skin.

In all his years as a soldier, he could never understand why, when standing at the edge of a fight, his mouth would feel like it was filled with ash and his bladder would be bursting. He swallowed and forced the muscles of his shoulders and arms to relax, easing the iron grip on his sword. He looked with surprise at the white-knuckled grip he had on the dark wood of the banister. He did not remember reaching out to grab it. *Relax, Panos, my lad,* he thought with a half smile. *Would be embarrassing if you shit your britches in front of all these people.* He almost laughed as he slowly started up the stairs.

"Are you mad?" Jasuf hissed. "Get back here, man."

Panos ignored him and continued to climb. He flinched as a step creaked under his weight. He blinked away a droplet of sweat that stung his eye. Three more steps and he had climbed high enough to see down the passage. It was empty, the dull yellow light of the lamps casting deep shadows in the recesses of the doorways. *There are the things that hide in the dark, things that crawl into your mind to drag you down into the place of nightmares...*

The swordsman stood rooted to stairs, his eyes flicking from one dark doorway to the next. *There's the space where the monsters hide, in the cloying, sucking black that seeps into your soul.* He shivered as the images of flame and ash and agony flashed through his mind. He would not... could not go back to that. He would not see anyone burn for him ever again, even if that meant his death.

Panos stepped into the passage and felt the cold trickle of sweat down his spine. His heart hammered, but his arm felt rock steady; the three feet of razor-sharp steel was unwavering. He would face whatever chose to step into this passage. There was only one way to the people huddled in the common room below, and that was through him.

He froze as the creature stepped into the light. It moved slowly on all fours, low to the ground. Its large, jet-black eyes were latched on to his. Thin lips peeled back from wicked-looking teeth, and then it hissed, the sound low and filled with malice. It was the size of a large dog but completely hairless. The skin was milky white, with grey mottles on the shoulders and back. The creature's limbs were long and powerful, each ending in a three-toed foot, each digit punctuated with a long black claw, hooked and sharp. It was something that stepped out of a nightmare, filled with hunger and hate.

Panos took a slow, deep breath and readied himself. The attack would come fast. He would have no chance for anything but a single thrust, with the creature running into his blade. If he missed, he would be dead. He tried not to imagine those teeth sinking into his flesh, the claws rending and tearing.

He crouched and slowly extended the blade. His senses felt painfully acute as he took in every detail: the flicker of the lamps sending the shadows dancing across the walls; the warm, dusty smell of the air; the taunt, excited readiness of his muscles. He had experienced this before every fight, the flow of each second slowing to that of molasses.

Panos watched with a detached fascination as the creature exploded into motion, the muscles of its shoulders bunching and rippling as it hurtled down the passage. And then it launched itself at him, all claws and teeth and death. The swordsman, wrapped in his hyperaware state, held his ground, blade extended, waiting for the impact.

The point of the sword took the creature high in the chest, punching through its body to exit between its shoulder blade and spine. It slammed into Panos, twisting the weapon from his grip, its claws raking across his shoulders and neck. The impact swept the swordsman from his feet. He flew through the air, landed hard on the top of stairs, and flew backward into space.

Panos hit the stairs on his back, rolled, crashed into the banister, and rolled again. He twisted, trying to arrest his fall, but hit the wall hard before crashing face-first into the floor. He grunted as something heavy landed on top of him, followed by a blinding jolt of pain as he felt a rib snap.

Hot, fetid breath fanned his neck, and he tried to scramble away, frantically punching at the thing that pressed him to the floor. He rolled and felt the weight fall from his back. Pain lanced through his chest as he dragged himself to his knees. The creature lay on the floor next to him, the point of his sword protruding from its back. It twitched and then lay still. He crawled quickly over to it and pushed the beast over onto its back. Grabbing the hilt of his sword, he twisted it and wrenched the blade free.

"Stay back! Back!" he barked hoarsely at the others, who had snapped out of their state of shock and had started to move forward. "There are more."

He forced himself to his feet and staggered to the foot of the stairs as another creature stepped into view in the passage above. This one was larger and more heavily muscled at the shoulders. The eyes were narrow, hateful slits, and the mouth filled with jagged yellow teeth. Behind it, a third crept into view. This one was similar to the first, milky white and mottled. Its eyes were the same hungry, jet-black orbs. Panos heard one of the women stifle a scream, along with gasps from the others as fear rippled through the small group.

"Here, you bastards! Here!" Panos shouted at the creatures as he forced himself forward and onto the stairs. He held a white-knuckled grip on the banister and tried, with little success, to ignore the grinding pain of the broken rib. He raised his sword and the larger creature charged, hurtling toward the swordsman at an impossible speed. Panos had no time to brace himself before it struck. Agony seared through his chest as he found himself catapulted backward. This time, the point did not find its mark, the blade merely cutting through the pallid flesh of the creature's flank before being torn from his grasp.

He hit the floor hard, the air brutally driven from his lungs. Pain stabbed through him as ragged teeth sank into his shoulder and wicked claws tore into his sides and back. Panos tried to scream, but all he could manage was a breathless wheeze. With titanic effort, he pulled an arm free, dragging it in front of him to protect his face and throat. With the other arm, he fumbled desperately for his dagger. He managed to pull the blade free from the sheath as the jaws released his shoulder to sink deep and hard into his forearm. He shrieked as the bones snapped, stabbing convulsively at the creature's flank with the blade, finally feeling it sink between ribs, only to be twisted from his grasp.

The creature thrashed in pain and anger. All reason fled as Panos' world descended into nothing more than blood and pain and the crushing, clawing, biting weight of the nightmare pressing him into the floor. And then the weight was gone. He dragged a ragged breath into his lungs and groaned as jagged shards of pain ripped through his chest. Rough hands grabbed at his clothes, and he felt himself being dragged along the floor before everything went black.

The Watch House, the Upper City

Rake leaned heavily on the desk, trying to ease the ache in his lower back. It had been a very long, very busy day, and having finally made it to the top of the hour, he would be on his way home soon. He toyed with the idea of dropping into the Crow for a pint and a game of cards but dismissed it quickly. He was tired, and a quiet glass of red and a warm fire sounded far better than a blazing hangover and an empty purse.

He stifled a yawn and stood up to look around the watchhouse. It was quiet for once. Most of the men were either on their rounds or at home, with one obvious and irritating exception, Otho. That useless lump of lard was once again nowhere to be seen. *'Bout as useful as tits on a tomcat,* that one, Rake thought as he scratched absently at his bearded cheek. *Probably up to his ears in his cups.* He started as the door burst open and Nils strode in with a breathless Marol in tow.

"Nils! What's wrong?" the sergeant asked with a sinking feeling that the night was just about to get a lot less quiet. *Gods damn it... should have left earlier.* No sooner had the thought passed than his face twitched with a pang of guilt. He was not one to dodge his duty.

"How many men have we?" Nils asked, ignoring Rake's question as he looked into the empty office. "Shit. Is no one here?"

Rake shrugged. "There were a few inquiries regarding disturbances, so I sent a few men to check those out. The rest are on rounds." He paused and looked at a particular desk. "Otho was supposed to—"

"Gods. That useless…" Nils bit back the rest with visible effort. "Tibero. Is he still here?"

Rake nodded. "Hasn't been out of his office the whole afternoon." He looked down the passage before continuing, "Probably blind drunk."

Nils' face darkened, and Rake could see the man's knuckles whiten as his fists balled. "Get your sword," Nils said simply. "And give young Marol here a shot of emberwyne. I'll get Tibero."

Tibero sat slumped forward over his desk with his head in his hands, his fingers threaded through his unruly mop of ginger hair, touched with grey. He stared into a glass of emberwyne resting on the desk in front of him, watching the flickering reflection of the oil lamp dance across the golden liquid. He had poured it hours ago, but for some reason, he had just left it there untouched. Since talking to Nils, he'd had every intention of getting utterly obliterated, but it looked like he could add that to the ever-growing list of things he had fucked up in his life.

He sighed and sat back. *No point in hanging around here,* he thought bleakly. *Might as well drag my sorry arse back home.* But the prospect of the empty house filled him with dread. Too many memories, too many blank spaces that were once filled with warmth and light and love. He reached for the glass but still could bring himself to lift it. He was scared of being sober and scared of being drunk. He didn't want to sit in his office, and he didn't want to walk past the front desk, where he could feel the eyes following him, judging or pitying. He wasn't sure which was worse. And he definitely did not want to be in that empty house.

His hand strayed down to the hilt of his dagger. He was just so gods-damned tired. There really wasn't any point to it all anymore. Maybe it would be for the best if he just…

He pulled the blade from its sheath and held it up to the light. His distorted reflection swam in the silvery metal.

"You can't even do that, can you?" he growled as he tossed the blade to the desk. "Useless, useless bastard."

Tibero jumped at the loud rap of knuckles on the door.

"Enter!" he shouted, not bothering to hide the glass.

It was hardly a surprise when Nils pulled open the door and strode into the office.

"Tibero," Nils said firmly. "We need you. Now."

"What?" Tibero blinked and then shook his head. "Wait... what's happened?"

"There is no time. There's . . ." Nils's face darkened as he visibly struggled to control himself. His voice was soft and measured when he continued, "I sent Sev and Marol to the church. They found two dead temple guards. Rake and Marol are with me. Sev is on his way to the temple. I think... no... I know he's in real danger. We need to go to meet him there now." He paused. "The answers are there, Tibero. This city is on a knife's edge, whether you want to believe it or not."

Tibero stared at the younger man for a long moment. *By the gods, this is impossible,* he thought. *Right or wrong, you're going to get me killed —or worse, into a world of shit.* He looked at the firm set of the younger man's jaw and the grim determination in his eyes. Then he thought of Sev and Rake, watchmen he had known for decades. They were solid, dependable men. He thought of young Melon, so annoyingly... fresh. These were men he had once led. Men who had once looked to him for guidance and support. Men he had abandoned.

Tibero nodded slowly, feeling something he had not felt in a long time. He pushed himself to his feet and straightened his rumpled tunic with a sharp tug at the hem. "Good. I'll get my sword."

The Crow Inn, the Market District

Jasuf saw the monster emerge from the passage. It's flat, tooth-filled face turned slowly toward him, and he felt a vicelike grip of fear that he had never experienced before. It was deep and debilitating. It dragged at his guts and turned his legs to jelly. Its cold, icy fingers gripped his chest and squeezed until each breath felt shallow and tight. *By all the gods, what is that thing?* he thought as he fought down the surging need to turn and run, only succeeding because there was nowhere to run to. They were in a corner, trapped like rats. And he could not leave these people, his girls. His large, meaty hands felt weak and sweaty as they wrung the handle of his cudgel, but nonetheless, he took a step forward.

"Here, you bastards! Here!" Jasuf started at the swordsman's sudden shout.

The creature's head snapped forward at the cry, and it sprang. Jasuf watched in horror as the swordsman was swept from his feet, slamming into the floor with the beast on top of him.

"Jasuf! The stairs!" a man to his left shouted. Jasuf pulled his attention away from the frantic struggles of the swordsman to see the other creature climbing slowly over the banister. It hung above them like some nightmarish spider. *Gods, it's going to jump right into the middle of us!* Without thinking, he snatched an oil lamp from a table and, in one motion, threw it at the beast. It shattered against the wood of the banister and exploded in a ball of flame. The creature shrieked and fell back.

He turned to the struggling swordsman and saw the creature's jaws clamp down on the swordsman's arm. The man screamed in pain but still stabbed at the beast's side with his dagger. *He's going die!* The realisation hit Jasuf like a hammer, and he ran forward, swinging his cudgel in a murderous arc. The heavy wood slammed hard into the side of the creature's skull, the force of the blow reverberating through his hands and snapping the creature's head to the left. Still, it held on to the man, but those slitted black eyes were now on him. Jasuf swung the club again, this time aiming it upward and under the creature's jaw. The blow landed cleanly and punched the beast from the swordsman in a spray of black blood.

It landed heavily on its side but was already scrambling to its feet as Jasuf grabbed at the swordsman's jerkin and started dragging him back to the group. "Help me, you bastards!" he roared. Two men snapped out of their shock and ran forward. One of them grabbed at the swordsman's legs while the other grabbed an arm, and they hauled him back to where the women huddled, terrified, against the wall.

"Is he dead?" the young red-haired barmaid asked, coming to kneel next to the still form of the man. Jasuf looked into her wide, frightened eyes. In the insanity of the moment, her name escaped him. *Gods! She had been working at the Crow for months…*

"I don't know, lass. Stay here," Jasuf said quickly before turning back to the fight. He nodded in grim approval as he noticed the girl move to stand next to him. In her hand, she held a short kitchen knife.

"I'm not going to wait like some rabbit," she said softly, holding the small blade in front of her defiantly.

Jasuf nodded and turned back to see that the larger creature had recovered and was moving toward them. It crept low to the ground, blood dribbling from its damaged mouth and running down its flank where the dagger jutted from its flesh. Jasuf saw with some satisfaction that the blow he had landed had snapped off several of the creature's teeth. The smaller creature had also descended the stairs, the skin on its shoulder and left arm blackened and blistered where the oil had burned it. He raised the club and realised that the fear had vanished. In its place was a burning rage.

"Come on in, you sons of bitches," he growled, raising the cudgel. "Come on in."

The creatures moved closer. Both bore painful wounds and were now far more wary, knowing that their prey would fight back. Jasuf flinched as the smaller of the two suddenly lunged forward. Its claws sank deep into the man standing to the left of the innkeeper. The man screamed and pitched forward as the weight of the beast dragged him to the floor. Jasuf swung his club down hard, the impact sending a shudder up his arms as the weighted wood crunched into the beast's shoulder, shattering the bone of the joint.

The creature shrieked in agony but somehow still held on, managing to drag the struggling man away even though its left arm now hung uselessly at its side. The larger creature sprang forward, sinking its teeth into the damaged shoulder of the wounded beast, driving it away from the struggling man. Then they watched in horror as the man's screams were cut short in a spray of blood as claws and teeth ripped him apart.

The injured creature slinked closer, dragging its limp left arm, but the larger beast snapped at it, hissing angrily and sending it scurrying back. Then it dipped its head to once again tear flesh from the ruined body. The small group stood in stunned silence and watched, unable to pull their eyes from the grisly spectacle; sweaty hands gripped weapons as they waited for what might be their turn to be torn from the pitiful safety of the group.

When the beast finally looked up, blood dripped from its flat, menacing face. Its black, slitted eyes latched on to Jasuf, and it bared broken and jagged fangs, hate palpable in its low, shuddering hiss. Jasuf carefully pushed the redheaded girl behind him. If the creature meant to take him next, he would not have one of the others be caught between him and that thing.

"All right, then, you ugly bastards," he rasped through clenched teeth, taking a half step forward. "Let's get it over with."

Water's Edge Road, the Waterfront District

Sev ran up the hill, feeling his lungs start to burn. It had taken him longer than anticipated to reach the road, inching his way forward through the inky darkness, and the relief had been palpable once he'd stepped onto the cobbles of Water's Edge. By comparison, the narrow, winding thoroughfare seemed like a broad, brightly lit avenue. In reality, though, the flickering street lamps were still too far apart for his liking, and there were too many deep shadows and narrow, jet-black alleyways between the small houses. He had no idea what had killed those men, and he had little wish to find out.

Sev slowed to a walk and sucked in a few deep breaths. The night was cold, but sweat beaded on his face and trickled down his back. Although in his early forties, he was still whip lean and fit, but he had begun to notice the dull ache in his knees and lower back whenever he exerted himself. He scowled and forced himself into a loping run. Marol would have reached Nils by now, and with a measure of luck, they would be on the way to the temple with a few men. Sev had no idea what they would do once they got there, but he would leave that to Nils's sharper mind. One thing was for certain: those guards had little business at the Quay Road church, and something had butchered them. If there were any answers to be found, they would be at the temple.

He rounded a bend and stopped, suddenly finding himself face to face with a startled cart horse that snorted in surprise. Three equally surprised men who were busy unloading the wagon stopped and looked at Sev. The closest had a heavy sack of what looked like grain draped over his broad shoulder; the others stood silhouetted in a narrow doorway that spilled bright-orange light into the street.

"Evening, gentlemen," Sev said casually.

"Shit. It's the bloody watch," he heard one of the men in the doorway hiss.

Bleeding hell. What're the chances I stumble across these jokers tonight? Sev thought as he moved slowly forward. *Bootleggers, by the looks of it.* There were quite a few of these operations in the city, not big enough for severe measures but not small enough to completely ignore. "I'm not here for you," Sev said, holding up his hands to show he carried no blade. "I need you all to go inside. There's… a wild animal loose in the city, and it's not safe."

A short, incredibly round man stepped from the shadows. He stroked a neatly trimmed goatee with a pudgy hand and looked at Sev with small, malevolent eyes. "A wild animal, you say? An' you want me 'n' the boys to go inside?" He paused and looked to the three men. The one on the wagon shrugged the heavy sack from his shoulder, turning to face Sev as it landed with a dusty thump. The other two were moving slowly to block Sev's path.

"Not bloody likely," the fat man continued. "You expect us to just go inside 'n' wait around over a cuppa for you to come back with a couple of your friends? Next we knows, we's clapped in irons. I don't think that's a particularly good idea. What you say, boys?" The others growled in assent, and Sev could see blades being drawn.

Idiots… I don't have time for this shit, Sev thought as he held up a hand. "I'm going to say this once more. I'm not here to arrest you. It's not safe." He pointed slowly back down the road. "There are two dead men back there lying in an alley. I can guarantee you lads have no wish to meet whatever did that. I need you all to—"

"Get him!" barked the fat man, and the three men charged forward.

Damn them! Sev thought as the first blow came in low and hard. Sev twisted from the path of the blade, feeling it snag at his jerkin as he hammered his fist into the man's jaw. The man crashed face-first into the cobbles, senseless. The next attacker was upon him, and he barely had time to parry the wild slash with his forearm. The man staggered off-balance, and Sev kicked out hard at the inside of his knee. The joint broke with a loud crack, and the man screamed and collapsed to the ground, writhing in agony. Seeing his two companions on the ground, the third drew up short and backed away, holding his blade stiffly out in front of him.

Sev drew his sword and pointed the blade at the fat man, who had retreated and now stood against the wall, placing the wagon between him and Sev. "Now I don't know if you and your lads are hard of hearing or just plain stupid, so I'm going to say this once more, and slowly. Get this pair of arseholes and yourselves inside before I lose my patience."

The fat man nodded vigorously, his jowls jiggling. "Get 'em inside, Jake."

"What about the horse?" the man called Jake asked, not looking away from Sev and not lowering his blade.

"Gods damn it!" the fat man barked. "Get those two—" The words were cut short as blood sprayed across Jake's face. The fat man staggered and clutched at a ragged wound that split his throat. His eyes were wide, and blood spilled from his mouth as he collapsed to the cobbles. The horse reared back in its braces and snorted loudly as something pale flashed past into the darkness.

Jake stood rooted to the ground. He touched his bloody face with a trembling hand. "What the fuckin' hell?" he whispered.

Sev ignored him and raised his sword, trying desperately to see any movement beyond the pitiful light cast by the sparse lamps and the open doorway. The man with the broken leg had managed to push himself up against a wall and was sucking in short, sharp breaths. His face was covered in sweat, and he gripped his thigh with both hands, the lower part of his leg bent at an odd angle.

"You broke… my leg… you bastard," he hissed through clenched teeth. "You…" He stopped as he noticed the fat man lying facedown in a dark pool of blood. "You killed him! Gods—"

337

"Shut it," Sev snarled as he reached down and grabbed the unconscious man's belt. He dragged him over to the wall next to the one with the broken leg. "I didn't kill anyone, you fool." Sev looked up as the horse snorted. The animal's ears were flat against its head as it stamped its hooves and fought against the leather braces. Sev picked up the man's knife and dropped it into his lap. "I think you're going to need this." He straightened and walked slowly to the terrified horse. He held his sword ready as he stared into the thick shadows. He reached out carefully to stroke the animal's neck. He could feel the muscles twitch and tremble beneath his fingers.

"There's a good boy," he murmured as he slid his hand down the horse's flank to the girth buckle. He tugged at the leather strap, pulling it free, all the time whispering to the frighted animal, never taking his eyes from the darkness.

"Was happenin'?" Jake hissed. "What you doing with the bloody horse?"

"I'm letting it go," Sev said softly.

"What? What for? Fucking leave it." Jake's voice had an edge of hysteria to it.

Sev ignored him and moved his hand slowly to the buckles of the trace and neck strap. Pulling the straps free, he finally reached up and pulled the crown over the horse's head, allowing the bit to fall from the horse's mouth. The terrified animal stood rooted to the ground until Sev slapped it hard on the flank, sending it rushing off into the darkness with a clatter of hooves.

"I'd move a bit closer if I were you," Sev called softly to Jake.

"Why? What did you see?" Jake whispered, wide-eyed, as he started to move slowly forward.

"Movement." Sev pointed into the darkness with his sword. "There… near the entrance to that alleyway." He stepped closer to the man with the broken leg. "I have a feeling we are going to need more than one blade."

The Temple Precinct , the Upper City

Nils walked to Tibero's right as they strode up to the gates of the temple precinct. With Rake and Marol following close behind, he took a moment to consider the determined stride of the older man. There was also a new sharpness to the eyes under the bushy brows and an uncharacteristic jut of the man's stubbled chin. It spoke of a purpose that had been missing for a very long time, and Nils could not help but smile.

"Open up!" Tibero called out to the two guards who stepped out from behind the tall, ornate iron of the gate. "We have business with the Primatus!"

"No, you don't," the tall guard on the left grunted. "Not at this hour. Come back in the morning and make an appointment."

"I'm the captain of the watch," Tibero snapped. "We need to speak with His Grace urgently." He stepped closer to the gate, eyes blazing. "This is a matter for the Primatus alone. I am sure he would not want the details to become public knowledge."

"I said come back in the morning," the guard huffed, an edge of annoyance and self-importance creeping into his voice.

Nils was about to step forward as he saw Tibero's frown deepen, then stopped as the captain nodded slowly. "Have you ever seen a leper?" he asked quite suddenly.

The tall guard paused, caught off guard by the odd question. "No. Can't say I have. What's that got to—"

"Terrible," Tibero cut him off with a shake of his head. "Bits of rotting flesh falling off them. They're like walking corpses. But the smell is the worst."

The guard blinked and opened his mouth to reply when Tibero grabbed at his own jowls and squeezed. "When it gets to your face, that's when it really gets bad. Your lips and nose just sort of slough off. I'd imagine that makes it quite difficult to eat." He paused, letting that sink in. The guards exchanged glances with looks of disgust settling onto their faces.

"You don't see many of them here in the city," Tibero continued. "You know why? We round them up. We've got a special cell for them deep under the watchhouse. The day cell on the first level is for the general troublemakers and drunkards. We use the second for the really nasty pieces of work. Murderers, rapists . . . complete scum." He stepped right up to the gate and leaned forward, lowering his voice as if to share a secret with the two men. "Then there's the third. It's completely dark down there. Couldn't see your hand in front of your face if you tried, and you would not believe the smell." He scratched at his ginger stubble as if wondering how to phrase the rest. "Now if I were to throw someone into that particular cell for... oh, I don't know..." He looked to Nils and waved a hand for inspiration.

"For obstructing a watchman in the line of duty, sir?" Nils replied, stone-faced.

"Yes! Exactly!" He jabbed a finger in Nils' direction before turning back to the first guard whose face had visibly paled. "I'm not sure how long it would be before anyone would come for a person like that. Not many visitors go down there. The stench, the risk of infection. It's far too much for most folks. He'd be stuck down there in the mud and rotting dark for a very long time. No light, no hope, and definitely no *God*. Now what you say you open the gate and show us to the chambers of the Primatus?"

The guard swallowed, then nodded stiffly, pulled a key from his belt, and worked the lock.

"You can't—" the other guard started to protest.

"Shut it," The tall guard growled as he pulled the gate open. "Follow me," he said gruffly and turned away to walk along a path of white gravel.

"Good lad," Tibero grunted at the man's back. "You watch the gate," he said to the other guard, who stood still with a look of bewilderment on his face.

They had not walked a dozen paces when Nils felt Marol step in close to his shoulder. "What is it, Marol?"

"The third level," the young man whispered. "Gods, that's horrible. Those poor people. How can we—"

"We don't have a third level," Nils heard Rake hiss, cutting off the young man's question.

"We don't have…" Marol's eyebrows shot up and he glanced at the gristled bulk of Tibero striding in front of them. "Oh."

"Watch and learn, young Marol," Nils said softly with a ghost of a smile, and behind them, he heard Rake's dry chuckle.

The shadow beast slid into the darkness at the foot of the wall. There were two of the man-creatures standing near a heavy, iron gate. It could see the bright plumes of heat swirling around them. The pungent reek of their flesh drifting through the cold night air sent the creature's nostrils quivering. It sucked in a deep breath through clenched jaws, fighting off the raging need to feed. The prey was very close now. It tore its eyes away from the easy meat and turned to the dark stone of the wall. Soon, it would feed to bursting.

It moved quickly, flowing like an oily shadow up and over the wall, dropping into the darkness of the garden beyond. There, it paused for a brief moment, staggered by the maddening congestion of hot flesh in the building that towered before it. Hundreds of rooms where it would gorge itself. It shuddered, narrowing its eyes to mere slits as it forced down the ravenous pangs that stabbed at its guts. First, the prey—only then would it be allowed to hunt. Ropes of salvia dripped from its chin, and it bared its long, jagged teeth. With a low, burbling growl of frustration, it forced itself to turn away from the feast.

It moved fast and low to the ground, sliding silently through the damp undergrowth and deep shadows between the trees. It skirted the first building, keeping well away from the pools of golden light that spilled from the many massive, arched windows. The prey was not in that building. It could sense the throb of that particular plume of life very clearly now. It blazed like a beacon to the beast. It was a maddening, pulsing light that needed to be crushed.

It froze at the sound of crunching pebbles under boots. Its great muscles twitched and spasmed as it watched the stinking glow of two guards grow brighter. Their meat stench oozed and roiled from the edges of their armour and from their mouths. They passed so close to its hiding place that the beast could hear their low ape mutterings, and it was all it could do not to fall upon them and tear them to shreds. It burned as it forced itself to stillness, just a shadow within shadows, the desire to kill causing it to sink its claws into the soft earth as it watched the guards move slowly away and turn a corner to disappear from sight. It dragged its head from the path, and with a low growl, surged towards the throbbing call of the prey.

It had crossed another path and climbed over another low wall when it once again paused. It was very close now. A small stream babbled close by, lazily tracing its way over smooth white rocks and between drooping ferns. Beyond that, it could see the white stone of a wall edged with dense shrubbery. There was a hint of soft light from a window. The beast bared its teeth and shook itself, sending droplets of water flying from the matted fur of its great shoulders. Finally, it had found the place of its prey.

Water's Edge Road, the Waterfront District

When the attack came, it was so fast that Sev didn't have time to lift his blade. Something pale and low to the ground flew from the darkness with terrifying speed, sweeping him from his feet. He slammed into the wall before crashing to the cobbles, his forehead cracking on the cold, unyielding stone with a splintering explosion of white light. His head swam drunkenly as he started to push himself up from the ground, only to have a crushing weight drive him back to the road. Pain surged through him as he felt razor-sharp teeth clamp down on his left shoulder like a vice. Claws sank into his sides, and he felt the skin and tendons of his shoulder tear as the creature shook him violently back and forth like a child's rag doll. Sev's reality shattered into a wild chaos of flashing light, claws and teeth, and pain. He was a leaf in the middle of a tempest. *Oh gods...* A single thought crystallised in his mind. *I'm going to die.*

341

Then it released him, and Sev flopped to the bloody cobbles with a grunt. He had just enough time to draw in a single, shuddering breath before he heard the screams. He forced himself up to his knees, his left arm hanging uselessly at his side, and turned to see the broken-legged man flailing under a pale, hairless creature. The creature's whitish skin was mottled with grey, like the scum on spoiled milk. There were several shallow cuts along its flank where the man had attempted to stab it, dribbling black blood. He had lost the knife, and now his empty fist frantically and uselessly slapped against the creature's side as it slashed at him with long, spider-like limbs. Sev could hear the man's clothes rip and tear. He could hear the wet splatter of blood as the hooked talons found flesh.

Sword . . . where? The desperate fragments of thought seemed to ooze slowly through his throbbing skull. His vision swam, and he blinked away a stream of blood that dribbled down from his hairline. His fingers closed around the hilt, and he managed to drag the blade upward as the creature's head dipped to the man's neck. The frantic screams cut off abruptly as the jaws clamped shut, and with a violent shake, much like a dog shaking a rat, the beast broke the man's neck with a sharp crack. Sev watched helplessly as the thing began to worry at the flesh, tearing pieces from the corpse as the legs twitched and jumped spasmodically.

Jake, who had been standing rooted to the ground, wide-eyed in horror, dropped his sword, the blade clattering to the cobbles at his feet. The creature's head whipped up, the ugly flat face smeared with fresh blood. Jake turned and ran.

"Get inside!" Sev shouted, waving at the doorway, "Inside!" His voice was hoarse, and stabbing shards of agony lanced through his head.

The creature's black eyes snapped toward Sev and then latched on to the running Jake. It exploded into motion, covering the distance in a heartbeat. Jake's shriek was cut short as he was smashed from his feet, the impact driving the wind from his lungs. He clawed desperately at the cobbles, mewling in terror as the creature's claws sank deep into his back. Sev gagged in revulsion as the jaws closed around the back of Jake's head, crushing his skull with a sickening crunch. Jake's body spasmed and then fell limp.

Sev dragged himself upward to stand on legs that felt like jelly. He forced the point of the sword upward and clenched his jaw. He was going to kill that monster if it was the last thing he did.

"Hey!" he shouted. "Over here, you ugly bastard."

The creature turned its blunt, blood-covered face toward the defiant watchman. The black eyes narrowed, and thin lips slid back from rows of wickedly sharp teeth.

"Come on, then," Sev growled. "I don't have all night."

It flew at him without any warning, and Sev had almost no time to lift the blade. He felt the point punch through hard, corded muscle before the sword was wrenched painfully from his grasp as the creature knocked him from his feet. As he hit the ground, he felt claws slice through his leggings and gouge deeply into his hip. He steeled himself for the snap of teeth at his throat, but this time, the creature scrambled backward.

It shrieked in pain, clawing at the sword that stuck out from its flesh. The point had entered just under its left shoulder, tearing up through the thick muscle and punching out through the creature's back. Black blood spouted from the wounds as the beast hissed in anger, biting and clawing at the hilt.

Sev grabbed at the deep wound in his leg, feeling the blood spill between his fingers. He pushed himself backward with his good leg until his back hit the cold stone of the wall. There, he grabbed at his dagger, pulling the heavy-bladed weapon from its sheath. The creature's black eyes snapped back toward him, and with a low, shuddering, hateful hiss, it moved slowly forward, its left arm held against its chest, the sword still jutting from its flesh.

His leggings were already sodden with blood, and his head swam sickeningly as Sev held out the wavering blade in voiceless defiance. He watched the face of death limp closer, ropes of bloody saliva hanging from its jaws. He saw the creature's muscles tense and wondered what Nils would find at the temple.

The House of the Primatus, the Temple Precinct

The woman groaned softly as she tried to move, pain lancing through her back and legs. She lifted her head slowly and winced at the white-hot pain that shot through her skull. She blinked in surprise to find herself pinned under the shattered remains of stone and splintered wood. She sagged back to the floor and coughed at the dust that hung heavily in the air of the kitchen. She lay still for a moment with her eyes squeezed shut the grit under her eyelids caused warm tears to run down her plump cheeks.

What on earth just happened? she thought. Perhaps an earth tremor, though they were very rare in Sarsini. She swallowed as she lay still, waiting for the pain to ease. She remembered she had been preparing the first course of the evening dinner with one of the other kitchen staff, a new girl by the name of Carla. A sweet young thing if not the brightest. She vaguely remembered a great crash of glass coming from the dining room. It had given her such a fright she had jumped back from the stove, knocking into the girl. *There was a clatter and splash of a pot hitting the floor and then...* She swallowed again, her mouth dry as sand. *And then... nothing.*

With a great effort, she managed to free an arm and gingerly touched the side of her head. Her fingers traced a shallow gash just above her right ear, coming away sticky with drying blood. Her shoulders and back ached with each movement, but thankfully, she didn't think there was anything was broken, but she wouldn't know for sure until she managed to free herself.

She lifted her head and looked around blinking in confusion. She could see most of the kitchen from where she lay. Shadows jumped and skittered in the flickering light cast by the fire that still burned low in the fireplace and the one remaining lantern on the far countertop. Utensils, food, and rubble were strewn all over the floor. A large pot lay on its side, the contents spilled out into a slowly congealing puddle. The decanter of Sarsinian red that she had planned to serve with the meal lay dashed in the far corner, the dark wine splattered on the floor and wall, already beginning to dry.

Her breath caught as she noticed the girl lying still on the floor, only a few feet away. She could not see the girl's face, and she lay at an odd angle, with one of her arms pinned under her body. She looked almost like a discarded doll carelessly cast aside by a child. She hoped the girl was not too badly hurt. Why could she not remember what happened? She tried once again to move from under the rubble that pinned her down. She groaned as the effort sent shards of pain lancing through her head.

"Carla," she called out in a hoarse whisper. "Carla! Are you all right girl? I need help. I'm stuck. I—" Her mouth snapped shut as she heard a low, burbling growl. *Oh gods,* she thought as she clamped her free hand over her mouth and stared wide-eyed at the dark entrance to the kitchen.

She watched in icy horror as loose rubble shifted and rolled across the tiles of the floor as something heavy brushed against the damaged wall. She listened to the heavy, wet snuffling punctuated by tearing and sharp crunches. Squeezing her eyes shut, she tried desperately to block out the sounds of what she could only imagine were those of something large that was feeding.

She bit down on her lip and prayed fervently to wake from the nightmare. She jerked at a sudden crash and splintering of wood, followed by a scream of terror drowned by a deafening roar. Blood filled her mouth as she bit through her lip. There was a shriek of agony, abruptly cut short by a sharp crack and the wet splatter of blood.

Icy fingers of horror gripped her as she ground her face into the floor, trying to somehow bury herself under the broken debris. The dreadful, palpable bellow tore through the air again. This time it was closer. She whimpered and squeezed her eyes shut even tighter, clamping her free hand over her head. She tried with every fibre of her being not to scream. With her chest pressed to the floor, she could feel the heavy footfalls. The stench of rotting flesh filled the air. Something rattled and then clattered to the floor.

She pressed her fist into her mouth and bit down hard on her knuckles. She was too terrified to look. She did not want to see what horror had stalked into the kitchen. She did not want to know what took those deep and ragged breaths. Something slid slowly across the floor.

After one last low and horrible growl, and she felt the footfalls withdraw. When she finally managed to open her eyes, the kitchen was once again quiet. A long, bloody smear marked the floor, and the girl's body was gone.

"By the gods," Tibero growled, running his fingers through his unruly mop of ginger-grey hair. In the dim moonlight that filtered down through the swaying branches of the trees, three temple guards lay dead—one cleanly decapitated, the other two lying in crumpled, bloody heaps, tossed aside like rag dolls. Tibero drew a slow breath and looked to the heavy iron gates leading to the home of the Primatus. The ornate metal was twisted and scored, the lefthand gate hanging lopsided on its barrels. Even in the matted shadows that now seemed to crawl and writhe, he could clearly see deep gouge marks in the cracked mortar of the stone pillar.

He turned slowly to Nils, who just shook his head. "I think you may just be right," Tibero said with a half-smile. "I'm beginning to think that this was not a dog."

"We need reinforcements," the temple guard whispered, backing away from the carnage as he fumbled with his sword. "We…" the man started as he backed into Rake, who scowled at the frightened guard as he pushed him away.

"Calm yourself," the burly sergeant hissed. "Your orders, sir?" he called softly to Tibero, who stood rooted in place.

"We go in," Tibero replied, reaching down to loosen his sword in its scabbard. "Nils, Rake, with me. Melon, stick close to the sergeant. Be quiet and keep your eyes open."

He watched as Marol fumbled with the pommel of his sword. "Be calm, lad," he rumbled. Marol looked up with a pale, pitched expression.

"Mouth's dry and bladder's full?" Tibero raised a bushy eyebrow, and Marol nodded. "Same here, lad. Just stick close, and you'll be all right."

"What about me?" the temple guard whispered, his face ash white.

"Guard the gate. Go get reinforcements. Piss your pants . . . I don't care." Tibero shrugged and turned toward the doors to the house, his boots crunching loudly on the pebbles.

Here, Tibero paused again and carefully drew his sword. The great double doors of the house had been flung open, the dark wood splintered and torn around the heavy brass locks. It looked like something huge had burst through them, as if they were made of paper. Tibero carefully pushed at the closest door and winced as the buckled hinges groaned softly as it swung inward.

He wiped away a trickle of sweat from his face and waited for his eyes to adjust to the gloom. A single torch hung askew in its sconce, the feeble, flickering light chasing shadows across a hellish scene of utter carnage. Furniture was strewn in all directions, some broken to kindling. Tapestries had been torn from the walls, and blood lay in dark pools on the white marble tiles.

Tibero stepped quietly forward and motioned for the others to follow. Three more guards lay torn and broken on the floor, and a fourth lay sprawled at the foot of a broad, sweeping staircase. *What, by all the gods, could have done this?* Tibero thought as he carefully threaded his way through the remnants of the slaughter. He gripped his sword tighter and fought down the cold worm of fear that had started to squirm in his guts. The wounds of the dead guards were horrific, white bones jutting from torn flesh, limbs broken and twisted, all lying in puddles of congealing blood. But for Tibero, the eyes were the worst, dull and unseeing.

He shot a glance back to the others; Nils and Rake were close behind him, firm jawed and rock steady, but Marol stood rooted in the doorway. "Melon!" Tibero hissed. "Move! Gods damn you!" The young watchman blinked and then moved quickly to stand right behind the broad bulk of Rake. His eyes were as wide as saucers. "Stay close, lad," Tibero growled and then waved them forward.

Tibero took a deep breath as he started to climb the stairs, carefully stepping around the fallen guard. The leather grip of his sword felt slippery in his sweating palm, and the blade felt woefully inadequate for whatever beast had smashed through the front doors and butchered four trained and armed men like they were children. Each step was a force of will, and each seemed more difficult as he passed splintered furniture that had been cast aside like toys.

Once he reached the top of the stairs, he paused, dragging in a deep breath and trying desperately to slow the hammering of his heart. He felt a little lightheaded and suddenly thought of the bottle of emberwyne in the drawer of his desk. *A little shot of the good stuff would work rather well at this point... would probably work for young Melon there, too,* he thought with a wry smile as he looked back to the others.

"There," he whispered, gesturing to a dark doorway with the point of his sword. Nils nodded, and Tibero noticed Rake reach out to squeeze Marol's shoulder before edging forward. *Good men,* he thought. *But what the hell am I leading them into?*

Nils watched as Tibero stepped through the dark doorway. He could see the sheen of sweat on the older man's forehead, but his step looked sure and his blade looked steady. He turned to Rake and Marol. The sergeant's face was grim and hard; the younger man looked pale and frightened. But to his credit, he stood with them, sword raised.

"Nils," he heard Tibero say, his voice low and urgent.

He stepped into the high-ceilinged dining room and almost gagged at the stench of blood and emptied bowels. He blinked at the insanity that lay before him. A massive hardwood table had been smashed in two, and two bodies lay crumpled against the far wall in a tangle of broken limbs. The red and gold of their robes, which were torn and sodden with blood, marked them as two of the Chosen.

He was about the step forward when he jumped at the muffled clatter of a sword hitting the thick carpets of the floor. He turned to see Marol on his knees, retching. *Gods damn it...* Nils shook his head, knowing he had been close to having the same reaction.

"Marol," he heard Tibero hiss. "Marol!" The young man looked up with bloodshot eyes, vomit flecking the front of his shirt. "Your sword. Pick it up. Now!" Nils watched as Marol groped for the blade and pulled himself off the floor. The young watchman wobbled unsteadily before taking a deep, shuddering breath. He gagged once again and groped for Rake's shoulder. The sergeant gripped Marol's upper arm, helping to hold the younger man upright.

"Steady, lad. Steady," Nils heard the low rumble of Rake's voice say. "We need you." Marol blinked as the words seemed to slowly sink in, his mouth a grim line in a face that was bone white in the gloom. Nils let out a slow breath as he watched the young watchman wipe his mouth on his sleeve before looking up and nodding slowly.

They found the body of the Primatus up against the far wall, his chest splayed open, white shards of ribs jutting from the ruined flesh. His throat and lower jaw had been torn away. Tibero pointed his sword at a door that most likely led to the kitchens. Nils could see dark smears of blood on the floor and the low, flickering orange light of a lantern or torch.

Tibero moved slowly forward, and Nils raised his sword and followed. He did not look back, trusting Rake to hold Marol together. He blinked at the sudden trickle of sweat down his face. Whatever had killed those people was probably still in the house. Given what they had already seen, they would not be able to stop it. He thought suddenly of Cilla. He had made sure she would be well taken care of, but still, there was a sharp pang of sadness. He might have seen her for the last time.

Tibero had stopped just inside the doorway, his gloved palm held up. Nils stopped and motioned for Rake and Marol to hold their position. He watched as the older man scanned the room, his face illuminated by the dull, juddering light.

"Here," Tibero called softly and motioned for Nils to join him.

Nils glided forward and stepped into the kitchen. A single lantern stood on the far counter, and a small, low-burning fire hissed and popped in a stone hearth. He quickly scanned the rest of the room; smashed crockery, copper pots, and utensils lay scattered around on the floor. A large pot with what looked like the evening's dinner lay upended, the contents already cooled and congealed.

To his left, a door leading to a dark passage hung drunkenly on a single hinge. He swallowed as he noticed a long, dark smear of blood that tracked into the darkness. Tibero slowly extended his sword toward the doorway and then pointed to a woman who lay facedown, trapped under a pile of broken wood and stone. Nils nodded and moved quickly to the woman. He knelt down and reached to touch her shoulder. He almost fell backward in shock as her head came up, eyes wide with terror.

"Shhhh!" He quickly held a finger to his lips. She clawed at his arm.

"Help me," she hissed. "Help me!"

He grabbed her hand and squeezed it. "We are here to help," he whispered. "Calm. Stay calm. We'll get you out."

She shook her head. Her eyes flicked from his to the doorway to the dark passage. "Its there. We must leave... *now!*"

"Tibero. Wait!" Nils called softly as he pulled his hand from the woman's grip. He stood and raised his sword.

"Don't leave me!" she sobbed, grabbing at his leg. "Don't..." Her voice trailed off, and Nils felt her fingers tighten on his leggings. He looked down to see the trapped woman looking beyond Tibero to the passageway. Her eyes were impossibly wide, and the muscles of her jaw worked as if she were trying to swallow a scream.

Nils froze, his mouth suddenly bone dry. He tightened his grip on his sword, drew a deep breath, and turned slowly to face a nightmare that had moved from the shadows. Great clawed hands closed around the edges of the doorframe as the beast pulled itself from the darkness. Its great horned head towered over Tibero, and burning red eyes latched on to the older man, who stood defiantly with his sword raised.

The beast's grinning jaws opened, spilling thick, bloody saliva down the matted black hair on its chest, and then Nils was moving, sword raised. "Rake! Marol!" His shout was almost immediately drowned out by the deafening bellow of the beast as its head snapped around. Nils swung his sword as the creature's arm slashed out. He felt the blade glance off the corded muscle and bone, and then the blow slammed into his chest, sending him flying across the kitchen. He careened off the counter, feeling ribs snap and the wind blast from his lungs.

Nils heard Tibero roar, followed by the crash of splintering wood and a deafening bellow of rage. He pushed himself up from the floor, gritting his teeth against the shards of white-hot pain that stabbed through his back. The trapped woman was screaming as he clawed at the floor, looking for his sword. His hands closed around the hilt, and he dragged in a painful breath, sagging backward against the wall.

He looked up to see the creature lash out at Rake. Wickedly sharp claws scythed through the sergeant's jerkin, sending a spray of blood against the wall. Rake staggered backward, clutching at the wound, his legs bucking as he fell. Tibero was lying on the floor, his face a mask of blood. *Gods, no!* Nils thought as he forced himself to his feet, ignoring the grinding pain of his broken ribs. The beast turned and roared, and in an instant, it was upon him, its crushing weight driving him to the floor. Nils screamed in pain and horror as its hot and fetid breath fanned his face. Saliva dripped onto his face, thick and wet, and he watched in horror as the jaws gaped and dipped toward him.

The beast suddenly roared in pain and surged upright. Nils sucked in a deep breath as the crushing weight was lifted from him. He kicked himself away from the flailing creature. A sword jutted from its side, buried to the hilt. Marol was scrambling to his feet, pulling his dagger from its sheath. The beast roared and lashed out at the young man, its claws raking across the countertop, sending splintered wood and fragments of pottery flying.

Nils watched with mixed horror and pride as the young man stood above the still forms of Rake and Tibero with the pathetically small dagger raised. The creature drew itself to its full height, the sweeping horns almost touching the ceiling. Black blood ran down the creature's side where Marol had plunged his sword into its chest, matting the coarse hair. A ragged, burbling growl burst from its lips, and Nils knew then that none of them would survive.

The Chamber

Bariuz held up the burning torch, his gaze following the stone stairs as they spiralled down into darkness. He shook his head, wondering what was down there in the darkness. *By the Dark One's balls, this does not make one ounce of sense,* he thought as he looked back to his men. Four of them had faces like stone; they were fighters, hard men that he had recruited from the streets, but he could still feel their unease.

The other two, who carried the unconscious woman, looked decidedly sick. They were the fools that the old monk had almost killed. He would have dealt with them already, but he knew they could be put to good use. With them carrying the woman, it left the others with their hands free, and the gods alone knew if they would need the blades. He hoped they would not, and if they did, that they would be enough.

"What are we waiting for?" the priest snapped, pointing at the spiralling stairs. "Move! Move! We need to go down."

Bariuz struggled to keep his face impassive. This arrogant prick was fast becoming a serious irritation. He fixed an icy glare on the priest before gesturing for his men to follow him. He stepped into the stairwell, not failing to notice how the priest almost scampered behind him. The pathetic ass made sure he was behind Bariuz, with the guards at his back. *Gods, what are we walking into here?* Bariuz thought sourly and reached down to loosen his sword in its scabbard.

The woman had been delivered to the warehouse gagged and bound, her face bruised and bloodied from the blows she had taken from the two fools. He had not been willing to risk good men on a task that could see them arrested by the watch, and he had to admit that he was more than a little surprised when they had actually managed to complete the task. But they had needed to beat her senseless to do so, and it had taken most of Bariuz's self-control to not to kill them out of hand.

Who is this woman? he thought as he climbed down into the darkness. *And what in the seven hells does the damned priest want with her? A witch, maybe? But even then, why are we bringing her here? What's down there?* He squeezed the pommel of his sword with his gloved hand. He hoped he wouldn't need the blade but took comfort in the feel of leather and steel between his fingers.

In the dancing light of the torch, Bariuz could see patches of moss begin to appear, clinging to the mortar between the rough stones. They were already deep below the street. The trip to this abandoned church had been thankfully uneventful. The streets were unusually quiet, with few people to question why a detachment of temple guards were escorting a cart down to the docks. The damned priest had been even more twitchy than before, clutching his cloak around him and snapping instructions from the moment he had arrived at the warehouse.

They had waited until nightfall and then followed the priest through narrow side streets to the church. Bariuz had watched as the man jumped at every shadow. The priest was terrified, and not for the first time, Bariuz had wondered about what gods-forsaken scheme they were now part of. If this got his men killed, he would drag a blade across the priest's throat himself. It certainly would not be the first time in the city's history that someone of importance would be found floating facedown in the harbour.

The stairs ended abruptly, and Bariuz found himself standing in front of large, braced wooden doors. They hung from heavy barrel hinges and stretched to the ceiling. Bariuz hesitated and then reached for one of the thick iron rings and pulled. The door groaned and swung open. Bariuz held up his torch, but the feeble light did nothing to pierce the deep, cold darkness that lay before him.

"What is this place?" He turned to the priest.

"There are sconces on the sides. Light them." The priest pointed into the dark, ignoring his question. Even though the air was cold, the man's face glistened with sweat.

Once again, Bariuz felt a surge of anger but crushed it as he motioned to his men. "Find the sconces. Light them all."

Vasilios stepped into the chamber. His heart was hammering, and it took all of his waning self-control not to turn and run up the stairs. The guards were moving quickly along the dark stone of the walls, lighting the sconces as they passed them. He was thankful for the dim, flickering light that sprang up; anything was better than the crushing darkness.

The altar stood at the far end, and he quickly walked over to it. The stone looked strange in the dancing light—almost like liquid. Tentatively, he reached out to touch the stone and recoiled immediately. He rubbed convulsively at his fingers. The stone had been hot and strangely pliant. It reminded him of putrefying flesh, bloated and obscene.

He turned to the two men who carried the woman. "Bring her!" he shouted far louder than he intended and turned away quickly to hide his growing fear. The two guards, faces red from the effort, lumbered forward and were about to lift her to place her on the altar when he waved them back. "No. On the floor." He stepped aside. "Here, you fools!" he snapped when they hesitated, pointing at his feet.

She groaned as they laid her down but did not wake.

"Get back." He waved them away. "Back! Against the wall, all of you!" He saw them look to the captain, who nodded slightly. He turned away and pulled the dagger from his sleeve. He had done this before. There was no difference. *I managed before; I can do it again. I must do it again,* he thought, remembering Relic's words. He would not burn, not for anyone or anything. And if that meant killing this woman, so be it. Nothing would stand in his way.

He knelt down next to her. The hilt of the dagger felt slippery in his sweaty palm. *Do it quickly. Get it over with,* he thought as he raised the dagger. He froze as her eyes flicked open. They were a beautiful, almost luminescent green and utterly devoid of fear. This terrified him. She nodded slowly, not looking away for an instant. Vasilios sucked in a deep, shuddering breath, then gritted his teeth and plunged the blade downward.

Pain seared through Jasmijn as the dagger sank deep into her chest. Her muscles spasmed, bringing her face so close to the priest's that she could see the sweat beading on his forehead, and the flecks of spittle at the corners of his mouth. She clawed weakly at his shoulder, warm blood filling her mouth as he twisted the blade. Then, slowly, the flickering light of the torches started to fade, and she fell back, her last breath bleeding from her lungs.

And there it was, a pinprick of light that grew steadily brighter. She felt herself being drawn toward it, faster and faster, until she found herself floating under a great expanse of stars. Far below, moonlight glistened off the Great Sea as it stretched to the far horizon. There, she drifted, in-between space and time.

Is this the end? She pulsed. *Is this my end?*

"No, it is not." A strangely familiar voice rumbled from the void. "It is just another beginning."

A beginning?

"You have had many," the voice replied softly. "The weight of each building on the last."

Many?

"Don't you remember?" the voice asked gently and she looked down to see that the ocean had given way to the vast sands of the Akhbari desert. She drifted lower, becoming aware of the acrid smell of smoke. All around, the tents of J'dah were burning, and a young girl lay dying on the sand.

Yes, she pulsed, *I am...*

The girl named Seya lay on her back. The pain was almost unbearable, but she tried to stay still. They would leave her alone if they thought her dead. The knife wound in her belly was deep, and she could feel her blood slowly pooling beneath her. All around, shadows flashed past, starkly silhouetted by the flames.

She could hear the hoarse cries of terror as the cruel, curved blades of the Tahuti tribesmen hacked at flesh and bone. The screams would be cut short, and outstretched arms would drop away in a spray of blood. She would hear the barking laughs of the Tahuti then. She imagined their blue-tattooed faces twisted in cruel and savage grins.

A tear ran down her cheek, cutting through the dust and blood, as she watched bright embers race up into the sky. She found it strangely beautiful, like thousands of tiny fireflies darting frenetically upward into the night. It was like they were trying to escape from her parents' burning home. Tiny, delicate beings of light fleeing from something so horrible.

Seya groaned as the pain clawed at her insides, and she fought against the instinct to curl up and press the wound closed. Her fingers were stuck together with the grit of sand mixed with coagulated blood. She did not know where her father lay. He had run out into the night, sword in hand, as the tribesmen had struck. Her mother had dragged her and her brother from the small house, and they had tried to run into the desert. They had not made it very far.

Her mother lay right next to her. Seya could still feel her hand holding onto her abaya. The girl could see the flames reflected in her mother's dark eyes as they stared blankly up at the night sky. The tribesmen had just ridden them down. They had tried to get up, only to be kicked back to the ground. A tribesman had grabbed her mother by the hair and pulled her head back before cutting her throat. The girl had tried to fight them off with her bare hands, but it had been utterly futile. Her brother lay just beyond her, face down in the sand, with an arrow jutting from his back. He had been struck not a dozen paces onto the dusty road. Her mother had been dragging him when the horse had smashed them to the ground.

Seya had tried to pull the man away from her mother. She had beat her small fists against his shoulders and the side of his face until the back of his fist had sent her flying. She had lain on her back as the world seemed to spin sickeningly around her. Then he was there above her, his bearded face, dark and terrible, blotting out the stars. His rough hand closed around her throat, and she felt something slam into her belly. There was a terrible ripping sensation, followed by blinding pain and a hot rush of blood down her legs. And then he was gone.

The air seemed cold now, and the noises and screams seemed very, very far away. Each painful breath was short and shallow, and her hand had fallen away from the wound. She found she could not lift her arm any more; it seemed far too heavy. She didn't want to die. She was very afraid. She took a deep, shuddering breath, and as she felt it seep out from her mouth the sky above her suddenly felt incredibly vast. She began to feel the odd sensation that she was no longer looking up but rather looking down into its unfathomable depths. All she needed to do was somehow let go, and she would fall forever into the stars.

And then she did...

The stars wheeled in the heavens as she tumbled into the void. The pain and the flames were gone, and as she fell, she became aware of a brightening light unfolding before her, opening like the petals of an incandescent flower. Onward she rushed until she was enveloped in blazing brightness that seemed to permeate throughout her entire being. She felt herself slow and then stop, and then she was hanging in an endless ocean of light.

"Welcome, little one," Seya heard a deep and resonant voice say.

Where am I? She felt the thought pulse from her being.

"Where you have always been," the voice rumbled. "You are just seeing things... a little differently."

Differently? the girl pulsed.

"Yes. You are used to seeing with eyes. That can be quite limiting."

Am I dead?

The girls felt, rather than heard, the rumbling laugh. "Oh no. You have just let go of an ill-fitting garment. What is your name, little one?"

I...I am... she pulsed feeling a new, but elusive, energy flow over her and through her. She tried to hold on to it, but it kept slipping away. *I am...*

"No, little-one," the voice said softly. "You are not ready. Return..."

The woman named Maisara watched sadly as the boy raised his hand and then swept it forward. Her head snapped back as the stone hit her forehead, and pain seared through her skull as she tried to blink away the sudden flood of blood. The boy who had thrown the stone stood a few paces away, staring down at her with angry, dark eyes. The mob behind him howled and shook their fists at her. Even now, all she wanted was to wrap her son up in her arms, but she could not move. She knelt in the hot, dry dust of the town square with her wrists chained to an iron ring between her knees.

"Hadi," she called to him, but the boy just turned away from her and walked slowly back to his father, who lay a large hand on the boy's shoulder.

"Close your mouth, whore," the boy's father shouted, his bearded face twisted in righteous anger. "We will hear no more of your lies."

"But I did nothing…" she started to say, and the man hurled a stone at her face. It cracked against her cheek, a glancing blow but still hard enough to tear the skin.

"Be silent!" he screamed with such vehemence that flecks of spittle flew from his mouth. She watched as he dropped down and began to claw at the gravel at his feet, looking for another stone. She had loved him once. Or rather, she had loved the façade he had deftly created. But over the years, he had proven to be petty and cruel, a small man driven by small, self-serving goals. *Just a shallow, broken soul… a gaping wound that will never heal,* she thought sadly.

Maisara knew now that he had never loved her. She had just been tolerated long enough for her to provide a son, and now that son was of age, he didn't need her anymore. She swallowed down the bitter taste of the truth. She was nothing to him. She never had been. She dropped her head. She could not watch the man grubbing in the dust, looking for another stone, a stone he would throw at her as easily as he would a stray dog.

The charges he had levelled against her were fabricated and backed by the testimony of four of his friends. *Weak men, all of them… weak, fearful, and empty,* she thought. There was nothing she could say in her defence. What better way to get rid of an unneeded appendage that had fulfilled its need?

She heard a change in the seething mob and looked up to see a tall, stick-thin man with a long grey-beard step in front of the seething mob holding up a hand. He wore the black robes of a cleric and quickly they fell silent. The priest reached down and offered a hand to the boy's father who had stopped his scratching in the dust. Gently he pulled the wild-eyed man to his feet. Orange dust clung to the man's beard and sweat beaded his face. Maisara had no doubt he wanted this to be over. Then he could move forward from this distasteful inconvenience.

She watched as the cleric placed his hands on the man's shoulders and waited patiently for him to calm himself. The priest then turned to her. His dark eyes were cold and utterly unforgiving. He reached into his robe and removed a smooth white river stone. She knew the very spot where he had found it. She had played in the deep shaded pools there with Hadi.

"Maisara bint Khalid al-Farah, you have been found guilty of adultery," he said in a clear and even voice. He then turned to the man and pressed the white stone into his hand. "You are the qua'hadi, the accuser," he continued, his voice carrying to all in the crowd. "It falls to you to cast the first stone."

Hudad stepped forward, eyes wide and filled with an anger that did little to hide his fear and self-loathing. Maisara felt a deep sorrow well up inside her. A tear cut through the blood and dust on her face as she dropped her head and waited...

The woman named Hagga felt the damp soil between her fingers. Her gnarled, arthritic fingers ached, but she was happy as she pushed the small seedling into the earth. She could hear her grandchildren running and laughing. They were a delight. Much like her seedlings, she thought. All they needed was love and care, and they would flourish.

Her weathered face split with a gap-toothed grin. It had been a very good life, filled with love and joy, as well as loss and sorrow. But she had come to know that you could not have one without the other. The hardest had been the loss of her husband. He had been a gentle and loving man, but he was never weak. He had been a pillar of strength to her.

The loss she had felt at his death spoke of the depth of her love. She knew now that her sorrow was just that love needing a new place to go. And she always found new places. Her children, her neighbours, and now her grandchildren. She looked up at a squeal of laughter and managed a smile just as a sharp pain stabbed down her left arm. She gasped as pain clawed at her chest. The small plant that she had been holding gently slipped from her fingers as she fell forward onto the soft, yielding earth...

The woman named Signe felt fear surge through her as the man threw the torch on the tangle of wood piled around her legs. The wood was dry, and the flames took quickly, greedily lapping at the twisted heap.

"It was me... it was... my fault," she could hear Mikha say as he pleaded with the men, with the fat and arrogant Trygve. But they just stared at Mikha with disgust, comfortable within their cloaks of righteous wrath.

The smoke grew thick, and the biting fumes clawed at her lungs and eyes. She bent over in a fit of coughing, the ropes tearing into the flesh of her wrists. She pulled herself upright, away from the heat of the growing flames and watched as one of the men grabbed a fistful of Mikha's hair and dragged his head backward. *No, no, no...* A blade flashed followed by a spray of blood, and Mikha collapsed forward. *My poor, gentle Mikha... my love...* Her vision swam with tears as cold fingers seemed to crush her heart.

The flames now lapped close to her legs, and the heat was quickly becoming unbearable. Thick smoke enveloped her, and no matter how shallowly she tried to breathe, her head spun from the hot, acrid air that enveloped her. *Mikha...* she thought as the pain started to stab into her legs. *I'm so sorry...* Her nightdress ignited with a low, throaty roar. Her hair followed in a wild flash of flame, and she threw back her head, dragging in a breath to scream, a scream that never came as her lungs filled with flame...

Echo drifted through the smoke of the fire until she floated above the being she had known as Mikha. This new being watched the remains of her last physical body burn. His essence so raw, so radiant with a new and terrible power—and so utterly not ready. There was no learning that only the weight of lifetimes could bring. There was only the explosion of savage, voiceless rage as his essence had been torn free.

She watched as the shadows cast by the fire danced across this new Ascendant's face, the flames reflecting in dark and sadly familiar eyes. He did not remember the woman hanging from the tree. The memories of years of love had been burned to ash and replaced by unspeakable rage and unquenchable fire. Her eyes welled with tears as she noticed the fresh blood dripping from his hands and the shattered bodies of the men he had killed.

She drifted closer. The shapeless anger that radiated from him was terrifying. It would spill from him to set the world to flame. It raged, voiceless, with no memory, fuelled by an elusive echo of a life and love cut short. Her fingers brushed his face, but he did not notice; he was unable to tear those terrible and dark eyes away from the burning woman. When the rope burned through and the body fell into the fire, she saw him flinch, and for the briefest moment, the rage flickered as something tugged at his core. But then it flooded back in a roaring torrent.

I love you, Mikha, Echo pulsed, running her fingers down his cheek. *Come back to me, my love. Remember...*

The essence of Moloc floated above the priest, but he couldn't look away from the body of the woman that lay on the floor next to the altar. The frustrating echoes of memories that had begun to tug at his mind had not left him since he had spoken with the old man. In fact, they were even more prevalent as he watched the slowly growing pool of her blood. The priest had staggered back, dropping the dagger as he collapsed to his knees. Moloc watched with disdain as the pathetic creature started to claw at his cloak, finally dragging a small leather pouch free. The priest was tugging frantically at the drawstrings as Moloc drifted closer.

Somehow, this woman was tied to the annoying, elusive reverberations that seemed to skitter off into the mists whenever he tried to grab hold of them. *Who are you really? Echo... E'kia... Jasmijn... Relic?* None of the names seemed to fit anymore. They were like an ill-fitting skin waiting to be shrugged off, to be replaced by something more. Once again he fought down the frustration. *More what?* he thought angrily as he drifted closer to the dead woman.

He could see no trace of the Ascendant left in the broken shape. She lay still, her hands bound with a rough rope and her mouth gagged. Her face was bruised from where these men had struck her, and a smear of blood ran from her nose across her cheek. Her eyes, once emerald green, were now glassy and unseeing. Her blonde hair was a wild tangle, and for the briefest moment, Moloc imagined running his fingers through it, gently easing away the knots. He saw her face turning to him and laughing. *But was it her face? Or that of another?* There was the briefest of moments when he felt her warm skin against his and he was enveloped in the soft, intoxicating scent of flowers… And then, just as swiftly, it was gone.

Why did you not listen? he thought angrily driving the images from his mind. After all, he had warned her, but she had paid him no heed. She had chosen to wear that… *weak*… form. She had chosen to feel. *Why would you choose that?* Suddenly, fire and smoke flashed through his mind, and he impulsively reached out to touch her face…

There was a loud clatter, and Moloc snatched back his hand and turned angrily to the priest. The stupid ape had managed to open the bag and had spilled the stones on the cold slabs of the floor. He watched as the priest clawed frantically at them with palsied hands, trying to arrange them into a line. The priest pressed his bloody hands to the stones and looked up with wild eyes, staring at the woman he had just killed. The stones started to glow brightly then, and Moloc noticed that other men, whom he had ignored to this point, had drawn their swords and had started to back away.

The Ascendant looked away in disgust. What did he care if the priest burned the world to ash? These pathetic fools would be the first to die when the gate was opened. They had no idea what waited for them on the other side. The pitiful creatures that Moloc had first allowed through were like mice compared to the beasts that ruled in the pit.

The altar burst into flame, and Moloc watched with mild disinterest as a great horned head split the black, distended skin of the rock and started to rise from the oily, burning surface. He heard one of the men cry out in terror. He waved a hand at the massive doors. The heavy iron barrels and pins of the hinges glowed brightly and then fused together.

Now you will learn the price of your ambition, Priest, he thought before dismissing the man from his mind as he looked back at the body of the woman.

He settled onto the floor next to her and willed himself to take form. Kneeling next to her, he reached out and touched her cheek. The great beast towered above them. It threw back its head and roared, but Moloc hardly noticed because in the dancing light of the flames that now touched the woman's face and rippled over her arms and the ropes that bound her wrists, he finally saw her.

Vasilios staggered back from the dead woman; the blood coating his hands was warm and sticky. He dropped the dagger, hardly hearing the sharp clatter as it hit the stone floor near his feet. He fell to his knees and looked at his hands. The woman's blood looked almost black in the flickering light of the torches. He quickly wiped them on his robe but only managed to remove some of it. It had caked under his nails and run between his fingers. *Finish it, you fool,* he thought and desperately tugged at his robes, looking for the pouch that held the stones.

He dragged it free and clawed at the leather drawstrings, but they seemed frustratingly tight. *Finish it. Put all this behind you. You did what you were told. You brought the woman here, and you… killed her.* A bead of sweat hung from his nose as he strained to open the bag. He could sense Bariuz and his guards shifting behind him, but he ignored them. In a few moments, it wouldn't matter what they thought. It wouldn't matter what anyone thought. He would be the Prime, and he would be untouchable.

Finally, with a last hard tug, the bag pulled open and the stones spilled to the floor. He quickly arranged them into a line and, with a deep breath, pressed his shaking, bloody hands to them. They felt warm—hot even—and as he looked up to the black altar, they started to glow. Behind him, he heard a sharp intake of breath, followed by the cold grate of blades being drawn from scabbards. Vasilios ignored them, and with clenched teeth, he stared at the stone of the altar and waited.

Bariuz took a sharp step backward as the altar burst into flame. He looked to his men. Blades had been drawn; even the two fools stood holding swords, but they looked ready to run and had inched backward until their backs thumped into the unyielded wall. *Pathetic cowards,* the captain thought with scorn as he turned back to the burning altar. He sucked in a sharp breath as the black stone bulged upward. It looked as if something was forcing its way up through the rock, something massive and terrible.

"Captain?" one of the men shouted.

"Hold," Bariuz snapped without turning to the man. His voice was iron-hard and steady, despite the growing horror of what was unfolding before him; the legacy of years of discipline kept the fear from turning his bowels to water. But as the surface of the altar split apart like distended skin, even that started to waver. *By the gods, what have you done, you son of a whore? What have you DONE?*

Bariuz felt his breath catch as a hideous horned head pushed itself through the torn membrane of rock like some obscene birth. Long pale arms, thick with muscle were followed by wickedly clawed hands as the beast pulled itself upward until it towered over them. He felt as if his feet were nailed to the floor, but when the beast tilted back its head and roared, Bariuz staggered back at the reverberating shock of the sound.

He heard the terrified cries of his men and more than one sword clatter to the ground, but he could not tear his eyes from the creature. His men were already clawing at the doors when it turned its burning yellow glare toward them. The creature bared fangs as long as daggers as it moved toward them. Then, quite strangely, all fear left him because he knew he was already dead.

Vasilios screamed as the Demon Lord stepped from the altar. The ground trembled at its enormous weight. He fell backwards as a thunderous bellow erupted from its gaping maw and burning yellow eyes turned to the men cowering against the far wall. Blinding panic surged through him, and his feet slipped on the smooth stone as he tried to push himself away from the towering nightmare.

Even in his mad scramble, he watched in sick horror as the beast's clawed hand snaked out to grab at one of the guards. The man swung his sword desperately, only to see the blade bounce off without so much as leaving a scratch on the pale skin. The guard shrieked as the fingers closed around him, long claws punching through his armour as if it were made of paper. Blood burst from the man's mouth as his bones shattered. The beast raised the limp, dripping body to its mouth before turning toward the group of screaming men pulling in desperation at the iron-rings of the heavy doors that refused to open.

Get away, get away! Get AWAY! Vasilios' mind screamed, his arms groping at the stone, his legs pumping spasmodically as he crawled away backward from the creature. His back slammed into the wall, but he could not stop his feet from pushing uselessly at the flagstones. The creature reached the men at the door with two great strides. It swept them aside like rag dolls; their bodies flew through the air to land broken and twisted on the dark stone.

Vasilios dragged his legs upward and hugged them tightly to his chest as the beast turned to the captain who stood with his sword raised in utterly impotent defiance. The air seemed to compress as the creature roared, and Vasilios clamped his hands over his ears. He wanted to shut his eyes but found he could not.

"Come on, you bastard!" Bariuz shouted as he threw himself forward. The captain's blade arced downward in a silvery blur, but the creature merely swatted him aside with contempt. His shattered body slammed into the wall before crumpling to the floor, his sword clattering to the stones somewhere in the distant darkness.

Vasilios' bladder loosed as the beast turned its hate filled eyes toward him. He started to shake uncontrollably as the warm liquid soaked through his leggings. He pressed himself into the wall, willing it to swallow him as the creature's black lips peeled back from its bloody fangs in a grotesque smile.

"We meet again, summoner." the harsh voice rumbled. "I see you have learned the folly of your ways. Even the mighty and brave can be humbled by blood and fire. But you, *summoner*"—it spat the last word— "are neither."

"Wait! Stop! I… I command you!" Vasilios cried. "The stones. I have the stones!"

The beast laughed its hideous, rolling laugh and stepped closer to the cowering priest. The burning eyes narrowed into hateful slits. "I am not one to be commanded by a pathetic thing sitting in its own piss," it growled with contempt.

Vasilios screamed as the enormous taloned hand opened and reached for him.

The being once known as Mikha did not see the Demon Lord step slowly from the altar, nor did he hear the thunderous bellow of insatiable hunger that erupted from its cavernous maw. He groaned and crumpled forward as a thousand images pinwheeled and exploded behind his eyes. His forehead cracked into the cold stone of the floor. His body twitched and writhed, his eyes wide but sightless as the raw memories of Signe's death tore through him.

His body spasmed as he felt cold steel once again bite into his neck, his mouth filling with blood as his dying body flopped forward onto the grass. Once again, thick smoke burned his nostrils, and he could hear crackle of the ravenous flames as they crawled inexorably towards her. Once again, he lay helpless, his life draining into the earth. Once again, he was just a useless, broken thing that watched his love burn in the fire.

His back arched and his face contorted at the memory of the crushing darkness, the blinding, unimaginable surge of power that flooded into his new being. A power that had obliterated the weak and useless Mikha and filled him with an exquisite inferno of rage. A rage capable of beautiful and terrible retribution.

Once again, he felt the hot spray of blood and heard the screams of agony as he tore at their flesh and shattered their bones. Once again, he faced the fire. But this time, he felt her fingers on his face. This time he heard her voice.

"I love you, Mikha. Come back to me, my love. Remember…"

Signe… my love… was the last thought that roared through his mind before all the vast power of his ascendance burst forth in a colossal, incandescent flash of light.

The ground heaved, and the dark stone of the chamber cracked and groaned. The altar shattered with a sharp detonation, sending razor shards of obsidian hissing through the air. The Demon Lord staggered as the ground buckled once again and then shrieked as the light tore through its flesh. Shredded fragments of the beast's body created brilliant arcs of flames before burning to ash.

The blinding light then raced outward, expanding and searching. In a small tavern, a group of people pressed themselves against a wall. A large man held a cudgel out in mute defiance as two lesser demons stalked forward. The light tore into the demons, and they howled in agony before their bodies exploded.

Onward the light raced, ripping through dark alleyways, where it found a bloodied man pressed against a wall, and waiting to die. The creature, stalking closer to its prey, stiffened and then screamed as it was incinerated in a tempest of flame. Upward the light flashed, toward the temple with its towering minarets. Here, three men lay broken on the floor, and one stood defiant with a dagger in his hand. The mighty beast of shadow tensed its great muscles, ready to fall upon the dagger-wielding man, when the light simply ripped it to pieces.

With no more of the demon spawn to find, the light raced back to the chamber, where it found a man kneeling over a woman. The light filled the man until he shone like a star. This new incandescent being, knowing that it could not hold the light, reached over to the woman and placed its hand on her cheek, where it lingered, allowing all of the light to pour into her. When it was done, the being once known as Mikha slumped back and smiled, then slowly crumpled into ash.

Vasilios squeezed his eyes shut and rolled himself into a tight ball, hugging his knees to his chest. He sobbed through clenched jaws as the ground heaved under him. Dust and fragments of stone fell around him, broken free from the vaulted ceiling, and he mewled in terror and clamped his arms over his head, waiting to be crushed by the unimaginable weight of rock above them. His body jerked at a sudden light so bright, it burned yellow red through his tightly shut eyelids. He squeezed his face into his knees as something exploded, filling the air with sharp pieces of stone that hissed past him and shattered against the walls.

The ground buckled once again, and he heard a piercing shriek of agony from the great beast that was suddenly cut short. Then, as quickly as it started, the ground was finally still. His ears rang in the sudden silence, and the air was filled with the stench of burned flesh and dust. He lay pressed against the wall, clinging to his legs, completely unable to move, hardly able to breathe.

He opened his eyes and blinked away the dust and grit. There was no sign of the creature. With a great effort, he forced his hands apart and relaxed the death-like grip on his legs. He was trembling violently as he pushed himself up. The broken bodies of the guards lay scattered on the floor. In front of the shattered altar, a cloaked man knelt in front of the dead woman.

Who? was all Vasilios managed to think before a brilliant pulse of light flowed down from the ceiling and into the man. Vasilios held up a hand to shield his eyes from the blinding nimbus. He could barely make out the vague silhouette of the man as the light pulsed and danced around him. *What is he doing? Why did he touch the woman's face?* Despite his trembling legs, Vasilios found himself taking a step closer, but he stopped as, quite suddenly, the light blinked out.

Vasilios watched in fascination as the figure slumped backward and fell to ash. The fascination turned to terror as the woman sat up and slowly turned to him. Her eyes blazed as they latched on to his and a pale-blue light shimmered around her. She stood slowly, those terrible glowing eyes never leaving him. He took a teetering step backward as the broken and bloodied woman shimmered and melted away, to be replaced by a dark, lithe figure. She took a step forward and crouched down to run her fingers gently through the ash at her feet.

Vasilios looked over his shoulder to the doors and began backing away, holding up his shaking hands. "I'm sorry. I didn't know," he whimpered, spittle hanging from his trembling lips. "I didn't know."

She ignored him, slowly lifting her hand and allowing the powdery grey ash to spill through her fingers.

"I didn't…" The words died in his throat as she looked up. She blazed with a terrible fury as she stood. Vasilios turned and ran.

He almost collided with the door in his mindless panic. He grabbed at an iron ring and heaved at the door. It refused to open. He threw his weight at it and felt a muscle tear in his shoulder. Pain exploded down his arm, but still, he tore at the handle in his desperate need to escape. He screamed and slammed a fist into the door. He clawed at the dark, ornate wood, feeling fingernails snap and tear from their beds.

Then he felt iron fingers close around his neck, and his face was slammed into the unyielding wood. His nose broke with an explosion of pain. He whimpered, blood and spit hanging from his chin, flailing helplessly as the powerful hand ground his face into the door. Then he felt the fan of her breath on his cheek as she leaned in close.

"But you did know," the woman whispered.

Vasilios felt himself being dragged back from the door. "No. No! Wait!" he blubbered, his legs giving way, his hands slapping ineffectually against the vice-like fingers. She flung him aside, and he scrambled away from her.

He watched in mute terror as she lifted a hand toward the massive doors and closed her fist. The doors groaned and cracked, then shattered, collapsing in on themselves in a heap of tortured iron and splintered wood.

She turned her icy, glowing eyes to him, and he held up a shaking hand as if to ward off the coming wrath. "Leave," she said simply.

Vasilios dragged himself to his feet and ran. He threw himself up the stairs, taking two or three at a time. More than once, he missed a step to fall heavily. Each time, he clawed himself to his feet, mindless of the pain. Each step took him further away from the incandescent vengeance that poured from the chamber below.

He almost sobbed with relief as he saw the top of the stairwell. He pulled open the door and burst into the dusty interior of the church. He slammed the door shut and finally paused to drag in a shuddering breath. He needed to get back to the temple. He would be safe there. He would be the Primatus. He would be… untouchable.

Vasilios then noticed his sodden leggings, cold and sticking to his legs. He wiped carefully at the crusted blood beneath his nose, wincing at the sharp stab of pain. Luckily, no one would see him in this state. He sucked in another deep breath and pulled open the door to the street, stepping into the cold night air. He looked up at the pale moonlight that shone through the gaps in the scudding clouds and was about to step from the top stair when something hard struck him in the throat.

He staggered back, hitting the doorframe behind him. He couldn't breathe. He clawed at his neck and was astonished to find the smooth shaft of an arrow. He tried once again to breathe but could not even drag the slightest breath into his lungs. He sagged to his knees, his mouth filling with the metallic taste of blood. He tugged weakly at the shaft and then fell forward onto his face.

Kratos stood in the deep shadows of a doorway, his ear pressed to the weather-beaten door, and listened intently for any sign of movement— the brush of cloth on stone, an unguarded breath, the creak of a floorboard. When satisfied that all was quiet, he slowly poked his head out and looked quickly up and down the narrow alley. It was devoid of life. To his left, the dim light from one of the flickering street lamps filtered into the gloom, creating a small splash of light on wet and muddy stone.

He eased back into the darkness, pulled his dagger from its sheath, and turned to the door. The lock was old and rusted and no match for the heavy blade; it yielded with a soft and almost tired snap. The hinges creaked in protest as Kratos eased the door open to peer inside. The small room was dusty from disuse and filled with old wooden furniture piled carelessly against the walls. A doorway on the far side revealed a narrow staircase.

Kratos picked up his bow and quiver which were resting against the wall, and stepped into the room, pulling the door shut behind him. Once again, he waited, listening intently. He had learned early on that caution was a valuable trait. No need to walk blindly into a blade in the dark. He moved quietly toward the stairs and began to climb.

He flinched as the old stairs groaned and creaked under his weight. But the house was otherwise silent, the brooding shadows and dusty rooms empty of any threat. He quickened his pace, taking two stairs at a time. Just beyond the third landing, the stairs ended abruptly at a door. He pressed his fingers to the rough wood. It felt cold. *Must lead to the roof,* he thought. He pressed an ear to the door and held his breath, listening intently. Satisfied that no one waited on the other side, he nevertheless dropped his hand to his dagger and pushed the door open.

The cold night air washed over his face as he stepped slowly onto the roof. It was caked with years of bird droppings and crusted mud. *No one had been up here for an age.* He looked around at the tiled roofs of the house nearby. In front of him, he could see the dark, narrow gap of the alleyway; to his left, the soft, diffused light from the lamps of the cobbled road outlined the low wall that skirted the roof.

The woman, Relic, had mentioned the old church, and he had chosen the house well. He could see the weathered stone of the steeple and the black arches of the belfry. He would have a clear view of both the courtyard and the door at the front from the corner. Crouching down, he moved quickly toward the edge of the roof. He dropped to his haunches and carefully looked down.

He could make out the overgrown courtyard. It was mostly shrouded in deep shadow, with only patches of moonlight illuminating the remnants of an old long-dead oak in one corner and the moss-covered stone of a well near the centre. If anyone came from that direction, they would step into the road from the alleyway that skirted the edge of the church. It was well lit, and they would be clearly visible.

He shifted his attention to the doors. They were closed, with several semicircular stone stairs leading up to them. Here as well, anyone leaving would be clearly visible, with no cover. He took a breath and let it bleed out from between his pursed lips, feeling his heartbeat slow. If nothing else, he was a patient man. He slid a long arrow from the quiver and checked the shaft and the fletching before nocking it. He eased back on the bowstring, hearing the soft creak as it came under tension. He sighted down the arrow, moving slowly from the alley to the doors. Then, satisfied that he had a clear line of sight, he slowly relaxed the drawn bow and settled back to wait.

Vasilios pushed himself upward. The street was dead silent. Clouds hung motionless in the night sky. He touched his throat, feeling only flesh. He blinked in surprise. He noticed he was naked, but the cold of the night didn't touch him. And then he noticed the body at his feet. The arrow jutting from the neck, the eyes dark and lifeless, staring blankly at the stone of the stairs. Fear gripped him then.

"Yes, Priest…" came the whispered voice; it slithered over this naked skin like icy serpents. "Now you are mine."

He looked up and saw the monstrous female presence, the writhing black hair moving like oily smoke. Behind her, there were other forms, shadows within shadows that moved low to the ground, with red, hungry eyes. He opened his mouth to scream as they surged forward. Claws and teeth dug into his flesh, and he felt himself being dragged down into the cloying, crushing darkness.

367

Dacian walked his horse down the narrow forest path. The cold night wind hissed and sighed through the needles of the pines, biting into the exposed skin of his hands and face. He could just make out the glowing lights of the estate through the swaying trees as he pulled on the reins. He sat in the saddle and tried to still the sudden rush of rage. He had no need for its fire tonight. He needed to be like ice if he had any hope of success. He leaned forward and patted the horse's neck, murmuring soft words to the tired gelding.

Finally, he swung from the saddle and, holding the bridle, he stretched his back, ignoring the protests of muscles that had been tortured on the hard ride from Sarsini. He moved to the horse's head, gently loosened the bridle, and pulled it free, patting the animal's neck. He moved to the saddle cinch, tugged the leather strap from the buckle and pushed the saddle from the horse's back allowing it to fall to the ground.

Taking the animal by the mane, he pulled its head around until it faced away from the estate. He ran a hand over the velvety nose and rested his forehead on the side of the horse's head. Then he stepped back and smacked the animal's rump with an open hand, sending it walking into the forest. He would not be needing him after tonight. There was nowhere to run, nothing to return to.

An icy calm settled over Dacian as he turned to the twinkling golden lights of the estate. He took a deep breath. One way or the other, it all ended tonight. This man would never stop hunting him. He unbuckled his sword and dropped it to the ground. If he needed it, he would have already failed. He pulled his dagger from its sheath and examined the beautiful etching on the gleaming blade. He had bought this on the day he met Arianne. It would be with him when he met her again.

He looked up at the explosion of stars visible through the forest canopy, remembering so many nights when he had sat with Arianne nestled into his chest, looking at these very stars. She had always seen the expanse as an endless ocean that somehow transcended time; to her, it was like watching the slow breath of all creation. But to him, they were just twinkling lights, and she was all creation.

His heart ached now because all he could see was the vast void between the lights. She had ignited the sky. She showed him the stars. Dacian sighed, his heart heavy as lead. A very wise man had once said that if you took and eye for every eye, eventually, the whole world would be blind. But there were no stars in a world without Arianne; there were no colours, no warmth—so what did he care?

He slammed the dagger back into its sheath and moved quickly forward, crouched over as he ran toward the old tree at the boundary wall. He paused at the edge of the undergrowth. Satisfied that the perimeter guards where nowhere in sight, he ran across to the thick gnarled truck and hauled himself up into the branches. He moved across the thick branch that crossed over the wall and dropped silently onto the soft lawn on the other side.

Dacian froze as a guard moved from the shadows into the soft moonlight, not ten paces from where he crouched. The man's back was to him, and no other guards were in sight. Dacian slid forward behind the man. His left arm snaked around the man's neck, and with his right, he wrenched the man's head violently to the side, the neck breaking with an audible crack. The guard went limp, and Dacian dragged the body back into the shadows of the tree.

Dacian moved quickly across the lawn to the wall of the house. He expected there would be more guards from this point onward and eased his dagger from its scabbard. Holding the blade low, he moved quietly to the corner of the house. He stole a glance around the corner and saw another guard walking toward him. He ducked back and waited. The sound of the man's boots crunching on the gravel of the path grew louder. Dacian raised the dagger. The guard stepped into view, and Dacian struck. He dragged the man's head back and rammed the blade to the hilt under his chin. The guard stiffened, twitched, and then slumped against Dacian. He twisted the blade and wrenched it free, feeling the gout of warm blood over his hand.

He left the corpse in the shadow next to wall, and moved back to the corner to listen for other guards. Hearing nothing, he moved quickly to the door to the guard room. He pulled it open and crept quietly down the narrow staircase toward the glowing orange lantern light below. He slowed as he heard voices. There were at least two guards in the room below. *Gods, let there be only two,* he thought. *More than that and this ends here…*

Dacian stopped at the bottom of the stairs and glanced into the room. Two guards sat on either side of the small wooden table, a half-empty bottle of red wine between them. The one closest to him, a heavyset man with a shock of black hair, had leaned his sword up against the edge of the table. He sat resting his elbows on the tabletop with an earthenware mug in his hand. The other was a sandy-haired, gangly youngster. He had a narrow, pockmarked face with the wispy beginnings of a beard.

This one was sitting back, smoking a pipe, his helmet and sword lying on the table.

Dacian eased back into the shadows and took a steadying breath. He stepped into the room and threw the dagger at the younger guard, the blade taking the man in the throat and pitching him from his chair. The heavyset guard had just managed to turn and was surging to his feet as Dacian struck, his fist crashing into the man's face, snapping his head backward in a spray of blood.

The guard staggered back, crashing into a small iron brazier, knocking it to the stone floor in a spray of sparks and hot, glowing coals. Dacian ran forward and smashed the man against the wall, grabbing his wrist to stop the guard from dragging his dagger free of its scabbard. He pounded his free fist into into the guard's ribs, feeling the man grunt at each impact; blood and spittle sprayed Dacian's face.

But the man was built like a bear, and Dacian felt his grip on the dagger hand loosening. He surged forward, slamming his shoulder into the man's midriff, hearing a painful grunt of wind being punched from the man's lungs. But still, the guard did not wilt, and still, Dacian could feel the dagger being dragged slowly, inexorably from its scabbard.

Suddenly, the guard twisted and Dacian lost his footing, staggering to his left. He felt his grip on the man's wrist being wrenched free, and then something white-hot slammed into his side. It tore free, then slammed in again. Shards of molten metal seemed to tear through his stomach.

Falling backward Dacian punched the heel of his hand under the man's chin just as the blade snaked out again, this time gouging a shallow wound across his ribs. The guard stiffened at the blow, momentarily stunned. Dacian forced himself forward despite the pain and slammed stiffened fingers into the man's throat. The man fell backward, his eyes bulging, and Dacian surged forward, swinging a fist into his jaw, snapping his head violently to the right with a gout of blood. The giant guard's eyes glazed, the dagger clattered from his nerveless fingers, and then he pitched forward, crashing to face-first to the floor.

Dacian swayed and sagged to a knee. He grabbed at the wounds on his side and felt blood pouring through his fingers. *No, no, no!* Desperate thoughts ran through his head. *Not yet, not yet…* Suddenly, his head spun, and he fell backwards to the floor. For long seconds, he lay staring at the wooden slats of the ceiling, his life blood pooling under his back. *No… not here… not like this, you bastard…*

He grabbed at his shirt with both hands and tore it, grunting at the burning pain of the effort. Sweat ran down his face as he sucked in a deep breath and ripped at his shirt again, tearing a strip free. Each breath was sharp and shallow as he wadded the cloth and pushed it into the first wound. He sucked in a deep breath and tore off another strip of cloth, bracing himself before he pushed it into the second wound. The pain at his side felt like hot coals being pressed into his flesh. But the bleeding had stopped.

Dacian dragged in raw and ragged breaths, waiting for the pain to subside. *Move, gods be damned!* he thought as he gritted his teeth and forced himself up from the floor. The large guard groaned and started to move. Dacian picked up the guard's discarded blade and rammed it down hard between the man's shoulder blades. The man stiffened and then sagged.

Dacian dragged himself around the table. As he leaned over to pull the dagger from the sandy-haired guard's neck, a wave of nausea washed over him, and he sagged back against the table. His vision narrowed alarmingly into a dark tunnel, and he clung desperately to consciousness, his face wet with cold sweat. *Gods... not yet...* He forced himself to breath slowly, deeply. *Not yet.*

He pressed the sodden cloth deeper into the wounds, grunting at the burning pain. His breath was once again short and shallow as he reached carefully for the dagger jutting from the sandy-haired guard's neck. He twisted the blade and pulled it free before dragging himself upright. The room seemed to tilt and spin, sickening him again, and he clung, white-knuckled, to the table, waiting for the wave to pass.

Not much time. Move! Dacian thought as he hauled himself up from the table and moved toward the door. There was little time for caution, and he pulled it open, staggering into the narrow, dark passage. The kitchen lay ahead, and he hoped it was empty. Blood still dribbled down his side, and his leggings were sodden. He would not be able to fight.

At the junction, he turned left into the scullery. It was deserted. He moved quickly through the small room to the double doors that lead to the kitchen. Here he paused, pressing an ear to the door. He waited, straining to hear any movement. *Nothing...* He pushed at the door and peered through the opening. A fat man was sitting slumped forward at a wooden table, elbows on the tabletop. The man's round, ruddy face was resting in the palm of his hand, and he was snoring softly.

Dacian eased the door open and slid into the kitchen. He slipped past the sleeping cook and moved to the large wooden doors. There would be stairs, then the dining room; he remembered this from the scullery boy. The antechamber would lie beyond that, and the staircase. *But how do I get up the staircase unseen?* he thought as he pushed at the door. With a quick glance at the still-sleeping cook he slipped through and, clutching at his side, forced himself up the short flight of stairs. *And then how do I find the bastard?*

The dining room was dominated by a massive table. The dark, polished wood gleamed in the soft candlelight thrown by three ornate silver candelabras. Six high-back chairs lined each side; the chairs at each end were markedly higher and gilded. *As if the bastard would need to remind guests of who he was,* Dacian thought darkly as he moved slowly forward. The pain was now just a dull, grinding, burning pulse through his stomach. The bleeding seemed to have slowed, but it had not stopped. He was getting weaker with every passing minute.

He leaned against the doors leading to the antechamber. He would need more than his fair share of luck from here, and he hated relying on luck. He had never factored in luck during the years he had served in the legion, and yet here he was, hoping against hope. He took the polished doorknob in his hand and turned it slowly, pulling the door open just enough to glance through the narrow gap.

A lone guard stood in the centre of the antechamber with his back to the dining room door. The wide marble staircase stretched upward to the man's left, and Dacian could see no one else. He drew his dagger and moved quickly forward, ignoring the clawing pain in his side. At two paces from the man, he lunged, grabbing the peak of the guard's helmet and pulling his head back, exposing his neck. The man started to cry out and stopped abruptly as the cold steel of the blade pressed against his throat.

"Shut your fucking mouth," Dacian hissed, drawing the blade slightly across the taunt skin, just enough to produce a trickle of blood. "Where's the duke?"

The man paused, and Dacian pulled at the blade again, cutting a little deeper. The man hissed in pain, and then quickly said, "Upstairs. Upstairs in the study."

"Where?" Dacian grunted at the sharp pain in his side. The wounds had started bleeding freely again from the exertion.

The man pointed a shaking hand up the staircase, gesturing to the right. "That way. First door... on the right."

Dacian ripped the blade across the man's throat, and blood sprayed into the air. He dropped the dying man to the floor and groaned as the effort pulled at the wounds. He grabbed at his side, feeling the blood seep though his fingers. He stood rooted to the ground as his vision blurred and a powerful wave of nausea hit him. Sweat dripped from his face as he forced himself to lurch toward the stairs, where he clung, white-knuckled, to marble banister and consciousness.

You need to move. Move now or die here! The cold, hard words echoed in his mind as he once again pressed the knuckles of his fist into the blood-soaked wadding. He had used the same words before while dragging men to their feet in the middle of a battle. He had used them to focus terrified and frozen men. He could not die here. Not when he was so close. Not yet. He groaned at the relentless, jagged shards of agony as he started to drag himself up the stairs.

Viktor d'Verana sat on the soft leather of the chair and sipped at a thick, sweet dessert wine. He stared at a large painting of his father that hung above the grey stone fireplace where a fire spluttered and popped as it ate away at the logs. The man was a cold-hearted bastard who had never shown him or his mother any love or affection.

He had tried to be different with Antoine. The boy had had many faults, but he had always tried. Viktor had attempted to support him but had fallen short in many cases. *If only the boy's mother had lived longer.* He had sorely missed the softer touch of a woman. Viktor's only role model had been an iron-fisted arsehole who would rather swing a switch or a fist than waste breath on a word.

He was dragged from his thoughts as something hit the door hard, and followed by a grunt of pain. The door rattled again, and then something heavy hit the floor. The duke watched as the handle turned slowly and the door swung inward. A man stepped over the slumped body of the guard he had posted outside the door. The man's face was chalky white, his left hand was pressed to his blood-soaked side, and his right held a long, dripping dagger.

"Who the hell are you?" the duke growled, looking about for something to defend himself with as he backed away. "How did you get in here?"

The ghost of a man only smiled as he took an unsteady step forward. His pale face had a sickly sheen, but his dark eyes blazed.

The man stopped and teetered on unsteady legs.

"Who are you?" the duke asked again.

"You know," the man grated through gritted teeth, trying to force his broken body forward. His face twisted in pain. "You know… who," he started to say, then pitched forward and crashed heavily into the floor.

The assassin tried desperately to push himself up, but his arms were weak, and his body felt like lead. He slumped forward and watched as the duke's slippered feet drew closer; they stopped just out of arm's reach. He gripped the hilt of the dagger and willed himself to follow through with one last, desperate attempt—the man was right there—but there was nothing left. All he could do was weakly wave the point of his blade at the man's legs, but then even this proved too much for his fast-ebbing strength.

The dagger fell from his fingers, hitting the carpet with a dull thud. Still, he clawed at the hilt but then finally sagged back as he realised he could no longer lift his arm. He lay there staring at those hated feet as each jagged, pain-filled breath snagged and rattled in his throat. And then the pain was gone. He found himself marvelling at how soft the carpet felt against his face. Almost as if he were melting into the floor. Such strange a thought as the last of his life drained away. He was cold now and so very tired. *So close... so very close...*

"Fool." he heard the duke say, and then the darkness took him.

"All endings are merely beginnings."
—The First Book

Epilogue

*"There is no beginning, no end.
No good nor evil.*

"There is only the endless ocean of time.

*"And the ripples
of light and shadow."*

—The Songs of E'kia

The skiff knifed through the dark waters of the sheltered cove as the four Akhbari slavers heaved at the oars. Salim sat in the stern, hand on the rudder, and skilfully guided them through the low, rolling swells. He prayed silently to the Great One that the damned smuggler would be there.

One the last trip, they had spent several long, boring hours waiting to rendezvous with the man. Mareq had a great many faults, but his patience, particularly when bolstered by the prospect of gold, was legendary. *Damn the man's eyes, the bastard smuggler had better be there tonight,* Salim cursed silently. The narrow strip of beach that lay a few oar strokes ahead was sheltered and far enough away from the main roads to avoid idle detection. They weren't trading in bales of wheat, after all, and the *commodities* they carried were generally less than willing to cooperate and very open to rescue.

But for all the discomfort they might be asked to endure while waiting on the beach, they dared not complain. Mareq was neither a forgiving nor an understanding man. And that love of gold, of which the smuggler had proved to be a steady provider, reached far beyond the scant love he felt for his crew.

Salim sat a little straighter as the low hiss of waves breaking reached his ears. He strained to see where the rolling white water began. One day, he promised himself, he would poke a damned hole in the smuggler's belly and be done with it. The idea died as fast as it formed as Salim imagined Mareq cutting his throat and feeding him to the fish. *Possibly not in that order, knowing the captain,* Salim though bleakly.

"Steady now," he instructed the oarsmen softly as a larger swell picked the stern of the skiff up and the bow started to slide down the glassy face. "Ship the oars!" he snapped and allowed the wave to drive the skiff almost all the way to the beach. As the wave started to die away, it took only a handful of strokes from the oarsmen before the hull crunched into the round grey pebbles of the beach. The slavers leaped over the sides and drew the boat up out of reach of the waves.

Salim stepped onto the loose stone, drew a longbow from an oilskin bag, and carefully strung it. He ran a loving hand down the beautifully polished wood. It was almost as tall as he, and not a man among the crew, apart from himself, could draw it. The leather quiver held a dozen two-and-a-half-foot-long arrows, each of them tipped with a wickedly barbed steel head capable of punching through all but the heaviest of armour.

"Kalib!" He called, picking out one of the oarsmen. "Take the others and collect some wood. I'll be damned if I spend the next few hours waiting in the cold." He nocked an arrow and jogged up the beach through the low scrub and onto the narrow, dusty path that the smuggler would be using. Apart from the cold wind blowing mournfully from the east, all was quiet.

He turned back and watched as Kalib and the others gathered twisted cords of old drift wood from high up the beach, where the last spring tide had dumped them. With a final irritated glance down the track, Salim made his way back to the men; they had already piled wood to heroic proportions.

"Gods... enough," he grunted. "We need to warm ourselves, not rival the pits of hell."

Soon a fire roared in a small hollow a little ways off from the trail to shield it from the wind and prevent any unlikely passersby from seeing the flames. Salim and the others sat close together and enjoyed the warmth.

"A pox on that bastard!" one of the men growled, pulling his cloak more tightly around his shoulders.

"I wager you would not say that to his face," one of the others sniggered. "Remember what he did to Fahad and his two apes?"

"Ahhh...that was years ago, and Fahad was a fat, slow idiot who my mother could have gutted with a soup ladle," the first one said with a snort. "And as for those two morons, she wouldn't even need the ladle."

The men laughed.

"Quiet!" Salim hissed, even though there was little likelihood of them being heard by anyone. Most legitimate travellers would not be out at this hour, and if they were, they would use the main highway, which was wider and cobbled for the most part. Why would anyone willingly choose a little-traveled dirt track that meandered its way along the coast?

"Fahad was always a useless bastard." Salim half smiled when the men had settled. "Remember his face when that vikingar hit him with the axe?"

"Looked like he was killed more by the surprise than anything else," one of the others chortled.

"I'll wager he—" one of the others started to say when Salim held up a hand, silencing him.

"I hear something." Over the crackle of the fire, Salim could hear the sound of hooves, slow and steady, approaching from the east. *The smuggler and that damned donkey of his. Thank the Great One!* He thought with a rush of relief. He had no desire to spend another night on this god-forsaken beach.

"Someone's coming." Salim rose and readied his bow. "It's likely the smuggler, but prepare yourselves. No surprises. Move!"

The slavers quietly drew swords from sheaths and slid into the scrub on either side of the track. Salim strolled casually out into the middle of the path, holding his bow low. The sound of hooves was much closer now.

"Get ready," Salim called out softly, drawing back the arrow a few inches. A rider on a horse came into slowly into view. He was tall and wore a dark cloak. He was not the smuggler.

"Stop!" Salim called out as he raised the bow, pulling back on the arrow so that the fletching rested against his cheek. "Who the hell are you?"

Kratos rode slowly along the narrow, winding coastal road. The very road the man he had hunted had taken only days before. He could not help but savour the irony. He had done what the woman, Relic, had asked of him—no more, no less. He had no idea of the identity of the man he had killed, but he was quite sure he didn't want to know. He'd sent the shaft into the man's throat and watched him die on the steps of that old church.

It was not the first arrow he had loosed that changed the course of his life. It would certainly not be the last. This one, though, had not been his choice. He hated nothing more than the feeling of being in someone else's control. He wondered for the thousandth time about the woman, Relic.

Obviously a sorceress of some form, he thought, remembering the dagger. *Or worse.* He shrugged off the sudden chill and turned his attention back to the narrow road. He had ridden hard for the first few miles but then slowed to a canter and eventually to a walk. There was no hurry now, and he began to turn her cryptic message over and over in his head.

"You will take the coastal road north until you find an old wych elm," she had said. "It's an hour or so ride from the city. You will know it because it was struck by lightning, and the bole has split. One half leans over to the west, and the branches point to a small stone path. It is difficult to spot, so ride slowly. You must take the path down to the sea before the second bell."

"Who will I meet there?" he had asked.

"You will know him when you see him." She smiled. "You will give him the bag. He will know what to do."

"This is not very reassuring," he complained.

"You could always head east to the Kurg." she shrugged. "I hear they have charming customs involving campfires and outsiders. If the duke doesn't find you first."

He shifted, stretching his back, and glanced down at the leather bag that hung from the saddle horn. He had not opened it, as she had instructed. Somehow, he knew that he had to follow her every instruction to the letter if he was to have a hope of escaping the duke with his life. Once he was across the Great Sea, there would be ample work for someone of his skills, and the empire was vast. A man with the right talents would never be found.

He rounded a narrow bend, passing a fall of rock, and saw the old tree she had spoken of. One half stretched upward into the night sky while the other leaned low over the road, the branches pointing seaward like gnarled fingers. *Now to find this path,* he thought, dismounting.

Tariq led the donkey down the narrow path, careful of the loose stone that threatened to slide underfoot. With luck, Mareq would be anchored in the bay, and there would be no need to spend a day or two waiting on the beach.

"Just a few days at sea, girl," he said softly to the donkey. "Then retirement. This time for good. I promise." The animal snorted softly as if to say she had heard it all before. Tariq smiled, mildly embarrassed at his lie but very conscious of the weight of the purse beneath his cloak. It had been a very lucrative trip. With the gold he had made, and his substantial investments, there would be no need to ever set foot on this side of the Great Sea ever again. *As a smuggler,* he quickly added. Perhaps there would be legitimate opportunities in the future, and it would be unwise not to consider each one carefully before just turning them down on principle.

He had turned to rub the donkey's nose when he caught a glimpse of movement behind him on the trail. He froze, and his hand dropped to the dagger at his belt. A tall man leading a horse came into view. The man stopped, his hand resting on the pommel of his sword. *Shit... is he with the watch?* Tariq thought. Getting thrown into a Sarsinian dungeon was not part of the plan.

Can I bribe him? Everyone has a price—well almost everyone, Tariq conceded. "Greetings stranger!" He called out. His voice was clear and sounded far more confident than he felt. "How can I be of assistance?" His mind raced. There was no way he could explain why he was taking a narrow, seldom-used path to a secluded bay that was, in all likelihood, populated by a group of slavers waiting for him to arrive.

"Good evening," the man replied. He lifted his hand from his sword, presenting the open palm. "I think I have something for you." Moving slowly, the man lifted a leather bag from his saddle horn and held it out to Tariq.

The smuggler looked at the bag with deep suspicion. "Who are you? I don't know you."

"My name is Kratos," the man replied. "I was asked…" He shook his head with a dark smirk. "I was *told* to give this bag to you. You will apparently know what it means."

Tariq walked slowly forward, his hand still gripping his dagger. The man held out the bag, and Tariq took it by the straps and stepped back. He opened it and took a quick glance inside. He looked back at the man with a look of surprise and then knelt and reached into the bag.

The bottle of wine was sealed with a deep-red wax threaded with gold leaf. The crest of the Sarsinian royal family was unmistakable. Tariq grinned broadly. Along with the wine was a small bag of coins; from its weight, he guessed it was filled predominantly with gold. "Alia…" he said to himself shaking his head wondering how in the world she could have gotten her hands on this bottle. He looked up at the stranger. "So, Kratos. What do you need?"

"Passage to Akhbar would be good," the tall man said simply.

"All right…" Tariq nodded slowly. "How does Abuzara strike you?" he asked, returning the bottle to the bag.

"As good as any." Kratos shrugged.

"Good. We're meeting some men at the end of this path. They're slavers and probably nervous, so let me do the talking. I think we have enough to buy your passage." He pointed at the bag at his feet. "Mareq, the captain, tends to do pretty much anything if you have enough gold. You'll have to leave your horse. Sorry—not much space after this old girl is loaded." He patted the donkey's flank.

"I'm fine with that." Kratos shrugged.

"Good. Let's go, then."

"Who the hell are you?" Salim sighted down the arrow, ready to send the shaft into the man's eye. The man had come to an abrupt halt and stood frozen, holding the reins of his horse. He was tall and thin and seemed more annoyed than frightened.

Before the man could answer, he heard a familiar voice. "Salim, wait, please." The smuggler stepped carefully into view with his hands held upward. "He's with me. He has gold. I'm quite sure Mareq would be interested in making a few extra coins."

Salim slowly eased the tension on the string and lowered the bow. He shifted his attention to the nervous smuggler, who now stood next to the tall man. "He's an... *associate* of mine. His name is Kratos. He needs passage to Abuzara."

Salim frowned. *Damn this man's eyes,* he swore inwardly, feeling the irrational urge to send an arrow into the smuggler's throat. Now he needed to make a decision, and Mareq would gut him if he made the wrong one. Bring him aboard and risk the wrath of the hell-toad of a captain, or leave the man, and his gold, behind and risk the same.

Fuck, he swore silently to himself. *Then again,* he thought quickly, *erring on the side of profit is always a good yardstick when it comes to Mareq. And the smuggler has always made good with payment. Why wouldn't he now? Maybe just kill them both and take the gold. But the men would know, and I'd have to share it. No doubt one of these stupid bastards would be sure to talk, and if that got back to Mareq, we'd all be dead. Shit!*

"Where's the gold? Enough for both of you?" he asked.

The smuggler brought out a coin pouch and bounced the heavy bag in his hand. "More than enough," he replied. "Probably enough for a bonus for you and your men, too. I'll put in a word for you with Mareq."

A bonus? Now this is starting to sound a bit better. "All right." Salim nodded reluctantly. "But you have to leave the horse." He pointed to the tall stranger, who merely shrugged and started to remove the saddle and reins from the animal. Salim looked up at the sky, still feeling mildly queasy about his decision. But the prospect of not dying and even earning an extra coin or two tempered his unease. He turned to his men, who had been watching the exchange with great interest. "Come on, you lazy bastards. Back to the ship!"

Sarsini
The Thirty-Seventh Day of 389, Morning

Panos groaned and slowly opened his eyes. He blinked and winced in pain as the bright morning light streaming in from the open window stabbed at him. He could smell a faint salt tang hanging on the cool breeze that blew in from the sea, and he squinted at the soft white clouds that drifted lazily across a deep-blue sky.

Gods alive... everything hurts, he thought as he closed his eyes carefully. He swallowed and took a slow, painful breath. *But it looks like you're still kicking, old son...* A brief, weak smile flickered, only to be replaced by a grimace as another stab of pain lanced through his chest.

Bloody hell... ribs took a pounding. He opened his eyes again and this time tried to lift his head, only to be greeted by a bolt of blinding agony.

"Carefully now, old horse," he chided himself.

He was tucked into a soft bed, and in the brief moment before his brain seemed to explode, he saw that his left arm was splinted and wrapped in bandages, resting above clean white covers. He had no idea where he was, though, nor how long he had been lying there. But he was clean and warm, so someone had apparently taken very good care of him. His last memory was being smashed into the floor by that... *creature.* He remembered his arm snapping and then... nothing.

He heard the door open and risked opening his eyes. A young redheaded woman stood in the doorway with a steaming bowl and clean white cloths. She stopped, her eyes wide with surprise. Then she dropped the bowl, the loud clang and splash of water drowned by a squeal of excitement that seemed to stab through his skull like a dagger.

"He's awake!" she shouted down the passage. "Get Jasuf!"

Panos raised a hand and waved feebly at her. "Shh, girl... gods above... my head."

She ran over to the bed and knelt beside him, tears in her eyes.

"Where?" he asked hoarsely, once again trying to lift his head, only to hiss at the sudden jolt of pain that shot through his ribs.

"Hush. Lie back," he heard her say, her hand gently pushing his head back onto the pillow. "You're at the Crow. It's been touch-and-go for a few days. The healer didn't think you were going to make it at one point."

"The Crow?" He squinted at the girl. *Gods alive, I must owe Jasuf a bloody fortune!* "And what of the... creatures?"

"Gone. All burned up," The girl said. "But not before you saved us all." He felt her soft fingers brush his hair back from his forehead.

"Saved?" Panos blinked as he tried to piece the fragments of memory together.

"Yes. If it wasn't for you and Jasuf, we'd all be dead." She paused and then continued shyly, "But mostly you."

More than a hint of promise in those last three words, my lovely lass, Panos thought with a sudden surge of excitement. *Now if old Panos here hadn't been trampled by an elephant...* The thought died as someone stomped into the room.

"Lad! You're alive!" he heard Jasuf's voice boom with pleasure. "Thought you'd become a great, hairy, permanent fixture in this room."

"You know me... anything to please." Panos smiled weakly. "What d'you mean hairy?"

Jasuf's laugh boomed out. "You need anything, lad, just ask young Tess here. She's been takin' good care of you." The big innkeeper nodded and then left, pulling the door quietly closed behind him.

"A pint of ale would be marvellous." Panos smiled, turning to the girl.

"And then?" She pursed her lips with a mischievous twinkle in her eyes.

"Gods, girl... I've just returned from death's door! Everything hurts!"

"Not everything, I'll wager... and I'll be careful."

Panos looked at her for a moment. "All right, you mad wench, but you better make that two pints, then."

Nils pushed open the door to the noisy reception area of the watch house and grimaced at the pain that simple effort caused. Cilla had bound his shoulder and chest and forced him to drink an evil-tasting tincture before allowing him to leave their house. It was truly a vile concoction, that may have been punishment for ignoring her advice to rest, had it not actually worked. The pain was not gone, but the dull, grinding ache was manageable.

One pain it had no effect on was that of losing his friend Sev. He had been found by the morning watch halfway up the Water's Edge Road, his body propped up against the cold stone of a wall, having died of his wounds. Nils dragged in a slow, painful breath as he hung his cloak and sword on a hook.

Rake was alive, but it would be weeks, if not longer, before the burly sergeant would be seen at the front desk of the watch. Tibero had been bloodied and bruised but had managed to limp from the temple precinct almost unaided.

"A line. Please, people, form a line. One at a time," he heard a voice ring out over the milling crowd of people. "One at a time, and we will get this done."

Nils could not help but smile as he saw Marol behind the front desk, gesturing with the open palm of his left hand for the line to form, paper and quill in the other. The young man had a new, steely look in his eyes.

"Nils!"

He turned to see the scruffy, ginger-haired figure of Tibero limping closer. The captain's left eye was bloodshot and still half-closed, a line of coarse black stitches splitting his eyebrow. He leaned heavily on a wooden cane, but he looked as if he was on the mend.

"Good to see you back," Tibero grunted. "Thought Cilla was never going to let you out of the house."

"Well, she did try to poison me," Nils said with a wry smile and laughed at Tibero's expression, holding his protesting ribs. "No... it was something for the pain."

"They all say that," Tibero said and then smiled as he looked over the jostling crowd. He scratched at his ever-present ginger stubble. "You know... I think young Melon over there is going to be all right."

"Sergeant Melon?" Nils prompted.

Tibero shook his head slowly. "Maybe after another monster or two... but it does have a good ring to it, doesn't it?"

The Akhbari Coast
The 182nd Day of 394, Night

The rain lashed the small stone house perched almost precariously on a rocky head of land that jutted out into the dark, storm-driven sea. Massive waves, driven by the howling gale, boomed and crashed into the rocks far below, and heavy clouds scudded across the black sky. Tariq lay asleep, oblivious to the hiss of the rain and the low, sporadic grumble of thunder, oblivious to the dark figure that moved silently to the side of his bed to stand over him.

Water dripped from the hooded cloak as a flash of lightning briefly illuminated the smuggler's face. He lay on his back with an arm tucked under his head. He was snoring softly. The dark figure reached up and pulled back the hood. Echo sniffed, and tucked a wet strand of hair behind her ear, and smiled. Tariq could sleep through almost anything.

She reached out and lightly touched his cheek, feeling the coarse white stubble under her fingertips. She remembered when that beard was full and dark and those eyes were bright and mischievous, the deep etchings of time and loss yet to be carved. She remembered watching the speckles of grey start to salt his beard and the crinkles around his eyes grow deeper as they laughed together, sharing almost countless baskets of cheese and bread, olives and wine.

She smiled as she thought of the multitudes of bottles of wine she had stolen from the cellars of kings and dukes and fat princes who wouldn't miss a hundred bottles, let alone one—rich, spoiled men who would never dream of enjoying those priceless sips from rough earthenware mugs while watching the gulls wheel above the rolling waves. She loved the wild, boyish delight he displayed at each gift. How he would shake his head in disbelief and then set three mugs on the table, fill them to the brim, and then sit holding Razia's hand while staring at the sea, savouring each cup.

She remembered that for a while after Razia had died, he would still fetch three mugs, sometimes even filling them before catching himself. He would stare at the third for a long moment, as if trying to shrug off an unwanted reality that slowly settled around his shoulders like a heavy blanket. He would scratch at the ever-present stubble on his chin and then look up to smile sadly at her.

She glanced at the small wooden table next to the bed and found a simple gold ring. She recognised it immediately. It was Razia's, and he always kept it close. It was too small to fit on any of his rough, gnarled fingers, so he would mostly keep it in his pocket or place it on the windowsill in the kitchen while he cooked or on the table while they ate.

He had given it to Razia as a wedding gift. She picked it up and rolled the band around and around and around. *It is time to go… and there are things to take,* she thought, her face hidden in the shadows. For a long moment, she looked down at the simple ring as it lay in her palm, and then she slipped it onto her finger. *And there are things to give away.*

She laid her hand on the smuggler's forehead. Tariq stiffened but did not wake. He took a sharp breath, held it for a second, and then released it in a shuddering sigh. His skin glowed where her fingers had touched him. She then leaned over and kissed him lightly on the cheek. "He is coming. You must be ready," she whispered with a sad smile, and then turned slowly away. She was halfway to the door when she hesitated. She looked back at the sleeping smuggler. "Shave, you rouge," she whispered and then left the room without looking back.

Tariq woke to find the morning light streaming in through the window. The storm must have passed in the night, but the sea was still wild. He could hear the deep roar and crash of the surf. He scratched at his beard as he dropped his legs over the side of the bed and sat up. He had expected the dull ache of protesting bones and muscles, but instead, he felt marvellously clear-headed and well. He took a deep breath and smiled.

He stood and walked over to the window, opening it wide. The ocean stretched out to the horizon, glistening like polished silver, and a salty tang hung on the cool morning breeze. His stomach growled, and he realised that he was famished.

"Eggs, my son," he said to himself, scratching at the stubble under his chin, then immediately added hot bread with melted butter and a strong mug of *khafja* with far too much honey to the list. He hadn't felt this good in years. He felt like a young man. *It is going to be a good day…* He grinned to himself as he opened his door and was enveloped in the rich, aromatic smell of his favourite dark brew.

Tariq paused, suddenly confused. Who was brewing the khafja? *Alia? Is she here?* he thought with a broad grin. The day was getting even better. *Wouldn't put it past her to break in and just start breakfast...* Still grinning, he ran his fingers through his hair in what he knew was a poor attempt to make himself presentable. *Should have shaved,* he thought absently as he stepped out of his room.

"Alia? Is that you, girl? Wasn't expecting you for at least..." The words died in his throat as he froze. The smile dropped from his face.

A stranger sat at the table with a steaming mug in front of him. The man was tall, his bearded face fierce and angular... and oddly familiar. His head was wrapped in the white gh'utr scarf of the desert tribes, and he wore a long flowing to'ab of the deepest black. Something long and slim, wrapped in oilskin, leaned against the table to the man's left.

The man looked up from his cup. "Good morning, Tariq."

Tariq blinked at the sound of his name. "Do I... know you?"

"Sit down." The man ignored the question and gestured to the chair opposite him. His voice was low and full of edges. It reminded Tariq of the desert, all scorched sand and rock. *There's no give there,* Tariq thought, feeling a sudden flash of fear. *No compromise...*

Tariq's mind raced as he forced himself to move forward. *What does this man want?* He was acutely aware that the air of calm he was fighting to maintain was perilously thin. *Who the hell are you?* he thought as he tried to remember where he had left his dagger. The man sipped at the khafja as Tariq pulled back the chair and slowly sat down.

"You won't need it," the man said suddenly, looking up from his cup. His eyes were a piercing blue and a truly frightening power radiated from him.

"Need what?" Tariq barely managed to ask. He swallowed, his mouth feeling bone dry. "What won't I need?"

"The dagger." The man pointed casually over his shoulder to the shelf near the stove.

"Well, that settles that, then," Tariq said and breathed out slowly. He pointed at the man's mug. "Besides, stabbing a guest is usually frowned upon. Any chance I could pour myself a cup, then?"

The man nodded with a ghost of a smile as he extended an open hand toward the steaming pot on the stove.

Tariq pushed back the chair and walked as casually as he could to the stove. He looked at the shelf, where the mugs stood next to the dagger. He shot a nervous glance at the man who sat quietly sipping at his drink, watching him with what looked like mild amusement. Tariq reached out and fetched a mug. He filled it and returned to the table, still wary, but much of the raw fear had begun to ebb away. If the man had meant him harm, he would have done it already. He doubted he would be able to stop him, dagger or not.

"So…" Tariq sipped at the brew. "How can I help you?"

The man said nothing but lifted the long package and placed it in front of Tariq. It was bound with strips of leather. Tariq untied them and unwrapped the oilskin. He flipped over the last fold and gasped. A sword of unspeakable beauty lay on the table. The long, subtle curve of the scabbard was white leather and silver; the pommel and guard were polished silver-steel, and the hilt was wrapped in a coarse and intricately plaited skin that he could not place.

"Where?" Tariq managed to say as he ran his fingers lightly over the scabbard.

"To the east," the man said simply.

"The east? Ras-al-Salah? The Naravasi? Further?" Tariq asked, not bothering to look up from the sword.

The man chuckled dryly. "A bit further than that."

Tariq lifted the beautiful weapon from the table. It was remarkably light, and he slowly pulled the blade free, holding it up to the light. He marvelled at the beautiful swirls in the metal. *I've never seen that on a blade,* he thought as his eyes followed the mesmerising patterns… *How in the seven hells could they—*

"It is called folding," the man said. "The metal is folded over and over to create the layers."

"This is… exquisite," Tariq breathed, reaching for the blade.

"Ahh… I would not do that," the man warned. "Not if you're accustomed to having fingers."

Tariq jerked his hand away from the gleaming metal as if it were a scorpion. He turned to the stranger. "Why are you showing me this?" Tariq asked, the remaining residue of fear burned away by the magnificent blade.

"I have heard you are a man who can acquire swords," the man said simply.

"I've been known to find a blade or two." Tariq nodded, feeling a familiar surge of excitement. "At a price." He leaned back and squared his shoulders.

"No doubt." The man smiled. "I need you to acquire twenty of these swords."

Tariq blinked in surprise. "Gods, man…" He shook his head and moved the sword slowly through the air, feeling the perfect balance of the weapon. "That would cost"—Tariq shook his head—"thousands. Tens of thousands." He looked up at the man. "And that's in gold," he added firmly, remembering a distant argument with an old friend. *Izem, you bloody pirate,* he thought absently as he turned his attention back to the blade and waited for the man's response.

The man merely shrugged and reached into his robes. He pulled out a bulging leather pouch and dropped it onto the table, where it landed with a weighty metallic thud; several golden coins spilled out. Tariq gaped at the small fortune that lay on the table in front of him. He reached out and picked up one of the heavy coins and examined it. It had what looked like a strange serpent on one side and an odd pictogram on the other.

"A down payment," the man said. "You will need a ship."

Tariq placed the coin on the table, his mind racing. If he could find a way to bring these swords back to Sarsini, he would be unspeakably rich… but even that was nothing compared to the excitement of finding the person who made this sword. *Gods…* His breath caught. *The secret to creating such a blade would be priceless!* He shook his head and looked up at the stranger. "When?" he finally managed to ask.

"Soon." The man replied as he pushed his chair back to stand.

"No, wait. You're leaving?" Tariq asked incredulously as he pushed himself to his feet while trying to sheath the sword.

"Yes," the stranger said simply and moved to the door.

"The sword!"

"Keep it. The mark on the blade near the hilt is the swordsmith's. You will need it to find him." The man paused. "Keep it safe, and make ready, Tariq. I will call on you when the time is right."

"Have we met?" Tariq called out as the man opened the door. "You are familiar. I am sure our paths have crossed. But apologies, your name escapes me."

The man stopped and turned slowly. For a moment those ice blue eyes glittered dangerously, and once again, Tariq caught a glimpse of that dark and terrifying power.

Tariq swallowed, wondering if he had somehow overstepped a line. "Forgive me… but who are you?"

The man paused as if weighing the question. Then, with an odd half smile he said, "I am Dacra."

Printed in Great Britain
by Amazon

32701221R00220